Force Majeure

E. N. CHANTING

Edited by J. Tylee Ertel

Cover Art by www.AmpersandBookCovers.com

ISBN: 979-8-9893509-3-3

Contents

Dedication	1
Trigger Warnings	2
1. Peyton	3
2. Peyton	9
3. Peyton	16
4. Peyton	19
5. Micah	21
6. Peyton	28
7. Micah	44
8. Peyton	50
9. Micah	59
10. Peyton	66
11. Micah	72
12. Peyton	76
13. Micah	84

14. Peyton   89

15. Micah   100

16. Peyton   105

17. Peyton   110

18. Micah   119

19. Peyton   128

20. Peyton   136

21. Micah   154

22. Peyton   173

23. Micah   184

24. Peyton   198

25. Micah   210

26. Peyton   220

27. Micah   229

28. Peyton   248

29. Micah   257

30. Peyton   262

31. Peyton   266

32. Micah   277

33. Peyton   283

34. Micah   294

35. Peyton   303

36. Micah   321

37. Peyton	332
38. Micah	341
39. Peyton	348
40. Micah	361
41. Peyton	370
42. Micah	376
43. Peyton	378
44. Micah	386
45. Peyton	388
46. Micah	392
47. Peyton	395
Afterword	399
Also by E.N. Chanting	400

Dedication

I want to thank the people who helped me get through this beast of a book, starting with my incredible husband who always supports me. My kids, who make great suggestions, I use so many of them. The Beta Readers, you guys offered such fantastic insights into the characters and the plot, you rock! My friends who know I write and listen to me vent about writing. My dogs, especially the one who follows me everywhere. To the band Volbeat, whose music keeps me sane while I type, thank you. My editors, you're awesome, no one else could possibly unjumble my words like you. The best cover designer, who makes my thoughts a stunning reality. Most of all, thank you enchanting reader, this book wouldn't be worth anything without you to read it.

Trigger Warnings

Language, sexual situations, violence, murder, human trafficking, kidnapping, animal corpse abuse, reference to rape, reference to sexual assault.
Recommended for adults 18+
No cliffhanger, no cheating, HEA, suspense, romance, each book in the series can be read as standalone, but for a more enjoyable experience read them in order.

Peyton

My new *almost* sister-in-law is so cool! I didn't want to be a bridesmaid; Paige is making it easy. My big brother, Rhett, is marrying a great person. She's been so kind and welcoming to me and I love the way she's handling our bridesmaids' dresses. She just asked us to get a purple dress, everything else is up to us. There's only two of us, so Nova and I are shopping together.

Nova is a trip, she's an older lady, and she smokes pot, *for glaucoma,* wink-wink. Her dead husband was a gangster, and he haunts her house. She's hilarious, I can't stop laughing.

She has on a one sleeved dress and is flapping her arm flab in the mirror. I want to agree it's not the dress for her, but I can't catch my breath and tears are pouring down my cheeks.

"Oh my God! Nova, you have to stop. I can't breathe!"

"You've got to breathe through your nose, haven't you learned that yet?" She's smiling at me with such mischief, waiting for me to get her joke.

I gasp when I catch on. "Nova! Aren't you past things like that?"

"Of course not, dear. I think about blow jobs all the time!"

"Nova, you're killing me!" My cheeks ache from laughing so hard. My face must be glowing red, and I'm pretty sure the sales associate thinks we're insane.

Shaking my head, I go back inside my changing room. One more dress to try on, I hope this one looks okay, I'm about out of options.

I squeeze my ass into the dress, it's a slim skirt with a tight waist making an hourglass silhouette overall. The bodice holds up my breasts and the sweetheart neckline highlights my cleavage. The fabric is so soft I love the feel of it, I think this is the one.

I step out onto the raised platform and look into the wraparound mirror.

"Oh Peyton! That's just lovely on you, please get it. The grape purple looks beautiful with your blonde hair and blue eyes. It's perfect!"

"Thanks Nova, I'm getting it. It's so comfortable and it looks pretty good, I can't ask for more than that." I smile at her. Oh shit! She's in her bra and panties in the main part of the store. In all honesty she looks pretty good, but holy crap! Men can walk into this part of the store.

Our salesperson, Katie, comes running over with a satin robe in her hands.

"Nova, I'm so sorry there wasn't a robe in your changing room. Here you go," Her face is bright red as she puts the robe over Nova's hand and guides it up one arm and then the other.

Before she's covered, I spot a tattoo on Nova's lower back, on anyone else I'd call it a tramp-stamp. Well damn, this lady keeps surprising me. I only caught a glimpse, but I swear her tattoo says: *Infinity and Beyond.* I cover my mouth and stifle a laugh.

"I'm going to try on these last two dresses, then let's get some cocktails. What do you say, Peyton?"

"I'm only twenty Nova, but I'll happily be your DD."

"Then, we'll just get our cocktails at my house. I have fresh baked brownies too." Her smile is conspiratorial, I love it.

"Sounds like a plan. I'm going to look at the shoes while I have this on."

Paige warned me to be cautious of Nova's brownies, her glaucoma medication ends up in them more often than not. The wall of shoes is overwhelming, I'm so bad at fashion, like all of it. I've always been a simple girl with simple tastes, fancy isn't me.

Katie comes over, "Do you need help, Peyton?"

"How did you know?"

"The lost look on your face gave you away. Don't worry, I have a few choices in mind that'll work. What size heel do you prefer?"

"There are different sizes?" Her eyes pop wide in shock, I smile.

"I'm only joking. I can't do anything too high. I'm five-foot-six so I feel like I don't need much, maybe three inches at the most?"

"Okay, have a seat in the chair right there and I'll grab your size from the back."

"I wear an eight or an eight-and-a-half depending on the style. Thanks."

Nova is on the raised platform looking in the mirror. This time she's wearing a strapless dress that has sequins covering the bodice and a sheer long sleeve jacket over it. She looks great in the dark eggplant color. It's formal and the wedding isn't, but I don't think anyone will mind. Everyone loves her, she's the team grandma for everyone who works at my brother's company.

Rhett and Paige had a gathering when I got to town, and a bunch of the guys came over. Every single one of them gave Nova a sweet hug and kiss, they doted on her all evening. She ate up the attention and entertained all of us with stories of *'My Henry'* as she calls her dead husband. I wish he was still alive, the two of them together must have been something.

Nova looks over at me and I give her two thumbs up. Her face lights up, I guess she likes the dress too.

Katie comes back with six shoe boxes balanced in her hands. "I brought both sizes in each shoe, let's try the 8 first. This one is a silver strappy sandal that I think goes well with the dress."

I slide my feet into them, and she buckles the clasps. I stand and pace back and forth in front of the mirror, the shoes are comfortable, the 8 fits great. Next, she has me try black pumps. I don't like them with the dress, and they rub my heels. Lastly, I tried a purple, peep toe pump that matches the color of the dress perfectly. I walk around in circles while Katie smiles at me.

Looking in the mirror I decide I like these best. They're comfortable and they look great with the dress. "I like these."

"Me too. I think you've made the perfect selection, Peyton. I'm going to ask Maria to come over and check the fit of your dress and see if you need it altered. Okay?"

"Sure. Thanks." Carrying my shoes, I joined Nova.

"What do you think dear? Is this the dress for me?"

"Definitely! It looks beautiful Nova. Do you need shoes?"

"No, I have the perfect shoes for this dress. I'm going to take it off before I mess it up."

"Wait, if you need it altered, the seamstress is coming over here in a minute to look at my dress."

"Oh, I better wait then, I think it's too long. Even though it's petite sized, I'm still too short for it."

"Do you want a pair of shoes to put on for the seamstress?"

"Nope, the shoes I wore here will work. They have the same heels as my dressy shoes."

"Why don't you sit in that chair, and I'll get them from your dressing room?"

"Thank you, sweetie." There're two satin robes hanging in Nova's dressing room, I smirk and shake my head. *She's such a wild thing.* I pick up her heeled sandals, they have chunky two-inch heels. I help her put them on.

"Hola misses, I am Maria, I fix dresses." She's an older woman, has a Cuban accent, and gray hair. Her arm is cuffed by a pin cushion at the wrist. Glasses rest at the tip of her nose with a chain dangling from them and a measuring tape hangs around her neck.

Pointing, she asks me to stand on the raised platform first, in my shoes. Maria walks around me and has me turn as she checks the length and the fit. She keeps nodding and smiling.

"Muy linda! The dress, it is pretty on you."

"Thank you so much. I really like it," I tell her.

"No fix, is good."

"Okay. Thank you, it feels right and with the shoes the length seems good."

"Si, good."

Smiling, I touch her arm, "Thanks so much. Will you please check my friend?"

"Si, si, misses, please to stand up." She looks at Nova pointing at the platform. Nova gets up and holds her skirt to step onto the raised platform. I hold her elbow just to be safe. When she lets go of her skirt it piles at her feet. Even with shoes it's too long. Maria walks around Nova and starts lifting the hem and pinning, it only takes her a few minutes. She looks over the bodice and three-quarter sleeves of the jacket, nodding her head.

"Okay, is good, misses, you give to me. I wait."

"You got it," Nova steps off the platform and enters her dressing room.

"Nova, do you need any help?"

"I'm good sweetie. Thanks," she says.

"I'm going to change too; I'll meet you back out here in a minute."

"Okay." I smile at Maria, and she smiles and nods at me. I change quickly and hang up my dress and pack up my shoes. When I come back, Nova isn't out yet.

"Ay Dios mio!" Maria gasps and covers her mouth with her hand. I look in the direction she's facing and understand why she was so shocked. Nova's wearing her pants and a bra, no top. Oh shit!

"Nova! You forgot your top!" She looks down, touching her hearing aid.

"Huh, I guess I did."

"Do you need help?"

"No sweet girl, just need to get my head out of my ass." Maria chuckles, her cheeks pink. She shakes her head and says something quietly in Spanish and then crosses herself. I guess it was a prayer. I take Nova's dress from her hand and block the view of her from the rest of the store until she is back in her dressing room.

Turning to Maria, I give her the dress, "Muchas gracias, Maria."

"De nada, muchacha." We smile at each other, then she takes the dress.

I carry my dress and shoes to the register. I have Rhett's credit card. For a long time, I fought him on paying for everything for me. In my high school years, I worked at the coffee shop near my house as a barista, so I had my own money. I tried to work my freshman year of college; it was too much with my heavy class load. My big brother has always taken care of me, he's the only family I have left. But I hated not contributing. I've gotten over it now, he's very successful, and it makes him happy to take care of me. I don't take advantage and only ever purchase what I need, but every once in a while, it causes my stomach to clench. Today is one of those days, I take a few deep breaths and it settles. The dress and the shoes are over $600. That's a lot of money! I suck it up and sign the receipt. Katie happily wraps my items into an easy to carry bag. She gives me a claim check for the alterations on Nova's dress. Nova joins me and I pass over her paperwork then she pays for the cost of her dress and the alterations.

"Okay Miss Nova, your dress will be ready on Thursday. What time would you like to come in?"

"I prefer mornings, 11:30 is good for me." Katie types into her computer and then smiles, she's probably earning a good commission from us.

"All set. Ladies, it's been a pleasure working with you. Thank you so much for shopping at Francesca's! I hope to see you both again."

"Thank you, dear."

"Thank you, Katie, for all your help. I really love what I got."

"I'm so glad you like everything. Have a great rest of your day!" She smiles at us, with all of her teeth.

"You too!" Nova and I say at the same time, we giggle at one another.

"Let's blow this pop stand, fellow bridesmaid!"

I'm exhausted by the time I make it back to my hotel. Rhett and Paige wanted me to stay with them, but I didn't want to intrude. They're getting married this weekend and they need their privacy. Plus, their place is tiny, and it just wouldn't feel right. They would've had me in their faces at every turn. They live in the other half of a duplex that Nova owns. It used to be Paige's place, but my brother moved in when they got engaged. He has a large home not too far away, but they decided to move into the duplex to take care of Nova. She lives on the other side, with the ghost of her dead husband. Paige and Rhett swear they've seen some things that've convinced them Henry actually is around. I don't buy it; I think they're humoring Nova... it's sweet.

Paige loves my dress; I showed it to her when I dropped Nova off. We all had a cocktail and dinner; it was a pleasant evening after a fun day. I swear my abs are going to be sore tomorrow from all the laughter. I love those at home moments with my brother. Paige is rapidly becoming my sister, it makes me happy. I miss my birth sister so much, she was murdered when I was sixteen. We lost our mom to cancer when I was a toddler. I don't remember her. My big sister was a great mom and sister to me. Rhett is a great big brother too, even though we're eight years apart. We were never as close as Larue and I. After Larue died, our father died weeks later, and Rhett stepped up and took care of me. He left the military and came home as quickly as possible to be there for me. I had to stay with one of my teachers for a month while he took care of changing his career and tying up all the things our father left unfinished. He's been my only family for a long time.

Peyton

Paige looks amazing in her wedding dress as she walks down the aisle with her father. Her parents are genuinely kind, they love Rhett. Her mom nags her a lot, she obviously loves Paige very much, so it's kind of sweet. Nova and I stand next to Paige during the ceremony, it's in this beautiful little historic church. There's lots of exposed wood with intricate scrollwork. It's like a fairytale. Rhett looks so handsome, and my eyes water as I watch him, and Paige say their vows. I wish our parents and sister could be here.

Rhett's best men are his best friends. Ace and Thomas have been his friends since he got to boot camp. They all became Army Rangers. Ace left the Army before my brother, and Thomas left after him. The three of them opened their company together. Savage Enterprises is a *Security Company,* but it's more like a quasi-military/police department. They often work with the FBI. Their focus is rescuing human trafficking victims, breaking up the rings, and prosecution of all the bad guys. They rescue kidnap victims, provide security for high profile dignitaries, and celebrities too,

I'm proud of him. Paige used to be a police investigator, but now she works at Savage too.

The wedding reception is at a country club. The building is like a Tuscan villa. There're beautiful vines full of flowers draping the exterior. The décor transports you to a different place. It's July, so it's being held indoors. Florida doesn't lend itself to outdoor weddings most of the year. They chose to have it over the summer so I could be here. When they leave on their two-week honeymoon, I'm going to stay at their place and watch the cats. Paige has two. I love animals and I'm looking forward to it. I'll be babysitting Nova too. She's a handful.

Both best men make toasts that are funny and heartfelt. I can't do it. I know I'll cry, so Nova volunteered to handle the bridesmaid's toast. She looks great in her shortened dress. Thank goodness she's appropriately clothed. She dyed her hair purple to match her dress. It was a shock when I first saw her long white locks in a fluorescent eggplant purple, but I like it now. Everyone keeps complimenting her and I can tell they're being polite, after they're rendered speechless by the initial shock of it.

The guests set down their glasses as Nova speaks, "When I first met Paige, I knew she was very special. My Henry liked her right away. When Rhett first came around, I wasn't sure about him yet. I told him I'd shoot him if he hurt my Paige." She laughs, and everyone joins her thinking she's kidding. Rhett told me she threatened him, and he believed her.

"But Rhett showed me how much he loves Paige. He put her first, always, and that made me like him. Plus, he can cook, and he's nice to look at, too." She winks and more laughter fills the room.

"Now I love them both very much. They're my adopted grandchildren. I'm very blessed to have them in my life. I know they're going to have a long and happy life together. It makes me very happy to know they're so deeply in love. My Henry loves them too and he's a great judge of character. Okay kids, I wish you all the happiness in the world and please Rhett, knock her up on your honeymoon!" Everyone loses it, there's a bunch of whoops and whistles.

They kiss and Nova lifts her glass higher, "Cheers! Cobb! Come dance with your date. I've got my dancing shoes on!" She shouts looking over Rhett's shoulder.

Nova chugs her champagne. Then she takes Cobb's offered hand and spins into him before getting down on the dance floor. I have a huge smile on my face, that woman is something else.

I watch the guests dance while I sip my champagne. A tall guy I haven't met before approaches and he looks from me to the empty seat beside me.

"Hi. Do you mind if I sit here?"

"Go for it, I don't know what happened to the guy that was sitting here." Glancing around I don't see him.

He's tall with dark hair and pretty greenish bluish eyes and wearing a suit which seems like an uncomfortable experience for him. I think he's close to my age, though he's slender, and he has muscles stretching the sleeves of his jacket. As I appraise him, he looks back at me, probably cataloging my features like I am with him. We smile at one another. He's handsome, his jaw and cheek bones are sharp in the best way, he reminds me of Johnny Depp.

"You're Rhett's sister, right?" he asks.

"Yeah. Who're you?"

"Oh, sorry, I'm Micah Castleman. I work with Rhett sometimes. Have you met Samson Del Rey yet?"

"No. Who's that?"

"He's a Special Agent with the FBI, and my boss. We both do a lot of work with Savage."

"Oh, gotcha. So, are you an FBI Special Agent?"

"No, I'm a consultant. But I'm directly employed by the FBI. I'm a computer engineer, like Cobb and Paige," he says. I nod smirking, Paige explained in their world that means he's a hacker. He smirks back knowing I've caught on.

"This is my first wedding. How about you?"

"I was a flower girl when I was little. A friend of our family got married and didn't have any little girls in their family. He was our plumber actually. We had so many plumbing issues that he became friends with my dad."

He chuckles, "That's unusual."

"Yeah, I guess. He was really nice. They used to come by after they got married and had a baby. My sister used to babysit for them."

"That's cool. You're here from out of town, right? College?" Clearly, he's done his research.

"Yep. I'm starting my sophomore year next month at LSU."

"Louisiana? You're from there, right?"

"Yes. I was born and raised in New Orleans, LSU is in Baton Rouge, it's about an hour away."

"What're you studying?"

"Dual majors, psychology and pre-law."

"Holy shit. Sorry. Wow, that's intense."

"It's hard, but I'm motivated, I've always been a good student, and I have no social life," I admitted.

"That's cool, I haven't been to college. I didn't attend much high school either, although I graduated. I don't need college for what I do, so I didn't see the point of spending the money, you know?" he replied.

"I totally understand that. If Rhett wasn't paying for me to go, I wouldn't have been able to, unless I got about ten more scholarships."

Looking over his shoulder at the dance floor he asks, "Do you want to dance?"

"Um, I'm not much of a dancer, but I'll give it a shot."

His smile is wide as he stands and offers me his hand. It's so sweet. I take it and he guides us to the dance floor. A burst of electricity shoots up my arm and my nipples tighten, there must be static electricity or something weird going on here. They're playing a hip-hop song, *Shut Up and Dance*, we both move without moving our feet. I need more to drink for this.

"What type of music do you like?" he shouts to be heard.

"I mostly listen to country, some 80's rock, and a little alternative. How about you?"

"I like alternative. I'm pretty flexible. I always like to have music on in the background. My workout playlist is heavy metal."

"I like some 80's metal. Rhett and I grew up with mostly country, so it's my go-to. He likes old country, like from the 60's and 70's. Our dad used to listen to it." Our feet are moving a bit now, we're getting the hang of it, and I smile at him.

"This is fun."

"What do you want to do with your degrees?"

"I want to help victims of crimes. Mostly victims of sexual assault and human trafficking, help them get through the aftermath. Dealing with the legal side and the trauma."

"That's admirable, I really like helping in the rescues of those crimes. Some of it is difficult to stomach. But it's great when we save someone." He gave a small smile.

"Did you help when Paige was taken and that whole mess?" I asked.

"Yeah. That was especially rough since I know her. Thank God, we found her quickly and she wasn't seriously injured. Rhett probably would've ended up in jail if anything happened to her."

"Definitely. I've never seen him so protective, and he treats me like I'm still a baby," I chuckle. Big brothers are great until they want to run your life.

"Do you want to get a drink?"

"Yes! I'd love to."

We walk over to the bar and away from the loud music. I felt like I was yelling at him, it's a relief to be able to speak at a more reasonable level.

"What would you like?"

"Vodka and cranberry juice, please." He leans over the bar a bit.

"Vodka and cranberry please. Also, a beer." he says to the bartender.

"We have bottles of Budweiser, Stella, Corona, and a local IPA," the bartender says.

"I'll take a Corona. Thanks." The bartender makes quick work of our order. It's an open bar, but there's a tip jar, Micah puts five dollars in the container.

"Do you want to sit? Or walk around?" he asks. He squeezes the lime into his beer and takes a drink. I sip my vodka and cranberry, it's good.

"Let's walk."

He holds his hand out inviting me to lead the way. His hair is falling in his eyes a bit, I guess our dance made some of his gel wear off. He sort of flips it back with a little jerk of his head. We walk out of the room where reception is being held and explore the main building lobby.

"So, what made you get interested in working with victims of crimes?" he asked, taking another sip of his drink.

"I don't know if Rhett's told you, but our sister was murdered. It was when Rhett was in the army, and I was in High School. When Larue graduated, she was working at a bar and taking classes at the community college. She still lived at home with me and dad."

"Shit. I didn't know. Someone mentioned that his sister died, but I assumed it was a car accident. That's terrible, damn, I'm sorry." He looked at his shoes.

"It was awful, our dad died three weeks later. That's when Rhett left the military. He had to take care of me because we had no other family, and I was a minor. I had to stay with a teacher who was kind enough to take me in or I would've had to go into foster care until he was able to get home."

"Wow Peyton, that's terrible. I'm so sorry. I was in foster care for over five years, and it sucked. I'm glad you didn't have to experience it."

"Shit, now I'm sorry, Micah. Did something happen to your parents too?" He tenses and takes a deep breath. I open my mouth to tell him he doesn't have to answer, then he speaks.

"Sort of, my dad left when I was born. I had an older sister, but she disappeared when she was 15. My mom said she ran off with some guy, but it's like she vanished into thin air. My mom was an addict, and I was neglected. Never enough food, and never a steady roof over our heads. When I was 10, she said she was sick of me and went to live with her pimp-slash-dealer."

"Wow, that's so sad." And I thought I had it bad.

He shrugs, "I took care of myself on the streets for a while. I befriended this guy who was a hacker, Spider. He taught me how to hack and I stole food, we traded. I learned and he ate without leaving his place, he had some phobias. When I got caught taking food, I had to stay in a group home for a while. The people running it had no training to deal with kids, especially traumatized kids. It ended up being a *Lord of the Flies* situation, but the adults joined in, and stole from me too. Some kids were abused in care, some were turned out, forced into prostitution, and there were always lots of drugs around. The cops kept hauling the kids to juvie for no reason. I wouldn't wish it on my worst enemy."

"Wow, Micah, that's so horrible. I thought foster care was supposed to help kids. It almost sounds worse than the situation the kids are removed from." Now, I'm really glad my brother saved me.

We reach a door leading to a big patio full of tables and chairs with umbrellas. It's dark but it looks cozy in the twinkle from lights strung through the potted plants. Micah opens the door for me and I head to the railing that surrounds the patio. Looking over it, I can see the ocean, well, the Gulf. The moon is low in the sky and almost full.

"Oh wow, it's so pretty," I say, breathlessly.

"Yes, very pretty."

He's not looking at the moon or the water. He's staring at me with heat in his eyes, I clear my throat. "Ahem. So, what happened to Spider?"

"I'm still friends with him. I haven't seen him in years, we talk online. He's a little further from reality these days, but he's a good guy. He loves to disrupt criminal activities, he's skilled at intercepting illegal money transactions. He steals the money with sleight of hand and donates it to charity."

"Like Robin Hood."

"Exactly. By the time I was fifteen, I was running scams of my own. I was selling college tests and essays. I would hack into the college computer systems, steal the tests, or term papers, then sell them to lazy, drunk, college kids. I made enough to live on. Spider helped me get a place since he was over eighteen and I wasn't. But one day I screwed up and hacked the FBI." he laughed.

"Oh shit! Did you get arrested?" My mouth hung open in disbelief.

"Almost. SSA Del Rey came to interrogate me. He asked me a bunch of weird questions; I didn't understand what he was doing. He wanted to know about my family and my living situation. Then he asked about my skills, he promised I wouldn't be in trouble. He just wanted to know what type of places I hacked, how successful I was, and how much I knew about the dark web. Being a dumb kid and not understanding my rights, I answered his questions. I didn't get in trouble. I was lucky. He and Melanie took me in, and I started working with him. The rest is history."

"You started working for the FBI when you were fifteen? That's crazy!"

"Yeah, I guess it sounds that way now, he needed a hacker, and I needed a home. It worked out." He shrugs.

Peyton

Unfortunately, I'm back in Oakdale and it's only been a few months since the wedding. I'm supposed to be in class, but Nova passed away. Rhett found her resting peacefully in her bed. He and Paige are devastated. Some happy news, Paige is pregnant, only a few months, but I think it'll help them through this.

I've attended far too many funerals, I hate them. My heels keep sticking in the grass, I should've worn flats. The air is comfortable, which helps since we're all in black. The minister is droning on about religious stuff that Nova wouldn't have cared about. Paige thought it would be nice. Rhett won't let anyone argue with her. She's been very upset and he's worried sick. I think she looks good, healthy, and well rested.

All the guys from Savage are here. Cobb and Ace are crying, quiet tears on their cheeks. Cobb was close to Nova; he was at her house at least twice a week. I'm sad too. She was a lively person who was friendly and kind, but also crazy and fun. Her voice is still in my head. I'll certainly never forget her.

Listen here sweetie, don't you dare be sad for even a minute! Life is short, so go for it, do it, and have fun! I smile, then I remember where I am, and it's not appropriate.

I noticed Micah at the service, but I didn't have a chance to talk to him. When we get back to Rhett and Paige's duplex, he's in the kitchen talking with Samson. I watch him until Thomas talks to me.

"Hey Peyton. Can I get you a drink or anything?"

Thomas is one of the two partners in my brother's company and one of his best friends. He's extremely attractive and tall, like all of them. He has defined muscles, with a killer smile. My brother has warned me to stay away from him, I believe he warned Thomas away from me with threats of violence, too. Thomas's nickname is *TomKat* because he's such a manwhore. I look but never touch, yet charm oozes out of him. *Sigh.*

"Thanks, Thomas. I'd love a cold drink. Is there soda or lemonade?"

"There's definitely lemonade. It's all Paige is drinking lately." He laughs.

"That'd be perfect, thank you," I smile. He looks me over appreciatively, then shaking his head, grins and walks off presumably to get that lemonade.

Leaning back on the sofa I stare out the front window. Rhett told me Paige wants to move into Rhett's house now. She's having a tough time being here without Nova. They were with her daily. Paige misses her so much. I completely understand that.

Micah walks up to me and hands me a glass of lemonade, I smile at him and accept it.

"Thomas asked me to bring this to you. Hi, how're you doing?"

"I'm okay. It sucks, she was so sweet and funny. I'll miss her, but I'm more worried about Paige. I'm glad she went to take a nap."

"Yeah. She's having a challenging time. Rhett keeps reminding her that Nova wouldn't want her to be sad. Nova was all about living in the moment and being happy."

"How're you doing?" I ask him.

"I'm okay. I just feel bad for Rhett and Paige. Like you, I'm worried about her, but she'll be okay, she's tough."

"That's for sure," I told him.

"How's school?" He asks.

"Hard. But it's good."

"How's everything with you?"

"Good, I moved to a new place. It's so much better than my old apart-ment. It's two bedrooms and two bathrooms. I'm thinking about getting a cat."

"A cat's going to have its own bedroom and bathroom?" I deadpanned. His eyes snap to mine and after a rapid evaluation, he laughs.

"Yep. I'm going to install scratching pads on all the walls, and a cat spa in the bathroom." He smirks at me. It makes hummingbirds wake up and zip around in my stomach. My own face splits into a big smile. He's making my body come alive, and this is so not the place. I have the strongest urge to kiss his full, smooth lips. I realize I'm staring at his mouth. I clear my thoughts and force my eyes away.

Still smirking, he says, "I had a great time with you when you were here for the wedding. I was wondering if you'd like to go to lunch with me tomorrow?"

"Oh, Micah, I'd love to, but my plane leaves in the morning. I have to be back at school."

His face crumples for a second but he pulls it back into a smile. "Would you give me your number so we can keep in touch?"

"Sure!" I whip out my phone. I quickly put his number in my phone and texted him. I'm not sure I get the point of exchanging numbers when I don't live here, but I like him.

Peyton

Over the next two and a half years Micah and I develop a great friend-ship. We talk all the time, schedules permitting. I like him so much and I know I have feelings for him that I don't understand. We spend time together whenever I'm in town and he visited Baton Rouge twice. I always want to kiss him, but I keep myself from doing it. I just can't bring myself to be in any kind of relationship with anyone. Especially someone who is hundreds of miles away.

I have a few meaningless hookups from time to time, but they're nothing more than a quick physical release. Micah and I don't talk about our conquests, it's an unspoken rule. However, we share everything else.

More and more I realize he's my closest friend and he's often the light to my drudgery through dark library stacks and depressing case law. As the months march on I'm losing myself in my studies and find I'm looking for an escape.

I've finished my bachelor's degree in psychology and my first year of law school. I have two years of school left thanks to LSU's special program. I can finish with a law degree in six years instead of seven. But I'm restless and lonely. Rhett and Paige have a beautiful little girl now, Nova Larue, and they're expecting again. I want to be with my family. I can only admit to myself in the deepest part of my heart, under the covers late at night, I want to be closer to Micah too.

I've decided to finish law school in Florida. I'm moving in two weeks and I haven't told any of them yet. I want to be settled before I let the cat out of the bag. I just don't want Rhett to talk me out of it. Transferring schools is a big deal. Especially, going from well-known LSU to Wellington School of Law. Nobody's ever heard of it, but I don't care. It's done.

Micah

Eagle: Want to have lunch?

Me: WTF? You're here?

Eagle: Literally, I'm in the parking lot ☺

Me: Shit dude! Why didn't you tell me you were coming? I'll be out in a minute.

I'm stunned. Peyton usually tells me when she's coming to town. Hell, I'm usually her ride from the airport. I wonder why she didn't tell me. My stomach tightens like always, that familiar tickle starts in my chest. Peyton is my dream girl. Unfortunately, we've been stuck in this weird friendship zone for years. I regret not kissing her at Rhett's wedding. Somehow, we missed our window and became just friends. I want more but I don't know what she wants. Sometimes I think she would let me kiss her, but mostly I think she would punch me. Letting out a sigh, I close out of my system and go out the door.

She's leaning on her car. I swear she's more beautiful every time I see her. She has dark blonde hair like Rhett, and she's the perfect height for my arm to wrap around her shoulders. Her face, shit, she could make angels sing.

She has intelligent eyes, and her nose is cute with a few freckles sprinkled across it. Her lips are thick and full, so kissable. Dammit, now my dick is hard.

Her face breaks into a huge smile as she runs at me and tackles me with a hug. I grab her in a tight squeeze trying to avoid letting her feel what she does to me. I kiss the top of her head.

"Well, hello! What're you doing here?"

"I'm your new neighbor," she exclaims, surprising me.

"Wait. What?" I hold her away from me and examine her eyes.

"I transferred to Wellington; I'm finishing school here. Surprise!"

"What? That's awesome! Why didn't you tell me? I would've helped you move." I could barely believe it.

"I didn't want anyone to talk me out of it."

"Ah, you haven't told Rhett. Does Paige know?"

"Nope, just you. I'm telling them tonight." She smiles, mischievously at me.

"Oh shit, you're brave. I'm glad I don't have to tell him."

"I was hoping you'd join me. Please? You'll help be a buffer, so he doesn't kill me. You know, witnesses and all?"

I squeeze her, "You're making it impossible; you know I can't deny you when there's begging. Not fair!" I tickle her and she busts out a loud giggle pulling out of my reach.

"Is that a yes?"

"Grrrr... yes, it's a yes. You didn't give me any options." I grin at her.

Changing the subject I ask, "Where're we eating? I'm starving!"

"Come on Radiohead, let's feed you," she decrees.

The initial shock has worn off and we're sitting calmly at Rhett and Paige's table. Nova is in her booster seat eating strawberries, but mostly she's wearing them. Paige's pregnant belly is starting to show. She's past the morning sickness and has a motherly glow, or so I'm told. She just looks normal to me, opposite of when she had morning sickness and looked miserable. I'm happy to see her feeling better.

With my eyes, I encourage Peyton to just spit it out but she's ignoring my hints. I push my fist into her hip, pushing her slightly, and I raise my eyebrows at her, pointing my head in Rhett's direction.

She whispers at me, "I know! Quit it. I'm getting there." I decided to help her along.

"So, Peyton, are you ready for year two of law school?" I ask dramatically.

She shoots me a death glare. "Yes, Micah. I'm all set."

Rhett notices something's up, he looks between us. "Is everything okay with school Pey?"

"Yes, of course. It's just, I've made some changes." She looks down and takes a deep breath, "I transferred to Wellington."

Rhett looks shocked but Paige smiles. "What do you mean?"

"I moved here. I'm going to Wellington for my last two years." She lifts her head and faces him, her chin raised in defiance.

A huge smile breaks across his face, "That's terrific!"

He jumps out of his chair and grabs her in a tight squeeze, and she shrugs at me. Paige is beaming. "Can't breathe!"

"Oh, sorry." He lets her go and holds her out to inspect her.

"What made you do it?"

"I missed everyone. Law school is all consuming and I wanted to be here with all of you. I've already missed so much of Nova's little years. I didn't want to miss out on the next baby." She looks lovingly at Nova.

"Aunt Pey! Pey! Pey!" Nova holds out her sticky hands to Peyton. Peyton smiles and hands her a strawberry. Nova takes a big bite, pink juice leaking down her chin while she chews.

"I want to be around for you guys. I want to babysit and see her achieve her next milestone. I want to be at the hospital when the new one arrives. You're my only family. I love you."

Paige bursts into tears and hugs Peyton, "We love you too! I'm so happy you're here. We've missed you so much."

"Please don't cry Paige, you're going to make me cry," Peyton pleads.

"She cries over everything, it's the hormones. Don't feel bad Pey," Rhett comments, without taking any precautions. Paige punches Rhett in the arm, hard.

"Ow! What? It's true," he chuckles.

"Yeah, but you don't have to point it out. Sorry I punched you."

Rhett rubs his arm, "I'm used to it." He steps back before she can punch him again. I laugh. They're always very entertaining, except when they can't keep their hands off one another. They can get R rated, and then some.

"Did you know about this Micah?" Rhett gives me a hard look.

"No, found out today. I don't even know where she's living yet. She just said she's our neighbor. So, where did you move exactly?" I query.

"Well, I'm just outside Oakdale, over in Mystic Cross. I found a cute little cottage for rent. They used to list it as an Airbnb, but they aren't able to travel back and forth from their full-time home anymore. They wanted an annual renter to take it so it's easier to maintain. Less work for them, you know?"

"I love Mystic Cross, how close are you to the beach?" questions Paige.

"It's one block from the beach. I can't believe how low the rent is for the location. They said they wanted me as the tenant since I'm a law student and responsible. I guess they spoke to my dorm Supervisor."

"Where do they live full-time?" Rhett asks.

"Indiana. They used to come here for the winter and rent it out the rest of the year. They would be booked solid for scallop season," she laughed.

"Yeah, usually you can't touch a rental near the beach from July through September, it sounds great. When will I get to see it?" Rhett asks.

Rio, the cat, comes running into the room like a terror, with Bingo hot on her trail. The two of them race around the room and then Bingo tackles her. Paige and Rhett don't even notice. It's very entertaining to me because I only have one cat. His name is Beta. He's a calico with bright blue eyes. He tears around by himself sometimes, but he doesn't have anyone to tackle. I wonder if my landlord would let me get another one. I'll have to ask her.

Peyton notices me watching them and asks, "How's Beta doing?"

"He's great, but watching them, I wonder if he would like a partner in crime."

"He's friendly, the couple of times we watched him for you. He got along great with our pack," Paige adds.

"I'm going to ask my landlord." Paige smiles. She loves animals. Peyton does too.

"Maybe I'll rescue one too. Once I'm unpacked, I'll have to ask the Renaults."

Rhett takes Nova out of her booster seat and takes her to the sink where he washes her hands. "I think I'm going to get this one into a bath," Rhett announces, to Nova's delight.

"Yay! Bath! Splash boat! Splash boat!"

"Okay munchkin! You got it, we'll play boats. Do you have kisses for Aunt Pey and Micah?"

"Mike-yeah! Pey!" Little Nova reaches out her hands to me. I give her a hug and she splatters a sticky kiss on my cheek.

"Thank you, Nova, have fun in your bath."

"Splash boat, Pey!" Rhett hands her off to Peyton before she jumps out of his arms. She wraps her little arms around Peyton's neck and makes kissing noises as she rubs her face all over Peyton's cheek.

"Thank you, sweet girl. Have fun with your boats. I love you." Peyton smiles lovingly at the excited little girl.

She hands her back to Rhett, and he holds her over his shoulder, and she squeals in delight.

"Are you heading out?" Rhett asks.

"Yeah. You all need to get to bed. Paige looks sleepy." She smiles at Paige.

"I am sleepy. I'm so excited you're here though. Can we talk tomorrow? Maybe have lunch?"

"Sure, text me." Peyton hugs Paige and Rhett, patting Nova on her diaper. Rhett shakes my hand and Paige hugs me. We all say our goodbyes. Peyton and I wash the strawberry off of us before we go out the door.

I met Peyton here, so we step outside for our goodbyes. She leans against her car and I wonder if she's trying to look like a centerfold on purpose. My dick has been hard on and off throughout the evening. My stomach flutters with big bat wings and my skin heats. She has such an effect on me, I feel a bit out of control... not like me at all. She smiles her beautiful smile and I melt where I stand.

"Thanks for doing this Radiohead. It went surprisingly well, I honestly thought Rhett was going to murder me. I'm glad he's okay with it."

"You're his only family too, besides Paige and Nova. I know he's missed you; I didn't think he would be too mad."

"I guess," she agrees.

She stares at me, her eyes sparkle and focus on my mouth for a second. I look at her lips and the urge to kiss her is almost overwhelming. I smirk at her to cover my true feelings. I'm so scared of screwing up our friendship. I couldn't stand it if she wasn't in my life. I'm bad at relationships. I tried half-heartedly a couple times when I was younger, and it didn't go well. My fear makes me crazy and scares women away. I've never had a friendship like I do with Peyton with a guy or a girl. I can't see a way to take us to the next level, but I need to figure it out.

"What are your plans tomorrow?" I ask her.

"Maybe lunch with Paige, otherwise, unpacking. How about you?"

"Do you want help unpacking?"

"Really? That would be great. I have to go to the school on Monday. There's registration paperwork I have to sign and I have to buy books. Oh, I'm also getting a campus tour. I want to be done unpacking this weekend so I can focus on the school stuff."

"I'm your guy," I smiled at her, not elaborating. I am her guy, if she wants me.

"Thanks, Micah, you're the best." She hugs me and I try to keep my crotch from her, hoping she doesn't feel how hard I am right now. This is going to be a problem.

"Happy to help. Will you text me your address?"

"I'll text you when I get home, so you know I made it. Okay?"

"Sounds good. I'll see you tomorrow."

She gives me a quick squeeze and releases me.

"Okay, drive safe."

"You too."

I give her a weird little wave and we both climb into our cars. I wait for her to pull out first and I follow her until I have to turn. Mystic Cross Beach is about 20 minutes west. I live on the northwest side of Oakdale, so we're probably 10 minutes apart. My office is about 40 minutes inland, near Ocala. I work out of the Savage office a lot because it's closer. They have great Wi-Fi with VPN, and they have plenty of room, plus they don't mind if I'm there. I only go to my actual FBI office when I have to, which is more often than I like since I'm a Special Agent now. My boss, Samson, is great and he doesn't mind where I decide to work as long as the work gets done. We actually work directly with Savage all the time when a case warrants it. It's a good symbiotic relationship.

When I get home, Beta wraps himself around my legs meowing loudly, "I know buddy, I've got you." I opened a can of food for him. Then I scratch behind his ears, and he purrs while he chews.

My phone vibrates in my pocket.

Eagle: Hi, I'm home

Me: I'm feeding Beta

Eagle: 77 Sand Dollar Lane, Mystic Cross. It's an aqua cottage with white shutters. It's on stilts like everything over here on the beach. There's a mailbox shaped like a manatee. You can't miss it. You can park under the house next to my car.

Me: what time should I come?

Eagle: I have no groceries yet, so if you bring breakfast you can come at 8 a.m. and I'll buy lunch, even if we have lunch with Paige

Me: you've got a deal

Eagle: sweet dreams Radiohead

Me: back at ya Eagle ☺

I smile at my phone like an idiot, turn on the shower, and throw my clothes into the hamper. I wash my hair first, but my dick is still rock hard. When I soap my body, I grab my dick in my hand and squeeze it. I stroke it slowly thinking about Peyton with her long legs wrapped around me. I think about her perky breasts being squeezed in my hands, and my mouth on her nipples. I imagine they are rosy pink and stiff for me. With my eyes closed and Peyton in my mind, on her knees in front of me, I stroke faster. Her soft pillowy lips wrap around the head of my cock.

"Mmm, yes like that Peyton." In my mind she swirls her tongue around the tip. I rub gently around the head.

"Yeah, baby, don't stop." My cock hits the back of her throat while she sucks me down, her cheeks hollow. She's moaning, and she can't get enough of me. I speed up stroking from the base to the top.

"Fuck! Yes!" Electric tingles shoot down my spine and into my nuts, they pull up tight. "Yes! Peyton!"

My cum hits the tile wall. I lean my hand against cold ceramic to steady myself. I keep stroking my length slowly as shivers flit through my body, until the last bit of cum drips to the shower floor. My body is covered in goosebumps and I'm panting. Damn that was good. I imagine the real thing is like heaven.

Peyton

It's 8:05 a.m. and there's a knock at my door, I look through the peephole. Micah's there with his hands full. I open the door for him and observe two coffees in a tray, a bag of food, and four grocery bags.

"Good morning, what's all that?"

"Home delivery, I got you a mocha latte, croissant breakfast sandwiches, and I come bearing gifts of groceries."

"Holy shit, Micah. Wow! Thanks." Taking the coffee from him I place it on the sofa table. The place came furnished since it was a vacation rental. It's a little too cutesy for me and ocean themed to the max. Not having to buy furniture is great though, because coming from a dorm, I don't have any. Micah sets down the bag of food next to the coffee and he puts the grocery bags on the sofa. I'm starved, so I open the bag, grab a sandwich, and take a huge bite.

"Mmmm, dis is oh ood!" Micah smiles at my lack of manners. Thankfully, he doesn't judge, I smile back, probably with egg on my teeth.

"Sorry, I'm hungry, this is so good!"

"Hey, I'm with you," he takes a huge bite, and his sandwich is half gone. I laugh, egg shooting out of my mouth and landing on his knee. My cheeks turn red as I wipe it off with a napkin.

"Shit, sorry!"

"I'll live." He gives me the sweetest smile. No teeth, so I don't have to see egg on his choppers.

When we're done stuffing our faces, I check out what's in the grocery bags. Aww, he's so thoughtful, he got me toilet paper, paper towels, liquid hand soap, window cleaner, some ready-made sandwiches, and a six pack of bottled water. Oh, and a few bags of chips, under the chips I find a small bag of bagels and cream cheese.

"Thanks Radiohead, you're the best." I kiss him on the top of his head as I walk by on my way to the kitchen to put the groceries away.

"This is a great place! You can't beat the location. You're only about ten minutes from Wellington, maybe twenty minutes to Rhett and Paige. You lucked out finding this place."

"I know, I was actually looking for an Airbnb until I could find a place, and this one said in the comments that they were looking for an annual renter. I called them right away and they sent me the application. I got approved the next morning and signed later that day. It was meant to be."

He grins at me. His eyes trace my face and sit on my lips for a beat. Then they slide to my chest and jump back to my eyes, his cheeks pink a bit. I grin back. He gives me a fluttering feeling in my stomach. My pussy clenches and my panties get damp. I sigh. He always makes me feel things, naughty things.

"I have a ton of boxes in the bedroom and office. There's only these three out here. The Renault's said I can put away any décor or books I don't want around. I plan to pack up their books on this bookcase and put them in these boxes when they're empty. There's a pretty big storage closet under the house."

"Where do you want me to start?"

"I was thinking you could start in the office. Maybe you can set up my computer since you're my tech support." I give him puppy dog eyes. "I'll start in the bedroom, and we can meet back here to tackle these books. How does that sound?"

"Sounds like a plan. How did you get all this stuff up here?"

"I lucked out. The Renaults arranged to have some guys collect the beds from the office and deliver the new office furniture. I told them I would buy it, but they insisted. They want to keep it in there when I move out. I got those delivery guys to bring everything up from my U-Haul trailer for fifty bucks."

"That's not luck, that's smiling your beautiful smile and getting anything you want," he snickers at me.

"Hey, I paid them. They didn't do it because I smiled," I frown at him.

"Did they ask you out?" My cheeks are getting hot.

"No...well, not exactly. They offered to show me a good place to get lunch since I'm new here."

He laughs, "Told you."

"Ugh! You're being such a man, Radiohead!"

"I am a man, want me to prove it?"

Giggling, I walk toward the bedroom, "No! I'm going to unpack, caveman."

He follows me, "I'll be in the office, since I'm the tech support, apparently."

I'm still giggling in my bedroom, when I pull out my Bluetooth speaker and connect my phone, then turn on some country music. I prefer the upbeat stuff and I dance around while I work. I quickly discovered dumping out the boxes on the bed works well for me. A bunch of my boxes are filled with clothes and linens. I'm going to repack the Renault's linens in the boxes when they're empty and put them in the storage closet. I don't want to use anything of theirs besides the furniture. It's not mine and I'm not a vacation renter.

As Micah comes into my room, I dump out another box onto the bed. When the contents fall out, I gasp, "Oh fuck!"

Micah is standing next to me staring at my lingerie and *vibrators*. I own two, a bright purple rabbit and a hot pink Womanyzer. Most of the lingerie is black, dark blue, or purple, providing the perfect contrast to highlight the vibrators. My face is flaming hot and bright red, no doubt. I turn the box over and cover everything with it. I can't look at him.

"I didn't see a thing," he swears.

"Liar."

"What do you want me to do here Peyton?"

"I want you to turn back time."

"That's not going to happen. What else have you got?" he says with a smile.

"I don't know. Please don't look at me."

He grasps my arm and turns me towards him. I'm practically breaking my neck trying to stare at my feet. He places his finger under my chin and lifts my face to his. I'm still looking down with my eyes. I can't face him; my heart is pounding hard in my chest. Sweat is breaking out on my body. I may actually have a heart attack.

He leans down and peers into my eyes. "Peyton, please look at me. You have nothing to be embarrassed about."

My eyes snapped to his. "Are you crazy? Of course, I have something to be embarrassed about. How would you feel if I saw a vibrator at your house?"

"I wouldn't be embarrassed because guys don't use those types of vibrators. It could have only been left by someone else or for some other reason that didn't involve me using it. That's not an equivalent comparison."

"Oh my God! Shut up, you're not helping!" My hands cover my face attempting to hide my embarrassment.

"Hear me out. What if I tell you something equally embarrassing? That would make us even, and that should help right?" he asks.

"I guess, it depends on what you tell me," I reply, intrigued by his offer.

I click off the music using my phone. I noticed a text from Paige. I guess I didn't hear it with the music and dancing, not to mention the embarrassment. Ugh! I shake my head, clearing the frustration out. I hold up a finger asking him to hang on. I read Paige's message and respond.

Paige: Hi Peyton, I'm so sorry I'm not going to be able to make lunch, Nova has a fever. I think it's just teething, but I can't risk getting everyone else sick.

Me: No worries

Paige: I'll give you a call this evening if that's okay?

Me: Of course! Give her a hug for me, I hope she feels better.

Paige: Thanks, me too, ttyl

"Where were we?" I ask.

I'm looking at him now, my cheeks are still heated but my heart has settled a bit. I can't imagine what he'll tell me. I wonder if it will be something sexy. I've seen him in swim trunks, and he is fiiine. He's long and lean with defined muscles. He has a tattoo across the right side of his chest below his pectoral muscle on his ribs, it says, *I have lived a thousand lives!*

There's a game controller next to it. A pretty stimulating tattoo for a gamer nerd. Thinking of it, my nipples peak and I can feel moisture pooling in my panties.

"I was going to tell you something embarrassing so we can get past this."

"I don't see how it will help but go for it." I'm smirking at him hoping he still thinks my cheeks are pink from embarrassment, and not arousal.

"When I got home last night, I jacked off in the shower. I didn't have any toys, but I didn't need them, my imagination did just fine." He has no shame at all.

"Holy fuck, Micah." My cheeks grow hotter, electricity shoots down my spine, and my pussy clenches. I have to look away from him, so he doesn't see the heat burning in my eyes.

"You're still not looking at me. Peyton, it's supposed to put us on equal ground, so you won't be embarrassed anymore. Please look at me," he begs.

I turn my face to him, but my eyes still aren't meeting his. I can't, he'll see how turned on I am. He's my friend, I shouldn't be attracted to him like this. *Come on Peyton, pull it together.* Finally, I lift my eyes. He's looking at my lips, but he meets my eyes when I move. There's desire burning in his expression. I tilt my head, am I imagining his interest? What if he feels like me?

I decided to ask him directly. I've learned to just go for the things I want. The older I get the more committed I am to that philosophy. What if I die tomorrow? My sister never had the chance to do everything she wanted, plus it's what Original Nova would advise. I let my desire show fully in my eyes, deliberately looking at his lips and back to his eyes. I want those lips on mine.

"Micah..."

"Peyton?"

"Do you, um, do you have feelings..."

He kisses me. I open my mouth a little surprised and he pushes his tongue into my mouth. I kiss him right back, tangling my tongue with his perfect one. His arms surround me, and he pulls me against his body. I connect my arms around his waist and rub against him while we explore one another's mouths. Warmth spreads across my skin as my heart pounds in my chest. A rush of wings flutter inside me. I feel his very hard cock against my stomach and arch into him. He slides his hands down my back and grasps my ass, squeezing gently. He lifts me against him, and I wrap my legs around his hips. I rub my soaking pussy against his cock moaning into his mouth. He groans and rubs on me too.

"Mmmm, Micah, I think I've wanted to do this for over a year. You feel so good."

My pussy is pulsing and clenching, I feel like there's a spicy current dancing in my veins. My skin is raised in goosebumps and warm at the same time. I want him so much that the desire floods me. My chest sparks electric, my heart is pounding, and a tingle makes its way into my lady parts.

"I've been wanting to do this since I met you. I didn't think you were interested. I tried to be happy just being your friend, because I like you. But..."

"I like you too Micah. I fought it because we lived too far apart, and I needed to focus on school. Mmmm..." We kiss some more, and the warmth continues to spread across my skin.

"Yeah, I understood and made myself follow your lead. You're okay with this?" His eyes search mine.

"Mmm, yes, so okay. I want you, Micah," I whisper, and trail kisses down his jaw.

"Thank fuck! I want you so much."

He leans over while supporting me by my ass and he swipes everything off of the bed. Then he lies down with me on top of him, my legs are straddled over his hips. Leaning over him I kissed him some more. He explores my body with his hands. He weighs my breasts and squeezes them together. I spread my hands on his chest and grind my soaking pussy against him. Then I sit up straight, locking on his eyes. I lift my top over my head. He sucks in a breath, hissing as he pulls his lip between his teeth.

"Your turn," I grin at him. He leans up and yanks his shirt over his head by the back of his collar. My hands scrape along his chest as he uses his on mine. My nipples feel like they're going to rip through my bra. I lean up, reach behind my back, unhooking it, and let it fall off my arms. His eyes dilate, he grasps my breasts squeezing, and gently pinches my stiff nipples.

"Mmm, Micah, yes." Flames singe across my chest and straight to my depths. We're frantic, I unbutton my shorts and unzip them. I unzip his pants next, unhooking them. I can't take either of our pants off, so I fall to my right and lie next to him. I yank off my shorts and panties. He takes his off too, then he pushes onto his side, looking intense and hot as hell.

He slowly peruses my body from my face to my breasts where he lingers. His eyes slide slowly, like a caress, to my feet and back to my face. I can see his twitching cock and it's perfect. I want to lick it, my tongue traces my lips. His eyes follow my tongue.

"Peyton, you are the most stunning creature I've ever seen. I want to kiss you all over."

"That sounds unbelievable, but if you don't climb on top of me and fuck me right now, I'm going to cry." He chuckles, then he slants over me. Placing one hand on my opposite side, he secures his knees above mine as I spread my legs for him. His body fits between my legs, and he holds himself above me. Reaching up I grab his hips pulling him down on top of me, wanting to feel his weight on top of my body. As he asserts his body onto mine, I grab his ass and drag him against me. He kisses me and I crush his taut ass cheeks in my hands. His stiff cock rubs against my clit and that delicious current shoots through my pelvis. We're both panting and grunting.

"You feel unreal. I want you so much."

"Yes, Micah, fuck me." I push my hips upwards.

"Hang on babe, let me put on this condom," he magically produces it, as if from thin air, he must have pulled it out of his pocket before he ditched his jeans. He tears open the package and slides it on quickly without crushing me. He looks deep into my soul and gives me a sweet kiss.

"I just want to make sure you're really okay with this," he says.

"I'm great, and I'll be better with your big, hard cock in my greedy pussy!"

"Wow, you're bossy in bed. I like it," he grins.

"You'll like it more when you fuck me!" I grin back. I guess he heard what he needed because he lines up his cock with my entrance and plows into me.

"Yes!" I mewl. He feels indescribable. I'm being stretched in the best way. All of my nerves are firing off like crazy.

"Damn, Peyton, you feel unbelievable, you're so tight and so wet. Holy shit, I need to move baby."

"Yes, please, move!" He begins thrusting into me. His cock is massaging my G-spot and it's incredible! I'm moaning so loud, but I don't even care. I'm done being embarrassed. I stretch my legs around his ass and move with each thrust.

"Oh my God! Micah! You're so... amazing! You feel...! Ooooh! Yeeeees! So. Fucking. Wonderful!"

"Fuck yes! Babe, so fucking gooood! So, fucking tight!"

He kisses my lips, my ears, my eyes; he's so sweet, and such a stud. I had no idea. He rests on his elbows and squeezes my breasts, pinching my nipples playfully. He bends and licks my left nipple. My head falls back in ecstasy, my nails scratch up his back.

His head lifts and he writhes in response to my marks on him. It's sending pleasurable twinges through me. We're transported to a cloud, flying through the air. If I didn't know better, I would swear I was high. I feel an orgasm developing, I'm so close. He's thrusting faster, and his strokes are hitting my clit just right. *Oh my God!*

"Micah, yes...I'm...fuck, going to come! Mmmm! Yes, just like that!" I yank on my nipples. My chest arches towards him, lifting from the bed in an arc.

"Aaah, yes, Peyton!"

He plunders me in earnest now, and I want him to find all of my treasure. I'm ready to walk his plank, and he's got my timbers shivering. What the fuck? I'm losing my mind. What's with all the pirate puns? Oooh, yeees, mmmm, Micah as Captain Jack Sparrow...*full speed ahead!*

My skin feels too tight, I want to rip it all off. Chills run over me and hot waves travel all of my nerve endings. My body tenses and I scream nonsense. I pull his ass into me as hard as I can. His thrusts stutter as he yells out. I can't control my movements; my nerves are overloading with sensation as an orgasm begins to shatter me. I feel his cock swell and sputter inside me. He fills the condom. A hot explosion travels outward from my lady bits, up my spine, down my legs, into my very spirit.

"Fuck! Peyton! Fuuuck!"

He slows and opens his eyes looking into mine. I'm panting and so is he. We smile at one another. I'm so happy I giggle. That was the best orgasm of my life. Is! Is the best of my life. It's still alive and sending out sparks to my nerves.

My chest feels tight in the best way, it's full of happy flutters, like sails aboard a ship, maybe a pirate ship, in a strong wind filling them with fuel for adventure and prosperity. We're both sweating, our smiles are huge all the way up to our glittering eyes.

"That was the most incredible, the best, amazing, fantastic... I'm out of adjectives, Peyton. I wish we did that a long time ago. It was hands down the most phenomenal orgasm of my life."

"Mine too. My heart is pounding so hard." I press my hand to my chest as if I can slow it down.

"Yeah, me too. I can't even express how I feel." He pulls out of me and rolls next to me.

"Let me go ditch this condom, I'll be right back." He pops a kiss to my temple. He returns a moment later with a washcloth, and he cleans me off. He's so gentle, more emotions overflow inside me. The very few guys I've done this with slid off me and left. I always wanted it that way. I don't want Micah to go anywhere. He takes the washcloth back to the bathroom, then he climbs next to me and pulls me to his side. I lean against his chest; his arm surrounds me.

"You doing, okay?" He looks at me with trepidation.

"I'm doing perfect," I smile.

"Do you want to talk about it?"

"We can, what do you think?"

"I'm incredibly happy, it feels right. How about you?"

"I agree. I'm happy, and it feels right." His blue-green globes aim upwards in thought. He eyes me next.

"Did you call me Captain?"

Startled, I rapidly blink a few times. "Did I?"

"You were making some really erotic sounds and I'm pretty sure you said something about, *Ride me, Captain!* I mean, it was hot, I'm just curious if I heard you right."

"Honestly, I have no idea what I said. But it was absolutely the best sex of my life. Do you really need to make sense of my brains being fucked out?" I laughed.

"I hope you have a little left for law school and trivia night at the bar and grill," he snickers at me. I shove him, while cracking up.

He tickles my ribs and I squeal, "No! Please no. I can't breathe!" I keep chuckling but it's hurting my lungs.

He gets more serious, "Sorry. You, okay? I'm willing to talk about feelings."

"Huh! Gotta catch my breath. Whew. Okay, I'm good. You know, I think I've had feelings for you for a long time. Maybe since we met. But like

I said before, I was worried about school and the distance. Plus, I don't have the best track record. My senior year of high school I had a boyfriend. It deteriorated quickly after I gave him my virginity. I haven't had a boyfriend since, just a few casual hookups. Of course, Rhett didn't help any. He found out about my boyfriend *and* my virginity. I'm thankful he didn't end up in jail."

"I can see that. Shit! Is Rhett going to kill me? He knows we're close friends, he should be okay with this right?" *Aw*, he looks nervous. His hand shakes a bit as he grips my hand.

"I'm an adult now. I'm sure he'll be fine," I say with a grimace.

"I've had feelings for you since we met. I wanted to kick myself for not kissing you on the patio at the wedding. But I'm kind of glad it worked out this way. We know each other so well now. I know my feelings are solid and I know you, which is nice. I've never had a girlfriend for longer than a week. You already know my virginity story, but I've only ever had hookups. Living on the street and in foster care didn't lend itself to relationships. When I moved in with Samson, I thought it would be disrespectful to bring any girls to his house, so quick hookups were all I ever did."

"I'm really happy I moved here," I grin at him.

"I'm happy about it too. So, are you my girlfriend now? I mean, do you want to be?" I turn to him, unable to wipe the smile off my face, I do want to be. This feels right, but what if I screw it up? *Ugh! Don't go there Peyton.*

"Yes, I want to be. So, you're good with that? You know once I start school, I'm going to be up to my eyeballs in law stuff. It's going to be tons of studying and I may be at the library on campus a lot. Are you going to be okay with me being super busy for a while?"

"We can make it work. I want to be with you, I won't mind if your head is always buried in a book. I can sit next to you working or gaming." He grins and his whole face brightens... he's so handsome.

"Great! Let's do this."

"I'm all in," he smiles brightly.

"Me too." We kiss. Wanting a shower, but remembering I need to unpack, I decide to wait, we get dressed.

"We better get back to work. I need to get this finished. What did you want when you came in here before I embarrassed myself?"

"Please tell me you're over that?"

"I'm good," I giggle like an idiot. Maybe he did fuck my brains out. It's okay, I'll flunk out happy as can be.

"Oh yeah, I came in here to ask you what I should do with your books. Are you putting them in any special order or anything, in the living room or the office bookcases? Also, what do you want me to do with the weird skull?"

"What weird skull?"

"It looks like some kind of animal skull. Is it a Halloween decoration?"

"I don't know what you're talking about. Show me."

Following him into the office, he points into the top open box. I look inside, and there is a weird skull. I reach out and touch it. Lifting it, I twist it around and look it over. There's a piece of paper inside, it falls to the floor. Micah picks it up and hands it to me. I hand him the skull. He looks it over while I open the folded piece of paper.

"This is so weird. I've never seen this before. What do you think it is?"

"It looks like maybe a cat, based on the teeth, but I'm not sure."

"Oh shit," I exclaim.

"What?" I showed him the paper.

You can't run from me. I'll find you.

"What the fuck? You've never seen this before?" he asks.

"No, never."

"Shit, I wish we didn't touch it. Put down the paper."

I set it on the desk, and he puts the skull next to it. He leaves the room, I'm uncomfortable being here alone with the skull. He comes back with a plastic baggie. Using the baggie, he picks up the skull and flips it into the bag. Then using just his fingernails on the edge he puts the note in with it.

"What are you going to do with it?"

"I'll send it for analysis through my office. They'll be able to tell us what it is or was, and if they're any fingerprints. Then they'll try to identify any prints they find."

He takes an index card off my desk and has me touch it with the same fingers I touched the note and skull with, so basically all of them. His prints are on file, so he doesn't do the same.

"Maybe it got in there by mistake or something. I can't imagine where it could've come from. My roommate was already gone for the summer when I was packing. Oh," I freeze remembering something.

"What is it?"

"I'm not sure. For the couple weeks before she left, there were some strange things that happened."

"What kind of things?" he asks, sitting up and putting on his FBI face.

"Stupid things, like stuff was moved or missing. I assumed it was my roommate, even though she denied it. I just figured she didn't remember doing it. She drank all the time. But it still happened after she left." I unconsciously rub my head trying to pull out the memories.

"The night she left, there was a stuffed animal on my bed. I thought she left it there. But maybe..."

"Did you have a disagreement with anyone?"

"No. I barely talked to anyone. Just a little in class and I had a study group, I probably talked to them the most, and my roommate, that's it. I didn't have a fight with any of them. I worked with a few people at the internship I did for eight weeks at the beginning of this summer, but I didn't have any trouble with anyone."

"Okay, let's not freak out. We can wait and see what the lab has to say and go from there. But obviously whoever it was is in Baton Rouge, not here. Who knows, it's possible it wasn't even directed at you."

"Yeah, okay," I agree, hoping he's right. I take a deep breath and focus back on what we were doing. Trying very hard to ignore the baggie on my desk.

"Alright, books. The ones in here I want in the office bookcases, and the ones in the living room should fit out there, I hope. If some don't fit in either place, we can swap them."

"I noticed a lot of them are true crimes. I didn't know you were into that," he points out.

"Yeah, I bought them to help me figure out what happened to my sister. The police never had any leads. She just disappeared and two weeks later they found her body. We don't know anything about where she was or what happened to her during those two weeks." I look around the office and realize he got a lot done in here. My computer is hooked up, my office chair is put together, and my desk accessories are all arranged. My files are in the filing cabinet.

"You got so much done here. Thank you."

He nods, then says, "Finish telling me about your sister." I sit in the chair, and he leans on the desk.

"Like I said, the cops had nothing, no leads at all. They found her dumped in a field. It was near the executive airport, maybe five miles from our house. She was strangled and raped. They even have DNA, but no suspects to match it. She had some bruises on her body in various states of healing. She had marks on her wrists like she had been restrained. I've been searching for information since they found her. Rhett never wants to talk about her, but I can't stop thinking about her. She was more than a sister, she was like a mother to me. I know Rhett feels guilty that he wasn't there, but it's not his fault. I think that guilt is why he won't talk about her."

"I have resources available that you wouldn't be able to access. Would it be okay with you if I looked at her file and investigated a little?"

"Yeah of course! That would be great. Here, I have a file with everything I've found out. It's not much." I open the filing cabinet and hand him her thin file.

"Will this tell me the police information, the time frame, and locations?"

"It's all in there. In fact, I don't mind if you want to set up a work area for investigating here. You could tack information on that wall if it helps. I'm picturing CSI, with red yarn pinned in a spider web of facts and locations, maybe some maps. I've never looked at photos of her body, though, and I don't want to. If you get any of those, please keep them away from me."

"Sure, I'll work on it. I may have questions... I promise you won't see any pictures," he adds.

We get back to work, I hide the vibrators in my nightstand and get the rest of my clothes put away. I put the cute picture of Nova's second birthday on the tall dresser. When I find a picture of me and Larue, I put it on the long dresser. There's another picture of all of us, me, Larue, Rhett, and dad. I study her. She was so pretty. When I was young, I never thought of her as pretty, she was just Larue. But looking at her picture, I see her natural beauty. She had dark blonde hair like me and Rhett with light green eyes. In different lighting they were different colors. Sometimes they looked almost yellow, green, or hazel. She had a dark blue ring around her iris that made her eyes stand out. When she got highlights in her hair it brought out her eyes, and they would almost glow. She had dimples like Rhett, but I have none. I remember she was tall-ish at five-foot-eight. I'm only five-foot-six. She had pale skin, where Rhett and I tan fairly easily, but she would burn. She took after our mother. Her cute nose and full lips gave her a stunning smile. People always say, *she just lit up the room with her smile,* when someone dies. It was true with Larue. People were drawn to her, when she entered a room all heads would turn, all eyes would follow her.

Micah pops his head in my door. "I got everything put away in the office and I packed the rest of their stuff up. Where do you want me now?"

I walk close to him and lean in, hugging him. He hugs me back.

I look up at him, "Thanks for doing this. Let's get these boxes down to the storage closet. Then I'm thinking lunch."

He squeezes me back. We heft a couple boxes and take them downstairs. After we get them stacked in the closet, I scan everything. We only have the books in the living room and two boxes in the kitchen. We're going to finish this today. Doing it alone would've taken me all weekend.

I examine Micah, appreciating his form and handsome face. Warm feelings swirl in my gut. He's been my best friend for at least two years. He's so smart, and he makes me laugh so much. I hope I don't screw this up. I need him in my life.

He scrutinizes my face. "You doing, okay?"

"Yeah, just hoping I don't screw this up. I need you. I have insecurities, you're my best friend, and now..."

"Now, you're my girlfriend, *and* my best friend. I think it's perfect, I won't let either of us screw it up. Just promise when you're worried, you'll talk to me, okay?"

"I promise." I smile wide, he's awesome and I'm lucky.

"I'm hungry, let's eat. Do you want to go out or order in?" He asks.

"Let's go out, that little place the movers showed me was good."

When we return from lunch Micah pulls under the house to park, and there's a guy standing next to my car. He's short, well, compared to Micah. He's stocky with muscles, and dark hair. I've never seen him before. Micah looks at me with lifted brows, I shrug.

"Hey, how's it going?" Micah asks the guy.

"Good, man, I live next door. Just wanted to introduce myself. I'm Orlando Diaz." He extends his hand, they shake, and Micah offers Orlando a friendly smile.

"I'm Micah, this is my girlfriend Peyton. She's your neighbor. Nice to meet you."

He looks from Micah to me. He looks me up and down, and my skin crawls. I hate that. Forcing a smile, I hold out my hand to him, he accepts and shakes it gently. His hand is clammy and feels like a slug in mine. Yuck, I don't like him.

"Nice to meet you, which house is yours?" I grilled him. He points next door to a house with wood siding and dark trim. I nod at him.

"Great, thanks for stopping by. We've got to get back to unpacking, so we'll see you later," I start walking to the stairs, Micah follows me. Orlando just stands there. Whatever.

Once we're inside, I turn to Micah, "I don't like that guy. He makes me uncomfortable."

"I didn't get a feeling either way. He's probably lonely or something. I wouldn't worry about him."

"I guess you're right. Let's tackle those books and get finished, then we can go out and do something fun tomorrow." I flutter my eyelashes at him. He chuckles and swats me on the ass, then pulls out of my reach.

"Hey, no fair!" I pout, folding my arms across my chest like a petulant child.

He snickers and opens up a box. I start taking books off the shelves and stacking them next to the box he's working on, while he empties the box, placing my books onto the shelves. We make quick work of it.

Sometime later the rumble of a motorcycle starts outside. I peek out the window. There's Orlando, my new neighbor, perched on a Harley. He's wearing a leather vest over a t-shirt. His vest is similar to what I've seen other bikers wear. On the back of his vest is a logo. It looks like biker insignia, but I can't read it from my window. The picture in the middle is an outline of the sun, with a skull that has horns, centered on it. I watch as he slowly drives away.

"What? You look like you've seen a ghost."

"It was Orlando riding a Harley. He had on a leather vest with a logo on the back. Do you know anything about the local bikers?"

"Yeah, I'm familiar with them. What did it say?"

"I couldn't read it, but I could make out the logo in the middle. It looked like a sun with a skull that had horns. Does that sound familiar?"

"Fuck." My eyes go wide at his reaction. I look out the window, Orlando's gone, the nerves clench in my stomach. I've got a bad feeling.

"You know them?"

"Yeah, that's the Southern Suns moniker. They aren't good guys. They sell drugs. Some have been involved in human trafficking and guns. We're watching them. Their VP, Buzzard, is wanted by the FBI. They were involved with the police chief that got arrested when Paige was taken. We caught a couple of pledges, but the guys we really wanted got away. Their President, Razor, is on death row, but he's still in charge from behind bars. We just can't pin anything on him, and even if we could, he's already on death row. He can't die twice." His face scrunches in thought. "I'm going to shoot a text to Samson and let him know about Orlando. I'll dig into him and keep you posted. Just stay away from him as much as possible for now. Okay?" he asks.

Wrapping my arms around him I nod. Shit, I don't need any more drama. I moved to this place because it's peaceful. I have to study a lot. I can't deal with any problems. He hugs me back and we stand there, in each other's arms. He rests his cheek on my head and we both squeeze tight.

Micah

I don't want to scare Peyton, but I won't keep anything from her either. She needs to stay safe. SSMC is bad news. I'm going to have a long talk with Samson and Rhett, then install an alarm with cameras for her. She needs peace of mind. She has a lot of work to do for her law degree and she can't be worrying about some asshole next door. Not to mention whoever put that skull and note in her things.

I hug her tighter and hope I'm giving her some reassurance. I'm overwhelmed with a need to protect her. I feel a strong urge to claim her publicly as mine and then be vigilant to keep her safe. I want to climb onto the roof and pound my fists on my chest. Some alpha male bullshit, I suppose. My feelings for her are fierce now, and I'm letting them loose. I may already love her. I know I've loved her as a friend for a few years, but is it any different now that we're dating? She pulls back and looks up at me. She seems okay, not worried, and I smile.

"There're only two more boxes in the kitchen. Then we can take all these boxes downstairs and be finished!" she grins.

"Sounds like a plan, let's get to it." By the time we finish and get everything stacked neatly in the storage closet, it's dinner time. I'm tired. We unpacked all day. Well, almost all day. A grin splits my face as I remember what we did earlier.

"Why are you smiling like that, Radiohead?"

"Just thinking we should order some food and maybe watch a movie?"

"My cable isn't hooked up yet, but we could watch on my laptop. Do you want pizza? The Renault's left a pizza brochure in the kitchen. Tony's, I think."

"Sounds good. You want me to do it?"

"Nope, I've got it. Just let me grab that menu." She types on her phone while she looks at the menu. We agree on pepperoni, mushrooms, and onions. When she's done, she says, "It'll be about 45 minutes. I think I'm ready for a shower. Want to join me?" She gives me a sexy smile and licks her lips. Fuck yeah, I do.

"Yes! Definitely."

She slowly walks backwards to the bathroom and lifts her shirt over her head, then she tosses it at me. I like this game, and I yank mine over my head by the back of the collar and drop it. She reaches behind her back unhooking her bra, then shoots it at me like a slingshot. It hits my chest and falls. Fuck! She's incredible. Her breasts are firm and rounded, her rosy nipples are peaked. My dick immediately swells in my pants. I can feel the moisture of precum on my boxer briefs. She's like a sex goddess.

She unbuttons her little shorts, and slowly slides the zipper down. She's killing me! My dick wants to bust out of my pants at this point. She slips her shorts down her long legs and then uses her foot to kick them at me. They hit my crotch and I groan. She looks at me expectantly, and I unbutton my jeans, rip down the zipper, and kick them off in record time. My dick twitches. She looks at my chest, and my abs, and then my dick. There's a sultry smile on her face and her eyes are filled with lust. I feel that alpha male inside me lift his head, he wants to claim her.

She hooks her thumbs into the sides of her tiny panties and slowly, so slowly, slides them down her legs. Then she uses her foot again to fling them at me. I catch them in my hand and stuff them into my mouth like an animal. I growl at her and chase her towards the bathroom, ready to attack, she squeals in delight as she runs. Once I have her trapped in the bathroom, I start the shower, tear off my boxer briefs, and let my dick free. He points at her and my arousal leaks from the tip. She licks her lips.

"If you keep doing that, I'm going to make you put that sexy tongue to good use."

She purrs at me, "Mmmm, sounds perfect!"

She steps into the shower. It's pretty big for a cottage, I guess the owners went all out on this bathroom since it's the only one. There's a soaking tub by a stained-glass window. It has a blue dolphin in a blue and green ocean. As far as stained glass goes, it's pretty nice and lets in a lot of light. We'll have to try out the tub sometime, it's big enough for two. I joined her in the shower. She wets her hair and steps aside so I can wet mine. She washes her hair and I wash mine, watching as bubbles slip down her breasts coating her nipples until the water washes them away. My dick keeps pulsing, and she watches with a suggestive little grin.

When she rinses the soap from her body, I rub my hands on her breasts, squeezing them gently. I caress her ribs and down her hips feeling her shape, she's perfect. I bend onto my knees and lift her leg over my shoulder exposing her to me. Her pussy is beautiful, pink and wet. I look up at her touching her clit. She sucks in a breath and watches me. I slowly circle her clit, she moans. I lean in and lick her clit, she moans louder. Her head falls back and she's panting.

"Oooh, Micah! Yes! Mmmm."

Her hips buck her clit further into my mouth. My finger eases to her entrance. She moves her hips so that my finger sinks in a bit. I press it into her, and she clenches squeezing my finger, I'm mesmerized. She's so tight, wet, and warm. I add another finger and she moans loudly. I run my tongue over her clit towards my fingers and back again. She's rubbing her clit against my mouth. My fingers pump faster in and out of her.

"Oh my God, Micah! Yes!" She grasps my hair in her hands and moves my head and her hips. She is so fucking erotic that my dick is about to bust. Damn!

"YES! MICAH!" Her pussy clamps down on my fingers and she jerks her hips. I watch as her skin breaks out in goosebumps, and a shiver works its way down her entire body. When she's done wiggling, I take my fingers from her pussy and lick the cum from her, then I lick my fingers clean.

Groaning, I tell her, "Babe, you taste amazing. You're so beautiful when you come, your pussy is the prettiest thing I've ever seen. I want to watch you come apart for me every day."

I lift her leg off of my shoulder and set it down, making sure she's steady before I stand. Her lids drape her eyes, her face has a satisfied pink glow, and her lips are drawn into a sexy grin. I wish I had my phone to take her picture. She looks more beautiful right now than I've ever seen her. Can she truly be mine?

I pull her in for a hug, she wraps her arms around my waist and squeezes my ass, pulling her body into mine. My throbbing dick presses into her hip. She leans back and looks up to my eyes. While she gives me a heated stare, her hand glides from the base of my dick to the head, and a groan hisses out of me. Fuck yes!

She falls to her knees, never taking her eyes off mine. She wraps her hand around the tip of my dick and then slowly moves back to my nuts. One hand continues to skate up and down my length while the other cups my balls. She leans forward, her tongue licks the precum from my tip.

"Yes, baby, just like that. Mmmm."

Her lips envelop the head as my dick slowly pushes to the back of her throat. She licks around the tip and shaft as she moves me in and out of her mouth. I can feel how tight her throat is as she sucks me down, her cheeks hollowed. Her hands grasp my ass as she pulls me further into her mouth. Her hands find my hands and she places mine on her head. She encourages me to control her movements. Oh, my fucking God, this is beyond my dreams. I start to feel tingles shooting down my spine, and my balls tighten and lift. A surge of sensation explodes from my nuts and into my dick.

"Peyton! Fuck! I'm going to...fuck!" Cum rushes from me, it shoots down her throat. She keeps licking me and sucking, swallowing every drop. I'm mumbling nonsense, shivering as I fill her. *Holy hell!*

"Damn! Babe! That was... holy fuck! That was amazing!" She smirks at me and licks her lips. Fucking hell, she's so damn sexy, like a porn star, only real, and so much better. I take her hand and lift her to stand with me, I kiss and hug her.

"I told you I jacked off in the shower, but I didn't tell you that I was imagining you on your knees in there with me. That was better than I imagined, better than I could ever imagine. You might have to marry me!" She laughs. I'm not sure if it's a joke, but I laugh with her.

We leave the shower and go to her bed. We're wrapped in towels with an extra towel on her hair. She looks adorable, and we snuggle on her bed. She curls up next to me with her head on my chest.

"Will you stay over, please?" she asks. Like she has to beg.

"Of course. I don't want to leave you, you're right where you should be." I squeeze her a little.

"Oh, what about Beta?"

"He has an automatic feeder and water, he'll be fine. Sometimes I get stuck at work so I had to set him up in case I can't get home. He gets mad at me, and he'll pout a little, but he gets over it if I give him a treat. He's pretty mellow."

"I can't wait to meet him. I didn't get the chance when I was here last time, remember?"

"Yeah, you ended up babysitting Nova when Rhett had to go out of town and Paige got Covid. Let's not repeat that any time soon."

"Yeah, I was so worried about her, of course we were terrified Nova would get it. Luckily Paige was able to quarantine on the other side of the duplex."

"That makes me think of Nova the First. I can't believe they found all that money in her house. I love their plan for it."

"Yeah, me too. Once the baby comes, they're going to dive into it. I think Nova the First would've loved their idea. It'll be really cool to see all of it come together." She has a big smile on her face just thinking about it.

"It's an excellent idea. The victims we rescue need so many services. Making that happen will help a lot of people. I love their plan to house them in Nova's houses too. The renovations are expensive, but I think they're going well."

"They are, Paige filled me in on how everything is progressing when we talked last week. She's so excited about it. I think being able to provide that link back to a good life will be a rewarding endeavor for them, and priceless for the women and children they'll help."

The doorbell rings, I collect our pizza and some paper plates and napkins, then bring everything back to her bed. She sits up and crosses her legs. I get us a couple bottles of water and we eat our fill. When we're done, we're content to just stay in her bed.

She yawns and covers her mouth. She looks sleepy. I decided to be quiet and let her drift off. I'm still thinking about the biker next door, not ready to rest yet. I texted Samson and we're having a meeting about it Monday. I need to talk to Rhett. I'm going to tell him about our change of status, the biker, and the skull. Shit, I hope he doesn't want to kill me.

Eventually I feel tired and let myself drift off.

Peyton

My eyes flutter as the morning sun brightens behind my lids. Stretching, I feel warmth behind me. Micah pulls me into his body pressing his morning wood into my ass. Mmmm, this might be heaven. I don't want to move, but my bladder has other ideas. I try to scoot toward the edge of the bed, but Micah holds tight.

"Baby, no, you can't get up yet," he begs.

"I don't want to, believe me, but my bladder is calling the shots right now. I'll come right back. Promise." He groans, frustrated, and gives my breasts a squeeze. Then he pats my ass, I guess that's permission to get up. I grin because he's so adorable.

I snuggle back in bed with him after I take care of business. I could stay right here all day. Unfortunately, I have things to do, plus, now I'm hungry. My stomach voices its needs right on cue.

"Mmmm, you're hungry. We better feed you," he laughs.

"All I have are the bagels you brought. I need groceries."

"Yeah. Let's go to my place and you can meet Beta, I can get some clean clothes, and we can eat breakfast. Then we can do something fun, and after that, groceries. What do you think?" As my stomach growls louder, I agree.

"Sounds like a plan, let's get dressed."

"I have to warn you, Beta might just run and hide with a stranger in the house or he might be mad at me, and you'll be his new best friend. He's not predictable." His face twists into a silly mask with his eyebrows raised and his eyes crossed, and his tongue out to the side. He's so funny and goofy, I hug him while placing a kiss on his cheek.

"What was that for?"

"You're just really cute," I smile at him. He makes a warm feeling bubble up in my chest. My heart sings a happy song. I'm glad we decided to push past our friendship because this feels right. I'm a little afraid it won't last, but my hope is overpowering my misgivings in this moment. Nova the First is in my head: *You have to jump on it when life hands you something good, or jump on him if he's good, sweetie!* I miss her.

"Okay, fingers crossed he's in a friendly mood," he opens the door, "Beta? Buddy? We have a special guest, come say hello. Here kitty, spspsps."

I follow him into a modern apartment, it has tile floors and black leather furniture. A cat tree and scratching post decorate the corner. There's a large box of cat toys. Beta must have one of everything at the pet store. An orange, black, and white blur comes speeding around the corner and meows loudly at Micah. Then he notices me and freezes for a second, the hair on his back lifting and his ears pulling down.

"Hi Beta, I'm Peyton. It's so nice to finally meet you."

I squat down and hold out my hand for him to sniff. He stalks over to me and investigates my fingers. I hold still, letting him choose what happens. He rubs his face on my hand. Taking that as a good sign, I rub his cheeks, he purrs and comes closer. I plop onto my ass and hold out my hands, inviting him into my lap. He climbs on to me and rubs his face under my chin. I scratch his ears and rub his back. He purrs louder and rubs his body against mine. I think we've come to a mutually beneficial agreement.

He's a beautiful large calico. He has bright blue eyes, with his sharp coloring he could be in advertising, he looks like a model. Micah watches with his mouth parted and his eyes wide.

"He's never been so quick to accept anyone. I knew you were special," he winks at me. I giggle, Beta is tickling my neck with his whiskers while he licks my chin with his warm sandpaper tongue.

"I'm gonna go get some clean clothes on. Then I'll start breakfast. Are eggs and bacon okay with you?"

"Sure, I'll eat anything for breakfast. You know me, cold pizza, cake, ice cream, mac and cheese. Hey, Beta, okay bud, you're getting a little fresh!" I pull his face out of my shirt. He comes right back rubbing his face on my neck, I can't stop giggling at him. Micah wanders off to change and I lie back on the floor with Beta on my chest. We're definitely going to be good friends.

My stomach is stuffed, Micah did a good job with breakfast. I helped him clean up and now we're just chilling on the sofa, while I type a list for the grocery store into my phone. Beta is curled next to him, asleep. Micah is looking up things for us to do. I'm actually perfectly happy on his sofa. Everything with Micah feels relaxed and comfortable. My phone rings in my hand making my ringtone play a parody of The Wall- by Pink Floyd. It's about lawyers. *"All we are is just another dick in the law..."* Micah cracks up.

"Hi Rhett, what's up?"

"Do you want to come over for dinner? Paige feels bad she couldn't meet you yesterday. Nova's okay, no fever today, we think it's just her teeth. She's drooling an ocean every hour," he chuckles.

"Hang on one second," I cover the phone and ask Micah.

"Do you want to go to Rhett's for dinner?"

"Sure."

Uncovering my phone I ask, "Is it okay if Micah comes?"

"Of course. What time works for you? We were thinking around five o'clock. Is that okay?"

"Yeah, that's fine, thanks. We'll see you then." Nova screams something and laughs hysterically through the phone.

"Oh shit! Okay, we'll see you later, Bye. Nova ... what did daddy say..." the phone disconnects. I laugh.

Micah tilts his head, "What's so funny?"

"Nova was getting into something; I could hear her laughing like crazy and Rhett kind of hung up on me to chase her."

"She's full of mischief, I hope this next one is a bit easier. You ready to go to Publix?" he asks, grabbing his keys.

"Yes! Let's get this over with, I'm not a fan of grocery shopping. But I love having a stocked refrigerator." He stands and offers me his hand. I say goodbye to Beta and we're off.

When we pull up under my house, there's no sign of Orlando, I'm so relieved. We lug all of the groceries upstairs and get everything put away. Micah had the great idea to get subs from the deli. Nobody makes subs better than Publix. We didn't have a Publix in Baton Rouge, so I only have them when I visit Rhett. Now, I'll probably overdose on them, and my clothes won't fit anymore. We eat our yummy lunch and then watch a movie. I just want to snuggle with Micah, I don't feel like going out. He let me decide the activity, so I let him choose the movie, The Avengers.

Around 3:30 p.m. a loud motorcycle starts up outside. Then another one and another, I look out the window towards Orlando's house and see a group of guys with motorcycles standing around. They're talking and drinking beer while two of them look over the engine on one of the bikes. Micah looks over my shoulder. They're all wearing the same leather vests. I hope this isn't a regular event or I'll have to study with headphones.

When it's time to leave for Rhett's, I'm nervous about walking outside with all those bikers out there. Micah tells me to ignore them, and I purposely don't look in their direction. We're taking Micah's vehicle, so I focus on getting inside his SUV. He has a tall, full-size Range Rover. I take the stairs as fast as I can without falling on my face. When I get to the door Micah has already unlocked it. I climb in and close my door so fast you would think there's a monster on my heels. When Micah climbs in, he starts the engine right away, but someone calls out his name.

"Stay here." He turns toward the voice, it's Orlando.

"Hey man, what's up?" he greets the biker.

"Hey Micah, I was wondering if you and Peyton wanted to come over for some beers and BBQ?" Orlando offers.

"Thanks, but we're on our way to dinner with family. Maybe another time."

"Okay. Have a good one," Orlando says, disappointed.

"You too. See ya." Micah climbs back into the truck. Orlando stands next to my driveway and watches us pull out. He waves, Micah and I wave back. What else can we do? He stares at me, and my skin raises with goosebumps.

"I don't want to eat with him, ever."

"I know. We'll just be polite when we have to be. I've no intention of ever actually having a meal with him either." Micah's face was stern.

We change the subject and chit chat about random stuff on our 20-minute drive to Rhett's. I put the bikers out of my mind. When we get to Rhett's I realize we didn't discuss telling Rhett about us. I guess we're going to play it by ear, I squeeze his hand and he squeezes mine back.

"Don't be scared of Rhett, he likes you a lot."

"That was before I was dating his little sister." He offers me an oversized smile, his nerves showing. I wrap my arm around his waist.

"It'll be fine and don't worry. I'll look after Beta if he kills you," I deadpan.

"Thanks! That helps," he gives me a sarcastic smile. We walk right in, and Nova comes running at me.

"Aunt Pey!" She tackles me around my legs. I grab her and pick her up for a hug. I swear she grows every time I see her, even if it's only been a day.

"Hi munchkin! You're so big! Did you grow again?"

"Yeah," she nods her head up and down. She's adorable, I love her so much. She leans on me giving me a hug and drools all over my cheek and shoulder. I don't mind, but I need a rag. Rhett comes around the corner and hands me a little towel. He's such a dad now, and I love it. Nova wiggles to get down, she slides down on me and hits the ground running.

"Mike-yeah! Mike-yeah! Up!" She charges him, he catches her and lifts her all the way to the ceiling and then into a hug. She squeals in delight.

"Hi Cutie, how's my favorite little girl?"

"Up! Up!"

"Okay, look how tall you are Nova!" Her hands touch the ceiling, and she squeals again. He looks like a natural. My heart warms in my chest and flying creatures unfurl in my belly. I look to my side and see Paige staring at me. She looks at Micah then back at me. She smiles wide and gives me a barely perceptible nod. Shit! She knows. That woman is so freaking smart.

"Hi Paige!" I wrap her in a tight hug. She's become like a sister to me.

"I won't say anything until you're ready. I'm so happy for you," she whispers in my ear.

"Thanks," I reply quietly and give her a conspiratorial smile. Nova wiggles for Micah to put her down. Then she grabs his hand and pulls him to the living room.

"Come, Mike-yeah, blocks!"

"Hey Paige, I'm being commanded to play blocks. Can we all move to the living room?"

"Her majesty has spoken; you better do what she says. Do you guys want anything to drink?" Paige asks.

"I'll get it, you go sit with them. What do you all want? I'm gonna have a beer. Lemonade for you, Turner? Micah?" It's so sweet my brother still uses the nickname he gave Paige when they met, *she's a real page turner,* popped into his head in our dad's joking voice. It's what he's called her since then.

"A beer sounds good," Micah says before he's dragged away.

"Lemonade sounds good. I'll go supervise the construction," Paige answers following them.

"You mind helping Pey?"

"Course not," I follow Rhett to the kitchen. He grabs out two beers and starts pouring lemonade.

"I'll have lemonade too please," I say, leaning on the counter.

"How's the new place?" I pick up the beers and start walking.

"It's great! Micah helped me unpack so I'm all set for tomorrow. I have some paperwork and a campus tour next." I smile. I'm happy to be here.

He follows me with the lemonades. When we get to the living room Micah is on the floor with toddler Lego's and Nova is in front of him telling him what to do. Paige is on the sofa with her feet up watching them. I place a beer on the table by Micah and the other one on the end table next to where Paige left room for Rhett. He hands me my lemonade and gives Paige the other one. This is so nice; this is why I want to be here.

"Tell us more about your place Pey," Rhett says.

"It's really cute. We unpacked everything and got it all put away. We packed the landlord's stuff and stacked it in the storage cabinet. I have two bedrooms, so one is an office now. They were sweet and took out the beds from that room and put in a desk. For a small place the bathroom is really nice, it has a huge walk-in shower and a soaking tub I haven't tried yet. Micah set up my computer and helped with all the books and lugging

everything down for storage. I'd still be unpacking if it wasn't for his help."
I smile at him in appreciation and Paige grins at me.

"We went grocery shopping this morning, so I'm in good shape."

Rhett smiles at Micah, "Thanks for helping her so much man, I don't
know when I could've made it over to help her. You're a good friend.
What's that saying about knowing who your real friends are because they
help you move and will pick you up at the airport?"

"I think you nailed it big guy," Paige giggles at him.

"I need to talk to you about some things, Rhett. Is it cool if I talk here?"
Micah asks indicating Nova.

"Yeah, it's fine, just be mindful of language because she's repeating
everything. But she won't know what you're talking about. Is it work
stuff?"

"Yes and no."

Micah looks at me with his brows raised in question, I take a deep breath
and nod. May as well jump right in. He can't kill Micah with Paige, Nova,
and me watching. Hopefully he won't want to kill him. I may have to
remind him that I'm an adult and I can do what, or whom, I like. Ugh,
awkward.

"As you know, ahem, Peyton and I have been friends for several years.
We've grown very close, and we've decided to change our relationship."
Rhett tilts his head and raises his eyebrows while squinting a bit. I'm
holding my breath, and my heart is pounding. Adrenaline floods my veins
and I feel myself tremble. Micah has pink cheeks and his hand shakes as
he waits for Rhett to catch up. Suddenly, Rhett's mouth pops open, his
eyebrows raise comically, then his eyes go wide. He gasps.

"Oh! Are you?" He looks back and forth between us. My lips are pressed
together, and I think I completely forgot how to breathe.

"Are you together? Since when?" He moves to the edge of the sofa, and
he places his fists next to his thighs. I take in a quick breath and his eyes
dart to mine. They're once again narrowed as he examines me. I plaster a
bright smile on my face and nod subtly. He shoots his gaze back at Micah.

"Technically, since yesterday. But we've been interested in each other for
a long time. I was afraid to get involved with Peyton because I really like
her, and my past relationships have not gone well. I didn't want to ruin
our friendship, which is very important to me." Micah smiles at me and I
smile back. Something settles in my chest, and I can breathe again.

"I felt the same way. I've liked Micah since I met him, but I forced myself to hold back because I lived so far away, and I don't have the greatest track record either. Plus, Micah and his friendship are important to me too." We looked at each other, then Rhett.

"I don't know how to feel about this. I love you both and I thought you were just friends. If I think about it too hard, I might flip out. I'm just going to set it aside for a minute while it sinks in." His fists open and clench several times. Then they stay open but it looks forced and far from relaxed.

"You said there's something about work?" Rhett asks to change the subject.

"Oh, right, you're familiar with the Southern Suns. It turns out there's one living next door to Peyton and we met him yesterday."

"What the fu...fudge?" At Rhett's raised voice Nova looks up at him and her face turns red and crumples as tears begin to fall. She runs to Paige and puts her head in Paige's lap.

"It's okay sweetie, daddy isn't mad, he just heard something he didn't like. Please don't be upset, everything is okay." Paige rubs Nova's back and glares at Rhett. He mouths *sorry* at Paige and gets on his knees behind Nova and rubs her back.

In a soft soothing voice, he tells Nova, "Oh baby girl, don't cry, daddy was just surprised by something at work. I'm not mad at anybody. Okay?"

She lifts her head, and her eyes search his face. Seeing the smile he pasted on for her, she smiles back.

"Daddy happy?"

"Yes, daddy is happy. Give me a hug?"

She jumps at him and wraps her little arms around his neck. All is right in her world once again. He hands her a block. She takes it and goes back to playing blocks like nothing happened. Kids are amazingly resilient.

"Sorry, she's going through a phase. You were saying?"

"I'm going to research him specifically. I called Samson and we're having a meeting in the morning. I want to add him to the Southern Suns surveillance. I also want to install security with cameras at Peyton's. We can actually film him, and his friends, and he'll just think it's her security system. I want the very best security installed for her, so she'll be safe when I'm not around."

"Absolutely, spare no expense. If it's not safe, we'll find her another place." Gasping in surprise, I hadn't thought about having to move or being unsafe. I guess I'll have to do whatever becomes necessary, but I love the place and the location. I don't want to go anywhere else. Micah didn't tell me he planned to install security; I suppose it makes sense. Especially if they can improve their surveillance on a case that involves human trafficking. We're all dedicated to fighting that evil. It'll also give me peace of mind. I sigh, resigned to whatever we have to do.

"What time are you meeting with Samson?" Rhett asks.

"We can meet at your office. Does eight thirty tomorrow morning work?"

"Yeah, I'll be there. Do you mind if I bring in Ace and Thomas?"

"Not at all, we need to be on top of this since Peyton is suddenly exposed to it. We've just been quietly watching for Buzzard; we know he's still around. We're watching Razor closely, but we haven't been able to catch how he's communicating with the rest of them."

"Racer! Racer! Racer!" Nova screeches.

I scoot next to Nova on the floor and pick up a red block, "Look Nova, this red block snaps into this blue block. How cool is that?" Ugh, she's listening even when we don't think she is. We don't need her talking about murderous bikers, geez.

"So, tell me what happened with this guy. How did you meet him?" Rhett continues his interrogation. I look at Micah encouraging him to tell it. I'd rather focus on the adorable bundle of joy on the floor, as she builds a tower of colorful blocks.

Micah accepts my nonverbal request and fills Rhett and Paige in on our encounters with Orlando yesterday and today. When he's done and has answered all of Rhett's questions, a timer buzzes from the kitchen. Rhett has us move into the dining room. Micah helps Nova get into her booster seat. I get drinks for everyone. Paige quickly sets the table, while Rhett gets our dinner out of the oven. It looks and smells delicious. He made meatloaf with macaroni and cheese. Nova loves broccoli, so he steamed some, and Paige made a salad. Everything is set out and we dig in.

Conversation turns to much more exciting topics. Paige is having an ultrasound this week and they may be able to see what she's having. I hope it's a boy, so they have one of each. I'd also love for Nova to have a sister to grow up with. It's such a special relationship. I'm excited to find out, either way, it'll be wonderful. My brother and his wife make super cute kids.

Micah

When I left Peyton's this morning I went home and spent some time with Beta and began my research on Orlando Diaz. He has a record, mostly misdemeanor drug charges. There's one arrest for armed robbery, but charges were dropped due to lack of evidence when the victims refused to testify. He also has a domestic violence arrest. A girlfriend claimed he beat her up and filed a restraining order, then dropped everything two weeks later. It's common when the couple makes up or if it never happened at all. Her injury photos only show a tiny scratch on her arm, so that might've been blown out of proportion from the beginning.

When I pull up at Savage, both Rhett's and Samson's vehicles are in the parking lot. I have full access to the building since this is where I work most of the time. It's more convenient than our field office over by Ocala. I like everyone who works here, I can't say the same for the FBI office.

When I get to the War Room, my preferred spot, Thomas and Ace are seated at the big conference table talking with Rhett and Samson. I plug in my laptop at my usual desk against the wall with my sweets stash, then take a seat next to Thomas. Everyone greets me and I respond. I notice there's a pile of bagels with cream cheese on a platter in the middle of the table. I only had coffee at home. I grab a plate and smear an everything bagel with whipped cream cheese.

"I hope you don't mind, I've already told them everything you said about Orlando yesterday," Rhett states.

"No, that's great," I swallow and continue. "I looked into his history a bit this morning. Just pulled his Florida record, there's not a lot. Mostly misdemeanor drug charges. He had two felonies that were dropped."

"What charges?" asks Samson.

"Armed robbery and DV."

"Wife or girlfriend?"

"Girlfriend. She recanted after two weeks."

Thomas makes a face, "Isn't that always the case? They make up and the asshole gets away with it?"

I considered his input, "Yeah, usually, but she only had a scratch on her arm. It might've been exaggerated from the get-go." Thomas shrugs.

"Witnesses refuse to testify in the armed robbery?" Samson speaks up.

"How did you know?"

"All of the Suns seem to get away with shit when the witnesses refuse to testify, or they just disappear. I'm still shocked we were able to bust Razor," Samson elaborates.

"Well, he was on camera, and we had dead bodies with his DNA and fingerprints. It wouldn't have helped him to make witnesses disappear. You know it's the only reason he was prosecuted, boss," I reply.

"That, and the new prosecutor at the time was looking to make a name for himself and couldn't be bought off or black mailed," Ace adds.

Paige walks in, "Hey guys, how's everything going?"

"Good."

"Great."

"No complaints."

"Good."

"I'm still good from when I left you this morning," Rhett winks at her.

She blushes. She's been working here since everything blew up at her old job for the Oakdale Police. I work with her a lot; she's a hacker like me. I mean, *a computer specialist*. She's good at her job. There's another computer specialist here, Cobb, but he's out in the field right now.

I can't help wondering how Peyton is doing. Her appointment was at 8:30 this morning at her new school. I asked her to call me when she finishes. A memory from last night pops into my head, damn, my girl is something.

"Micah? Did you hear me?" Samson asks in his boss voice.

"Oh, sorry, my mind wandered for a minute. What did you say?"

"I asked when the security system will be installed at Peyton's."

"I called the team Savage uses. They were able to squeeze us in as a priority. They'll be out tomorrow, and I'll be there to supervise. I can confirm the camera angles work for the surveillance we need for the Southern Suns case. Were you able to get the warrant lined up?"

"Yeah, I'll have it in hand this afternoon, we're set on our end," Samson confirms.

"Have you had a chance to see if any of the guys you saw yesterday are on our radar?"

"Not yet, I'm going to work on that this morning. Thomas, can you go over the photos with me since you have the most experience with them?"

"Yeah, sure."

Thomas went under cover a few years ago and infiltrated the Southern Suns in another state. He wore a disguise and they think he's dead. He hasn't had any issues working on the case here, but I imagine there's a Sun out there somewhere who will recognize him and cause a problem. He knows their organization better than anyone from his experience with them. He put pictures and names together for us as well as the State Attorney he was helping. His efforts stopped some of their drug and weapons business. There were some fascinating trials. He testified from a different room behind a black screen with a voice changer.

It was surprising the judge agreed to the protection of his identity. With Thomas being a war hero, and since he was working for the state, they went above and beyond to honor his service by keeping him safe.

"Micah, do you want to use my office to go over the IDs? Or use the big screen here?"

"Here's fine, thanks Thomas. Give me a minute and I'll pull them up on the big screen."

"Cool."

I stuff the last of my bagel in my mouth and move to where my laptop is plugged into the wall. I pull up the Sun's files and open the *Known*

Member's file. An ugly bald guy covered in tattoos fills the giant screen on the wall. Damn! He has two teardrops tattooed under his right eye. His neck has a Southern Suns insignia, the outline of the sun and the horned skull in the middle. The side of his head has a swastika, and the number 666. The other side of his shaved head has a gun tattoo, looks like a .45. I think there's something on his eyelids too. I'll have to check further into the file for the rest of his tattoo pics.

"That's Roach, aka Jason Bivens," Thomas says "He's a real piece of work. I think he has priors for strong arm robbery on a person over 65, GTA, fraud, DB, and possession. I don't remember what else, but if it's something that makes your skin crawl, he's your guy."

I click on the next one and shrink back from the mug on this guy. He's got blonde-gray hair, brown eyes, and I only see one tooth. His skin is wrinkled up like a hotdog that's been spinning on the griddle at the movie theater for far too long.

"Shit Thomas, these guys are hideous. Let me guess this one. Hmm, possession, DV, attempted murder, battery on law enforcement, resisting with violence?"

He chuckles, "Wow, you got pretty close. You missed distribution and soliciting."

"Ha! How sad is that? They're not just awful, but predictably awful," I chuckle. Sometimes we just have to laugh otherwise this job would push us over the edge or off a cliff.

We spend the rest of the morning looking through the photos we have and identifying them. Orlando isn't in the photos as he wasn't on our radar. Two of the guy's Thomas identifies were at Orlando's yesterday. They definitely aren't the worst of the bunch, but none of them are good.

I'm ready for a break and some lunch, the Red Vines aren't cutting it. Thomas went to his office for a call, so I'm finishing up, then going out for some food. As I close out my laptop my phone vibrates.

Eagle: Hi, I'm done with the paperwork and buying my books. I'm grabbing some lunch now, then I have the tour at 1 p.m. How's your morning?

Me: I'm heading out for some food. It's been busy, but productive. Your security system is being installed tomorrow.

Eagle: Great! You coming over after work?

Me: absolutely!

Eagle: Okay, I'll text when I'm done and ready to leave ☺

Me: thank you, sorry to make you check in, but for now it's the safest way.
Eagle: I agree. I'll keep you posted. Enjoy your lunch
Me: you too

After lunch I get wrapped into some other work and time flies. I love it when that happens, especially when I'm waiting to see Peyton. When I come up for air and a bathroom break, I check the time. It's just past 3:30 p.m. Peyton should be finished soon.

I notice an email pop up on my screen, it's from the lab at my office. The results from the skull and note are in already. I read it over and it just confirms everything we thought. No fingerprints, it was a cat skull, and we got nothing from the analysis. Hopefully she won't hear from this person again and we won't need to worry about it.

I seek out Rhett and find Paige leaving his office, "Any word from Peyton?"

"Yeah, I heard from her earlier after she finished her paperwork and bought her books. She should be finished with the tour any time now."

"I'm so excited that she made this move. Rhett won't admit it, but it was hard having her so far away. He's so happy and Nova is beside herself. Last night she was naming all of her stuffed animals, Pey. Except her big bear, that one is Mike-yeah," she imitates Nova's adorable way of saying my name.

"Aww, she's so cute. I feel honored," I grin at her.

My phone rings in my pocket, I pull it out, "It's Peyton. Hey, Eagle, everything okay?"

"It's good. I'm finished with the tour. I got to meet two of my professors. One's Dr. Maryanne Bertman, she's incredible. I'm so excited to take her class. She's teaching Social Justice Advocacy. She's the lawyer who won that case where the foster care system had to be reformed to prioritize the children's mental health care, and it requires each child on mental health medication to have legal representation during all court proceedings. The whole state was subject to that reform. Sorry, I'm rambling."

"No, it's interesting, I'm happy to hear you so excited. It's great that you'll have such an experienced professor." Paige waves at me to indicate she's going back to work. I smile and signal I understand.

"Oh, and you'll never guess what happened! One of the girls from my study group at LSU is here. She transferred too! Some family drama caused her to move. So, I already know somebody, and she's a great study partner.

How cool is that? I'm in my car and ready to go home. I'm going to cook the spaghetti, okay?"

"That sounds great. I'm going to run home, feed Beta and grab a change of clothes, if you're okay with me sleeping over?"

"Yeah, of course. I'll text when I get home, and I'll see you later."

"Sounds good, see you then, bye Eagle."

"Bye, Radiohead." She hangs up the phone first.

"Why do you call her that?"

"Shit! Dude! Don't sneak up on me," I admonish.

Ace chuckles, "Good to know I haven't lost my touch."

"You're lucky I didn't punch you!"

"Like you could catch me! Seriously man, why do you call her that? It's weird. Most guys call their girlfriend babe or something."

"I've been calling her Eagle since she started studying law. Instead of *legal beagle*, she's *legal Eagle*."

"Oh, that makes more sense. I was thinking it was some sex thing and I was a little afraid to find out more."

"What's wrong with you? You sound like TomKat!" I laugh at him.

"Do not compare me to Thomas, he's a devout manwhore. I have respect for the women I date. I actually take them out on a date, and I usually call the next day."

"He claims he has respect for them, and they're well informed it's just a hookup. I had to listen to an entire lecture, *How to Hook-Up Without Guilt 101*, or maybe it was *Hookups for Dummies*!" I chortle.

"Good one!" he burst out laughing.

"Hey assholes! I can hear you, ya know?" Thomas yells at us from his office.

"Why do you think I brought it up, dickhead?" Ace retorts. Chuckling at their antics, I say my goodbyes to both of them.

I stuck my head in Rhett's office, "You busy?"

"Come in. What's up?"

"I was wondering if you're going to be at Peyton's tomorrow during the security install?"

"Nah, I can't. This case I'm working on is going to take me into the field tomorrow. Is everything okay with it?"

"Oh yeah, I was just wondering, I'll be there. I'm going to work from there tomorrow. I was also thinking, I just wanted to...well..."

"Micah, spit it out brother," he chuckles.

"Are we cool? I mean, I want to make sure you're okay with me dating Peyton. I really like her, but you're one of my closest friends, I don't want anything to mess that up."

"Yeah, we're good. Paige and I had a long talk, and she's thrilled by the way. She explained how much you care about Peyton and how long you've held a torch for her. I didn't have a clue. Apparently, my wife used her sixth sense, woman's intuition or some shit, and always knew you two would end up together."

"Really? Because I still can't believe it."

"I'm guessing I don't need to threaten your life, so you don't do anything to hurt her, correct?" His face hardens into a stern mask.

"Obviously! I would never do anything to hurt her. Honestly, I have very intense feelings for her. I'm afraid to jinx it, but I think she might be it for me."

After he inspects my face, he stands up and comes around his desk. He holds out his hand to me with a huge smile adorning his face. I shake his hand and he pulls me in for a man hug, with a hard pat on my back.

"Dude, that's awesome. I'm so happy for you both. I couldn't pick a better guy for her."

"Thanks man. I haven't told her how I'm feeling yet, but I will. There's a couple other things I wanted to talk to you about."

He steps back and his brows raise in question, "Okay, go for it."

"Peyton says you never want to talk about it, but I feel like you should know. I hope I'm not overstepping..." I proceed to explain how I'll be helping Peyton investigate their sister's death, and about the skull.

"That's definitely weird. At least whoever it was, it sounds like they're still in Baton Rouge, hopefully they stay there. I appreciate you letting me know... about everything."

"Sure. I'm heading out, I'm running home then to Peyton's. I'll keep you updated on the install, Larue's case, and the rest. See you."

He pats my back, and we smile at each other, "See you later."

Peyton

As I stir the sauce, I drop the spaghetti into the boiling water. The oven is preheating for the garlic bread, and a Cesar salad is chilling in the fridge. All I need is for Micah to get here. There's a knock at the door. Speak of the devil. When I open the door, he leans down and kisses me on the lips, a bottle of red wine in his hand.

I smile at him, "Hey, thanks for thinking of wine, it's perfect." His other hand holds a small duffle bag, just big enough to contain a change of clothes and his laptop. Taking the wine from him I suggest, "Go put your bag in the bedroom. Everything's almost ready, just five more minutes."

I pop the garlic bread into the oven and dump the pasta into the colander in the sink. It smells like Italy in here, well, what I imagine it smells like. He returns, opens the wine, and adds wine glasses to the table I set.

"What can I do?" he asks.

"Grab the salad from the fridge?" While he gets the salad bowl along with the pecorino cheese, the grater, and Cesar dressing, I pour the pasta and sauce onto the largest platter I own. It must weigh five pounds when I carry it over to the table. I quickly pull out the garlic bread before it burns and we're ready.

"Peyton, this smells incredible. I can't wait to dig in!"

"I hope it tastes good. It's one of my favorites and I've been craving it. I couldn't cook in my dorm, so this is a huge step up."

Right when I lift my loaded fork to my mouth in anticipation, the freaking doorbell rings, wtf?

"Dammit! Who the hell could that be?" My stomach voices its frustration.

"Why don't I get it, you go ahead and start eating babe."

"No, I don't want to start without you." He gets up and looks through the peephole. He mouths, *Shit!* at me. I can only assume that means Orlando is at my door.

"Hey, Orlando, what's up?"

"Hey, Micah, I got this package for Peyton by mistake. Just wanted to give it to her. Wow, what smells so good?" He peeks around Micah.

He takes a box from Orlando, and answers, "Peyton cooked a special dinner for me, we just sat down."

"Oh, sorry, guess I'll let you get back to it. Smells amazing!" He calls out towards me.

"Yeah, it does. Thanks for dropping this off. We'll see you around."

"Yeah, okay. See you." Micah closes the door, puts the box on the island, and sits back at the table. Finally, I take a bite of my dinner.

Micah voices my thought, "This is delicious. Thanks for cooking this for me. Wine?"

"Yes, please," I agree as he pours, I take a sip. "Oh, this wine is really good. Have you had it before or was it a lucky guess?" I ask Micah.

"I confess, I asked the guy at the store to recommend something that would go with spaghetti. I'll have to post a good review for him."

"Yeah, this is perfect."

After we have all the dishes cleaned up, I take a look at the box Orlando dropped off. Hmm, that's odd. My address is correct on the box. The address of his house and mine are very clearly marked on the mailboxes and houses. Somehow, I doubt this was delivered to the wrong place. I opened it and it's some of the school supplies I ordered. I'm almost ready to start school next week, I'm nervous but excited.

I'm starting as a 2L (*2nd year Law student*), I finished my 1L while I completed my bachelor's degree last year. I didn't walk for my graduation since I wasn't done. I didn't want to make Rhett and Paige come to Baton Rouge with baby Nova. He tried to talk me into it, but I had already decided to move here, it seemed unnecessary. Plus, I dove right into an eight-week internship at the public defender's office. I didn't have time to worry about graduation or out of town company.

Micah is in my office setting up his laptop for work, when I enter to put away my school supplies. He also has the file about Larue's case on the desk. I wonder if he plans to work on it too.

"I need a shower. Want to join me?"

"How can I say no to that?" He smiles at me, heat entering his gaze.

"I guess you can't," I smile in what I hope is a seductive way.

I lift off my shirt and throw it at him. He catches it before it hits his face. I reach behind my back and unhook my purple lace bra. Turning away from him, I throw my bra in his direction, then walk towards the bathroom. I peek over my shoulder and spot him following me. I step into the bathroom and start the shower. Keeping my back to the door, I slide my pants down my legs. I leave my purple lace thong in place as I bend over to slip my pants over my feet.

He whispers, "Fuuuck!" I smirk, I have him now, I flip my hair around and smile at him over my shoulder.

"You doing okay there?"

"So very fine. You are the sexiest thing I've ever seen, babe. May I?"

He approaches me from behind and he places his hands on my hips. Then he rubs his warm fingers over my skin. His thumbs drift under the sides of my barely-there thong. He pulls it down my legs at a pace that makes me ache. When he's bent over, his lips meet my lower back. He kisses down my ass cheek and then takes a soft bite where it meets my thigh.

"Mmmm, Micah, I want your tongue on me."

He grasps my hips and gently turns me towards him, kissing my lips and then following my neck to my shoulder with more soft kisses. He uses his teeth again, biting my shoulder in the barest nibble. Then he kisses down my breast and licks my erect nipple. My head falls back as I moan.

"Yeeeees, mmmm."

His strong hands squeeze my hips as his tongue circles my nipple. Moving to the opposite side, he treats my other nipple to gentle sucking, finishing with a teasing bite. He kisses across my ribs and then licks a circle around my belly button. His hands pull my hips towards him. Falling to his knees he lifts my leg over his shoulder.

"Babe, this gorgeous pink pussy is so wet for me."

It clenches and more of my arousal leaks from me. His finger circles my clit and slides through the slick moisture. I play with my own nipples while he places kisses on my little bundle of nerves. His finger traces my entrance. As his tongue flicks out at my clit, his long, agile finger pushes inside my pussy. He stretches me and licks hard against my delicate, but oh so sensitive, nub.

He adds a second finger and it's divine. Sensations shoot through me, I'm panting and pinching my nipples, tugging on them. His machinations speed up and my body hums in reply. My hips buck into him, my clit hungry for his attention.

"Yes!! Micah!! Oh my God! Yes!" He thrusts his fingers in and out brushing my needy G-spot, as his lips and tongue savage my most electrified skin.

"Holy, fuck! Micah!" The culmination of his endeavors leaves me twitching in satisfaction. Warmth and pleasure travel my veins. His tongue licks up my climax while I tremble with each touch. I hold onto his head, so I don't fall over, my knees are weak.

"Mmmm, that was amazing! You're really good at making me come," I smile wide. My face must be glowing red, I can feel how warm it is, like a furnace.

He slips his fingers from my pussy and pops them into his mouth, sucking up my release. He licks his lips and smiles at me as he lowers my foot to the floor.

"You have the most perfect pussy. You taste delicious, sweet and tart. I could do this every night and never get tired of it, but my dick is about to rip out of my jeans. I need to be inside you, now."

As he stands, I entwine myself around him. He yanks his shirt over his head, and I admire his perfectly sculpted torso. I kiss down his chest and lick his tattoo. He kicks off his shoes, while I unbuckle his pants then unzip them. His hard cock bursts from its confines.

Grasping his pants and boxer briefs, I pull them down on his legs. I kiss his skin wherever it meets my lips. He smells good, like soap, musky cologne, and man. He kicks out of his jeans and then uses his toes to remove his socks. He stands before me erect in all of his toned glory. I release a satisfied sigh. He's so incredible, I can't believe he's all mine, yum!

Pulling him into the shower we both stand under the hot water. I pour shampoo into my hand and then rub it into my hair. Next, I pour shampoo into his hand, and he does the same, while I rinse and apply conditioner. Soaping up my hands I place them on his chest, and I work my way down his torso leaving bubbles in my wake. Then I grasp his perfect cock with my hand, and it glides up and down his length. My other hand squeezes his balls, and he groans deeply. I lean up and kiss him, tasting myself on his lips. His tongue slips into my mouth, and we explore one another while my hand makes certain his cock is cleaner than it's ever been.

His hands grasp my hips and slide to my ass squeezing me. As we continue our passionate kiss, he lifts me against the cold tile. It heats quickly as my hot body presses into it. My legs encircle his hips, and I slide my pussy up and down his granite-hard length. He notches his head at my entrance, and I wiggle until he enters me. The stretch caused by his girth is otherworldly. I'm moaning and panting, I can't keep up with our kisses and get enough oxygen into my lungs. He lifts me up and down while he thrusts. My hands hold his shoulders to lift myself in sync with him.

He growls into my ear, "Babe, you are so tight, and so slick. You feel so good, all my fantasies come true with you."

"Yes! Micah! Mmmm, keep doing that."

I'm writhing in pleasure as he thrusts faster and harder. I swear his cock was made for me; it's never been this good. There's a warm tingle in my chest that sends electric shocks outward. I'm moving in a furor trying to get him as deep inside of me as possible, while his pelvic bone rubs deliciously on my clit. So, fucking scrumptious.

He speeds up again becoming frantic with me. I think I'm yelling or mumbling; I don't even know anymore. Vibrations tickle along my body, the enjoyment warms my soul. My climax evolves fast, we race to chase the feelings between us.

"Micah! I'm so close! Don't stop!"

"I'm going to come, babe! Yes! Fuuuck, you feel unbelievable. Yeah! Oh God, you're squeezing me so tight!"

"Oh! Yes! Micah!" My finish hits like a charging bull and I'm moving erratically, trying to capture every bit of friction. I scream out my glee. He thrusts upward as hard as he can and buries himself deep. I feel his cock twitch inside me as he fills me with his emission. It's warm and lights up my G-spot with sensations that sing through my center. Electricity travels across all of my nerves in warm sparks. My chest feels like fireworks are exploding in my heart. I tremble as I come down from my climax, and I hug him close. He cuddles me to his chest. I realize he's moaning sweet whispers to me.

"Peyton?" I gaze into his eyes; he's looking at me with emotion filled pools of faded blue and green. His face is pink, his eyes a bit glassy, shimmer in the scarce light, a smile plays on his lips.

"Yes, Micah?"

"I think I'm in love with you."

A flock of birds take flight in my chest, big ones, like Canada geese or swans. Tingles travel my body, setting all of my nerves on fire. Warmth fills me, while chills run along my skin as I continue to look into his mesmerizing blue-green eyes. I know I love him, truly, with all my heart.

"I think I'm in love with you too."

He kisses me and holds me close. I hug him back and kiss him hard, it feels so right. I'm so happy and satisfied that my body hums with joy. I've never felt like this before and it's awesome.

He lifts me off of his cock and gently sets me on the tile floor, but he doesn't let go. I'm smiling so hard my face hurts. He's smiling back at me and I hope he feels this amazing feeling I'm experiencing inside. I hope he feels this joy that is cuddling my heart in my chest. Feeling loved, safe, and serene, I want to shout my good fortune to the masses.

"I can't explain how I feel, but it's incredible."

"I feel it too. Say it again, Micah."

"I love you, Peyton. I think I've loved you for a long time. I just squashed it and told myself it was friendship. But this feeling, it can't be anything else. I want to shout it from the rooftops. I want to protect you and take care of you. Am I crazy?"

"No, you're not crazy, I feel the same way. I love you too, Micah. I absolutely love you."

Micah

As I admire her gorgeous, firm body, I notice my cum dripping down her thigh. My chest puffs up, and something very alpha male inside me feels satisfied that I've marked her as mine. My eyes widen and panic grips my gut as I realize our mistake.

"Oh shit! Peyton, I just came inside you, without a condom."

"Oh, yeah. Oops! It should be okay, I'm on the shot. I'm also clean, I saw my doctor right before I left Baton Rouge."

"I just had my physical for work last month, I'm clean too. Are you sure you're okay with this?"

"Yeah, I'm alright. I've never done it without a condom before, it was so good. Of course, that may just be you." She grins at me and pats my back. She washes off while she talks.

"Oh, it's definitely all me. I never did it without a condom either. Even when I was a stupid kid, I didn't want to make the mistakes my parents made. Not that I would ever abandon my kid, but it was always in my mind. Not even teenage boy hormones could override my conviction."

"Well, you are kind of a genius."

"I know, but you helped," I raise my brows at her and give her a cheeky grin. She smacks me on the arm.

"Ow! Hey! That's what Paige does to Rhett, I'm not okay with violence." My brows pull down and my mouth is clenched into a line. But I can't fake a stern look for long, I'm too happy. I grab her ribs and tickle her; she bursts out laughing and steps out of the shower. She picks up a towel on her way out and takes off. I turn off the water, pick up my own towel, and chase after her. I find her in the bedroom, digging in her drawer for clothes. She squeals when she sees me and backs up holding her hands out at me while laughing.

"You think that will stop me? I'm still going to get you!" I lift my hands and approach her; I screw my face up in what is probably a ridiculous look. I'm trying to appear menacing, but I keep laughing. She eventually backs into the edge of her bed and falls on it. I've got her now. I jump on the bed and bounce up and down making her fly up in the air. She's cracking up, which makes me laugh too. We both fall onto our backs to catch our breath.

"Oh my God! I can't breathe. You can't tickle me, I'll pee my pants," she gasps.

"You aren't wearing any pants," I give her a goofy grin.

She turns her sparkling light blue eyes on me, "Good point."

"Oh, I'm sorry your bed is wet now. Maybe we should dry off huh?"

"Yeah maybe." She sits up and begins drying her shoulders, then her arms, and finally wraps the towel around her hair.

"Do you want to watch a movie?"

"Yeah, that sounds good. I'll let you choose, Radiohead."

"Cool! Let's get dressed. I'll put on my PJ's."

"Okay, me too."

She finishes drying off and finds her clothes. I collect my bag and dig out my pajamas. We get dressed and cuddle on the sofa. I chose a Netflix movie about the end of the world. It's not long before she drifts off in my arms, I carry her to bed after the movie ends. When I lie her down and climb in next to her, she scoots close to me and snuggles her head into my chest. As I hold her, I feel happier than I've ever been. My chest has warm blooms of blissful joy shooting across it, and my heart pounds a satisfied beat. I feel like everything is right in the world as I drift to sleep with a content smile on my face.

When my eyes pop open in the morning the warmth of a softly curved ass is cradled against my morning wood. I grind my dick into the valley between the plush globes.

"Mmmm, babe you feel so good. I never want to move." She presses her ass back into me, I tighten my hold on her. We lie there for an extra 30 minutes before my alarm goes off.

"Crap! Sorry, Eagle. The security guys are coming at eight. We better get dressed and eat some breakfast."

"Nooo, it's so cozy, I don't want to move." I kiss her temple and ear, I squeeze her a bit, wiggling my hips against her.

"Come on baby, aren't you hungry? Don't you want your coffee in peace? They're going to be stomping all over, drilling holes and hammering."

"All right! I'm going," she sits up and her hair is an adorable rat's nest of a mess. It sticks up in blonde spikes in every direction, her eyes aren't even open. She looks so cute I want to jump on her and squish her in my arms, but time is ticking. Her eyes flutter and I give her a commiserate smile.

"Come on cutie, let's go."

"I'm moving, aren't I?" she asks groggily.

"No babe, you're sitting still, looking very cute, like a lost puppy."

"Then have pity on me," she breaks out the puppy-dog eyes. Oh no. My resolve is fading, I can't fight the puppy eyes. She's been able to control me with those for years. I turn away so I don't cave.

"Nope, I'm not looking. Go on, go use the bathroom and I'll put the coffee on, deal?"

"Fine, but I'm going only because I need to pee. Not because I'm letting you tell me what to do."

"Of course. I would never attempt to tell my beautiful Eagle what to do." I wink at her.

"You're ridiculous. You know that right?"

"I thought I was a genius?" I snicker.

"Ugh! I can't argue intelligently before coffee."

I continue to chuckle as she stumbles her way to the bathroom. In fresh clothes I make quick work of the coffee maker. Thankfully she has one of those k-cup machines and I know how to use it. I have two cups of coffee ready by the time she enters the kitchen. Her hair is brushed and pulled up into a ponytail. She looks smokin' in her jean cutoffs and little white tank top, it shows off her tan skin. Her feet sit in white leather flip flops, and her toenails are sporting bright blue polish. She's not wearing a stitch of makeup, and she's stunning.

"This one's yours," I hand her the blue cup that says: *Law School. What? Like it's hard?* Mine is black and says: *May the Force Bean with You!*

She takes a careful sip, "Mmm, thanks Radiohead. This is so good."

"Yeah, it is. I like this salted caramel white mocha flavor, it's my favorite."

"Yeah, my roommate always got them for me and now I'm addicted. Do you want something for breakfast? Remember, I have pop-tarts," she smirks. She's very much aware of my sugar addiction; I love sweet snack food.

"That sounds perfect. You got strawberry right?"

"I got strawberry, cinnamon, and chocolate. I'll make you strawberry and I think I'm going to have chocolate. It'll mix well with my coffee."

She puts the pastries in her toaster right as the doorbell rings. Shit, they're here. Hopefully I'll get the chance to eat my breakfast while it's hot. She answers the door and I stand behind her, just in case.

Peyton

Micah stands with me at the door, I know he's worried it might be Orlando. But it's a few guys I don't know wearing uniforms. Definitely the security guys. When I open the door, the tallest one smiles at me and introduces himself.

"Good morning, I'm Zach Asher, with Vaultech, we're here to install your security system. Oh, hey, Micah."

"Hey Zach, Reggie, Logan. Hey man!"

"Hey Micah. Didn't know you'd be here. They just told us Savage needed a rush install."

"This is Peyton, my girlfriend, she's also Rhett's sister. Come in guys."

"Peyton, this tall guy is Zach, this is Reggie," he points to the blonde as he walks in. "And this ugly guy is Logan."

He fake-punches Logan who puts up his hands like they're going to box. He's not ugly, he has dark hair and eyes, with a square jaw and dimples. Actually, none of them hurt my eyes. It's cool to see some friends of Micah's. Each of them offers me a hand to shake. The toaster pops in the kitchen, with a *ding*.

"Hi guys, it's so nice to meet you. Thanks so much for coming out so quickly, it's kind of urgent. I'm sure Micah will explain. I just heard our breakfast finish cooking in the kitchen. Are you guys hungry? Or do you want coffee?"

Zach speaks up, "Thanks Peyton, it's very kind of you to offer, but we just had breakfast. We might accept some coffee later though. You go ahead and have your breakfast. We're going to look around and map out where we need to put what. I take it the wood house next door is the one you want some cameras on?"

I smile at them and go to the kitchen. They can figure this out and I want more coffee. I put Micah's breakfast on a plate next to his coffee cup and sat down with mine. These chocolate pastries are so good with my coffee, it's like dessert. After a few minutes Micah joins me. He takes a huge bite out of his strawberry tart.

"Is there anything specific you want them to do while they're here?" he asks.

"No, whatever you think is fine, I'm good with anything. When I called the Renaults about it, they were thrilled to be getting a free security system. It gives them a break on their homeowners insurance too. They said to let the experts do whatever they think is best. That's you, and I guess them," I pointed in the direction I saw the security guys go.

"Okay, I'm going to do some work until they need me to check the cameras on my computer. Do you have anything you want to accomplish today?"

"Actually, yeah. When I spoke to the Renaults, I asked them if they'd let me get a cat. Turns out, they have four and they love cats. I want to go to the cat rescue I found online, Furry Paws of Mystic Cross, and see if they have one I like."

"I'm so glad they said yes, maybe I'll go with you. My landlord said I can have another one too. She suggested I get a female because Beta will be more likely to accept a female, since he's king of the castle right now."

We cleaned up from breakfast and headed out while Zach and the guys hauled around ladders to mark the locations for the cameras. We made it downtown and easily spotted the building marked on the GPS.

The rescue is so cute. It's in an old Victorian house. This area became a town in 1855. It was initially a vacation spot for the wealthy. They built beautiful Victorian mansions near the water and came here during the winter to escape the cold. Many of the old mansions are refurbished and have businesses in them. One is a restaurant, and another has a medical office. This one is painted in bright colors and has paw prints painted up the wall and onto the roof like a cat climbed up there. I love it when people get creative, I have no artistic talent at all, but I definitely admire art.

When we walk into the lobby, I'm expecting a bad smell of kitty litter, but it smells good in here. It's decorated in a combination of antique furniture and cutesy cat stuff. The furniture is upholstered in bright patterns with cats and little fish. The art on the walls depicts all sizes and shapes of cats and kittens. It's all for sale so it must be from a local artist. I may have to find out who they are and purchase one of these paintings.

A man at a desk stands when we come in. He looks young, maybe seventeen or eighteen. He has on a cat t-shirt that says: *The cat's meow!* With a picture of a black and white cat wearing a Hawaiian shirt and sunglasses.

"Good morning, folks. I'm Connor Montgomery. How may I help you today?"

Micah speaks up, "Hi Connor, I'm Micah and this is Peyton. We're both interested in adopting a cat. I'm looking for a female. I have a male, calico."

"Hi Connor. I'm interested in either sex, a fairly young and healthy cat, I'm a student," I tell him.

"Great! I love people who have an idea what they're looking for. It makes it easier for me to match you up with the right cat. Come on back this way and I'll show you our females, and young ones," he smiles and guides us through a door.

He leads us down a long hallway with several doors on either side. The floors are all hardwood, I bet they're original to the house, it's warm and inviting.

"These are our medical rooms for exams, surgery, evaluation, quarantine, and so on. All of our mature cats are fixed. If you adopt a young one, you'll be required to sign a contract agreeing to have them fixed as soon as they're mature enough. We do the procedure here, and we give a discount to our rescues."

"Wonderful. I definitely agree with having them fixed. One of my former college roommates used to trap and fix feral cats with a group, then return them to where they were found. I went out with her a few times," I informed him.

"We have a group here that does that. They're called *The Nightcrawlers*. Good group of people. We help with some of the surgeries if we have the time and space," he says as he opens a door at the end of the hall. It's a huge room with crates, pet beds, cat trees, and scratching posts. There are cats everywhere, from kittens to seniors, most are roaming free. There's a pile of sleeping kittens in one of the round beds. A few run by us in a blur.

I immediately spotted a youngish black cat with green eyes off by itself. It's on a windowsill watching the other cats. It's fluffy instead of sleek, it looks like a teenaged cat, if that's a thing. Not a kitten but not an adult.

"Micah, the three cats playing with that purple toy over there, are females. They're sisters and tend to hang out together, they're fixed. They were surrendered when their owner was diagnosed with terminal cancer. They're very agreeable and mild tempered. They wouldn't do well alone, but since you have a cat, any of the three would do well. They're about 18 months old."

"Miss Peyton, you can pick any one you like. You can see we have many younger cats and kittens they're all healthy. We have a few who aren't, but they're in our special needs playroom."

"Thanks Connor, what can you tell me about that black one? In the window?"

"That's Ebony, you don't have to keep the name if you take her, it's a little obvious. She's a great cat, she seems a bit reserved and watches the others. But she's friendly with humans and affectionate. She's around seven to eight months old, at our best guess, and she's fixed. She came in as one of a litter of kittens and for some reason, no one wanted her, all of her siblings were adopted months ago. We tend to have that issue with black cats. I think it's that superstition about bad luck."

I walk over to her and watch to make sure I don't frighten her. She perks up her ears when she sees me and meows. When I reach out my hand, she sniffs it then she rubs her cheek against my fingers. I scratch her and she rubs against me purring. I'm in love, she's coming with me.

I turn around and Micah is sitting on the floor with the three sisters in his lap. Two kittens are playing with his shoelace and another cat is rubbing against his back, I laugh at him.

"Micah! You can't take them all."

"Aww, how can I choose? They're all so cute. What's this one's name?" He's petting a sweet, fluffy white and black sister. She's pretty. Beta will fall in love with her in no time.

"We call her Kate. Those three are named Mary, Kate, and Ashley. I know it's ridiculous, but we run out of ideas and have to start using celebrities or comics, or foods, we even did cars one time. Be thankful she's not called Volkswagen." He chuckles at his joke.

"What do you think Kate? You want to come home with me and meet Beta? I bet he'll love you," then he whispers to her, "I promise to change your name to something cool."

Ebony climbs into my arms and curls up on my chest purring. I rub my face on hers and she purrs louder. Oh my God, yeah, she's coming with me.

When we pull underneath my house, Reggie is on a ladder installing what I assume is a camera. The other two must be inside. I'm so excited about Ebony. I have to decide if I want to keep her name. It's a bit too obvious, like Connor said, and I prefer more creative names. I can't believe we can pick them up on Saturday. Micah is getting 'Kate' but he's definitely changing her name. He just hasn't decided what to do, yet. We stopped at the pet store and loaded up on supplies though he didn't need as much as me.

Micah helps me carry everything upstairs. Then he seeks out Zach to check on the installation. I head to my office to look up interesting names. Micah has his laptop set up next to mine. He pulled a dining chair in here and has a few things tacked to the wall. I look them over. They're note cards with headings, *Suspects, Witnesses, Timeline, Evidence, Contacts,* and a few others. He has my *Larue File* next to his laptop underneath his ever-present Red Vines. It looks a little thicker. I'm afraid to look inside. I'm going to need another office chair in here. He'll never be comfortable on that wooden chair for any amount of time.

Firing up my laptop, I start searching and quickly narrow it down to: *Spirit, Echo, Mystery, or Storm.* I'm going to wait until she's here to decide which fits best.

"Hey! I was wondering where you went," Micah says as he joins me in the office.

"I'm looking up new names for Ebony. I have it narrowed down but I want to see which fits best once she's here. How's the install going?"

"Good, they have the cameras up. I need to check the angles."

"Here, you can have my chair," I stand up, but he holds his hand out.

"No, I'm good. You stay there, we can work together."

"Are you sure? I can find something else to do."

"I'm sure. Didn't you tell me you already have assignments to work on for school?" he asks.

"I do. 2L is already starting out at warp speed. I think I'll stay," I pop a kiss on his lips.

"Now that's why it'll be nice to work side by side," he flashes me a bright smile.

It makes my heart speed up a bit. I sigh in satisfaction; man, he makes me happy. I sit back in my chair and pull up my student portal so I can get to work. Micah sits next to me with a camera interface open on his screen.

After a while, Micah calls Zach on his phone so he can direct him to fix the camera angle on one of the cameras pointed at Orlando's house. As I watch, Orlando pulls into his driveway. The rumble of his motorcycle is on the screen and live outside, the window vibrates with the sound. Orlando looks at what the guys are doing, then his face turns to inspect each camera. He frowns and his brow furrows.

When Micah is satisfied with the images, he hangs up and continues adjusting settings on his screen. My stomach lets out a growl, my hand grabs it, like I can make it be quiet. I roll my eyes at myself.

"I'm going to get a snack; do you want anything?"

"Will you bring me a red bull please?"

"Yeah, you got it." When I return, he's on a different screen. It looks like something official. I don't want to pry, so I get back to my own screen. Before I know it, I'm immersed in social justice once again. I have a paper due, and I need to read this case first.

"Babe?" He startles me from my reading.

"Yeah?"

"Do you know if Larue was dating anyone?"

"No, definitely nobody special, she would've told me. Why?" I asked, now distracted.

"This guy keeps popping up. He's a witness, and it looks like he was one of the last people to see her before she disappeared. I've been working on the timeline of her last week. She was with him every day. Does the name Mark Ramsey mean anything to you?"

"No. She was working at the bar then, so he could've been someone she knew there. It still makes me mad they let her work there when she wasn't even twenty-one."

"He didn't work there, but maybe he was a regular customer. His street name is *Saint*, I'm going to need to talk to a few of the people who worked with her."

"Oh, wait, Saint? That name is familiar. I don't think they were dating, but he was definitely around. She mentioned him several times. I think I even met him once, but I'd need to see a picture to be sure."

"Here, I have his mug shots," he aims his screen at me, and I lean over to look at him.

"Huh, I recognize him. She called him *Monk*. She might've been dating him because her face used to light up when she talked about him. She loved his tattoos and his dark eyes. He was nice to me, kind of charming. I always thought he poured it on a bit thick. He took us both out once for her birthday. She didn't want to leave me home alone, even though I was more than old enough. She always worried about me being lonely."

"Where did you go?"

"Like I said, he was charming, over the top sweet. She loved to paint, and he took us to one of those places, you know, where you take a class for two hours and then everyone leaves with a cute painting? Then we went out for dinner. He told the restaurant it was her birthday, they sang to her and gave her a free dessert."

"You're saying he was charming, but I'm getting a feeling you thought the opposite."

"Well, he was extreme. He went out of his way to be charming and chivalrous. Opening doors, pulling out chairs, checking on me. It was too much for a young guy with a bunch of tattoos. It seemed like an act to me. Sometimes I would catch him looking at her, or me, with a creepy look on his face, it was lecherous. Like, he would be staring at her chest, or her thighs, or her ass. I caught him staring at my chest too. Trust me, back then there wasn't much to see," I chuckled at his face. He's staring at my chest.

"I'm up here, stud."

"Oh, yeah, sorry. There's plenty to look at now," he grins an innocent smile.

"I remember wondering what she saw in him. But he completely fooled her. She looked at him like he could do no wrong. I tried talking to her about my concerns, but she wouldn't hear it. She thought he was great. Yuck! Do you think he was involved in her murder?"

"Don't know. But you're not gonna like this," he says. My eyes snap to his, my mouth open, eyes wide.

"He's a Southern Sun. New Orleans chapter of the club."

"No! You're kidding. I didn't even know they were in New Orleans." My mind quickly jumped to Orlando next door. Glad we have the cameras up now.

"Yeah, they've got chapters throughout the south... Georgia, Alabama, Mississippi, Arkansas, Louisiana, and Texas."

"Shit! That can't be good. I knew that asshole wasn't what he seemed."

"Yeah, I need to find out how much time she was spending with him, and his role in the Suns. I think he's fairly high up, but I can't find anything with his title in the club."

Logan sticks his head in the door, "Micah, can you come out here for a minute?"

He stands, "Sure," and follows Logan out. I rack my brain trying to remember anything I can about Monk or *Saint*.

Micah

Logan leads me outside; we stand underneath the house where our cars are parked. He points up at a camera. I scan the rest of the underneath of the house, I don't see any other cameras.

"I got this one installed and then realized the way the wood is under here I won't be able to aim any of these at the neighbor's house. That trim," he points along the edge. "Right there will block the view. So, I can put them all on the far edge and aim them in that direction, but it may give you a cut off view, or tip him off."

"Hmm, I see what you're saying. Yeah, go ahead and put them on this side. They can capture the vehicles under here and if they get anything else, great. If not, oh well. They'll still pick up the sound, regardless, so that should work."

"Yeah, okay. We'll get these finished up as soon as they get the doors and windows finished. Your girl will be better protected than a bank."

"That's the idea. You want to stay for dinner?"

"Sure, Peyton won't mind?" Logan asks with a wink.

"Nah, she's cool with you guys."

"Thanks man," he fist-bumps me.

I rejoined Peyton in her office. I need to send out some feelers to Larue's former co-workers. I need more information about Saint or Monk. I look through the folder, find the name and number for a female witness that worked at the Crescent City Pub with her. Kristen Gilmore, her number's in the file. I wonder what the odds are of her number being in service. The quickest way to find out is to dial it.

"Yeah?" A male answers.

"Good afternoon, I'm looking for Kristen Gilmore."

"You got the wrong number," he hangs up on me.

That answers that. I try putting her name through a program I use to find people. She's still in NOLA according to this. I found her number, email, address, and place of employment to start. I try again, dialing the new number and it goes to voicemail. I leave a message identifying who I am and requesting she call me back as soon as possible.

One minute later my phone rings, "Agent Castleman."

"Hello? This is Kristen Gilmore; I'm returning your call."

"Good afternoon, Miss Gilmore, thank you for calling so quickly. I'm investigating the murder of Larue Baker. I have you listed as a witness. You worked with her at Crescent City Pub, correct?"

"Yes sir."

"Do you have a few minutes to answer a few informal questions?"

"Yeah, sure. I'm happy to help. It was just awful what happened to Lou."

"Thank you. I'm specifically wondering about any men she may have been friendly with or dating. Do you recall anyone special?"

"Well, Lou was a lot of fun. She flirted with the customers for better tips, we all did. But she didn't actually date much, she was always worried about taking care of her little sister. But she did have a crush on this one guy who used to come in all the time. His name was Monk. He was pretty cute, dark hair, dark eyes, tattoos, muscles, but she was way out of his league. She was a good girl, you know? Responsible. He was a bad boy type."

"Do you know if she ever dated him?"

"She had a crush on him, he flirted with her and hung around, she was too young for him and too sweet. But he did take her out a few times. I remember one time he even took her little sister out with them. But he didn't show any interest beyond friendship that I saw. Well, until..."

"Until what?"

"It was only a day or two before she disappeared. She went home with him; he offered her a ride when her car wouldn't start. The next day she wasn't herself. She was really quiet. I sorta kidded her about going home with him and asked what happened. She wouldn't tell me. She said not to ever mention him again."

"Go on."

"I wasn't working the night she disappeared, and she was still having car trouble. I heard he was at the bar that night, I don't know what happened or if she left with him. But Percy, one of the bartenders, said she was outside with him after she left work for the night. I'm pretty sure they questioned him though, and he was never arrested or anything."

"After Miss Baker disappeared, did you notice if Monk was still around? Or did you notice any change in his behavior?"

"He didn't come around after she disappeared. I think he only came around because of her in the first place. Once she was gone, he never came back. His friend still came in once in a while. Oh, what was his name? Give me a minute. He was tall, shaved head, tattoos, and a piercing in his nose. He was always wearing a leather vest. It had a sun on the back with a skull with horns in the middle. Oh! His name was *Zombie*. I guess that's not his real name, but that's what everyone called him. Does that help?"

"Definitely. Did she have any other men that hung around? Or anyone she was interested in?"

"No, not really. She was popular, a lot of men made advances, but she always turned them down. They didn't continue to pursue her once she said no. Many of them were regulars. They still came around and were nice to her. Everyone liked her, she was sweet, and very pretty. But there isn't anyone I would say was particularly interested or that she was interested in either."

"Okay, thank you Miss Gilmore. Please call me if you think of anything important. I may call you again if I have more questions. Will that be okay?"

"Yes, of course. Like I said, I want to help so you can catch whoever killed her. She was my friend," her voice cracks on the last word.

"Okay, thank you, have a good day."

"Thanks, you too. Bye." She hangs up the phone.

I add the name Zombie to a card and attach it under the witness column on the wall. Then I add Monk to the suspect column, and Kristen Gilmore to the witness column. Peyton is next to me, and she's engrossed in whatever she's reading. She didn't move an inch when I turned to the wall and back.

Her eyes are locked on her screen. She has her bottom lip pinched between her teeth, and that does something to me. My dick grows in my jeans. Her beautiful blonde locks are lifted in a ponytail exposing her delicate neck. I wish I was an artist, and I could capture how elegant she looks right now.

Zach sticks his head into the office, "Hey, we're almost finished. Will you check all the angles one last time?"

"Sure, I got you." I pull up the camera feed, they all look good. Logan was right about the ones under the house, but I can see Orlando's yard and driveway in them.

"Looks good Zach. I'm going to order pizza for dinner. You're staying, yeah?"

"Yeah, thanks for the invite. We like pepperoni and mushroom," he grins at me. Peyton looks up. She looks at Zach, then me.

"It's cool if they stay for dinner, right?" I asked, realizing I hadn't gotten her permission yet.

"Of course, I want pepperoni, onions, and green peppers," she flashes me her puppy eyes.

"No need to beg, gorgeous, I like it too."

"Oh, great. We won't have to argue about pizza, I liked what we got last time, but peppers and onions with pepperoni is my favorite. I was afraid I might find out you're one of those nuts that like pineapple on pizza, and that you've been keeping a terrible secret about your sick preferences all these years. We would've had to throw down."

"That's blasphemy. Never!" We chuckle together. Zach smiles at us and shakes his head as he walks out. Peyton notices the new cards on the wall. She looks them over for a couple minutes, her hand moves under her chin and her head tilts a bit.

"Who's Zombie? I haven't heard of that one," she queries.

"Apparently, he's a friend of *Monk-slash-Saint*. Kristen Gilmore said he continued to frequent Crescent City Pub, after she disappeared. Monk-slash-Saint never came back."

"Hmm, that's a little bit suspicious. I'm not loving calling him two names though. We need a shortcut, how about Mosa?" She asks.

"How about Samo?" I counter.

"Flip a coin?" she asks as she pulls out a quarter from her pocket and hands it to me.

"Okay, heads Samo, tails Mosa." I flip the coin, *yes!*

"Heads, Samo it is," I announce triumphantly.

"Okay, Samo. Now, get to ordering! I'm hungry!" She smiles brightly at me. I'm a bit bedazzled for a moment. I sigh. She smirks. That little minx knows exactly what she does to me.

I spend the rest of the week at her place only going home to take care of Beta, and grab clothes, working next to her while she studies. On Friday, right after breakfast, she has a brilliant idea.

"Why don't you bring Beta here? It might help to introduce him to his new friend on neutral territory. If you get him today, he can adjust a little before the girls get here tomorrow."

"You're so smart, that's a great idea. Do you mind if I pick up an office chair for in here while I'm out?"

"No, that'll be much better. I've been feeling bad about you sitting on that wooden chair. But you're so stubborn, and I refuse to have our first couple's fight over a chair."

"Wow, Eagle, that's a lot of baggage for one little chair," I smirk at her.

"I tried to offer you a better chair. You insisted on sitting in that wooden monstrosity. You're so stubborn. Remember the time when you wouldn't listen to me?"

"Which time?" I give her my poker face.

"You're funny. You know the time when we were in New Orleans and I knew which way to go and you argued with me?"

"All right, I surrender. Please don't bring that up. You realize we sound like an old married couple, right?"

She smiles, "Yeah." I smile back and we no longer recall what we were talking about. She places a kiss on my lips.

"Okay, I'm going to head out. Do you need anything?"

"No, but you should bring some of Beta's food. I only have the stuff the rescue recommended."

"Okay, text me if you think of anything. We'll be back as soon as possible."

Peyton

I'm tucked into my computer reading a brief for my Criminal Procedure class. It's pretty interesting, so I'm absorbing the material at a fast pace. My doorbell rings and a pop-up showing the front door camera view opens on my screen. I click on it, and it opens to full size. Orlando is at my door with a box in his hands. I roll my eyes.

"Ugh! Did he just wait until Micah left? You're talking to yourself Peyton. Quit it."

I call out through the door, "Who is it?"

"Hi Peyton, it's Orlando, from next door."

"What's up?"

"I got a package for you again. I'm sorry, will you please open the door?"

"Yeah, give me a second. I'm not sure how to work the new alarm."

Me: Orlando is at the door. I'm gonna open it.

Radiohead: okay, I'm pulling up the cameras, go ahead

Me: 10-4

Punching in the code, I wait for the green light and open the door. "Hi Orlando, sorry about that, I was afraid I would set it off. So, what's going on?"

"I got this package for you," he holds it up for me to see, "it's weird. It has your name, and my address."

"That is weird. But you're 79 and I'm 77, maybe it was just a typo. It's probably more of the school supplies I ordered."

"School supplies? Are you a teacher?"

"Nope, I'm a student. Law school."

"Wow, you must be really smart."

"Or really dumb, depending on how you look at it," I chuckle, and he joins me.

"So, here you go. If it's not yours, let me know. But I think you're probably right. Okay, see you," he hands me the box.

"Thanks, bye." I lock the door and reset the alarm.

Radiohead: all good babe?

Me: yeah, he was fine

Radiohead: what's in the box?

Me: probably school supplies

Paige: Are you busy? Can I call you?

Me: yeah sure

Me: Paige just texted, she's about to call me. Ttyl love you

Radiohead: love you too

"Hello?"

"Hi Peyton, guess what?"

"Oh! Your ultrasound was this morning. Am I having a niece or a nephew?"

"A NEPHEW!! Ahhh! I'm so excited!"

"Congratulations! That's great news. Is everything good? Did you get a due date update?"

"Everything's perfect! He's due January 12th." We both squeal into the phone.

"Wonderful! I'm so excited for you all. How's Rhett? He must be thrilled."

"He's beside himself. He just left to take cigars to everyone at the office. I have to think of boy names. Oh my gosh, I'm crazy excited too."

"Well, you should be, it's really great. I'm so happy for you. My face hurts, I'm smiling so hard."

"How's everything with you? Any issues with your neighbor or anything?" she asks.

"No, it's been fine. He actually just dropped off a package of mine that was delivered to his house. He was polite and appropriate even though Micah isn't here."

"That's good. Maybe he won't cause you any trouble. You're getting your cats tomorrow, right?"

"Yeah, Micah went to get Beta. We thought it might be easier on him if we introduce them here instead of his home turf."

"That's a great idea, I'm sure he'll do fine. He's always been good for us with our crazy crew, he's a really sweet boy. Uh oh, I hear Nova waking up from her nap. I better go. Let me know how it goes with the girls."

"I will. Congratulations! Give my brother a kiss for me. Bye."

"Bye, sweetie." I take the box to the coffee table, with a knife from the kitchen and sit on the sofa. Looking over the box, I notice it has no return address. That's kinda weird.

I slice into the tape and lift the flaps. There's packing paper bunched up in it, I pull it out and set it on the table. I see something black, and I have no idea what it could be. As I lean in closer an awful smell hits my nose and I jerk back. My mouth fills with saliva and I gag.

"Ugh! What the fuck?" I drop the box on the floor and slowly lean over it holding my breath. I don't want the sickly-sweet smell of death to fill my nostrils again. I examine the black object and I still can't figure out what it could be. It looks like something made of fur, but it's horribly matted and there's something clumped in it that looks like it's hardened.

I don't want to touch it, so I find a long handled wooden spoon from the kitchen, wrap the dish towel in my hand, and hold it over my face. I poke at the furry black thing while I stand as far away as I can and still reach. When it moves a bit, I can see an ear, and what looks like an eye that's only slightly open.

"Holy fuck! It's a motherfucking dead animal!"

I drop the spoon into the box and run out the front door. The alarm beeps at me and I have to go back inside and type in the code to make it stop. I run back out and vomit over the porch railing. I collapse on my ass and cry. Who the fuck would send me a dead animal? Oh my God, did they kill it?

I pull myself back up to the railing and vomit again. I spit a few times when I'm done. My vision is blurred by tears. Fuck! I need Micah. Taking some deep breaths, I steel myself to enter the house. I keep my eyes down and walk directly to the kitchen where I get a drink of water and rinse my mouth spitting into the sink. I gulp a few sips and wipe my eyes with a paper towel. I snag my phone from the island and take my water back outside. I sit on one of the chairs on the porch, take some more deep breaths, and a few more gulps of water, then call Micah.

"Hey babe, what's up?

"Micah…" I burst into tears again. My voice hitches as I try to tell him what happened.

"Peyton, take a deep breath, I can't understand you sweetheart. Please, tell me, what's wrong?"

"There's…a… d-dead…animal in th-th-the box!" The tears start again.

"Are you safe?"

"Y-y-yeah."

"I'm two minutes from you, just hang on for me, okay?"

"Okay."

"I'm gonna call Rhett, you'll be on hold for just a second, then he'll join our call. Just hang on for me."

"Okay." A huge hiccup escapes me. There're a few clicks on the line and then it rings.

"Hey Micah…"

"Rhett, I have Peyton on the line, I'm almost to her, she got a package with a dead animal in it. She's safe, but I think you need to be included in whatever's happening."

"Fuck! I'm on my way. I'll let everyone know. Call me back if you need anything else. Pey, hang in there, okay?"

"Okay. I'm Okay."

"I can tell you're not, but you will be. We're coming."

"I can see Micah's car," I tell them.

"I see you too. Come down the stairs."

"I'll be there in a few. Thanks for calling Micah," Rhett hangs up.

I stumble down the stairs. Micah whips into his parking spot and runs to me. He hugs me and I cry, again. I feel childish, but I'm so upset. The smell won't leave me, and that poor animal! I'm hiccupping and my body shakes. Micah holds me, rubbing my back, he whispers soothing words until I settle.

He holds me at arm's length and looks me over. His finger swipes my tears away. I try to smile at him, he's so sweet and comforting, I feel better with him here.

"Are you alright?"

"Yeah, now that you're here. Except, I threw up over the rail so don't walk past the stairs."

"I won't. Let's get Beta out of the car and go upstairs, okay?'

"Yeah. But you have to get that box out of the house before we take him inside."

"I will. Come on, he's so excited to be here."

Micah brings Beta's travel carrier to the porch. I sit in a chair and he places the carrier at my feet. I slide down to the deck and look in at Beta, he's watching me. I reach out and scratch his cheek through the grate. Micah's inside, he comes back out with the box and places it at the far side of the deck. He put the packing paper back in the box but didn't push it down, it's just laying at the top.

Beta meows at me. I look back at him and keep rubbing his face. "It's okay buddy. Your daddy is fixing everything. We'll go inside in just a minute. You're such a good boy." He purrs at me, and I feel better. I'm calm now. Micah is spraying air freshener inside and I can smell it out here. Beta sneezes.

"I know, that stuff makes me sneeze too. But I promise it's better than the alternative." I give him a serious nod. My nose begins to itch.

"*Achoo*! See Beta? Me too."

"Okay, I think we're good now. You doing okay?"

"I'm okay. What did you do with the spoon?"

"It's in the box. I just placed everything in there and brought it all out. I didn't look at any of it. I wanted to get it out and you two in."

"Thank you. I'm sorry I freaked out, but that was a shock." He offers me his hand and I let him help me up.

"You have nothing to apologize for. I'm sorry I wasn't here. I didn't think it could be anything nefarious or I would've asked you to wait for me."

"You don't need to apologize either. Now that we know any box could be scary as shit, we can be more prepared in the future. Let's get Beta inside."

He brings Beta's carrier in and I direct him to the bedroom. I don't want to be in the living room right now. The air freshener is too strong and the memory too fresh. Micah sets the carrier on my bed and unhooks the door for him.

Beta strolls out like he owns the place. He immediately sits on my bed and looks around. Micah moves the carrier to my closet, and I lean in and pet the beautiful cat. He purrs and I smile. Nothing like a happy cat to soothe a distressed soul. I sit next to him, and he rubs against me, purring louder. Micah stands by and watches us. He keeps examining my face. I'm okay now, so I give him a real smile.

"I'd like to brush my teeth before Rhett gets here. Are you two okay if I go to the bathroom?"

"We're fine as long as you are, babe."

"I'm okay now. Thank you."

I brush his arm affectionately as I walk by. I close the door behind me, go to the bathroom and scrub out my mouth. After I'm done I check out the living room. The smell of air freshener is dissipating, thank God. There's a loud knock on the door and I jump, it's possible a small squeal left me too. Micah exits the bedroom and closes the door behind him.

"That's Rhett. I'm going to leave Beta in your room for now, so he doesn't try to dodge out the door while we're busy."

"Okay." I followed him to the door. Micah opens the door, but Rhett's not there.

Micah sticks his head outside, "He's checking out the box. Thomas is here too."

I follow Micah outside and stand as far from the box as I can. Rhett and Thomas have gloves on and some large evidence bags are hanging from Rhett's back pocket. They're bent down investigating the box. Rhett hands Thomas an evidence bag and Thomas holds it open. Rhett puts the packing paper into the bag and then adds my wooden spoon.

"Sorry, that's mine. I was using it to touch stuff in the box, I dropped it when I saw what was in there."

"Hi Peyton. Sorry to see your new place under these circumstances," Thomas greets me.

"Hi Thomas, thanks for coming. Hey Rhett."

"Hey sis, Micah."

"Thanks for coming," Micah says. Rhett moves something around, I guess the dead animal, in the box and frowns. I have to look away, I don't want to puke again.

"What is it?" Micah asks.

"Looks like a small, dead dog. It's a bit flat, so I think it's probably road-kill."

"Oh God," I fight my gut and keep it from revolting.

"What's that?" Thomas asks.

"I don't know. Looks like...a knife. Hmmm..."

"Is that a note?" Micah questions.

"Yeah, Micah, can you get a picture before I remove it? Thomas, can you get another bag ready?"

Micah leans over them and takes a picture with his phone. Thomas holds open another bag and Rhett places a knife in it. It's a pocket knife with maybe a four or five-inch blade. It's in the open position, the blade gleams silver. The handle is dark, maybe wood. I can see it when Thomas holds out the bag.

"I got a couple pictures before I brought it out here too." Micah takes a couple more pictures now that the knife is removed. Rhett reaches in and pulls out a folded piece of paper. He slowly and carefully, unfolds the page.

Rhett holds it up and the three men read it to themselves. All of their faces twist in an array of anger to confusion, and concern. They all look at me when they finish.

"What?" I swallow hard, I'm afraid to know what it says. They clear their throats and Thomas looks down. Rhett gives me a sympathetic look. Micah looks almost sad.

"You guys are freaking me out, what does it say?" Rhett speaks up and Micah comes to me and places his arms around me.

"It's a threat. It says they or he... knows you're here, and they're going to punish you for running from them."

My eyes jerk to the box. Then I look at Rhett. He looks sick. Micah is rubbing my back while he holds me. Goosebumps trail across my skin and I feel myself tremble. My vision gets a bit wavy for just a second as I fight against the panic that wants to pull me under.

"It's going to be okay. We'll keep you safe. I'll keep you safe if I have to be your personal bodyguard," Micah earnestly tells me.

"Yeah Pey, we'll guard you twenty-four-seven if we have to, nothing is going to happen to you. I promise. You can stay with me and Paige any time Micah can't be here or any time you want. You'll always have a room in our home."

"Thanks Rhett, I appreciate it. Should we call the police?" Micah speaks up, "Nah, I'm going to open an FBI case. This has followed you across state lines. I can take jurisdiction without any issues. I'll take all the evidence in and have the lab process it. But I have a feeling we won't find any fingerprints."

Thomas adds, "Probably not, there wasn't anything on the last note so I doubt there'll be anything this time."

Thomas seals the note into the evidence bag. He looks in the box and leans in closer. I don't know how he can stand the smell, but he doesn't seem to react at all. Maybe it's because of his years in the military. I know he has a few medals for things he did overseas, he's a hero.

"Rhett, look at this."

"What the fuck is that? Shit!" Thomas looks up at me, a sheepish look on his face. Micah is looking at them. Rhett is digging in the bottom of the box with his gloved hands.

"Gimme another bag will ya Thomas?"

Thomas grabs one from the pile next to Rhett and opens it holding it out for him. Micah lets go of me and takes my hand. He stretches out my arm trying to get a little closer to see what's so disturbing. Rhett lifts out a handful of small pieces of paper, they look like pictures. The old-fashioned kind from a camera that uses real film.

"What are they?" I ask.

"Sorry Peyton, they're pictures of you," Thomas answers, not meeting my eyes.

My stomach lurches, my heartbeat picks up, and my head throbs. My mouth goes dry and my eyes bulge wide. Micah envelopes me in his arms. I take some deep breaths fighting off the panic pressing against me again.

"Pictures of me doing what?" My voice shakes; it's almost a whisper.

Rhett answers, "They're mostly close ups, they look zoomed in. But, there's at least one that looks like a view through a window and you're getting undressed. I'm sorry." He gives me a sympathetic look and clears his throat.

I gasp at that revelation. What the fuck? It has to be from Baton Rouge. I was on the third floor in the dorm and I wasn't always careful about the blinds because nobody could see up that high, I thought. Here the blinds have been closed since I've been in this place. I was worried about my neighbor seeing in, we thought he was the one to be concerned about. Orlando, the biker next door, definitely seemed like the most obvious threat, but this isn't him this is someone else. I feel like someone kicked me in the gut.

"I need to sit down." Micah guides me to the chair and makes sure I'm seated in it before he lets go of me.

"What can I do babe?" He looks ill. Poor guy. He's so worried about me. I need to pull myself together. I don't want him sick with worry over me.

"I'm all right. Let's get this over with, okay?" Thomas continues to hold open the bag of photos. Rhett lifts the dog and looks underneath it. He pulls out a couple more pictures. After he places them in the bag, Thomas seals it.

"I don't have any evidence bags big enough for this whole box. Have you got a trash bag Pey?" Rhett asks.

Micah speaks up, "I'll go get one." He leaves me after a squeeze of my hand and goes inside. Rhett closes up the box. Thomas removes his gloves. Micah returns with a big black trash bag. Thankfully they were here when I got here. I didn't think I would have any use for them, and I almost put them in the storage closet.

Rhett places the box into the bag that Micah holds open for him. Micah seals it and Rhett removes his gloves. Thomas puts both of their used gloves into another evidence bag. Then everyone looks at me.

"I'm okay guys. I promise." I emphasize my words with my hands. Rhett comes over and hugs me. I remember he found out he's having a baby boy today, I smile.

"Hey, congratulations. Paige told me about the baby."

He smiles at me and hugs me again. He squeezes me pretty hard, but it feels nice, it's reassuring. I love my brother so much, and I'm lucky to have him. He and Paige and little Nova are my family. I'm glad I'm here despite this incident. Oh my God, I could've been dealing with this alone in Baton Rouge. I have a little trouble swallowing the lump in my throat.

I'm successful just as he releases me. He looks me over and seems satisfied that I'm okay.

Thomas speaks up, "Micah, I have to go to Ocala later. Why don't I drop this stuff off for you. Otherwise, you're going to have to figure out cold storage for the box."

"Yeah, good point. Thanks man," Micah responds.

"No trouble, I have an appointment over that way. But we're going to have to head back soon so I can get on the road," Thomas says, glancing at Rhett.

Rhett responds, "No worries. We can leave in a few minutes. Micah's got this under control." He smiles at me and Micah.

"Is Samson going to be around any time soon?" Rhett asks.

"Yeah, he's back from his trip today, and he'll be back at work Monday. Do you want to have a sit down with him? I'll get this all written up and send him a report. I can ask him to meet with us at Savage on Monday," Micah answers.

Rhett replies, "Yeah, that sounds good. I'll pull Ace in too if that's okay?"

"Yeah of course."

Thomas speaks up, "I won't be able to be there Monday, but if you guys call me, I can attend virtually. We'll put together a plan to get a handle on this. Are you going to speak to the neighbor who brought the box over?"

Micah replies, "I have to, he touched the box. I don't think he has anything to do with this though. Since Peyton was having trouble in Louisiana, I think he's just in the wrong place at the wrong time on this one."

"I agree with you," Rhett adds.

Micah decides to keep the note and photo evidence, he sends the box and the packing material with Thomas. I don't want to see the photos. He promises he won't make me look at them, for now. But I may need to identify locations at some point. We're assuming they're from Baton Rouge.

We all hug each other before Rhett and Thomas leave. They both hug me extra tight and extra-long; I appreciate it, and their affection bolsters me.

After they go, Micah carries up some more things he brought for Beta. He also has his laptop and a bag of clothes so he can spend the weekend.

He puts the evidence away and I do my best to put it out of my mind. I'm excited about picking up the cats tomorrow and I focus on that. Not to mention the exciting news of my nephew.

Micah

After getting Peyton and Beta settled, I walk next door to speak to Orlando. I resolutely climb the stairs to his door and knock. Orlando peeks at me, his brows lifted and eyes wide, "Micah, hey man, what's up? You want to come in?"

"Thanks," I step inside, "I'm sorry to bother you, we've had a bit of an incident. Do you mind if I ask you a couple questions?"

"What about? No offense, but you sound like a cop right now."

"Sorry 'bout that. The box that you brought to Peyton?"

"Yeah?" His eyes scrutinize me.

"It wasn't anything she was expecting, it was actually a threat. We've turned it over to the authorities. Since you touched the box, I wanted to give you a heads up. Your prints may be on it and they know you dropped it off. We told them we don't have any reason to think you're involved."

"Shit dude! Is Peyton, okay?" He surprises me with Peyton's wellbeing voiced as his first concern.

"She'll be okay. It was a shock and she's upset, but we're lucky her landlord just put in a security system. It should help keep this person away from the house."

"The mailman dropped off the box. I thought it was something I ordered. But when I saw Peyton's name and my address, I figured I better check with her first. It was weird, but I figured it was probably hers, since it was only one digit off on the address and it wasn't heavy enough for motorcycle parts. I told her if it wasn't for her, to let me know. That's it, I left it with her."

"That's pretty close to what we told the cops about your involvement. If I find out they're coming to talk to you, I'll let you know," I tell him.

He looks me up and down suspiciously, "I notice you didn't deny being a cop, Micah. Anything you want to say?" His arms cross his chest, his chin lifts.

"I do work with the police sometimes, but here, I'm Peyton's boyfriend before anything else. I'm in your house as her boyfriend, to see her neighbor about a situation that happened at her home, period. If you hadn't touched the box, I wouldn't have involved you. I'm not questioning a suspect; I'm just talking to a neighbor. You cool with that?"

His nose twitches and he looks at me, his brow pressing down.

"I guess. We can call our yards neutral ground, no shop talk." Even though his eyes narrow, he holds out his hand for me to shake.

I look him in the eye and raise my own chin, "Okay, I'm in," I grasp his hand, and we shake. Nodding, he lets go of my hand, and smiles.

"What should I be looking out for? I mean, I have a great view of Peyton's house," he gestures toward a window. Sure enough, there's her porch, living room, kitchen, and bathroom windows.

I turned back to him, "Anyone you don't recognize, lurking around or behaving suspiciously, let us know."

Fishing a card out of my pocket, it's for a sandwich shop. For some reason I usually have cards in my pockets, people are always handing them to me. I pull a pen out of my other pocket, scribble my cell number on the card with my first name and hand it to him.

"Call me any time, day or night if you see something suspicious. Even if you're not sure, call me anyway. I appreciate your help; extra eyes will keep my girl safe." I inch my way to the door.

Smiling, I add, "I guess I better head out. Thanks Orlando, I'll see you." He stays rooted there, only his eyes follow me. A small smirk cracks his stern face.

"Yeah, see you, Micah." I close the door behind me and go back to Peyton's.

"Hi," Peyton smiles at me. Her head tilts to the side, she looks better. She was fighting off anxiety earlier, but she's winning now.

"Hi, doing, okay?" My eyes trace her face.

"I am. Mr. Beta here, has been curled into my side offering therapeutic cat rubs and purrs." She looks good. Eyes bright, her face relaxed, and I believe her.

Smiling at her I agree, "He takes his job seriously. Everything went fine with Orlando. We agreed to a neutral zone, no shop talk between your yard and his."

"That's very interesting. So, he knows you're FBI?"

"I didn't tell him. I didn't deny being law enforcement either. He knows I'm something. Our neutral zone means I don't have to admit it and he doesn't have to admit anything either," I shrug.

When Peyton and I arrive at the shelter all of our outside concerns go out the window. We visit the playroom and there's Kate, my new little girl. She'll be known as Qwerty from now on. She runs to me when she sees me, her sisters follow. I plop onto the ground, and she climbs right onto my lap and rubs her cheek under my chin. I made the right choice with her. She's going to be great with Beta.

Peyton is on the floor near the window with Ebony in her arms. She hasn't told me what her name will be yet. She narrowed it down to about three choices, I wonder what she'll choose. She looks so happy, her eyes sparkle, and her smile is ethereal. She's a vision, like a beautiful faerie with her magical animal counterpart. How am I so lucky to call her my girlfriend? I'm so in love with her. *Please, whoever answers prayers or grants wishes, don't let me screw this up.*

Qwerty licks my neck with her sandpaper tongue. She sneezes at me. Poor thing probably got too much of my cologne. I scratch behind her ears and she purrs which elevates my happy heart all the more.

"Okay, I've got your paperwork. They both had a checkup this morning in preparation for your adoptions. They're both spayed, so you don't need to sign the Stop Unwanted Felines Contract. I have a carrier for each of them like we discussed. Have you decided to purchase the carriers? Or return them?" Connor, the rescue employee, asks.

Peyton speaks up, "We're going to purchase them. I also want to buy more of the food you guys feed them. We've been transitioning Beta, Micah's cat, to the new food. We want to keep feeding all of them the better food. We researched online and really like everything we read about it. Also, Micah's vet just retired, we both want to use Dr. Ree. We liked her when she called us, plus since she runs this place. We can't really ask for anyone better."

"You most definitely can't get anyone better. Dr. Ree is fantastic. She loves the animals so much, she's great to her staff, and she's young, so she'll be around a long time. You're making an excellent choice," Connor praises us while plugging his boss.

"Both of the girls are up to date on their shots, and they don't need to be seen again for a year. Micah, your boy, Beta, right? Is he up to date or do you need an appointment for him?"

"I just took him for a checkup and shots about a month ago, so I'll probably just get them a combined appointment in a year," Micah answers.

"Perfect. What name did you decide on for Kate? I'll get everyone entered into the computer, so you won't need to do that when you come back," Connor smiles at us.

"I'm going with Qwerty." I wait for his response.

"How do you spell that?" Connor asks, suddenly an old hat at this business part.

"Q.W.E.R.T.Y." His head lifts and meets my eyes, there it is, he gets it now.

"Oh! I see it, that's cute. Are you an IT guy?" Conner asks.

"Something like that. I thought it would go well with Beta."

"Yeah, it's great. How about you, Peyton? Does Ebony have a new name?"

"Ugh! No, I can't decide," she scrunches her face in mock frustration.

"What're you debating between?" Connor queries.

"I keep changing my mind, I don't think I can name her until I spend some time with her. I switch between Spirit, Echo, Mystery, and Storm. I want something unique, but I'm not sure which fits her best."

"I vote for Mystery. I've only met one other cat with that name," Connor adds.

"That's funny, on the way here I was leaning towards Mystery. But I'm still undecided. Just leave her as Ebony for now and I'll call you when I make a decision."

"You got it. Do you have any questions for me?"

I answer, "I'm good, no questions."

"Me too," Peyton adds.

"Great, I just need your checks for the adoption fees and the carriers."

Connor approaches Peyton to collect hers first. She digs it out of her pocket. I hand mine over and he marks everything down on a receipt for each of us. He has carriers ready to go with a care package for each cat. There's a small bed in each carrier with a toy. He also puts all the paperwork for each of us in a folder. The folders go into the care packages. After we load up the cats, we trail behind him to the front where he grabs the food. He follows us outside and loads it into the back of my SUV.

We fasten the cat carriers into the back seat with them facing each other. Ebony is crying, and her meows aren't happy. Qwerty meows at her and she settles. I don't know what she said, but it was impressive. I hope they'll be okay with Beta. I think he's going to be excited to have someone to play with.

Peyton

When we let the cats out to investigate the place and each other , it's anticlimactic. They sniff at each one of their new friends then they all go separate ways. We show them the kitty litter box, their beds, and where to find water, but they find the cat tree on their own. Ebony immediately climbs to the highest platform.

Qwerty hops up on the sofa and curls on the back towards the corner. Beta claims the platform below Ebony, then he tries to join her at the top but she pushes him off. He gives her a dirty look and stomps off pouting. She curls up and flicks her tail like she's staked her claim to the throne. Beta sits on the chair and watches the girls while feigning indifference. When Ebony hops down, Beta takes her spot, I swear he's smirking. I giggle because they're so entertaining.

"Aww, don't laugh at him. He's totally a badass, despite being shoved off the top by a girl. Ow! No hitting, Eagle," he flinches. I chuckle at Micah and go after Ebony. I find her in my closet, with a flip flop in her mouth.

"Hey! That's not yours," I scolded, taking it from her. She snorts at me and leaves the room. I looked around and made sure she didn't chew on anything else. Thankfully it was only this shoe, but she left serious teeth marks in it. I hope this isn't a regular thing. I decided to hunt for her again.

This time she's in the office, standing on Micah's keyboard, all kinds of letters and symbols flash across his screen as she steps on the keys. It's nonsense but hopefully she doesn't hit anything that'll cause damage, I scoop her up.

"You're a little troublemaker, aren't you? I don't think any of my name choices are going to fit. I guess we'll have to see how things play out today. But now I'm thinking Chaos or Freyja."

She meows at me and wiggles for me to put her down. I bring her back to the living room and set her on the back of the sofa. Qwerty and Beta are playing with a cat toy on a string that dangles from the tree. Ebony watches them but she doesn't participate.

"Your two seem to be getting along. That's great. I hope Ebony will settle in and join them. You won't believe what the little stinker got up to in the short time she was gone."

"Oh yeah? She seems so small and quiet. Hard to picture her getting into something already." Micha smiled.

"I was surprised. She chewed up one of my flip flops. Then while I was looking for any more damage, she went into the office and pressed a bunch of keys on your laptop. Hopefully she didn't do anything too crazy, like email the head of the FBI," I chuckled, shaking my head.

"I'm sure she didn't cause any damage or send any emails, it's locked. She just needs a little time. She'll be okay." He smiles at her and I swear her little chin lifts in triumph.

I sit on the sofa near her, but not too close, I want to see what she'll do. She comes over behind me and sniffs me. She steps on my shoulder and crawls down to my chest where she nestles in and starts purring. She's affectionate with people as advertised, but I want her to befriend the others. I'm hoping they'll spend a lot of time together. I need them to get along. I guess it's fine if she ignores them as long as there's no fighting.

Beta wanders away from the toy and jumps onto the sofa right next to me. He looks over Ebony and then takes a cautious step onto my lap, her ears twitch. He presses against me and rubs himself on me and Ebony. She swats at him, then her ears lay flat on her head. She opens her mouth and gives him a halfhearted hiss.

He ignores her attitude and collapses in my lap. Qwerty watches from the top of the tree. I scratch Ebony and she purrs. She pays no more attention to Beta, I guess that's good. I scratch him with my other hand.

"Are you thirsty? I'm gonna grab a soda, what would you like?" Micah queries.

"I would love a big glass of ice water, thanks."

Qwerty follows Micah, Beta lifts his head and watches them go, but he doesn't move. Interesting. I think he's trying to improve relations with Ebony. She continues to purr and pays him no mind. I scratch both of them and wait to see what they do. Micah returns with my water.

"Thank you. This is perfect," I gulped my water. I was thirsty too. I didn't notice with all the excitement of the three fur-balls.

Micah sits next to me on the sofa. He takes my hand in his. I smile at him and he smiles back. The familiar warmth fills me. He makes excited sparks jump through my chest. The nerves in my hand shoot excited tickles up my arm from where his hand touches mine. He drifts closer and I'm about to grab him for a kiss, when his phone rings in his pocket. He slides down a bit so he can fish it out of his jeans. He doesn't let go of my hand and I squeeze his.

He winks at me as he answers, "Hey Samson, what's up?"

I can hear his reply, "Hi Micah, I was reading this report about the package Peyton received. The lab is rushing their examination. We should have results by Monday morning. I was wondering about her neighbor."

"What about him?" Micah asks.

"I read everything from your reports about him and Peyton's proximity and the security system. I see that you don't think he's involved with the package. Why do you think that?"

"Mostly because of the trouble she had in Baton Rouge. We think this is unrelated to the bikers and the biker next door. It seems to be a stalker who was harassing her before she moved here. It's an odd coincidence that he brought the box over, my thought is the actual stalker probably saw the security system and decided not to risk anything coming directly to Peyton. But that's just a guess."

"I suppose that makes sense. I just hate coincidences, especially when they involve someone who has a record and associates with a gang. It makes my gut clench." I could hear Samson say through the phone.

"I know, but honestly, he doesn't have anything to do with it. Are you available Monday, for a meeting at Savage?"

"Yeah, I'll work from there Monday so I'll be available any time. Are you doing okay?"

"I'm great," Micah says.

"How's Peyton doing with all of this?"

"She's hanging in. She's strong and she's distracting herself with her boyfriend and a new cat."

"That's good. I'll see you Monday."

"Okay, see you."

When I wake up Sunday morning, there's a very insistent meowing at my door. I don't want to open my eyes, but it's not stopping. I open one eye and look at my phone, it's 7 a.m. *What the hell?* I reach out for Micah and he's not there. Both eyes open and I sit-up. Looking around I see a note next to my phone, and Qwerty is in my doorway meowing at me.

"Hi pretty girl, what's with all the loudness?" She lets out the loudest mewl yet.

"Okay, okay, show me," I drag myself from bed and walk towards her. She turns and walks down the hall to the kitchen. She meows incessantly. She's definitely agitated. I swear she's trying to tell me something.

When I enter the kitchen and look where her face is aiming, I'm shocked to see Ebony. She's on the island chewing up some mail. There are three envelopes in shreds and she's working on a fourth.

"What're you doing? That's not yours! You, young lady, are a big troublemaker. You're a little felon." I grab her and hold her face to mine.

Looking into her eyes I ask, "What shall I do with you, little miss? You're going to get a felony charge before you're even an adult at this rate." She meows in answer, pleading her case.

"Listen here my little walking felony, you better cut it out or you're going to end up in time out in a little kitty prison. You don't want that right?" She tilts her head at me listening intently, "That's what I thought. You're going to be a good girl now, right?" She's so cute I can't be mad. I hug her and place her on the ground.

"Are you girls hungry?" They both meow and Beta runs into the room meowing too. I feed them, and everyone quickly shoves their face in a dish. Finally, the noisy meowing comes to an end. *Peace at last, ahh.*

Micah comes in the door; his hands are full with a tray of coffee and a bag of food.

"Have I told you how much I love you?" I ask him.

"You might've mentioned it," he smiles and kisses me.

"I was wondering where you were."

"I left you a note. I just ran out to get food and coffee. Surprise," he gives me a cheesy grin.

"I didn't get a chance to read it yet. Qwerty woke me up to tell me my little felon was committing a crime."

He laughs, "What? How did she do that?" He says looking her over.

"She was meowing at me until I got up. Then she led me to the kitchen where my problem child was in the process of committing a crime. Seriously, she destroyed some mail. I think that's a federal offense, probably a felony."

He laughs, "That's a good name for her. *Felony*. I like it."

I laugh with him, "Oh my God, you're right, it's perfect."

"I wonder if she'll like it. Hey, Felony, what d'you think?" She finishes eating, licks her lips, and walks over to Micah like he called her.

"I guess that answers that, huh, Felony? You like your name, don't you?" *Meow!*

"Sounded like yes to me. Is that her name, Eagle?"

"Yeah, I knew something would come up once I got her home. I have to remember to call Furry Paws and tell Connor."

We enjoy our last day before I start school. I finished all of my assignments and the required reading over the past week. I think I'm ready to get started. We watch a couple movies and enjoy the cats. Micah goes home after dinner and takes his cats with him.

As I get ready for bed, I realize I miss them. This is the first time I'll sleep alone in weeks, I'm not a fan. I want my handsome guy here keeping me safe. I want the cats here keeping Felony company. I look at her, and see she's coiled on Micah's pillow. She watches me until I lie down. Then she puts her chin on the pillow and closes her eyes. I closed mine too.

Peyton

I'm so proud of myself. I found both of my morning classes and I didn't fall asleep in either one. Actually, my second class was my favorite. Social Justice, with Dr. Bertman, she's an incredible person. I hope I can be like her when I grow up.

"Peyton! Hey!"

"Hi Anisa! How're your classes?" I'm so excited to see her. A friendly face on a college campus is a blessing. I immediately relax, a tension I didn't notice before, eases.

"I made it through torts without killing anyone. How about you? Are you going to lunch now?" she asks.

"Yeah, I have 55 minutes until my next class, I'm going to the cafeteria. I love my social justice class. Are you taking it?"

"It's my class after lunch. So, you like Dr. Bertman? I heard she's tough."

"I don't know yet. We're so lucky she's here though, and she agreed to have two classes so everyone who applied could take the class. She's an amazing person. She's my idol in the social justice realm. Dr. Bertman has accomplished so much for the betterment of society. I want to find a way to do that."

"Not me, I want to earn lots of money and retire young so I can enjoy it," she laughs and I'm not sure if she's serious or not. She's a bit quirky, I like it. She's taller than me, and she's got beautiful auburn hair. She wears it in a shoulder length, layered style that suits her face perfectly. She has dark blue eyes, similar to my brother's. Her hair color makes her eyes stand out against her pale skin.

We buy pizza in the cafeteria. Anisa and I have never been more than partners in a study group. She's pretty funny and I'm hopeful we can become friends. I'm so lucky she had to transfer here, especially with me starting as a 2L, since I'd be the odd one out. Everyone else has already spent a year together. The two of us are in the same boat so it eases some of the stress of being a second-year student in a new school.

Both of my classes and the clinic tomorrow are with Anisa. That'll help us study together. She's in Social Justice also, but not at the same time as me. She's taking Campaign Finance and White-Collar Crime. I'm taking First Amendment Law and Pretrial Procedural Practices in Florida. To-morrow, we have Wills and Trusts and Criminal Defense with a Criminal Defense Clinic. In my head I refer to it as *Criminal Defense Against the Dark Arts.* Harry Potter was my favorite as a kid.

By the time I finish Pretrial Procedural Practices in Florida I'm bouncing on the balls of my feet, my chest pounds a joyful rhythm, and I can't stop smiling. As I walk to my car, I'm practically floating on air. I love my classes and professors so far. I've always loved school but I'm in my element and it feels great.

"Excuse me. Hello. Hi, I'm Jake Waverly. We have Pretrial Procedural Practices in Florida together."

Startled and confused, I responded, "Okaaaay?"

"You're Peyton, right?"

"Yes?"

"I wanted to meet you. The TA is my cousin, he said you turned in the best essay for the required reading. I just wanted to introduce myself and I'd love to form a study group with you."

"Oh. Um...Hi. Sure, Jake?"

"Yep," his smile is big.

"That'd be great. I'm in a group with my friend, Anisa, so far, but you're welcome to join us. We haven't set up a schedule yet or anything yet."

"That's okay. Maybe we can exchange numbers?" he asks.

"Yeah, of course. Sorry, you caught me off guard. My mind was someplace else."

"It's fine. Here, enter your number and I'll text you." When I look up, he's smiling radiantly at me, causing dimples to decorate his cheeks. It makes him very attractive, but I feel nothing. I smile back. Taking his phone, I quickly type in my number. I press message and text myself. My phone vibrates in my pocket.

"Okay, I texted myself. So, we'll talk soon about study group. Thanks."

"Thank you! I look forward to hearing from you, Peyton."

Smiling back at him, I say, "Me too, Jake."

When I get home, I look around before exiting the car. I check all the shadows carefully, still anxious from the box incident. Seeing nothing of concern, I gather my things and trot to the stairs. Rushing to the front door, I get inside as fast as I'm able. Anyone watching me would think a monster is breathing down my neck.

Once inside with the alarm engaged, I finally relax. All my school stuff gets dropped on the table. A fluffy little girl comes charging at me meowing. I'm starving, apparently Felony is too. She rubs my legs even as I walk. I make my way to the fridge and tug open the door.

I gasp, "Holy crap! Oh Micah, you're the best!" I say to no one but Felony. Inside my fridge is a beautiful Publix sub with my name on it and a heart. I love that man. Feeding my poor starving actress quiets her while she inhales her moist food.

I find some chips and pour myself a grape juice. Right when I take a huge bite of turkey and cheese heaven, my doorbell rings. Someone is holding the button down, shit!

After a quick peep, I fling the door open, "Mwat-tha-hwell?" Orlando is pale, his eyes are wide, and he is so tense he looks ready to pop something.

"Are you okay? What's wrong?" I blurted out, having swallowed.

"Are *you* okay? Nothing's wrong here? Nobody's been inside?"

"Orlando, come inside, you're scaring me. What happened?"

"You weren't home yet. Your car wasn't here. I saw movement at your place in my periphery, when I looked over there was a guy on your porch. He saw me when I saw him and he took off running. He went through the backyard and the neighbor's yard, then I lost him. I spent a while looking for him, but he got away. Now I come back and you're home."

"Oh my God! Nobody came in the front, I mean, I had to unlock it and disengage the alarm. I'm gonna call Micah."

"I already did."

My head snaps in his direction, "What? Why?"

"He asked me to let him know if anything happened, before I knew you were here, so I called him. I saw your car while he was still on the line and he's on his way. Did you check around?"

Embarrassed, I admit, "I was starving when I came in, I went to the fridge and sat down to eat. I didn't look anywhere else."

"Is it alright if I check?" he asks.

"I guess. I mean, if Micah's on his way…"

His face is serious and amicable, "It's all good. But I'm going to wait with you, if that's okay?"

"You can check, I guess. It's just awkward having a stranger looking in my closet and under my bed, you know?"

"Really, Peyton, it's fine I truly do understand. But I want to make sure you're safe until Micah gets here, okay?"

"Yeah, that's fine. So, um, do you want something to drink?"

"Nah, I'm good, you can go ahead and eat though."

I roll my eyes at myself and answer, "I'm too nervous to eat or drink until someone checks the house." He cackles. Seriously, he lets out a loud, authentic movie witch cackle.

"Not cool, Orlando." I narrowed my eyes at him. Felony rubs his legs and he squats down to pet her, never breaking eye contact with me.

"Oh, shit, I'm sorry. You just remind me of my little sister. She wants to be all brave and not let me protect her one minute, then she cuddles with me because she's scared the next. You're funny."

"Great, my fear is funny." I tilt my head and widen my eyes in exasperation at him. It's mostly mock annoyance, he seems kind of sweet about his sister. Felony likes him, she's rubbing all over him while he scratches her with two hands. He acts like an animal lover and if he's passed Felony's inspection, I can accept him. Maybe he's not so bad. Micah comes in without knocking. He almost tackles me with his worried hug and kiss. He holds me at arms length and looks me over.

"I'm fine. I promise. But no one has checked the house," I inform him.

He stares daggers at Orlando, "What the hell man? Why didn't you check...?"

I interrupt, "It's my fault Micah. I didn't want a stranger in my room. He was very polite, and he wouldn't leave until you got here to make sure I was safe," I plead with my eyes for him not to think I'm crazy. Micah looks between me and Orlando a few times. Then he smiles sheepishly at Orlando.

"No worries, dude," Orlando cuts in before Micah can apologize. They sort of give each other a nod and we're past it. Men have some strange rituals.

Before anyone else can say anything, Micah and Orlando walk to the back door. They investigate the lock and handle. I hang back and look around me, honing in on things I've never noticed before. The pencil marks on the door frame to the office look like someone was measuring a growing child. There's a nail in the wall without a picture or anything else hanging from it. I spotted a chip in the wood floor close to the office door. I hope those movers didn't do that, I might get blamed. I need to look at my move-in walk-thru photos.

They walk toward my room next. I'm about to stop them, stranger in my room, hello! But with Micah here, somehow, it's not so weird. I step into the office. Nothing looks out of place or tampered with. I even check under the desk.

They step into the office and I squish into the corner to stay out of their way. They check everything I did, and the window. Nothing is wrong. We all go back to the kitchen, and they look over everything there, but nothing is amiss. Felony voices her dislike of the intrusion. I shush her and she stops fussing. Huh, who knew a cat would listen?

"Do you mind showing me where he ran?" Micah directs to Orlando.

"Sure, see you later, Peyton."

"Bye, Orlando," I wave.

He turns back to Micah, "He went out the front, I saw him on the porch at first. Then he went that..."

The front door closes and cuts off what Orlando's saying. Feeling much better now, I sit back in my seat at the island and enjoy my sandwich, sharing a bite with Felony. My juice is a little watered down from the ice melting while we checked the house. But it's all right, still plenty of grapey goodness.

When I'm done eating, I clean up my mess, then spread out my books and look through everything. Checking what I've completed and what needs to be done. I compare everything with the syllabus I got today. I make notes of what our study group will need to accomplish. I'm hoping to join a team, either Law Review or Trial Team. They look great on a resume, plus I love the competitive aspect. I'm reading my to do list when Micah comes back.

"Did you find anything?" I look at him.

"A few people have video cameras. I'll have to check if they caught anything. Do you promise me you're alright?"

Hugging him I reply, "Honest, I'm perfect. I don't think he was inside. He was gone before I got here and we have no clue if it was even the stalker. Relax, please?"

"You're right. Tell me how was your day?" He forces a smile and I appreciate the effort.

"It was great, I love Dr. Bertman, you know the professor I told you about? She's amazing and I liked my other classes okay. Anisa, my friend? She's in a few of my classes, so we're planning a study group. Some guy approached me in the parking lot and introduced himself. He said his cousin is the TA and he told this guy that my required reading essay was the best one. So, now the guy wants to be in our study group. I shared my number and told him about Anisa."

"What's the guy's name?"

"Why?" I ask, confused why he would care.

"Because a stalker is harassing you and a stranger walked up to you in a parking lot, claimed he's a student, flattered you, and got your phone number, babe," he smiles a sarcastic smirk. My chin tilts up and my eyes narrow as I evaluate him, I'm pretty sure he's asking for safety's sake and not out of jealousy.

"He said his name is Jake Waverly. Please, don't get weird about me studying with people," I touch his arm. "I love you. I'm not interested in anyone else. I don't have any feelings whatsoever for anyone but you." I reinforce my words with an intent look right into his eyes.

He puts his palms on my hips and grasps chunks of my ass. He pulls me in for a kiss. I seek entrance to his mouth with my tongue. We make out for a few moments.

I break our kiss to say ... *MEEOWW!*

"Felony? What's wrong little girl?" She looks at me then proceeds to throw up on the floor, "Oh no! Are you okay sweetie?"

I quickly clean up the small mess. Micah holds Felony and declares her to be fine now, but we're going to watch her. She walks off and coils up on the couch, I watch as her eyes close. The mood is ruined, but that's okay for now. I can't keep my hands off him for long.

"Oh! I forgot to thank you for my sandwich. I was starving when I got home and you must have read my mind."

"What sandwich?" His eyes squint and his shoulders raise in a puzzled gesture.

"The Publix sub, you got it exactly right. Even when I write it down, I never get the submarine sauce I order. You get an A+ and a thousand good boyfriend points," I smile warmly.

"Seriously, Peyton, I didn't get you a sandwich," his face is pinched in concern.

"Well then where did it come...oh fuck!" I run to the trash and vomit. I can't stop until there's nothing left. Micah's holding my hair and rubbing my back as tears streak down my face. He runs and gets my toothbrush; he loaded it with toothpaste. He's a keeper, if I didn't have barf breath, I'd kiss him. My face crumples when I remember that I ate and vomited an unknown sandwich.

"Oh Micah! I gave a little bite of my sandwich to Felony and she threw up too. What if it had something poisonous in it?" Fresh tears overflow my eyes.

"I called nine-one-one, I'm sorry, but we have to be safe. *You* might have been poisoned. We need your blood checked, and maybe your stomach. How do you feel now?" Micah asks, his face serious.

"Other than really scared and sickened by the thought of it, I'm physically feeling okay. No pain or strange feelings anywhere," I take inventory of myself and nod in confirmation.

"I hear a truck, it's probably the EMTs. Why don't you sit wherever you'll be comfortable. I'll let them in," he guides me towards the living room. I fall onto the sofa, I'm tired. He looks out the peephole then opens the door.

Three guys come inside carrying various cases. They all have stethoscopes around their necks, gloves on their hands, and masks on their faces. They approach me slowly.

The redhead talks first, "Good afternoon, Miss?"

"Peyton Baker, please call me Peyton. I ate something that may have been left by my stalker not knowing it was from him. My cat ate a bite and vomited. Where is she? Micah?" I search around nervously.

"I closed her in the office so she wouldn't get out, or stepped on. I called Orlando. He's going to stay here and watch her while we go to the hospital."

"You think that's okay?"

"We've got the security system. I'll adjust it so we can watch him. Paige is going to help. If we need her, she'll come and get Felony and take her home to her house or mine, so Felony won't be alone. Okay?" He double checks with me.

"Yeah, okay. Thank you, Micah. I love you."

"I love you too," he squeezes my hand in emphasis.

"Sorry, Miss, um, Peyton, your blood pressure is elevated, along with your pulse. It could be nerves but, even for that, it seems high. Do you normally have high blood pressure?"

"No, never."

"I agree with your boyfriend, we're going to take you to Oakdale General." He nods at his co-workers then focuses on Micah.

"Mr., Uh?"

"Special Agent Micah Castleman, FBI," he lifts his ID from inside his shirt and shows the EMT. Dan Newbury, according to his name tag. All three EMTs nod in acknowledgment.

The other two EMTs have dark hair and big muscles. Dan is tall but he's pear shaped. The other two go outside, they come back without their cases and pushing a stretcher. Thinking about the stairs they'll need to carry me down; I'm relieved they have muscles.

They have me move onto the stretcher and lift it into a sitting position. Dan starts an IV in my hand. He hangs the bag of fluid on a hook just over my shoulder. They seatbelt me onto the stretcher.

Orlando comes in through the open door, his face is pale again, "What happened? Are you okay Peyton?" He inspects my face in a concerned way, I might be melting toward him a little.

"I hope so," I answered. Micah fills him in and explains further about having him watch Felony. Color returns to his cheeks when he realizes I'm not in immediate danger. He kindly agrees and settles onto the sofa.

"I've got people coming to look things over, they'll know you're here. Call me if you have any trouble. Thanks Orlando."

"No worries. Happy to help. Peyton, you get better and back home quick, okay?"

"I'll do my best. Thanks for helping. I really appreciate it."

"What're neighbors for if not to help in an emergency?"

"Good point, thank you."

The two dark haired EMTs wheel me through the door. I think one of them is named Tony? I wasn't really listening when they told me their names. Dan follows behind. Micah was next to me but he can't fit now, so he's actually behind Dan. I can't see him once they straighten the stretcher. When I try to look for him over my shoulder, I spot the top of his head and Orlando watching from the doorway.

"Are you riding with us SA Castleman?" Dan asks innocently.

Micah coughs before he answers, "Yeah, I'm going to ride with her." I can't see Orlando anymore, but I swear I heard a short gasp when Dan called Micah an agent.

So much for the neutral zone, I'm not going to worry about it. Orlando won't let anything happen to Felony. He's an animal lover and she likes him. I trust all of that and Micah likes him, though I'm not sure he's ready to admit it.

Micah

Motherfucker! My new friend Dan has just outed me to Orlando. I guess our neutral zone will cease to exist now. I don't care about anything but Peyton. I sneak a quick glance at Orlando, he looks sufficiently surprised. I'll deal with it after I know Peyton is safe.

When we arrive in the ER, they immediately roll Peyton into an examination room. They quickly assess her and take a blood and urine sample. The doctor explains he put a rush order on her tests, and he has a call in to the best toxicologist in the country. Peyton's asleep I'm watching her vitals as the light travels up and down across the screen relaying her heart functions in real time. Her blood pressure is still high.

I'm jolted from my thoughts when Paige runs into the room. "Oh, thank God, Micah! Is she okay?"

"She's okay so far. She vomited when she realized who left the sandwich, we didn't have to induce anything. We're waiting for test results, and they'll decide treatment based on anything she ingested."

"Sounds like they're doing what they can. Is she feeling all right?"

"She zonked out in the ambulance, then she woke up when they took her blood and urine and fell right back asleep. She hasn't complained about any pain or anything. She shared her sandwich with Felony so she's worried about her. She threw up too. Orlando's watching her."

"The neighbor?" Her eyes go wide.

I touch her arm so she focuses on me, "Felony will be safe with Orlando. He's an animal lover and he likes Peyton. No MC BS." She sighs. I offer her my chair with a hand gesture. She smiles and falls into it. Her belly isn't huge yet, but big enough she has to be uncomfortable hauling it around.

"I'm so confused. What happened? How did a sandwich get into the house?" She speaks quietly to keep from waking Peyton, her eyes tell me her intention. I give her an appreciative smile. We've worked together long enough that we have our own language of eye rolls and gestures. I consider her and Rhett part of my chosen family, and of course my *niece*, Nova.

"I'm not sure what happened. I didn't get a chance to review the security footage yet. I got a call from Orlando; Peyton wasn't home yet, and he saw someone on her porch. He chased the guy but lost him on the next block. When he got back, Peyton was home. He called me before he saw her car. I was on the line when he told me she was there. He checked on her and she didn't feel comfortable letting him search the house, so he waited with her for me to get there."

"I'm not hearing about a sandwich."

"I'm getting to it. She thought I left it for her. I went with Orlando to check out the direction the guy ran, so I can check the security footage from any cameras I spotted in the area. When I got back, she had eaten the sandwich and shared a bite with Felony. I called nine-one-one. You're all caught up."

"How do you think he got in?"

"No clue. Orlando and I checked the house, no forced entry. Everything was locked up tight. I want to check the security feed, but it will be too difficult to see it clearly on my phone. I need my laptop."

"I'm going to wait here for the test results and then I'll head home. I can take a look when I get back if you're still not able to get to a screen," she offers.

"Thanks. We'll figure it out, I've never been so scared. I'm trying to stay calm, but damn Paige, how do you let Rhett out of your sight?"

"It's not easy some days. When you love someone who's hurt and there's nothing you can do to fix it, it's the most difficult thing. She'll be okay. Thankfully she vomited pretty quick, so I doubt there's much, if anything, in her system. You're doing a good job of holding it together. She's a lucky girl, having someone like you love her," she gives me an encouraging smile.

Even though she's not that much older than me, she often fills my need for a mother figure. Melanie, Samson's wife, cared for me in a motherly way when I went to stay with them at 15. She's a very nice lady and I almost have more of a grandchild/grandmother relationship with her. I love her, but we're not as close as mother and child. I was a difficult teenage boy, I didn't open up much, so it's on me. But she has always cared for me no matter how much of a shit I was.

Paige is only five or six years older than me, but she has a mother's loving way about her, she took me in the moment we met. She immediately started to worry about me, offering me unconditional love and support. We're definitely friends, but she's at the top of my chosen family. She's the person I'd go to with any relationship questions. Anything a mother would normally help with, she's my go-to. I smile at her. She has no clue how much she means to me. I might need to rectify that. I'm getting old I guess, and thinking the people I love and appreciate should know it.

"Paige, do you know-"

The door bursts open and Rhett storms in, "Is she okay?" He slows his movements and lowers his voice when he sees she's sleeping. He drills into me with his gaze.

"She's okay, we're waiting for results. I'll let Paige fill you in, I'm going to see if I can find her doctor and speed him up a little."

"You good, dude?" He asks me.

"Yeah, just worried. Who's checking the house?"

"Ace is there with Double Mint. He's collecting samples, dusting for prints, and checking all the entry points."

"You warned them about Orlando?"

"Oh shit, no! I was worried about her, and just yelled stuff at Ace as I ran out. I'll call him now, Thanks! That could've been awkward or worse," Rhett pats his chest as he talks. I've noticed he does it if he can't roll his challenge coin over his knuckles when anything emotional happens. I think he's trying to soothe his heart. He takes out his phone and steps into the hall.

I signal Paige that I'll be back in a few minutes. The doctor is up ahead at the nurse's station. He's got a phone to his ear and his eyes are glued to a computer screen. His face is red and pinched, and his fingers jab at the keys making them click louder than usual. I take a few deep breaths and try to settle my nerves.

"Okay, I understand. Thank you, Dr. Kozlowski. Yes sir. Thank you, sir," Dr. Bronson acts like he's talking to the King of England. He sighs after he hangs up, then he notices me.

"SA Castleman. Is she awake?"

Shaking my head, I answered, "No, she was still asleep when I stepped out. Have you gotten any results yet?"

"Yes, I don't want to wake her just yet. She has ketamine in her blood and urine. I'm going to go ahead and guess she doesn't abuse illegal drugs?"

"No, of course not. If it's in her system, she was drugged. At least now we know what we're looking for. That'll help speed everything up. Did you speak to the expert? The Toxicologist?"

He points at the phone in front of him, "That was him. He says the cat should be perfectly fine. It's used as a tranquilizer or sedation for animals, if she was going to have an issue it would've happened fast, like within 10 minutes." I take a deep breath and he continues.

"The same for Peyton. If she was going to have a reaction it would've been within 20 minutes. I'm letting her sleep because the drug can cause hallucinations and it can be very unpleasant. If she sleeps through it, that'll be the best thing for her. I'm just going to keep her overnight so we can monitor the levels in her blood and in case she has a bad reaction to any hallucinations. I want to warn you as well, it can cause memory loss. Chances are she won't remember anything from just before she ingested the drug until after it wears off. If you don't mind, will you press the call button or stick your head out and get me if she wakes up?"

"Yeah, okay. She's going to be fine though, right?"

"Yes, sir."

"Please, call me Micah."

"I'm Richfield, I go by Rick," he smiles and holds out his hand for me to shake.

Gripping his hand, I tell him, "Thanks Rick, pleasure to meet you. Thank you for taking care of my girl." He gives me some more details about the drug and possible effects before I go back towards her room. When I'm two steps from the door, Rhett pops up from I don't know where.

"Any news?" Rhett speaks in a soft voice, so he doesn't disturb the other patients.

"Yeah," I answered. Then I explained what the doctor told me.

"We need to let her sleep then? Hallucinations can be pretty bad. I saw some bad reactions to hallucinations overseas. There was a guy who went on a shooting spree trying to kill the hallucinated zombies chasing him. Thankfully he only shot up some trees, but it could've been so bad."

"Yeah, I'm hoping she'll sleep through that part. Did you get a hold of Ace? Everything okay with Orlando?"

"He says everything is under control. Felony is doing okay, she drank a bunch of water, that's good, right?"

"I think so. Did the team from my office show yet? One of the EMTs outed me to Orlando, so I called in the crime scene team."

"He didn't mention them, so either it's fine or they're not there yet. I wouldn't worry about any of it. Remember it's Ace we're talking about, he can charm the habit from a nun," he laughs at his joke.

"That's true. We better go back inside. I want to make sure she's okay."

When we quietly enter Peyton's room, we find Paige sprawled out next to her on the bed, snoring softly. Peyton's IV is on the opposite side of the bed, and she's turned that way; I can't see her face. Rhett walks to the foot of the bed and looks Peyton over. He gives me a thumbs up and I relax a little. I sit on one of the chairs and focus on her vital signs, the bright light still flashes across the screen.

After a while, Rhett signals me to step outside. I silently walk out, and he follows.

"I'm going to go nuts sitting here. I know she's in good hands, but I need to do something, so I'm going to go to Pey's and see what's what. I'll make sure Felony is safe. I can bring her home with me if need be. Let me know if anything happens. I'll do the same."

"Thanks man. We'll talk later." He gives me a man hug and leaves. I look around for Dr. Bronson, I don't see him. I visit the vending machine and bring back a red bull.

Nobody's moved, but it's good. Paige needs the rest. Even better for Peyton because if she hallucinates, she'll sleep through it. *Does that make them dreams?* I wonder.

I need to get a look at the security footage because it's killing me not knowing what's on it. Clueless to how long I've been back in the room, I can't take the silence. I leave the room again.

I cave and pull out my phone. I was worried it would be too difficult to see the security footage clearly. It never occurred to me that the time frame for when we think he was there, would be completely blank. What the hell? I tried another way to access the footage. Nothing. Dammit! I want to throw away my phone. Not only did this asshole break in and drug my girl, but he also managed to stop the footage of him doing it, somehow. I'm grinding my teeth, fisting my hands, and my chest aches. My phone pops like cracking plastic, and I ease my grip. I need my laptop. I dial my phone...

"What's wrong?" Rhett answers. One of the things I like about him is how direct he is, other people don't like it. They say he's too abrupt.

"She's fine. I need my laptop. I tried looking at the security footage and it's blank. I need to see why."

"No problem, I'll send Double Two. He'll be there in less than 20 minutes. Wait, it was blank? How can that be?"

"That's what I want to figure out. I'll let you know if I find anything. Everything good there?"

"Yeah, crime scene techs just left. They said Samson has the case flagged as a priority. Orlando went home, but he said he'll be back later so we can go. He's been cool and he's good with Felony too. She likes him. I always trust our cats' opinions. DT is leaving now. He's got your laptop and the case."

"All right. Thanks."

"Later."

In under 20 minutes, I caught sight of Double Two. He finds me easily, since I'm pacing the hallway like I'm waiting for pregnancy test results. I never understood why we call him and his twin, Double Mint. He explained it to me, even had me watch the old gum commercial, but they aren't identical twins. It would be impossible since Double One is female. I get that they're the Mintus twins, but Adam and Eve Mintus don't equate to Double Mint Twins in my head, I just don't get it. They have enough problems with their parents naming a brother and sister Adam and Eve.

"Thanks DT," I blurted, taking my laptop case from him.

"How's Peyton?"

"Sleeping it off so far. She's going to be okay and probably won't remember this."

"That's good. She's a nice girl, I heard you're dating her. That true?" He looks me over, as if he's evaluating my worth, weighing my soul. He's an intense person.

"Yeah. For a couple weeks, give or take. But we've been on this path for a while."

"I know, 'bout time! I've had a bet with DO since we lost Original Nova."

"Pretty sure DO knew since last week. She was at the office when I was telling everyone."

"That snake, I bet she's just trying to get out of paying me," he rubs his hands together like a cartoon villain. He looks to be plotting something as he says goodbye.

I unpack my laptop and plug it into an outlet. Signing into the Wi-Fi and then my security account, I dig through the images. The recordings stopped at 3:18 p.m. The cameras have been off since then, I restart them and verify they're working.

I quickly reconfigure the reporting settings. Now I'll get notified anytime the recordings stop. I go through the half hour before the last image, not a soul crosses the view of any camera. I quickly peruse the log to see if I can find the shutdown code that was used.

"Gotcha! Sneaky bastard," realizing I said that aloud. I checked around to see if anyone noticed. Whew! I'm in the clear. At home I talk to myself all the time when I'm working, though it's a bad habit I need to shake. I follow the code. It's impressive work. I hate admitting it. I put in some roadblocks and closed his back door, so he won't be able to get back in the same way he did the first time.

I put some tracers on him and left them to search. I look through the neighborhood cameras. The only one that might have something useful is a cheap piece of crap. There's a view from the side of the house that's on the corner. A blurry, dark figure runs down the street toward a parked car. The car starts up and the headlights come at the camera, no view of the tag on the back of the car. I take a few screenshots and then send the video footage to the FBI tech lab. I put the still images through our identification system. While I'm waiting for those results, I skim back farther through the footage trying to pinpoint when he arrived.

Finally, I see him exit the vehicle. I go back further looking for footage of the car on the road. The car arrives from the far end of the block. I can only see the front view, nothing more. It's some type of SUV, a dark color, and that's all I can tell. The images are too grainy for any brand identifiers to come through. Florida doesn't require front license plates so there's no tag information. I'm back to trying to figure out make and model by the headlights. I send off more still shots for identification.

I go frame by frame checking over the images of our unknown subject. When he gets out of the car, he's wearing sunglasses and a hoodie, maybe a ball cap too. He's not particularly tall, maybe five foot nine or ten. He doesn't raise his head at all, I can't even see hair color nor any skin. His face is visible, in the pixelated shots, it's impossible to guess at his race in the grainy gray images. He seems fairly stocky; his legs and arms are thick. He doesn't appear to be someone who can run very fast. He must've had a pretty good head start to get away from Orlando. Peyton's door opens and Paige steps out quietly closing the door behind her. She turns, sees me, and gives me an encouraging smile.

"Hi, how are you holding up?"

"I'm gonna live. Take a look at this," I request, and she sits in the chair beside me.

Glancing over my shoulder she looks at my screen. I show her the code, then the images. She's especially interested in the subject, but she can't make out any more than I can.

"I'm going to go home. Why don't you send those to me and I'll look at them on my system? Please tell Peyton she's welcome to stay with us if she wants. Also, we can take care of Felony for her if she needs a place for her. Anything she needs, or you. Call us if you find out anything else. You know I love you right, Micah?" My mouth pops open in shock. I was just going to tell her that earlier. I guess I can credit it to great minds thinking alike.

I hug her and say, "I was going to say exactly that to you when Rhett got here earlier." She pulls back and looks me over.

"I love you Paige, you're like a big sister and a mom wrapped into one tiny badass package. I wanted you to know. I think I'm getting old," I explained, raising my hands and shoulders.

Paige smiles at me, "Not old, mature. Good for you. Thank you, I love you like a little brother. Hmm, maybe like a son too. Never really thought about it, but I think you're right," her smile gets even brighter.

"I'll call you if anything happens. Call me too if you find anything. When she wakes up, I'll talk to her about Felony."

"That'll work. I'll talk to you later," she kisses my cheek as a goodbye, and I ruffle her hair. It's a joke between us, since she's so small I always ruffle her hair. She always kisses my cheek, it's a whole thing because she can't reach.

"Bye."

"Bye, be a good boy," she chuckles, winks at me, and walks toward the elevator.

Peyton

My back feels cool, and it gives me a chill. I reach out for Micah, the bed is warm next to me, but empty. I roll onto my back and then look around. Oh, I'm not home. Why am I not home? What's burning?

There're rails on my bed and I have an IV in my hand. This is a hospital room. I can't think of any reason I would be in a hospital. I don't feel any pain. I don't see a bruise or a scrape anywhere. Doesn't seem likely it was a car accident.

There's a nurse call button, I debate pushing it. I hate to bother them when I'm not in any pain, but I need to know why I'm here and if Micah is okay. I press the orange glowing button.

A speaker on the wall crackles, "How can I help you?"

"Hi, I'm Peyton Baker, why am I here?"

"Oh Sweetie, you're awake! I'll be there in just a minute, don't move, okay?"

"Yes ma'am." The door swings open with a light knock. A large woman enters, she's wearing Wonder Woman scrubs, it makes me smile. She sees my grin and gives me one in return.

"Hello Miss Peyton. I'm Lashonda, your night nurse. Before we get you up for the rest room, I have a few questions for you. Do you feel dizzy?"

"Not dizzy, though kind of fuzzy," I reply.

"Okay, how about your environment? Do you see anything that seems odd or scary?"

"No," I answer with a confused tilt of my head.

She smiles at me, "What do you remember about today?"

"Hmm, I can't remember coming here. I remember being at school. I met that guy in the parking lot. I got home, and...um..."

"Take your time sweetie. No rush."

"Wait, I remember being really hungry and right when I started to eat, somebody was at my door. It was, uh, umm, oh! It was my neighbor, he...oh shoot, I don't remember."

"That's actually pretty good. Don't worry, you may not remember some things and that's okay. You were drugged. They found a drug called ketamine in your system. Since you vomited, you didn't absorb very much of it. Do you still feel sleepy?" she asks as she lowers the rail.

"I'd like to use the restroom more than anything else right now."

"Okay Sweetie, give me your hand and I'll help you up." I put my hand out and turn to the edge of the bed. Using her to balance, I slide to my feet. She pulls my IV pole next to me.

"Here, hold onto this pole, it has to go with you. I'll walk behind you in case you get wobbly. But I'm going to let you do it yourself."

"Okay, thanks," I smile at her and concentrate on not falling over. After my successful return from the restroom, I notice my stomach growling and realize I'm hungry.

"Are you hungry?" She hands me a menu. It has a heading that says: *Dinner Mild Menu.* That sounds appetizing, I roll my eyes at myself. Choosing a grilled cheese sandwich and baked potato chips, I inquired about drink options. She turns over the menu. I selected grape juice and a root beer. She promises my meal should arrive within thirty minutes.

My door opens again, I look up and am delighted to see Micah. His face is grim until he sees I'm awake. He rushes to me and his arms engulf me in a tight hug. He covers my head with kisses.

"Thank goodness. How're you feeling?"

"I'm hungry, and a little fuzzy, but mostly good."

"Did the nurse say she would order food?"

"Yeah, Lashonda is on it. What happened?" He looks down, his smile shrinking. He takes a deep breath and looks me over. He quickly filled me in on the events that brought me to the hospital.

"Holy shit. I remember the sub and Orlando was there, getting sick, and not anything after that. I didn't remember an intruder. Since I was drugged, what happens now?"

"You had a drug called ketamine in your system. It's an animal sedative. It is abused by addicts and rapists. It's a date rape drug."

My eyes fill with tears and my lip trembles. Micah sees my reaction and his face melts to sympathy. Sometimes he delivers information in his FBI agent voice and forgets about the person he's talking to. It's not on purpose or unfeeling. He's a very sweet guy. I may need to work on his expression of empathy though. I have some tools I learned in psychology classes.

"I'm sorry, I didn't think about how that would hit. Are you okay?" he asks me gently.

"I'm safe and I'm with you, so yes. I just never thought about that. Do you think my stalker was planning to attack me?"

"I don't know. But we won't let anything happen to you. We'll keep you safe, babe. Rhett and Paige were here earlier. I need to let them know you're awake."

"Okay. Please tell them I'm fine and not to worry. Will you please find out what's burning?"

The doctor knocks as he enters, "Hi Peyton. I'm happy to see you awake. How are you feeling?"

"A little fuzzy. Hungry too, but the nurse, Lashonda, said my meal should be here soon."

"I'm Dr. Bronson by the way. You haven't been awake during our previous interactions," he chuckles at his own joke.

I smile, "It's very nice to meet you. When will I be able to go home?"

"I think we're going to keep you until morning, just to be safe. As long as you feel okay after you eat, I'll be ready to sign your discharge papers. Okay?"

"Okay."

"Any questions?" he asks.

"Yeah, are there any long-term effects from the drug? Anything I should watch for?"

"We'd be worried if you had any reaction after ingesting the drug. Difficulty breathing, or other signs of an allergic reaction. If you hadn't vomited, I would've induced it, so you lucked out there. I don't think you'll have any lasting effects; this drug leaves your system quickly."

"I think you've answered everything else I was wondering except…what's burning? Did they burn dinner?"

"Hello! I've got a meal here for Miss Baker. I promise nothing is burnt." An enormous man in a hairnet with a big smile and dimples, sets my tray on the bedside rolling table.

"Thank you. You're my hero, I'm starving," I give him a grateful grin.

"Happy to be of service, Miss Baker. Usually people yell at me," he chuckles and we all join him before he leaves with a wave.

"Do you smell something burning right now?" the doctor asks.

"Yeah," I sniff the air. "You don't smell it?"

"No. It could be an olfactory hallucination. Let's see if it fades now that you're eating, okay? I'm going to let you eat in peace. I'll be back to check on you before I head home."

"Thanks Rick," Micah surprises me with his intimate connection to my doctor.

"Yeah, okay. Thank you, Dr. Bronson," I add.

After he leaves Micah pushes my dinner close and he uncovers the individual dishes. It looks edible and my stomach growls again. I take a big bite of the grilled cheese, then I shove a couple chips into my mouth. Micah opens my root beer and I take a sip of my grape juice. It's tart, making my lips purse. Micah spends my dinner time telling me about the doctor and the security footage. When I'm done eating, I'm ready for a nap. I convince Micah to go home long enough to eat, shower, and feed his cats. I must fall asleep immediately.

When I open my eyes the first thing I see is a woman's foot on my bed. I try to figure out who's foot it could be and I come up with nothing. Paige would never wear those combat boots, it's not her style. I don't have many friends here, but most of them work for my brother and they're all men, except for Double One. She could pull off those boots without blinking an eye. I look further up the leg and expect to see blue hair. I'm surprised when I find auburn hair on top of a pale neck.

"Good, you're awake, I was about to leave. I have class in less than an hour. How're you feeling?"

"Anisa? What are you doing here? How did you know I was here?"

"I called your phone. Imagine my surprise when a deep male voice answered. Your gorgeous boyfriend told me you were here. He went to grab some coffee. He's so fine. Does he happen to have a single brother?" she asks with a cheeky grin.

"Nope, sorry. He's the only one and he's very much taken," I give her a stern look, then giggle. I'm a terrible actress.

"I'm going home this morning but I probably won't be in class today. Will you collect all the info on what to read and share your notes, please?" I plead.

She smiles, having pity on me, "Of course. You need to call Wellington though and tell them you're going to be out. The professors will let you do everything online for a day or two. My roommate is in her second year here and she's filled me in on all of the important info. Plus, she heard me talking to Micah and told me what happens when you miss a day. So, you know, a hospital stay is about the only excuse they accept. She said if you have a good enough excuse, they'll let you attend virtually for up to a week. I'm sure they'll explain all that when you call. Micah told me you got food poisoning. I wish I could get that for a week and lose these extra twenty pounds."

Ignoring her negative comment I inject, "Thanks Anisa. You're in all my classes today, right?"

"Yep, I'll collect anything I can for you and tell the professors where you're hiding. I have to get going. Oh, I almost forgot, I called you to see about setting up our study group. I already need help. Can we start this weekend?" I struggle to think about what I need to do this weekend and decide setting up the study schedule is a good idea.

"Let's plan for Saturday at nine. Will that work? Where do you want to meet?"

"I can do Saturday at nine, but I don't know where. My dorm is out, the common room isn't available and my roommate makes my room unusable. Don't you have a house?"

"Yeah, you can come over. But...there's another person joining our group. We may need to move it to the library in the future. I'll text you, my address. Hopefully I'll see you tomorrow."

"Hold up, who's this other person? More importantly, is he hot?" She grills me aiming her intense stare at me.

"His name is Jake Waverly. I don't know him. He approached me and asked if we could form a study group. I told him about you and he agreed to join. Yes, he's good looking, I don't know his status," I smirk at her, she has a one-track mind I swear.

"Who's good looking?" Micah asks from the door.

"Nobody to get worked up about. You're most certainly hotter than some random study partner. I'm out. See you tomorrow, Peyton. It was so nice meeting you, Micah," she gives him a sultry smile looking him up and down, then she saunters from the room shaking her ass like a hooker on Front Street.

I laugh at the look on Micah's face. Poor guy looks so confused. He's fairly reserved in public, on the quiet side, and always appropriate and proper. Anisa says whatever pops in her head without a filter. I got used to her last year. She kept us laughing with her comedic relief. It made the difficulty that is law school a little more bearable.

"What the heck? Is she always like that?" he asks.

"Not always. She's kind of boy crazy. I told her we have another member in our study group and she immediately wanted to know his stats. I have no clue, all I could say about him is his name and the fact that he wasn't ugly," I shrug.

"Okay. Rick already signed your discharge paperwork. He wants you to eat and make sure one more time that you're okay. Your blood work looks good now. You can leave after you have breakfast." No sooner does he say that, then my meal is delivered. Thank God, I'm ready to get out of here.

"How's Felony?" I ask.

"She's at Rhett's. Orlando was fine to watch her but Paige insisted. Apparently, Felony spent the night with Nova, in her bed. Nova doesn't want to give her back. Rhett said he had to promise to bring Nova to see Felony at Aunt Pey's house to get her to go to preschool this morning," he chuckles, I join him imagining my feisty little niece making demands.

I'm so happy to be home. We stopped at Rhett's and picked up Felony along the way. She seems happy to see me and be home. She's sniffing everything in the house. I wish I knew what she thinks about. A shower goes a long way toward making me feel much more like myself. Micah keeps touching me and searching my eyes. It's so sweet how he checks on me.

"I love you," I spontaneously state, full of feelings.

He kisses my lips and replies in kind. He wants me to rest, but I feel rested enough. I want to work on my school requirements. I had such a different plan for last night and today. Stepping into my office I've got school on my mind. He's in the kitchen making me a sandwich, determined to feed me until I burst. My pocket vibrates, and I sit at my desk and take a look at my phone.

Anisa: I'm on lunch. You didn't miss much. Professor Jameson seems okay with you being out. There's at least four HAF guys in this class!

Me: Did you take notes? Will you send them to me?

Anisa: I'll send them all at the end of the clinic. Are you trying for Law Review?

Me: Yeah are you?

Anisa: Yeah and Trial Team. They start Interviews Friday. you have to sign up on the Student Portal and submit your resume.

Me: Cool, thanks. I'm trying for both, hopefully I'll get one.

Anisa: You said our study partner is Jake right?

Me: yep, Jake Waverly. Why?

Anisa: he's one of the HAF guys from class. I'm going to introduce myself. Ttyl

Well, that was abrupt. Anisa's a trip. I wonder how much success she has with her aggressive man crazed tactics.

I applied for The Law Review and Trial Team. Then I got busy doing everything I planned for last night. Maybe I should remind Anisa about the notes, "No nagging Pey. Remember you're trying to have friends and study partners and do well in class. No need to be a nag unless she earns it," I say out loud.

"I agree," Micah says from the doorway.

"Shit! You scared me. What do you agree with?"

"You said not to nag someone until they earn it. I think that's a profound policy. I agree." My cheeks heat, and I realize I was talking to myself out loud again. I've been trying so hard not to do that but for some reason, when I've got school, I talk to myself. Great, I probably need therapy. A smile raises, making my cheeks glow red.

"Why are you smiling, Eagle?"

"Just laughing at myself. I realize I talk to myself when I'm in school. I'll try not to do it; I know it's annoying."

"No, it isn't. It's cute, plus it probably relieves stress and helps you plot out your work. Don't try to stop for me, I like it," he grins at me. I noticed he brought me a sandwich and some chips. He remembered the sub sauce I like. This is why I was so excited about that stupid sub. Ugh! Don't think about that!

"Thanks Radiohead, have I told you that you're the best boyfriend ever?"

"Do I get to keep those boyfriend points you were handing out?"

"Definitely. This sandwich was made by your own two hands and you got it right, you get an extra thousand points. Hey, I feel like a teacher at Hogwarts handing out points. What house are you in?"

"Since you're my girlfriend, and I love you, I'll share my secrets with you. However, you must guard my secrets to your grave. Do you accept this responsibility?"

"I solemnly swear that I'm up to no good and I will keep your secrets to my grave." I hold up two fingers in a peace sign as I swear my loyalty. We both crack up.

Continuing in his conspiratorial voice, "I belong to the house of Ravenclaw. My dear lady, I imagine you're a member of Gryffindor, am I correct?"

I play along, when in Rome, "My good sir, you are quite correct. Please, I beg your pardon, but I'm going to wolf down my sandwich in a very unladylike fashion." My mouth opens like a boa constrictor, and I take a huge bite, I may have growled a little. He smiles and wraps an arm around me giving me a quick squeeze.

Peyton

"Seriously Anisa, I can't thank you enough. If you didn't take those notes I would've been lost. He said everything was online in his class journal and assignment files. But there was nothing at all on the Texas vs. Van Hoorgue case. I owe you."

"Perfect, now I've got you in my clutches. Where're we meeting them?" she chuckles.

I double check on my phone, "They reserved room 55. I see 52 over there." I point her toward the study rooms. We make our way over, through the biography stacks. Yep, I see Jake through the window.

"This is the place," I opened the door without knocking.

"Hi Jake," Anisa says with a bright smile just for him.

"Hi Anisa, hi Peyton, this is my friend Roger. He shares our Pretrial Pro class."

"Hey, I'm Roger Stanley. Are you guys new here?" The dark-haired guy next to Jake asks. Anisa steps forward, closer to them, I plop my bag onto the table and slide out my chair.

"Yeah, we transferred here from LSU. We both had family drama and ended up here. We ran into each other during orientation. What type of law do you plan to practice, Roger Stanley?" She looks seductively into his light brown eyes. He's good looking in a smart and nerdy way. Something about him screams money. I bet he's Roger the third or fourth. All the rich people I've met have numbers after their names.

I cut in momentarily, "Hi Jake, nice to meet you, Roger."

He looks at me while he answers Anisa, "I'm planning to join my father's firm. It's in Tallahassee, Stanley and Stanley. Likewise, Peyton." He looks Anisa over and she poses for his enjoyment. She's somewhat large boned, most definitely tall, probably about five-foot-ten. She mentioned needing to lose weight, but I think she has an attractive figure. She's the epitome of the hourglass shape. She has a large chest and shapely legs, she flaunts it well and guys' notice, Roger is no exception, his eyes repeatedly find her cleavage. Oddly, Jake doesn't seem interested in looking.

"That's so cool, I love legacy firms. It's so nice when a family works together towards a common goal," Anisa gushes at him fluttering her lashes. Jake looks at me with a forced smile that makes me think he's struggling to humor her. I curve my lips in response, faking it as well.

"The lighting is better over here, Jake sweetie, do you mind if I sit on this side? I have trouble with my eyes. Thanks so much." She doesn't wait for his answer and tosses her bag almost on top of his laptop. His quick reflexes save it just in time. He slides his stuff to my side of the table and moves into the chair next to me.

He leans to my ear, "Is she always like this? I have a lot of work to do. Can you and I start and leave them to their conversation?"

"Yes. I don't see why not. Do you know your topic for Practical Pro?" I ask.

Jake and I work for an hour before Anisa and Roger start working. I think they're touching each other under the table. My stomach speaks up eventually. Seeing the time, I can't believe it's almost 1 p.m. Looking at everyone, their heads are aimed at their laptops.

"Ahem, I think we need a lunch break, I'm going to call it. Do you guys want to go out together? Meet back here? Call it a day? What're you thinking?" I look to Jake first.

"I can have lunch but then I'll need to leave, I have a family obligation," Jake answers.

"I can go to lunch and study after," Roger adds, he looks at Anisa for her response.

"Yeah, I can do lunch, then come back after too," her eyelashes flap at him again, "What about you Peyton?"

I think before answering, "I probably need to get home. I have a new cat and she's not used to being alone. But I think we should set up our study schedule while we're all together."

"You're right, but let's do it at lunch. I'm hungry, yeah?" Anisa requests.

"Sounds like a plan. Where do you want to eat? The cafeteria is open," I reply.

"No, we can walk to the Mexican place on the corner of Broad and 7th. I'd kill for some of their tacos. They're the best ones I've had since I left Texas," Jake says as he stands and packs his items.

I pack my things and send a quick text to Micah. He's going to bring his cats over and spend the rest of the weekend with me. He tells me to text when I'm on my way. I refocus on the group seeing Roger is helping Anisa get her laptop to sign off. She says it's not responding, and my eyes roll without my permission. Thankfully nobody is looking at me.

Eventually we get it together and make it to the restaurant. It's called Tres Burritos. It's so good! Our server, Aishwaria, is lovely. Despite her musical British tinged middle eastern accent, she speaks fluent Spanish and does a great job getting all of our special requests correct. I chat with her every time she comes to our table. She was born in India, but she grew up in South Africa. She's had quite the adventurous life before getting pregnant, marrying her husband, and opening this restaurant. His family is half Mexican and half Greek. She shows me pictures of her kids, two little boys. They could almost be twins if it wasn't obvious, one is slightly older, they're adorable with matching smiles.

"I really hate the Day of the Dead décor in here. Those skulls freak me out," Anisa comments. I hadn't noticed, I was hungrier than I thought, and the food has all my focus. I look around and there's an awful lot of sugar skulls, but they're beautiful. They look hand painted. When Aishwaria passes by our table, I stop her to ask about them.

"My husband's uncle paints them. He sells them at the gift shop up the street. They're very popular, especially this time of year."

Maybe I'll get one to decorate for Halloween. I make a note in my cell to remind me about them on the weekend. Anisa shoots them a wary glance every once in a while. I'm learning she has a tendency towards the dramatic.

We work out our study group schedule in between delicious bites of meats and cheeses. We're going to meet Wednesday nights and Saturday mornings at the library. On Sundays, starting next weekend, we'll meet at my house. We're each going to make (or buy as pointed out by Roger) a dish on Sundays to eat during study time. After I say goodbye to Aishwaria, and say my goodbyes to the others, Jake and I walk toward the parking lot while Anisa and Roger go in the direction of the library.

As we spread apart, I say, "Bye Jake. I'll see you Monday." He stops, so I stop.

"Can I ask you something?" he asks.

"Sure, what's up?"

"I was wondering... do you have a boyfriend?"

I'm jolted by his question, "I, um, yeah, I have a boyfriend." I smile at him. I'm being awkward. He seems perfectly at ease, almost relieved, he smiles back.

"I figured you did. Is he back home or did he come with you?"

"My brother lives in Oakdale. I met Micah, my boyfriend, through my brother's work. He's local, in Oakdale."

"Oh, maybe you know your way around here better than us," he chuckles.

"That would be a no. I've been here a few times but whenever I came here there was always some big event, death, birth, wedding... I didn't have much chance to relax and look around. We're originally from Louisiana, but my brother moved here after the military. I followed because I missed him, my niece, and sister-in-law. They're having another baby and I didn't want to miss anything else. How about you? You mentioned Texas?" I ask him.

"I'm from San Antonio. I ended up here because my grandfather went to Wellington. My father went to Wellington. I got accepted to Stanford and Harvard, but my family pressured me to come to Wellington."

"That's kinda cool though, following in your family's footsteps. Nobody in my family has practiced law before so I'm the first to take a crack at it. What type of law do you plan to practice? Or does your family have a firm you're going to join?" I query.

"They have a firm. I'll be opening my own department, and we'll start working with immigration law. Right now, they focus on corporate law, real estate, divorce, and a little bit of white-collar crime. If one of their clients gets into trouble the firm will defend them, but they're not really into criminal defense. Mostly they deal with wealthy corporations and clients. I want to do something to help the community. My dad says they're always trying to find worthy pro bono cases, this way they'll have a department that has huge potential for pro bono work in-house."

"I love that. I want to help my community too. That's why I'm interested in social justice. I'm probably going to focus on human trafficking." I explained to him.

"Wow, that's admirable. That has to be very difficult work. What some of those victims endure is unfathomable." He shakes his head, and his eyes aim down.

"I know it'll be hard, but I can't stand that some of the victims get arrested and blamed. They often have other charges depending when and how they were taken. I want to help them with all of their legal needs. Really help them get their lives back on track. It's why I studied psychology as well. I want to help them in all the ways they need to start over or return to their former life."

"You seem passionate about it. That's really cool, Peyton. I'll see you Monday. I have to get to a family gathering. I'm going to spend the remainder of my day being compared to my cousin. I'll never measure up. Wish me luck!" He rolls his eyes.

"Good luck! Bye Jake," I smile at him.

Pulling under the house next to Micah's SUV, I wear a huge grin. I missed him today. I smile up the stairs and onto the porch where he waits with two cats in one carrier. I rushed him for a hug and a kiss. I blow kisses at Beta and Qwerty then unlock the door. I punch the code into the alarm while he brings the cats and his bag inside. Felony lets out a loud howl. She's on the kitchen island, where she definitely shouldn't be, twitching her tail angrily.

"Hi Felony, what's wrong?"

I try to pat her head, but she pulls away and narrows her eyes at me. I reach further to rub her back and she takes off. She stops just out of my reach. She sits and gives me a dirty look.

"Are you hungry?"

Raow, Meeeow!

"Eagle what did you do to her? She's furious with you. Is her water empty? Food dish?"

"I don't know what's wrong. I wasn't here so I didn't do anything wrong for her to be mad about."

"You sure?" he asks, his brows lifted and a grin playing at his lips. I get the impression he's trying to walk me to the elephant right in front of me.

"Oh! You think she's mad I left her alone?"

"What do you think?" His smile blooms.

"Maybe. I'm going to have to leave sometimes. She'll have to get used to it. Any suggestions? You had to leave Beta all the time, he was alone before Qwerty came along."

Micah gives me some ideas while the cats watch. They all retreat to the living room, each staking out their own spot, and start grooming. Felony ignores me.

"I brought a few groceries. I'm going to run down and grab them. I want to make dinner if that's okay?"

"Okay? Are you kidding? Absolutely! Put something yummy in my mouth." I smile realizing my comment may be misconstrued.

"What? You think I noticed what you said? You think it put images in my head? Maybe diverted some blood flow?" He smirks at me.

"Now I know it did." I smirk back and saunter to the living room to check on the three whiskateers.

There's a vibration and my text message alert sounds in my pocket. I retrieve it and lean against the back of the armchair on one leg.

Anisa: OMG I might be in love!

Me: Roger?

Anisa: What? No. He's nice enough, but no. I just met the most gorgeous bad boy I've ever seen! He actually pulled up on a Harley! I'm dying!

Me: Where did you meet prince charming?

Anisa: After I left the library, I was aiming for my dorm, but I decided to stop at the drugstore. When I walked out, he pulled up right in front of me. We talked for like five minutes!

Me: I'm astounded.

Anisa: He invited me to a party later. Do you want to go? You can bring your HAF boyfriend.

Me: I'll ask, but I think I just want to stay in. He's cooking dinner.

Anisa: okay let me know. Maybe my roommate will want to go, she's single.
Me: K ttyl

"Who was that?" Micah asks, a brown bag in each hand.

"Anisa. She's already moved on from her morning of groping our study partner, to the love of her life apparently. She wants us to go to a party the new guy invited her to."

"Do you want to go?"

"Not really. She's fun and I'm sure we would have a good time, but I was looking forward to our dinner. Maybe something fun for just you and me after dinner," I attempt a seductive wink.

"Now that sounds amazing. Let's skip this one," he smiles with some heat warming his eyes.

I surround his waist with my arms and hug him to me. He's warm and solid. He smells good, like fresh soap and something manly, it reminds me of leather and flannel, cowboy boots and horses. I don't know where that came from, it's like a cologne commercial in my head. I don't want to let go, but he reminds me he's meant to be cooking dinner.

I set up my laptop in the office while Micah works on dinner. I can hear pots clanging and the occasional curse word. I look over his notes on the wall. There's a few more cards than the last time I checked. I don't even know when he put those up. He must be continuing to work on Larue's case when he's not here. I spy the folder on the desk, I want to look inside, but I'm worried about accidentally seeing my sister's dead body. I could just open it a little and peek in to see if there's any photos. I lift the cover. When I can see the top page is just a report, I let out a relieved breath and open it all the way.

He made a log of calls he's made about the case. There are 27 so far. There's an envelope with something inside. I turn it over and in Micah's scrawled handwriting across the flap is a note to me. I'm shocked to see my name at first. *Peyton-DO NOT OPEN this envelope contains photographs.* Then my heart warms, he's so considerate. He's protecting me even when he's not in the room. I move the envelope to the side, definitely not wanting to see what's in there.

I read through the reports and notes. The arrest records for *Samo* are on top, then his 'friend' Zombie. Both have some fairly awful things in their history. I read Micah's report on the case. It's been forwarded to his supervisor, Samson, and further up the chain. One sentence grabs my attention,

Recommendation to consider Mark Ramsey aka Saint aka Monk primary suspect in the kidnapping, sexual assault, and murder of Larue Baker. I feel like I've been kicked in the gut, the air rushes from my lungs. My mouth fills with saliva and my skin breaks out in a clammy sweat. Darkness dances at the edges of my vision. Gasping in a breath I try to soothe my rapid breathing. I recognize my symptoms as the beginning of a panic attack. I close my eyes and count my breathing, in and out. I consciously attempt to relax each part of my body. My breathing normalizes and I open my eyes. The darkness has retreated. I used to get panic attacks when I was a teenager, after I lost Larue. I worked hard to get past them, but lately they keep trying to resurface. I close the file. I'll finish looking at it some other time.

"Dinners ready!" Micah calls. I guess I'm saved by the bell.

When I leave the office there's a delicious scent wafting down the hallway, I follow it to the kitchen. I have no idea what Micah cooked but my stomach is growling, and my mouth is watering. Whatever it is, I want some.

"What're we having?" I ask as I squeeze into my seat.

He carries over a bowl full of rice. Then he brings over a pot of some type of sauce, with meat. There's a salad and a bowl of shredded cheddar cheese on the table.

"You're going to be treated to my specialty, dum, dum, duuum! Chinese chili!" He smiles at me with mischief in his eyes. He's adorable. Warmth spreads in my chest, I love him so much.

"You're so cute, but what the heck is Chinese chili?"

"I learned how to make it when I was a kid. I might've invented it. You know what they say, *necessity is the mother of invention?* Well, when you have a mother who doesn't buy groceries very often, you invent shit to eat, or you starve."

He scoops a pile of rice onto each of our plates, he sprinkles cheese over the rice. Then he plops a big spoonful of chili on top. It's weird, but it smells really good. I'm game.

"That sucks. But I'm glad you were an inventive kid. This looks so good. Will you please pass me the Ranch?"

"Here you go, babe. Yeah, I had some nights without any food at all. I was really thankful when there was enough to put something together. This is made with ground turkey, but it works with any ground meat. I didn't put any beans in it either. I ate a lot of beans growing up, and I try not to have them on purpose anymore."

"I understand that. We had crawfish all the time growing up, I mean at least once a week. I try not to have it now. I don't hate it, but I would rather have anything else."

I crunch a big bite of salad as I watch him take a big bite of the main dish. His eyes close and he kind of hums, I guess it's good. I fill my fork and try a bite.

"Oh, you're right, this is so good. How's this not a thing?"

"I think Cincinnati Chili is similar, but they use spaghetti instead of rice. But I really like it with the rice, it's good with the ground turkey too. I've been trying to limit red meat. Gotta keep my figure up for my hot girlfriend," he chuckles at his joke and pats his stomach.

I laugh too, then happily stuff my face. Felony comes over and rubs against my legs under the table. I guess she's over her tantrum. Beta and Qwerty watch from nearby, but they pretend they aren't looking this way, like they aren't interested at all. We eat until we're stuffed. Neither one of us has any room for dessert. Micah's store-bought apple pie stays in the fridge.

After we clean up the kitchen we decide to work for a while in the office. Micah's new office chair is much more conducive to longer work hours. He digs into whatever he's working on, I decide not to ask if it's Larue's case. I have some reading and then some essay questions to work on. We toil away for a few hours.

When I break away from my computer for a stretch, I notice Micah is looking at me. I stare back and look deep into his eyes trying to figure out what he's thinking about. There's emotion there, some heat but also something sweet and loving. I smile at him trying to project my love for him.

"What ya thinking beautiful?"

"How much I love you. What're you thinking about?"

"I was thinking how nice it would be to take a walk down to the beach and watch whatever is left of the sunset. How about it?"

"Oh, that sounds perfect. I need some outdoor time, away from this screen. Let me hit the bathroom, then we can go. Will you feed the cats?"

He stands and salutes me as he says, "Yes ma'am. I'm on it. Come on kids, let's get some kitty food." The cats follow him toward the kitchen while I make a pit stop. I fix my hair and coat my lips in lip balm.

The cats are happily munching on their dinner when I enter the kitchen. I open the medicine and miscellaneous junk cabinet and take out the mosquito spray. It's supposed to be all natural, and it doesn't smell like chemicals. I sprayed him and myself with a good layer of the lemony spray. After we climb down the stairs, he grasps my hand as we make our way one block over to the beach entrance.

We made it in time. As much as I hate daylight savings time, I'm thankful the sun isn't down yet. I'm guessing it's after 8 p.m. I didn't check the time when we left. There are some clouds, so the rays of the sun reflect onto them in stunning shades of pink, purple, red, and orange. I'm speechless. Micah puts his arm around me, and we walk to the Gulf waves. I kick off my flip flops and step into the warm salt water. It's perfect.

"Did you ever wish you could save a perfect moment and enjoy it over and over?" Micah asks.

"I was just thinking how perfect this is right now. I love you," I smile at him and squeeze his waist a little tighter. He squeezes my shoulders and places a kiss on top of my head.

"I love you too. If you weren't standing here, I would say this sunset is the most beautiful thing I've ever seen. But it pales in comparison to you." He lifts my hand and kisses my knuckles.

"Shit Micah, are you sure you haven't had a girlfriend before? That was pretty sweet." His cheeks turn red, and he looks over my shoulder. I touch his chin and tilt his head back towards me.

"No getting embarrassed. I love you and you love me, and it's okay to be sweet," my smile is huge.

"Oh, duh, I'll take a selfie."

He aims at us, so our backs are to the setting sun. He takes a few shots, but they're dark because the camera is facing the sun. I hand him my phone.

"Here, use mine. I have it set up to get a good picture in these conditions," he takes the camera and aims at us again. The flash goes off but not at full strength.

"Let me see?"

He leans over and we both look at my phone versus his phone. The pictures on his phone have us in silhouette with the sunset brilliant behind us. On my phone, our faces are visible as well as the sunset. They're both really good regardless of if our faces are visible or not.

"Send me yours, I like them all. Can't really beat a beautiful sunset as a backdrop." My text alert goes off as I lean in for a kiss.

He meets my lips and plunges his tongue into my mouth. We move toward one another, and my arms slink around his neck. His hands clamp onto my ass. Sparkling faeries spring to life in my belly, their wings and pixie dust sending flutters through me. He presses his hard cock into my hip then my stomach. My panties grow damp.

"Mmmm, Micah, I want you so much," I moan and kiss him again.

He groans and squeezes me tighter. I adjust my hands and slide them to his waist. His hand moves around to my breast as he rubs his palm on my nipple then fills his hand with the whole thing. A zing of sensation shoots from my nipple and directly to my clit causing me to growl softly. I want his hands on my tits and my ass and my clit all at the same time. He just needs a couple more hands.

I bring one of my hands to the front of his jeans and rub my palm over the bulge there. I don't want to stop kissing him. He feels so strong and warm. The sea air and the last of the sunset fuel my fire. I remember my *go for it* philosophy. I think it's sage advice from Original Nova. I unhook the button on his jeans, and the zipper goes down slowly. Seagulls drown out the metallic click of the teeth. I thrust my hand into his boxer briefs and grasp his length. I stroke him and he moans into my mouth.

Not thinking for even a second about where we are I'm so lost in him; I fall to my knees. The sand is wet on my skin, I sink ever so slightly. I don't care. My heart beats so fast and I'm panting a little, breathing hard. My hormones must be on overdrive, because I'm not in control. I push his clothes out of my way and shove his hard cock into my mouth. I immediately push him as far as I can into my throat. My right thumb and forefinger circle him without being able to touch, and my left-hand tugs on his ass to move him deeper into my throat. My hand strokes him up and down in sync with my mouth. I swirl my tongue over his head in time with our movements. His palms grasp my face, firm but gentle. His thumbs rub against my cheeks in circles as if he's worshiping me. I breathe through my nose and swallow around him. The contraction of my throat has him murmuring incoherently. I use the palm of my right hand to envelope his balls and press them up. His movements become staggered. I suck and lick with what I imagine is all the skill of a porn star, and he seems to think so too. His head is leaned back his hands clutch my face and he thrusts his hips, fucking my throat. I'm moaning and sucking as he becomes tense all over.

"Yeeees! Babe, oh God, yeees!"

"Mmmmm."

His body stills as his cum squirts down my throat. I breathe and swallow, licking until he's finished. I keep swirling my tongue over his tip. He shivers and groans out again. I swallow down every drop of him. When his cock softens, he slips it out of my mouth, tucks himself away, and zips up. I lick my lips. His hand returns softly to my cheek. I look up at him and smile. He smiles back. The seagulls screech and we both look down the beach. Thankfully there's no one around. I completely forgot we were in public. How does that happen?

I stand. Over his arm, the corner of Orlando's house is visible. One window aims this way. I didn't know he had a water view, but it must be nice. As my eyes reach the window, a shape there moves the curtains and disappears out of sight.

"Crap!" Micah turns his gaze to the direction of mine. Not seeing anything he turns back.

"What's up?"

"Nothing, I just saw the drapes move at Orlando's place, like he was watching us. Now it's going to be awkward." I make a goofy face at him. He looks at Orlando's house. There's nothing there now. He wraps his arm around my shoulders.

"So, what brought that on? I can't believe you just did that," he states in amazement.

I shrug, my cheeks pink with embarrassment, "I just had the overwhelming urge to stick your gorgeous cock down my throat. Don't look a gift horse in the mouth!"

He pulls me into his chest, and we watch the last of the setting sun fade into darkness as we embrace in the sand. I'm a little overheated as our encounter has left me aching for more. I relay this situation to Micah with a pinch to his ass.

"Hey! What was that for?"

"I'm not done with you Radiohead, let's head back home," I give him an intense look, filled with desire.

His eyes widened. "Oh. Well shit, let's go." I grin to myself, he's extremely intelligent but every once in a while, it takes him a minute to catch on. We hold hands as we make our way back to my cute cottage in the sky.

After spending my weekend in Micah's arms and behind my computer, sometimes both at the same time, I miss him while in class.When I get to Pretrial Pro, Jake is waiting for me outside the door.

"Hi, Jake. What's up?"

"Hi, Peyton. I wanted to introduce you to my cousin. He's the TA and he's kind of an ass, but you'll have to be nice to him, I'm sorry. He gave me a hard time on Saturday because I haven't introduced you yet. I explained you were out sick, but he was annoyingly persistent. Are you cool with an introduction?"

"Yeah, sure. But why would he care about meeting me?"

"I don't know. I just gave in and tried to enjoy the short lived quiet," he makes a face and rolls his eyes. I laugh and open the door.

Our TA is sitting at the teacher's table working on his laptop. He has dark hair and eyes. He's fairly tall and well built, he's not ugly, but the vibe he sends out is anything but friendly. He looks very uptight and formal. His long sleeve button up shirt is closed with a necktie. His sleeves are buttoned at his cuffs. Hasn't anyone told him this is Florida and it's about ninety-five degrees on average? I'm wearing a short, sleeveless sundress with leather flip flops. My hair is in a high ponytail, anything to get as much air to my skin as possible. He notices us approaching and pastes a smile across his mouth. His teeth are shockingly white and straight.

"Hello, Jacob, who is your friend?" His voice is oddly formal and lacking in accent or dialect. He reminds me of someone, but I can't place it.

"Hey, Wesley, this is Peyton Baker. Peyton, this is our TA, and my cousin, Wesley Stanton. Our mothers are sisters."

I hold my hand out to Wesley to shake, "Hello Wesley, it's a pleasure to meet you. Jake and I are in a study group together."

"It's my pleasure, I assure you. I remember your preterm essay, it was excellent. I believe Professor Rothman gave you the highest score. What concentration do you plan to practice?"

"I'm leaning toward social justice right now. Dr. Bertman is an idol of mine." I offer him a smile. He smiles back but it looks fake and forced. He's beginning to make me uncomfortable.

"Oh, yes, I've heard good things about Dr. Bertman, I haven't met her yet. She's only offering 2L courses and our paths haven't crossed," Wesley replies.

"Yes, I was really surprised that she was here and proctoring two classes. The school must have really offered her something special, but whatever brought her here I'm thankful for it." Professor Rothman joins us at the table, he pointedly clears his throat. Wesley looks uncomfortable now.

"I guess I better find my seat, it was nice speaking with you, Wesley. Good afternoon, Professor," I smile in greeting and shuffle to my seat followed by Jake who sits beside me.

When I open my laptop there's an email from Wesley. It's our reading assignments for the rest of this semester and all of the writing requirements. Holy cow, it's so much.

Once Professor Rothman finishes his lecture leaving us to our own devices for the last thirty minutes of class, Jake leans over and asks, "What do you think about all of the reading for this class? I'm overwhelmed. Wes warned me it would be reading and writing heavy, but I think ten essay questions for each week plus the midterm project is overkill."

"It's certainly a lot of work, but I think it's pretty interesting. You and I are choosing concentrations that'll require courtroom time. Pretrial Pro will be important for success. But I could do without so much of it," I chuckled, agreeing with him even though it sounded like I was going to argue.

Anisa was missing at lunch time. I still feel a little lost from my hospital stay. If she's out sick I hope she had someone gather notes for her. I'm not in her Monday classes. I sent her a quick text to check in.

Me: Hey Anisa, missed you at lunch everything okay?

Anisa: You missed a great party. It lasted until this morning

Me: WTF? Wasn't it Saturday night?

Anisa: Yeah, it was at a beach house. We hung out all day Sunday at the beach. Then the party kinda restarted Sunday night. I'm still hungover or drunk?

Me: Are you at school?

Anisa: Yeah, not sure I've caught what's been said tho

Me: I just wanted to make sure you're okay.
Anisa: I'm good. Still alive. I still might be in love, for reals
Me: Wow.
Anisa: gonna head to my dorm and catch some Zs. See ya 2morrow
Me: peace ;-)

I pack up my things and Jake follows suit. I've got lots of work to do and I need to add things to my schedule. My brain is working to organize all of my tasks. Jake walks next to me towards the parking lot. He has an off-campus apartment. The dorms here are really small and old. The wiring is old, and the pipes are old. Hot showers are highly prized, and outlets are scarce. When they built the dorms in 1960-something, you didn't need to plug in so many electronics and hair products. The newer buildings on campus always have students clustered around their accessible outlets trying to charge laptops and cell phones. Anyone who can swing an off-campus apartment does so, even if they have to get a part time job to do it.

I'm thankful Rhett was able to pay for my school and rent. I understand the privilege I'm afforded, and I appreciate it more than he'll ever know.

All we are is just another dick in the law...

My phone blasts out my Pink Floyd parody ringtone. Note to self, I might need to change that now that I'm here. I fumble around getting my phone out. Jake stops and waits for me. I don't recognize the number.

"Hello, Peyton Baker speaking."

"Miss Baker, this is Professor Jameson, from Pretrial Procedure class? I'm calling about your application for Trial Team."

"Hello, Professor Jameson. Yes, I did apply for Trial Team and Law Review."

"Professor Manning is running Law Review. He should be calling you soon. I'm calling to invite you for a personal interview. Are you available Friday? I have openings at 2:00, 2:30, and 3:00. Any of those work for you?"

"Yes sir, two would be great. Thank you."

"Okay, I've got you on the schedule for 2:00 p.m. Bring your resume and any writing samples or other materials you think we should see. We'll meet you in the Teaching Hub, Conference Room B27. Any questions?"

"No sir, I'll see you there. Thank you, sir."

"You're welcome, Miss Baker. See you tomorrow. Good-bye."

"Yes, sir. Thank you, good-bye." I turn to Jake, and I jump up and down, "Oh my God! I got an interview for Trial Team! I thought it was a longshot. I'm so excited!"

I give him a hug and he laughs, "Congratulations! That's awesome. I applied for Trial Team and Law Review. Maybe they'll call me too. Fingers crossed."

"I also applied for Law Review. Maybe we'll get to work together. That would be cool. I like your work ethic," I compliment him, and it's true.

As we're about to step off the curb his phone sounds. He pulls it out of his pocket, looks at it, and aims the screen at me. It's Professor Jameson. I high five him and signal that I'm going to leave and give him a thumbs up for encouragement. I can't wait to tell Micah!

Friday couldn't come fast enough. I'm wearing a business suit. My skirt is black, my jacket is white with black details, and my camisole top is hot pink. My heels are also hot pink with a black scroll design. Wearing my favorite suit empowers me. My stride is purposeful as I enter the Teaching Hub. I quickly locate wing B. My shoes click on the marble floor as I make my way to the end of the hall where Conference Room 27 lurks.

There's a typed note on the door: *If closed, please knock.*

I inhale in a deep breath and knock softly. The door opens and it's Wesley from Pretrial Pro, also Jake's cousin. Awkward! I'm being awkward.

"Hello, Wesley," I try to recover with a smile.

"Peyton," he tips his head.

He stretches his arm toward the room. I remind myself to breathe. It's a long dark table surrounded by chairs of which six are filled. I only know Professor Jameson, Professor Rothman, and Wesley of course. Wesley sits in the seventh chair, and I take the eighth. Everyone is reading a paper or electronic copy of my resume. I fold my hands and wait patiently.

"Ahem. Hello, Miss Baker. We'll each introduce ourselves. As you know I'm Professor Jameson, I teach Florida Pretrial Procedures, Florida Pretrial Procedures Clinic, and I coach the Trial Team."

"It's a pleasure to see you again Professor Jameson. Please call me Peyton." He nods.

An older gentleman with a bald head surrounded by a halo of gray, looks at me and introduces himself, "I'm Professor Manning, Civil Procedure, Torts, Law Review Editor." His foggy pale eyes look to me through thick lenses, he nods. He looks to his right.

The woman sitting there is also older, but she's very pretty. She looks really great for being in her mid-fifties, her hair is blonde, and her skin is tan. I idly wonder if she was ever a TV weather girl. She slides the half glasses from her nose and looks at me hard.

"Peyton, it's a pleasure to meet you. I'm Dr. Landry. White Collar Criminal Defense."

And so, it goes around the table. I answer all of their questions and I think I do a good job. They're all smiling as I say goodbye and leave the room. Hopefully that means something positive. When I get outside the door to the building, I peel off my jacket. Ah! That's better.

I walk to the parking lot feeling confident. I'm finished for today. A loud rattling engine rumbles into the lot attached to a big old Harley. I stop and watch as the muscular guy in a jacket and a black helmet pulls up. From behind him a long leg in a high heel steps down. She's wearing a skirt, and I don't know how she doesn't flash everyone with her dismount. Her professional gray suit fits her figure like a second skin. Her chest is trying to burst free from her top. Her auburn hair is revealed as she removes her helmet, and it's pulled up in a flattering twist. I continue to watch as Anisa makes out with the Harley guy, and he squeezes her ass. She drags herself away from him and straightens her clothes. She looks great, a pink flush in her cheeks, a smile on her lips. She waves as he pulls off. As he passes me, I swear he gives me a long look, but it's hard to be sure with his dark helmet. She notices me and her arm waves like she's landing a plane.

"Peyton! That was him! Isn't he dreamy?"

"Yeah, amazing. What're you doing here? Aren't you off Friday afternoon?"

"Yeah, I have an interview for Trial Team. Did you?"

"Yeah, I tried to tell you, but all you talk about is Mr. Harley. I assume that's why you've been scarce? We missed you Wednesday," I say pointedly with my lips pursed and eyes narrowed.

"That wasn't his fault. I had really bad cramps, I wasn't making it up, I swear. I have really bad PMS, sometimes I have to stay in bed for a day or two. I've had surgery three times to remove cysts."

My eyes widen and I try to fight off pity but it's difficult. I know what that means, each surgery leaves scar tissue that could clog up her tubes. Each procedure could be the end of her fertility. I took a whole semester on loss and grief for my psychology degree. There was a series on fertility and loss of fertility. It's something that's common in long term sexual abuse victims. Drugs or physical trauma can cause damage to fertility. Though, one of my volunteer experiences would tell me the worst drug abusers seem to be more fertile than average and they can't seem to stop having drug addicted babies to abuse and neglect. I lock down my pity and push understanding-alone, into my expression.

"I'm sorry Anisa. That sucks. Let me know next time and I'll bring you a care package, okay?" I offer her a sheepish grin.

Her face brightens into a huge smile, and she says, "I'll definitely accept your care package. I'll burden you with my suffering next time, promise. I've got to get to my interview. I'll talk to you later, wish me luck!" She hugs me. I hug her back, with my eyebrows lifted in surprise. She's not usually affectionate. I mean, she rubs against guys, but no real emotional spontaneous outbursts of any kind.

"Good luck! Peace." I don't know what it is about her that I keep ending our conversations this way. I'm not sure if I'm saying it to wish her peace, or if I'm hoping she'll be hypnotized into behaving peacefully.

On my drive home I think about Micah. He told me his recommendation about Larue's case. He also explained just because they want to name Samo a suspect, it's still a long way from winning in court. They need a lot more evidence, and they need DNA from a suspect. They need a suspect to interview.

I smile when I remember that I gave him a key to my place. He can come and go as he pleases. I mean let's be honest he knows my alarm codes and how to work the thing better than me, and he can just pick a lock or break in anywhere. But something solidified between us with that key. I have that warm feeling of joy in my chest again. I let it overtake the thoughts of my family's loss.

He's there when I pull under the house. I'm nodding to myself and doing a weird dance in my seat. I collect up all my belongings and dance my way towards the stairs.

"Peyton?"

"Holy fuck! Orlando, you scared me!" I spin while I yell and come face to face with my biker neighbor.

He chuckles, "Well I don't want to interrupt, ahem, but I'm wondering if you and Micah are available for dinner? I want to find out if there's any updates. Can you spare an hour for some burgers?" He's giving me puppy dog eyes. It's oddly influencing my response, reminds me of my brother who does the same thing to me. I use them on Micah too.

"Ugh! You're not playing fair. Come upstairs with me and we'll ask Micah," I acquiesce.

Micah

I can hear Peyton talking to someone as she comes up the stairs. It's probably Orlando. We haven't really spoken since I was outed as an FBI agent. This should be interesting. The door opens and in walks my beautiful girl, followed by Orlando.

He steps over to me and holds out his hand as he says, "Hey Micah. How's it going?" I look him over. His face is earnest, and I don't detect anything suspicious nor any ill intent.

I shake his hand, "Hey Orlando, it's good. No sign of the stalker since she was poisoned. Maybe he got scared off, but we'll have to see." Orlando nods. He smiles. He seems sincere, so I relax. Seems he's offering to keep the status quo, that works for me.

"How was your day?" I kiss her cheek while she ditches her bag, jacket, and shoes. Then she scoops up her shoes and jacket.

"It was good, I'm gonna change really quick. Gotta ditch this suit. Orlando? You can ask him, okay?" He looks at Peyton and nods. I turned toward Orlando, curious as to what this was about.

"Yeah, uh, I asked Peyton if you guys could come over for a quick BBQ? I've got burgers and some salad. I think I've got baked beans too. What'd ya think?" Peyton and I don't have any plans, just work and school. She would've told him no if she couldn't or didn't want to go. I don't know what we would eat if not for the BBQ.

"Yeah, that sounds great. Should we bring anything? I think we might have some fries in the freezer. We can bake them before we come over."

"Why does that sound so good? Yeah, that'd be cool. How's Felony doing?"

Hearing her name, she comes out from under the chair. It's an old-fashioned chair, it spins around three-hundred-sixty degrees, and rocks. It bounces to a leaned back position but doesn't latch to stay reclined. It has a skirt that reaches the ground and the fabric is scratchy with starfish all over it. Most of them are blue except for a couple random green ones. It's not comfortable either. I guess the landlords just bought anything nautical they came across. It's like a cavern under the chair skirt for a little kitty who isn't at all social. When she comes out, she sniffs me then she goes to Orlando and rubs herself on his leg.

Meow! She declares.

Orlando squats down and scratches her ear and her cheek, "Hello little troublemaker. Your mama named you right. Felony is the perfect name for you. Yes, you're cute, okay, thank you." She licks him and rubs her face along his chin.

Peyton comes back wearing cutoffs and a tank top. I don't blame her, it's hot. But damn, I wish she didn't have to look so attractive in front of other men. I finally understand Rhett's protective streak. Felony runs to Peyton and rubs on her legs, meowing until Peyton picks her up.

"Who's mommy's good girl? I didn't find anything chewed up. I'm so proud of you." Beta and Qwerty are at my place so they can't be blamed. I don't have the heart to tell Peyton that I cleaned up toilet paper from one end of the house to the other when I got here. Only Felony was home.

"What's the verdict? BBQ or no BBQ?"

Orlando and I say simultaneously, "BBQ."

I preheat the oven and we say goodbye to Orlando for now. He wants us over in about a half hour. It's long enough for fries and kisses. She gave me a key to her place yesterday. I don't know why it was such a big deal, but we both got a little emotional over it. I'm really happy, but I hate to think about it. That's usually right when all hell breaks loose.

I hug Peyton and kiss the top of her head. She feels so soft and warm in my arms. She always smells so good. I asked her what fragrance she wears, and she told me she uses vanilla oil. I don't know what that means. But she smells incredible, honestly, I don't know if that's just her or if it's the oil. My heart beats in a happy rhythm.

"How did your interview go?" I ask her.

"It went as well as I could've hoped. The TA, Jake's cousin, I told you about? He was on the panel. I have no clue if he likes me or not. Professor Jameson, Professor Rothman and Professor Manning, Dr. Landry... Oh, she was a total bitch to me, she's really pretty. It's so weird she's in her mid-fifties, and she barely looks over forty. I don't remember the rest of their names, but at least one of them is an editor for the Law Review. They're really interviewing for both. I'm so sorry Radiohead. I'm just rambling on and on. How was your day?"

"Same old same old," I grin.

"Seriously, how was your day?"

"Let's see, I went to my actual office for a meeting first thing. Then I had a meeting with Samson about your case and your sister's case. Then I had to run three blocks from the office, to arrive just in time to watch a guy splat on the sidewalk, it was horrible. Poor guy was mentally ill and had stopped taking his meds. Such a waste, he was only 32. His parents came before they could get anything cleaned up. Someone called them who recognized what he was wearing. Can you imagine that being the final memory of your child?"

"Wow. I'm so sorry. That's a horrible day!" She hugs me close with her arms around my waist. She leans her head onto my chest. The preheat buzzer goes off. She watches as I place the fries in the oven and set the timer for 15 minutes. Just like the package says.

"May I get a drink for you, my lady?" Where did that come from? I'm so cheesy. No wonder I never had a girlfriend.

"Yes please, kind sir. May I have a root beer? I believe there are two on the top shelf if you would like one as well?"

"Nah, I'm good. I might take a sip of yours though."

"Go for it. I can share. Aced it in kindergarten." She gives me a cheesy smile. I guess that explains why she likes me. We're both cheesy weirdos.

When the timer sounds, I turn everything off. I wrap a sheet of foil over the top of the hot pan. We feed Felony and walk next door. I think about our neutral zone agreement. I'm going to assume it's still in place.

This is Peyton's first time over here. She's impressed but the cleanliness and modern style are at odds with Orlando's biker persona.

"Hi Orlando, thanks for having us over," she states. "What can I do to help?"

"Where do you want these?" I indicate the fries.

"Micah, the fries can go on one of the potholders on the table. Peyton, if you wouldn't mind setting the table? The stuff is out there, it just needs placing in the right spots."

We both go to the dining area, it's just a corner of the small living room. I set the fries on a potholder as instructed. Peyton starts setting the table. I walk back into the kitchen, toward the fridge.

"What about drinks? Can I fix them or grab them?" I ask him.

"Yeah, I've got beer, water, or lemonade. It would be awesome if you got that sorted. I'll take a beer. Thanks man."

"No problem." I reach in and grab out two beers. I spy a bottle opener nailed to the wall next to the fridge. The recycle bin resides beneath it. I pop off the top on both beers, the caps fall into the bin, then I take a sip from mine. Oh, that's good. Nothing like ice cold beer on a hot day. When I set the beers on the table, Peyton is just finished setting the places. There's four.

"What would you like to drink?" I ask.

"I'm fine with a beer," she lowers her voice to a whisper as she takes one from me, "Do you know if someone else is coming?" I shrug and walk back to grab one more beer.

"A friend of mine's going to join us, he'll have a beer too, if you don't mind."

He opened the door, so I asked, "What friend?"

"My buddy, Ax, he's like a brother to me. He wanted to meet you guys. I couldn't think of a reason to say no. Is there a reason not to?" I think about it. If we're going to do this, I need to trust him a little. He was quick to help Peyton, I feel in my gut that it's okay. Plus, Felony likes him, and that's gotta say something. She's not all that easy to get along with and she doesn't like just anyone.

"I can't think of any. I'm looking forward to meeting your friend." I try to appear as relaxed as possible.

"Cool. I'm gonna pull the burgers off the grill. We'll be ready in just a couple minutes," he walks off leaving us loose in his house.

I returned to Peyton with the two beers for Orlando and Ax, apparently. Peyton is peeking out the window. I sneak up behind her and put my lips close to her ear without touching her.

"Anything interesting out there?"

"Ahh! Shit! You gotta stop doing that to me. I'm going to end up punching you."

"Why would you do that?" I ask, truly curious.

"Rhett taught me a couple moves when I was a kid. Punch the face and kick the balls. It's been a while, but if I didn't realize it was you, I would definitely hit you." She grins at me. I may need to test this out a bit and make sure she does have some basics. Too bad Paige is pregnant, she would be the ideal person to work with Peyton. An engine rumbles in the distance as I listen to it approaching, I deduce it must be Ax.

"Orlando said his friend, Ax, is joining us. This might be interesting," I smile at my girl. I love calling her that.

Her mouth is open in surprise. My sneaking up on her started it, now she's surprised about Orlando's friend. I press my lips to hers and push my tongue into her open mouth.

"Mmm, Mmmhmm…" She kisses me back and makes some sweet sounds.

"Okay guys, the burgers are resting for a minute. Here's the salads, condiments and toppings. I didn't make the baked beans since I have a broccoli salad and a pasta salad. With your fries and these salads, I think we're set. Here comes Ax," Orlando tells us as he enters the room.

A loud engine comes to a stop outside. Boots clomp up the steps and then the door opens without a knock. I haven't seen Ax before. He wasn't in any of the previews we've done on the Southern Suns. That means they haven't caught him on camera doing something he shouldn't. That's good. He smiles at all of us. He has dark hair and light eyes. Like me, except where my hair is stick straight, his has a little wave. He's probably around my height too.

"Hey, I'm Ax. It's nice to meet you."

"Ax, this is Peyton and Micah. Peyton lives next door. He's there a lot," he offers me a goofy grin he's not wrong.

"Hi Ax, it's nice to meet you," Peyton thrusts her hand towards him to shake. He shakes her hand and smiles at her. He turns his attention to me. Not to be outdone, I also thrust my hand at him.

"Good to meet you Ax, I think we're ready to eat. Have a seat." We all load up our plates and deck out our burgers in condiments and toppings. I add a small puddle of ketchup to my plate for the fries. Peyton drowns her fries in a lake of ketchup and mayo. It turns a sickly pink as she dunks fries into the mixture.

"So, Peyton, Orlando says you're in law school? That sounds really difficult, you must be smart. When will you be finished?" Ax questions.

"I'm in my second year, and one more to go after this. Then I have to pass the bar. It's a grueling two-day exam."

"Brutal. I have a bachelor's degree. I thought that was hard, but I can't imagine three more years of high-level classes on top of that. Are you a masochist?"

"Some days I wonder," Peyton chuckles. "But I have high hopes for helping lots of people when I'm finished. Hopefully it's worth it."

"What type of law do you plan to practice?" Ax questions further.

"My plan is to practice social justice. I want to work with human trafficking victims."

"Wow, that's admirable. Seems like a path likely to lead to some painful situations. You must be tougher than you look," Ax pushes Peyton's buttons expertly. I wonder if he realizes his mistake.

"What's that supposed to mean?" Peyton retorts. He and Orlando cringe, too late, they grasp what Ax did wrong. He raises his hands in a placating gesture.

"Whoa, don't freak out and go all women's lib, please. I didn't mean anything by it. You're just not very big, so you don't appear tough. I was pointing out that you must in fact be tough, despite your size, because that sounds like a grueling job. I promise I wasn't trying to say anything at all about you being a woman," he gives her puppy dog eyes. Uh oh, she always gives in for that look. I think he might scrape by and avoid her wrath.

Her anger deflates as she says, "Okay. But watch it." She points her finger at him and narrows her eyes for effect. He appears appropriately chagrined.

"Well, that was close. Tell me what's going on with the stalker, any updates?" Orlando speaks up wisely, changing the subject.

"There's no suspects. There also hasn't been any activity. We don't know if they've moved on, or are just lying in wait. So, we're still being vigilant," I responded.

"Orlando told me about what happened. I'm glad you're okay, Peyton," Ax says.

"Thanks," she says. She takes our conversation in another direction when she asks about their weekend.

"Do you guys have any fun Saturday night plans?" she asks.

Orlando answers first, "We'll probably be at a club party. They usually host an event at our clubhouse every week." He stops talking and looks at me. I got the distinct impression he was about to invite us to the party and then stopped just in time when he remembered I'm an FBI agent. Not sure if that's good or bad. Maybe I should be offended.

"Uh, how about you guys? You have plans?" He asks, looking at Peyton.

"Nothing definite. A friend of mine at school always knows about the best parties. She'll probably try to make me go to one," she looks at me. "Well, us." She offers me a smile, and I return it.

"Thanks for having us over. This burger is good, and it's cooked perfectly. The last burger I ate was a hockey puck," I praise.

"Thanks for bringing the fries. They hit the spot," Orlando replies, patting his stomach as if he has a gut.

"Orlando says you have a cat named Felony. I guess it makes sense if you're a lawyer. He told me she's the cutest cat he's ever seen. I was almost offended because I think my cat is pretty cute," he whips out his phone and shows us a sleek white cat with gray around its ears and tail. It's pretty cute. Peyton feels her pockets and then gives me an exasperated look.

"Do you have a picture of Felony? I guess I forgot my phone." I pull up a picture of Felony with Beta and Qwerty. I show Ax and Orlando leans over to look also.

"The black one is Felony. The calico is mine, and the white one is my new girl. Peyton and I just adopted them."

"Yeah? Where did you adopt them from?" Ax queries.

Peyton pipes up, "The cutest rescue, Furry Paws, do you know it?"

"Yeah. Connor is my younger brother," Ax says with a grin.

"No way! I love him, he's a sweet kid. He was so helpful. He's not a part of your club?" Peyton asks innocently. God bless her, she's asking FBI questions in our regular conversation.

"He can't be any younger than you. He's twenty-three. Are you that ancient?" Ax chuckles as he grills Peyton right back.

"Really? Wow, I was having a hard time thinking he was even eighteen. I'm almost twenty-four if you must know." She gives him a hard look. Orlando looks at me and we both fight off the chuckles trying to burst free. She's indignant and it reminds me of a bird attacking a predator, the way they flutter around while the hunter continues on without a care. She's so cute, but wholly ineffective at intimidation. She may need to work on that before she ends up in a courtroom.

"Really? I was having trouble thinking you were even twenty-one. But I didn't want to card you for a beer," Orlando chuckles with abandon. She scoffs and then joins him, unable to maintain the ruse of anger. We all have a good laugh.

"Connor will be thrilled when I tell him I met you and saw pictures of your cats. He always remembers every cat and who adopted them. Are you keeping Dr. Ree as your vet?"

"Yes. We love her. Micah's vet just retired so it worked out well for us to meet her. Does Connor work there full-time? I thought he might be a volunteer in high school. But don't tell him that. I don't want to offend him."

"You won't. People don't believe his age all the time. He has a baby face. He works at the rescue full-time. He's also a vet tech, but he lives for the adoptions and works the desk anytime Dr. Ree doesn't need him."

"So, he's not in your club then?"

"Nah. He has no interest. I've known this guy forever; he grew up in the club. I joined in high school. Back when I was too young and recklessly naïve," his look turned introspective. His hand still rests on Orlando's shoulder.

"Yeah, I didn't know anything else. So, this friend of yours, is she single? Is she hot?" Orlando queries.

"I don't know how single she is anymore. Seems like she might be dating a guy she met this past weekend and I think she's been with him every day this week. She's usually serially single and happy to let you know it. But she seems wrapped up in this guy. I don't even know his name. I keep referring to him as Harley Guy," she shrugs.

"He has a Harley?" Ax questions.

"Yeah, it's flat black, even the exhaust. Looks kinda pricey. I've only seen him once and he had a full-face helmet. I've barely had two words with my friend since she met him." Peyton gets quiet.

Orlando bursts from his seat, "What the fuck!" He charges for the window. We all ran after him. He pulls back the drapes so we can see better. Yep, there's someone on the stairs at Peyton's place.

"Shit!" I exclaim and haul ass to the door. I yell across the lawn at the dark figure on the stairs.

"Hey! What the hell are you doing?" He startles and bolts. When I get down the stairs, I chase him going in the direction I last saw him heading. Orlando and Ax are hot on my tail. I catch a glimpse of him as he hops the fence at the edge of the property, and he disappears in the rapidly fading light.

"Freeze!" I yell at him. He trips and looks in my direction, I can't see his features. He speeds up and he's jumping the far side of the next fence when I get over this side. Orlando and Ax are right with me. I want to yell out FBI, I'm not sure how that will go over with the bikers. Ax gets ahead of me and Orlando, the dude is fast. He leaps over the fence and tackles our target. They struggle a moment; it stops when Orlando grabs an arm. Once we have him subdued, we drag him back to Peyton's.

Ax is a little dirty from wrestling with the guy, and the guy has a split lip. I yank the hat from his head. His brown locks flop to his forehead. Wait a minute, I recognize this guy. What the hell? I quickly think through what I know about him. I didn't think there was any chance he could be the stalker. Dammit, I let Peyton study with him.

"Stop! What the fuck? Why did you chase me?" The prowler yells.

"Why did you run?" Ax asks.

"Because I saw three big dudes running at me! I didn't do anything. The door was open when I got there."

My ears perk up, "Wait. What?"

"I didn't break in. The door was open when I got here. I didn't do anything! Fuck!" He touches his lip and inspects the blood on his fingers.

"Oh shit, you got this Orlando?" I question.

"Yeah, we'll catch up, go!"

I take off running for Peyton's front door. I fling myself up the stairs not even sure my feet hit the wood. I rush to the open door, draw my firearm, and enter the darkness. The reflection of the last of the fading sun paints the clouds a bright pink. It's just enough light for me to see that I'm not going to trip over any furniture. I clear the living room and kitchen. Then I sweep the bathroom, nothing out of the ordinary. I haven't found anything or anyone. I carefully and quietly walk to the end of the hall. I choose Peyton's bedroom first, nobody's here. Relaxing, I tread softly into the office. Peyton is standing inside the door, her hands cover her mouth. She's shaking, tears glisten on her face in the last light of the day.

"Are you hurt?" I ask gently.

Her head shakes and a sob escapes her open mouth. Tears gush from her eyes. She rushes to me and grasps me like I'm a life preserver in the middle of the Bering Sea. I wrap her in my embrace, aiming my firearm away from her. She crushes her face to my chest and bawls like a child. I ease my firearm back into its holster and inspect the room cataloging the triggers for her distress.

The gruesome photographs from the file of her sister's murder are taped all over the wall. Something red and dripping, slashes big letters across the photos. *You're next, cunt!* The pictures of Peyton from the stalker are also tacked to the wall. The most graphic autopsy image is front and center. It's held to the wall with a dagger stabbed into the drywall.

Orlando dashes into the room, "What can I do?"

"Will you please check her bedroom carefully? I only took a quick glance for intruders. I don't know where…" I silently mouth, "Felony."

"Might be." I try to signal him with my eyes that her cat is missing. I'm trying not to alert her to the possibility.

He nods, "On it." He leaves the room. I squeeze her tighter and kiss her head and along her temple to the corner of her mouth. I rub her back and whisper.

"Let's get out of here, okay?" She nods and makes a hiccupping, sniffling, whimpering noise. It crushes my heart hearing her pain. I gingerly guide her to the sofa and turn on some lights. I sit and she crawls into my lap. I sneak my phone from my pocket and over her shoulder I type with one hand, alerting Samson and Rhett.

Orlando returns with a fluffy black bundle in his arms. Thank fuck! She would've been inconsolable if anything happened to her first cat. She already loves Felony as much as she loves me. Relief washes through me easing some of the tension that was holding me hostage. Orlando sits next to us.

With great care he quietly tells Peyton that Felony is here and she's fine. Peyton hiccups again, though a smile graces her beautiful face. Relief is evident in her body. She almost deflates like a party balloon after the last goodbye. Orlando places Felony in Peyton's lap and she clings to her kitten as she's slowly recovering from the shock, grief, and fear plaguing her.

Orlando stands, makes a face, and then gestures that he's going back outside with Ax and the prowler. When Peyton settles, I want to go outside and check on what's happening there. But my need to protect Peyton and care for her, overpowers my need to solve the case. I'll wait with her as long as it takes.

Eventually Paige comes rushing into the room. She sits next to Peyton and me on the sofa. She leans into us and holds Peyton's arm. It's a bit awkward, but oddly soothing. She speaks softly to Peyton and eventually pulls her over to her own ever shrinking lap. Peyton leans on Paige more than she sits on her.

"Micah, go do whatever you need to do. Rhett's outside with your friends. I'm a little worried he may end up in jail without proper supervision. I'll stay with Peyton until you're finished. I've got all night. Nova is with my parents; they're visiting for the weekend. Don't worry, I've got her. Please, go do your job." She smiles and nods at me. I give Peyton a kiss and scratch Felony. I pat Paige's arm in thanks.

The scene outside is chaotic and slightly off the rails. Orlando is holding back Rhett. Ax is holding the prowler behind him to keep him safe. While Rhett is waving his arms around as he yells at the prowler. I step behind Orlando and face Rhett.

"Hey Rhett, she's okay. Why don't you go up and check on her. Take a break, okay?" I pull on his arm and lead him towards the stairs.

"I'm going to kill that mother fucker! He better hope you guys can keep protecting him! Dammit, Micah! I'm so fucking pissed off. What the fuck was that asshole doing in my sister's house? Is she okay?"

"Yeah. She's not injured at all. He never got near her. She's just extremely upset. Thankfully Felony is fine too. Paige and Felony are working to calm her nerves. Whoever was inside pasted the autopsy photos of Larue and the stalker pics of Peyton, all over the wall. There's a threat splashed across it too. Why don't you go check Peyton for yourself and ease your mind. Then check out the office, okay?"

"Yeah. Okay. I'm good, just keep that fucker away from me."

He stomps up the stairs, I turn to Ax and Orlando. I look over at a still bloody Jake Waverly. His hair is disheveled, his lip continues to leak blood, and his eyes are wide and fearful. He's trembling in fear from Rhett's reaction. Something is off about this whole situation. When I checked into Jake, I found no red flags. He's always been a good student and he's never been in trouble, not even a parking ticket. He lifts his chin, some show of bravado I suppose because he looks terrified.

"All right Jake. Go ahead and tell me what happened. Start with what you're doing here."

"Aren't you going to read me my rights?"

"I thought we'd just keep it civil for now. I'm Micah, Peyton's boyfriend. What were you doing in her house?"

"I told you, the door was open when I got here. I didn't go inside."

"Okay, start at the beginning. Why did you come over? Was Peyton expecting you?"

"No. I mean, yes, on Sunday," he sighs and tries to get his thoughts together, I can see the wheels turning while he procrastinates.

"Ahem. I called Peyton to ask about an assignment we're going to work on tomorrow. She didn't answer, so I texted and called again. I got worried since she's always quick to respond. I was nearby, so I figured I would just stop by and ask my questions. I just wanted to be sure she's all right."

"And..." Ax interjects. He and Orlando are standing on either side of me with their arms crossed over their chests. They're intimidating, by design.

"And, when I got here, I went up to the door and I was going to knock but it was ajar about 3 inches. I yelled into the house and nobody answered. I knocked and yelled louder, still with no response. I was going to call the cops when you guys came charging at me. I thought you might be the robbers, so I ran. That guy tackled me," he thrusts his finger at Ax. "And now I'm being detained. I don't understand what's going on here."

"May I look at your phone?" I ask.

"I don't see a search warrant. I shouldn't even be talking to you," his lawyer voice is steady and strong.

"I get that. I understand you're a law student and you know your rights. So far, I'm not inclined to read you your rights or arrest you, despite how this all looks. You also must know, without a search warrant anything on your phone will be inadmissible. So, please, your phone," I hold out my hand.

He acquiesced and handed me his phone. I point it at his face, so it unlocks. I quickly check his texts and phone calls. The calling app sits with a nine and one waiting for another one to be keyed into the queue. There're several texts to Peyton and they ask about tomorrow. Then become increasingly more concerned when she doesn't reply. The last one says he's coming over to check on her.

"Okay Jake, you aren't under arrest. But you're being detained as a witness, for now. I'm going to need you to come to the office with me. I need your fingerprints to rule you out. It's very simple, you say you didn't go in the house. You've never been here before, correct?" He nods.

"So, there's no way any of your prints would be inside. If none of your prints show up, you'll be cleared. Okay?" I told him.

Jake's eyes brighten as he sees my logic. He appears eager to come to the office with me now. He also has none of the red substance staining her office wall, on his hands or clothes. While answering my questions his behavior doesn't give any indicators of deception. He seems sincere in his concern for Peyton, and I've no reason to doubt his claims.

The front door explodes open and an angry bull who looks a lot like Rhett storms down the steps. All three of us jump in front of Jake to protect him. Rhett charges like he's seeing red. I wrap my arms around him and try to reason with him.

"Rhett, buddy, what's going on?"

"I'm going to kill that sick mother fucker!"

"What happened? Is Peyton okay?" Concern leaks into me, did I miss a threat inside?

"She doesn't know what that sick bastard did!" He shoves against me, and it takes all of my effort to keep him from killing Jake.

"What did he do?" I ask, clueless.

"That sick fuck put whatever that red shit is in her bed. It's under the covers so she wouldn't have noticed until she climbed into sleep. Jesus, Micah, he came on her fucking pillow! There's mother fucking cum on her pillow! What the fuck is wrong with you?" Rhett shouts.

Lunging towards him, he resumes his efforts to murder Jake. I physically push against his attempts and accept assistance from Orlando and Ax.

They each put a hand on one of his arms at the ready in case he gets past me.

"Rhett, chill! I don't think it was Jake. He was just in the wrong place at the wrong time. He's a witness, not a suspect. Please tell me you didn't touch anything."

He relaxes some and looks at me with something other than murder in his eyes, maybe it's confusion. Then he looks at Jake, then Orlando, and Ax. He looks at their hands on his arms and they each remove them.

"No, of course not, I know better. What the fuck is he doing here if it wasn't him?"

I give Rhett the details of what happened, "Anything to add Jake?"

Shaking his head side to side, he answers, "Nope, you covered it."

"Well, I'm not 100% convinced. When I see some evidence that clears him, I'll be on board. Until then, watch your back asshole." Rhett gives Jake a threatening look with his finger pointed at his face. He stomps over to his pick-up truck and leans against it. His challenge coin flips between and over his knuckles, his go-to stress relief.

"Are you guys cool?" I ask the bikers.

"Yeah, just tell us what you need. We're here for it," Orlando speaks for both of them, Ax nods his agreement.

"Thanks, I owe you. This is twice you've chased after a prowler. I need to speak to my boss, if you guys would just keep an eye on Rhett and Jake for me?" I raise my brows trying to convey that I want them to keep Jake alive and Rhett from jail. They both give me a nod. I walk back up the stairs and into the house.

Peyton is sipping tea, Felony remains curled in her lap. She's not crying anymore though she looks miserable, somewhat haunted. Paige is next to her with a glass of water. They're talking about construction plans and décor for Original Nova's properties. Peyton always gets excited about the project, she's sufficiently distracted to keep the tears at bay. I blow her a kiss on my way past.

The lights are on in her office and bedroom. It's a most unpleasant sight. I take pictures of both rooms and close ups of the substances left behind. My stomach turns, Peyton is going to have to stay at my place until we can get this cleaned up. Forensics is going to leave fingerprint powder all over everything too. I'll probably need to find a deep cleaning restoration service. I make notes as I list my tasks, then send an email request to a service that's worked with our office before.

In the office I carefully inspect everything. As I make my observations and document, I forward everything to Samson and the lab. Samson and I text back and forth. He offered to come here, but I declined. There's nothing he can do. I need his help with any red tape, policies, and search warrants, nothing on scene. We agree to a sit down on Monday at Savage. There's a commotion in the other room. I hear raised voices and laughter. I guess forensics is here. I make my way out to meet the techs.

Keiko McLain is in scrubs and has shoe protectors on her feet, safety glasses dangle around her neck, and her hands are covered by gloves. A face mask sits on her chin, and a cap covers her dark hair. Her usual partner, Vaughn Guthrie, is similarly attired. The main difference being her uncovered short white, blonde hair and piercings versus Keiko's long, straight, dark hair, and distinct lack of metal facial accessories. Keiko told me her mother is Asian and her father is American of Scottish descent. She says her mother is four-foot-eleven inches tall and her father, six-foot-one. The mixture of their ethnicity has made for attractive offspring.

Keiko is a closet gamer. I met her online and found out a month later she works in my office, one floor below my desk. We team up all the time online. I kick ass at COD, and she rocks GTA. I don't recognize the tall guy with them, he must be new. I've heard there were some budget increases, and we may see some new faces. I lift my chin to him, and he responds in kind.

Keiko smiles when she sees me, "Hey Micah. What's up?"

"Hi Keiko, hey Vaughn," I say as I walk to stand next to Peyton.

"This is my girlfriend, Peyton Baker. This is her place," I gesture to the room.

"Peyton, this is Keiko Mclain, and Vaughn Guthrie, they're techs with forensics. I'm sorry man, I don't know you yet," I shrug in apology at the new guy.

"No worries, mate. I'm Brighton Hughes, I've just come on board at the lab. I completed my technical training at university, got hired straight away after graduation, and here I am. Pleased to meet you both," he extends his hand for me to shake. After I do, he gives Peyton a polite nod.

Mastermind investigator that I am, and using the skillful art of deduction, I decide Brighton is from the UK. I chuckle at myself, watch out

Sherlock. I don't know what it is, but UK accents irritate me. It seems to be when it's a man speaking. I've tried to recall if I had a traumatic encounter with a Brit, and nothing comes to mind, but that doesn't mean it didn't happen. I've blocked out many of the worst memories from my childhood.

After the introductions I show them to the office and bedroom. I cringe when I see the red threat on the wall. Peyton did not need this. I have to figure out how they keep getting in without tripping the alarm. I was sure I had secured it to be hack proof.

Keiko whispers her sympathy, "Geez, Micah, I'm sorry this is happening to your girl, she seems sweet. What kind of psycho would do this?"

"This reminds me of the Stratford case," Vaughn whispers. Her eyes shoot to me, panic crosses her face.

"Shit! Micah, I'm sorry. I wasn't thinking about the outcome. Just that time he broke into her house and trashed it. Dammit, please don't listen to me. I'm sure this is nothing like that." She rubs my arm in a soothing manner.

My stomach is clenched in knots, I force a brave face to let her escape her guilt over bringing up a gruesome murder. Fuck, now I can picture that poor girl's body. My nightmares are going to come back.

"I'm going to let you guys do what you need to do. One thing to remember though is Peyton's sister was murdered several years ago and I'm working on the case. There're photos on the wall that the perp took out of my files. I had a folder on the desk with reports and everything we have on that case. The intruder went through it and plastered some of the pictures on my evidence wall. It's where the words are splattered. I just wanted to clarify that those papers and pictures were here, he didn't bring them into the house. I'll be with Peyton if you guys need anything. Thanks."

Feeling defeated and somewhat nauseated, I walk back to the living room. Felony is still coiled in Peyton's lap and Paige remains snuggled next to Peyton. They're speaking softly. I gesture to Paige that I'm going outside.

The fresh air hits my face and eases my bubbling stomach. It's dark now. Ax and Rhett are deep in conversation next to Rhett's truck. Orlando and Jake are chatting, more subdued. I let out a relaxing sigh. The yard is much calmer than the last time I came out here.

I walk towards Orlando and he asks, "How's she doing? Have they found anything?"

"She's okay. She's on the couch with her sister-in-law, chatting. I don't know yet if there's anything to find, other than fingerprints," I answer, giving Jake a pointed look.

Jake asks, "Where's your office? Just wondering how late we're going to be."

"It's near Ocala. But I think I'm going to ask the forensic techs to take your prints while they're here. When I was leaning towards you being a suspect, I wanted you at my office. Now, I think it'll waste four hours of our lives. But you're not free to go until I say, okay?"

He perks up, and nods as he says, "It's fine. I want to help, and if you can clear me, I'll be free to help. I'm here for whatever you need. I really like Peyton and she definitely doesn't deserve whatever is going on."

"No, she doesn't. Thanks for being cooperative Jake." I look at Rhett and Ax. They're laughing and oblivious to the rest of us as they continue their discussion. They're talking about motorcycles of all things; I shake my head. I've never been interested in motorcycles, dirt bikes, or cars for that matter. If it gets me where I want to go, I don't need to know anything else.

"I'll be back. Do you guys want anything? There's bottled water, not sure what else."

"We're good Micah, go take care of your girl. We'll wait until you tell us otherwise," Orlando says.

My phone vibrates with a response from the restoration service, our priority appointment is booked.

"Thanks Orlando, Jake," I nod at them and then climb back up the stairs.

I check in with Peyton and Paige. They're still discussing the plans for the properties, and it's a great distraction for Peyton. She loves what they're doing and wants to help. Paige is surrounded by guys 24/7. She told me once her favorite thing about Peyton is that she's a girl and she likes girl things. Not that Paige is very girly, but I can see how the guys at Savage can be overwhelming with testosterone.

"Do you ladies need anything?"

"May I please have another water?" Paige asks. I look to Peyton for her response.

"Me too, please. Thanks Radiohead."

"Of course, babe."

After I hand them each a bottle, I'm not sure what to do with myself. I sit on the couch on the opposite side of Peyton, from where Paige is pressed against her. Peyton leans on me, and Paige hops up.

"Sorry, I'll be right back. The baby is on my bladder." She walks down the hall and I hear her ask the techs if it's okay for her to use the bathroom.

"Are you doing okay, for real?" My concern coats my question like hot fudge on a sundae.

"Yeah. I'll be okay. We're going to have to stay with Rhett until we can get this cleaned up. I want a new mattress. I didn't have to buy one when I moved in, but I'm not sleeping on that one again. The sheets are trash too and those were new. I'm going to have to patch the wall as well. I'm dreading calling the Renaults about this."

Damn, she saw the dagger, so she also got a look at the autopsy photo of her sister. Thankfully she wasn't up close, but it's a disturbing enough image if she's not your sister. I can't fathom how it's affecting her.

"We can stay at my place if you want. Felony can come visit Beta and Qwerty. I've already put in a cleaning request with a restoration service, we're set. I can get a mattress here tomorrow too. What else can I do? What will help you feel better?"

"You're doing it. Just hold me." She climbs completely into my lap. I wrap her in my embrace and speak softly.

"I'm so sorry the alarm isn't keeping this asshole out. I'm going to rip apart the code and see what I missed. I promise to keep you safe. You're my everything, you know that, right?"

"Hey. Stop that. This isn't your fault. The alarm isn't your fault. We'll figure it out and you'll catch this asshole. I have complete faith in you, but no pressure. I'm just glad I was with you. Usually, these things seem to happen when I'm alone." She plants a kiss on my lips and looks into my eyes.

"You're my everything too. I'm okay, promise," she adds. Paige walks into the room looking relieved. She glances around then focuses on us.

"I'm going to check on Rhett. Yell if you need me."

"You got it, thanks for being here Paige," Peyton says.

"Of course, sweetie. We'll always be here for you, no matter what," she gives Peyton a smile and Peyton returns it with a genuine smile of her own. I feel my own chest ease slightly. The more Peyton seems to be coping the better I feel.

"Oh, Paige, thanks for offering your guest room. But I'm going to stay with Micah, okay?"

"Yeah, whatever you want. You're both welcome at our house any time you need. If you don't, that's okay too. But you're going to have to at least come for dinner. Nova's been asking for you, both." She looks between us grinning, then she goes outside.

I'm really thankful Rhett and Paige are okay with me dating Peyton. They're like family and if they didn't approve, I don't even want to think about it. Luckily, I don't have to find out what would happen. I really value my chosen family and I don't ever want to lose any of them.

Peyton

"Oh my God! This feels so good," I exclaim as I lie back onto Micah's mattress.

"I know. I started to think we wouldn't make it here before dawn. Thankfully the cleaning crew can pick up the key from Rhett's on their way. I had no clue they could replace the mattress. It makes it possible for us to stay here as long as we want tomorrow. I'm thinking we sleep until noon," he says grinning at me.

"Mmm, that sounds perfect. Considering it's," I glance at my phone, "It's three already! I'll probably sleep late without even trying." I stretch like a cat. Micah's bed feels heavenly. When you're so tense with worry for that long, it drains you physically. Once I felt better, and the tension eased, I was ready to collapse. Only four short hours later, and here I am, finally able to collapse. I snuggle into Micah. The cats are in their beds. Micah is the sweetest. He got a bed for Felony. How cute is that?

Placing a kiss on his lips I hug him. "You're the best. I love you. Please don't wake me in the morning."

"I love you too, and you're the best," he counters.

"It's a tie."

"Okay." His lips skim my cheek and land near my ear. I feel and hear his breath. It's reassuring as I let myself drift.

Meooow! Mowmowmow!

My eyes pull open and I'm grateful for the dim light. Micah truly is the best, and he's consistently considerate. The curtains and blinds are all closed tight. The door is only open a crack, just big enough for a bossy little girl to squeeze through.

"What's wrong Felony? Why are you in my face, hmm?" She rubs against me and purrs. I scratch her ears and her face. She rubs harder and purrs louder.

"So, you woke me up because you wanted me to pet you? Is that what I'm getting?"

Meow!

"Sorry girl, I've gotta pee. Feel free to follow me though."

She takes me up on my offer and almost trips me at the bathroom door. Luckily, I've always had good balance and I step around her without falling. After I use the bathroom and Felony sniffs every inch of it, we make our way to the kitchen. I'm thirsty and hungry. I forgot to check the time on my phone. Micah's not in the kitchen. I don't know where he went. I pour myself some orange juice and find a couple of Eggo's in the freezer. It's almost noon but I don't care. Once I get them cooking, I hunt for Micah.

Found him! He's focused on one of the four screens on his office desk. He doesn't notice me and I take a moment to appreciate him. His dark hair is mussed like he ran his hands through it a few times. His bottom lip is between his teeth. His blue-green swirled eyes move as he reads. He's dressed in his black t-shirt. I can't see what it says, but he has some funny ones.

"Good morning, Radiohead. Any updates?"

"Your idea of morning may be flawed, it's almost noon. There are some updates. I'm hungry though, so can we move to the kitchen?"

"I put Eggos in the toaster. We can share."

"Thanks Eagle. Let's eat," he stands and smacks my bottom on his way past me.

"Hey! That's not nice...ah, screw it I can't even pretend to be angry with you," I kiss him when we get to the kitchen. While we have breakfast, Micah fills me in on everything he knows.

"Jake wasn't lying. He didn't go inside the house. His prints are on the door, and that's it. Yeah, he could've worn gloves, but we didn't find any after a thorough search inside and out. The other biological evidence didn't identify anyone yet. Sometimes it takes them a while, so there may be updates. But the information they have so far, matches no one."

I think about the awful scene in my office and ask, "What was the red stuff they splattered all over?"

"Chicken blood mostly. It had something in it to keep it from drying quickly. It also had food coloring mixed in, that's why it was so red."

"What about the big dagger stabbed into the wall? Anything traceable?" I ask.

"Nah, it's a replica of an artifact that was made in Malaysia. It's mostly cheap steel and lead. Something you can order on the internet from hundreds of sites. I'm still working on the code for the alarm system, but I haven't found anything. The logs show that the alarm was disengaged, which seems impossible. You only gave the code to me and your family, right?"

I was startled, "Yeah, you, Rhett, and Paige. That's it. We know it wasn't Orlando or Ax because we were with them. The cameras don't show anything?"

"No. They were erased, and nothing in the cloud either. I have the USB connected to my computer to run diagnostics, but so far it hasn't found anything. Either this person is a computer whiz or they know one. The way everything was erased could have been accomplished by connecting a USB drive containing the coding to get rid of everything. Theoretically this guy could have gotten a program written by someone else. But they also had to be capable enough to disarm the alarm. If they didn't have the alarm code, it would have called the police. It's intuitive, any tampering and the police are called immediately."

"I don't understand how anyone could know the code. Oh. Shit," I shift my eyes to the ground, not sure how to broach the possibility that just popped into my head. I brave a look in Micah's direction. He's looking at me quizzically. My nose is scrunched and my eyes squint with my discomfort.

"What? Spit it out," he cajoles.

"How well do you know those alarm company guys? Zach, Logan, and Reggie?"

"Oh. I never considered them as a possibility. I've known Zach for probably four years. I've known Logan that long too, but we didn't talk much at the beginning. But I've known him pretty well for at least two and a half years."

"What about Reggie?" I question.

His eyes focus on the wall, then he answers, "I think he's been with the company over a year. But I don't know him as well as the other guys." He places his hand under his chin, a contemplative look covers his face.

"They background check all their employees. I mean, a minimum Level Four screening, depending on their position," he adds.

"Man, I hate to think any of them would be involved, but nothing else makes sense. What should we do?"

"I'll have to question them. Honestly, I don't suspect Zach at all. I can start with him and ask about the other two. Hopefully we can stay friends after this. Sometimes my job sucks," he states flatly.

"Do you think we're safe at my place?" I voice my fear.

"We can stay here as long as you want. Don't worry, I'll..."

Raooow! Beta runs into the room and jumps on the table. Qwerty chases behind him and follows suit. They both freeze when they notice us. We have a bit of a stare-off until they get bored and turn their backs on us. Felony prances into the room and hops onto a barstool at the kitchen island. She watches us out of the corner of her eye as she begins licking her front paw for a bath.

I decided to hold our Sunday study group at my place as scheduled. I want to face my fear and start having our weekly study group, as planned. I had to skip yesterday, I slept through half of the session in Micah's bed. My study partners are very understanding, and they chose to cancel the session. We'll work a few extra hours today to make up for it.

I check my face in the mirror and fix the smudge of pink lipstick next to my lip. They should be here any minute. Micah and the cats are tucked away in my office. My laptop is on the coffee table in the living room. The doorbell sounds and I open the door for Jake and Roger.

"Hey guys, how's it going?"

"Hi Peyton, it's good to see you. How're you doing after the other night?" Jake asks as he makes his way to the stove. He places a pot on a burner and sets down a grocery bag before looking me over.

"I'm okay. Catching up on lost sleep yesterday helped. Micah had a service clean everything and make repairs. They even got me a new mattress. When we got here this morning it's like none of it ever happened."

"Yeah, Jake told me about the incident. I'm sorry you had to go through that. Is Anisa coming today?" Roger asks eagerly.

"As far as I know. She texted once this morning, so it seemed like she'll be here."

Roger holds up a foil wrapped platter, "Where should I put this?"

"Anywhere in the kitchen is fine." My doorbell rings and I open the door.

"Speak of the devil! Hi Anisa, come on in. You can put the food in the kitchen," I point in that direction.

"We gotta eat this soon. It's more breakfast than lunch." She indicates the boxes and bags in her hands. Everyone greets each other. Roger looks ready to drop to the ground and kiss her toes, she smiles sly as a fox at me. After we load up plates full of breakfast goodies, we settle around the living room.

"This is so good. I love these little faux nuts, where did you get them?" I ask Anisa.

"Chicken or Egg. It's this great little breakfast and lunch shop," she answers.

Then she adds, "I noticed your neighbor up the street has some of those Day of the Dead skulls from the Mexican guy. Why do they have so many? They're absolutely hideous."

"That's harsh. They're works of art and each one is different. I understand wanting them all. But, yeah, that old guy did go a little overboard. Halloween must be his favorite holiday or something."

"Well, I still think they're awful. They're so tacky, it's embarrassing. Do you guys have any plans for next weekend?" Anisa asks with her smile aimed at Roger. His eyes watch her every move and he smiles like a fool any time she looks his way or acknowledges him. It's kinda sweet and sad at the same time. He's obviously smitten and she's oblivious or maybe devious, since she's not interested in him.

Jake answers first, "I have another family dinner on Saturday. My parents will be in town, so it should be especially tedious," he rolls his eyes.

"That blows. What about you Peyton?" Anisa asks.

"I don't have any plans besides studying and hanging out with Micah. Why? What are you doing?" I ask.

"I know about a party Saturday night that we should go to. How about you Roger? Are you free?" she asks.

"Yeah, I can make it. Where is it?"

"It's a party Rev told me about; his friend is hosting. You can bring your boyfriend, Peyton. You guys can bring dates too, if you want. It's going to be at a mansion on the beach."

"Oh, is it the same place you went to that other party?" I wonder.

"Nah, Rev says this is a good friend of his, Chainz."

"Is Rev the Harley Guy?" I ask.

"Yeah, didn't I tell you that before?" She giggles.

"What Harley guy?" Roger asks with concern.

"He's the guy I'm seeing. He rides a Harley and has a bunch of tattoos. He lives over in Oakdale," she replies with dreamy eyes.

Roger looks crestfallen, and his shoulders droop as he asks, "What kind of name is Rev?"

"It's his road name, he's in a club."

"A club? He's over eighteen, right?" Roger digs further.

Anisa chuckles, clueless that she's broken Roger's heart. "Of course, silly, it's a motorcycle club. He's a bad ass biker," she smirks.

"Oh, you mean like a biker gang? Isn't that dangerous? Is he a criminal?" Jake asks.

"I don't know. But he's fun, he's hot, and he's into me. All of my favorite things in a man," she winks at us. "The party is going to be a blast. They have a live band, and it's right on the beach. There'll be an open bar and you should wear your swimsuit under your clothes. I'll text you guys the address."

"I can't go, got that family thing," Jake says, shaking his head.

"I just remembered something I have to do, so count me out," adds Roger. I look him over and I'm pretty sure he's lying, but I won't call him out. I don't blame him after how Anisa's treated him, even if she's unknowing in her hurtful behavior.

She turns to me, "Peyton? Can you and Micah go?"

"I'll have to ask him, but I can't think of any reason why not, right now. I guess count me as tentative until I check with him."

"Yeah!" She claps her hands and bounces in her seat, like an excited toddler.

We get busy after that, and I forget all about Anisa's personal life. I dug into my Pretrial Pro project. We come up for air around 1p.m. Everyone's hungry so we dig into the food Roger and Jake brought. Jake brought burritos. His pot contains shredded chicken and rice in a spicy sauce. He also brought tortillas, veggies, cheese, sour cream, and guacamole to fill up.

Roger brought some queso, chips, and bean dip. It's a lovely fiesta of Mexican deliciousness. We stuff our faces and I bring a plate to Micah. He's up to his elbows in something and I try not to disrupt him too much. He's appreciative of the food since he forgot to eat. He hugs and kisses me then sends me back to my group.

Jake poses a question to the others. "Would you guys quiz us for our exam this week? I made some cards and one of you can use the questions in the book. Do you mind?"

Anisa jumps at the opportunity, "I'd love to! We can make it like a game show. Do you have any alcohol Peyton?"

"How's that like a game show?" I laugh. She's always so ready to do something over the top. I definitely want to go to that party next weekend. I need a night filled with alcohol and laughter. Things have been too intense lately. Between school and the stalker, I'm wound up tight.

"Whoever gets the answer takes a drink."

"I see a lot of issues with that. That leaves out you and Roger. Plus, won't we do worse as we go if we're drinking, and shouldn't we drink if we miss an answer?" Jake questions logically.

"Okay, let's choose a word. We'll drink any time anyone says the word."

"Sorry, I don't have any alcohol. We ditched everything after I got food poisoning. I haven't replaced the liquor yet. We might need to have a BYOB policy for study group." I smile at everyone. I'm hoping Anisa isn't as big a drinker as she seems at the moment. My last roommate was an alcoholic, and it wasn't fun trying to be her friend. I'm sticking with the food poisoning story at Micah's suggestion.

"Oh well. Let's get busy with the quizzing!" She recovers quickly from her disappointment in the lack of adult beverages.

We work for another hour before everyone heads out. I'm relieved to be alone in my living room. I'm on the floor in front of the sofa with my books and laptop spread on the coffee table. I let my head fall back onto the cushion and stare at the ceiling. I assess my feelings and determine that I'm doing okay regardless of what happened the other day. I feel comfortable here. I love this little house. I love Micah and I'm really happy with how things are going between us. I love Felony and I'm so glad I adopted her. Overall, I'm pleased with my move closer to my family. Seeing them regularly does my soul good.

For some reason Original Nova pops into my mind. I can hear her voice; *You stay strong, young lady. Don't you let some sick jackass ruin your happy home. You've got a keeper with Micah. You can't go wrong with My Paige and Rhett, and mini-me. You're going to be okay. You're going to be a kick ass lawyer, so don't let anything or anyone stand in your way.* I smile. Nova was always quick to offer unsolicited opinions. I'm going to accept the advice at face value, even though it's just my imagination. The front door flings open and a gust of wind blows some of my papers around. I hop up and slam the door closed, locking it.

As I lean against the door, Micah comes out of the office on alert, "What was that?"

"What was what?"

"The slamming and the wind? A bunch of stuff blew off the desk."

"I guess whoever was the last out the door didn't close it tight. Sorry it disrupted your work. Do you need help cleaning up?"

"No. It wasn't that bad it just... startled me. I don't understand how a gust of wind from the front door reached me in the office." He sniffs the air. I sniff it too. There's a weird smell, and it's kind of stinky.

"Do you smell that?" He asks.

"Yeah, what is it?" I look at him confused.

"Smells like marijuana. Did your friends have some?"

"Not that I know about. I didn't smell it until now," I sniff around trying to locate the source. I look out the window when I consider the possibility it could be coming from outside. It looks like nobody's home at Orlando's. I open the front door and step onto the deck still sniffing. Micah follows, sniffing with me. I don't smell it out here at all.

"There's nothing out here. Weird," Micah states.

"Yeah, it's weird. You know, I was just thinking about Original Nova. She's the person I associate with that smell. Maybe I smelled it and it made me think of her without realizing."

"Probably. You should explain to your friends that your boyfriend is a cop, and they shouldn't bring any substances to your house," he grins at me.

"Will do, officer," I salute him. He leans down and kisses me. I add my tongue, then we embrace and make out. Chills rush across my skin and I can feel a twinge in my panties. An alarm goes off on my phone. Breaking our kiss, I pull it out of my pocket.

"Oh, shoot, it's time to head over to Rhett's for dinner, rain check?"

He hugs me close and squeezes my ass, "You know it, Eagle." I pop a quick kiss on his lips and go inside to change.

We had a great dinner with Rhett's family. I got to play with Nova when she wasn't bossing Micah around. She's the cutest. When we get back to my place our minds are only on each other. We decided to shower and then climb into my bed.

I can't stop kissing him. He's such a good kisser. His soft lips and talented tongue send zings of sensation through me that light up my lady bits. We're already naked from our shower so it's easy to feel one another. Micah rubs his hands over my nipples and squeezes my breasts. His actions cause my nerves to light up. I smooth my palms over his nipples and grind my pelvis into his swollen cock.

He lays me on my back and then he leans over the edge of the bed. He lifts my womanyzer from my nightstand drawer. I watch as he figures out how it works. Then with a bright smile he traces it over my nipples. I arch into the vibration; it feels warm and fluttery. My clit throbs in arousal. He slowly guides it down my belly and to my sex.

He spreads my labia and lines up the womanyzer with my clit. The moment it comes into contact with my most sensitive nerves, I scream out in pleasure.

"Oh my God! Yes! Holy...yes...oh God!" I ramble. My head shakes from side to side, I don't know what to do with myself. The sensations are hitting me fast and furious. I squeeze my breasts and hold on for dear life as my orgasm builds quickly.

"Yes! Oh Micah!" He inserts his finger into my pussy and rubs against my g-spot. I detonate instantly. My body seizes and my back lifts, then my hips buck I can feel the gush of wetness as I come hard.

"Oh Micah! Wow!" I start to giggle, and I can't catch my breath.

He has a huge smile on his face, "Yeah, wow! That was awesome! You shot off like a rocket. I think you launched yourself four feet across the bed!"

"I did?" I look around, he's right, I'm not where I started.

"That was so good! Now I want to climb on top of you and have my way!"

"I'm all yours, Eagle." He leans back and holds his hard cock. He pumps his hand a couple times and I see the moisture at his tip. I lick my lips and crawl over his lap. I line him up and fall on him, piercing myself with his hard staff. I pull on his shoulders encouraging him to sit up. We wrap our arms around each other, and I kiss him. I move up and down guiding his cock to rub exactly where I want. He groans when I fall flush on his hips burying him as far as he can go inside me. I grind on his pubic bone while he's so deep.

"Mmmm, yes. You feel incredible, you're perfect for me. We're made to fit together."

I speed up my movements as we pant between kisses. I kiss his ear and he moans out. A shiver travels through him, setting off a shiver in my body. The delicious thrills grow, and another orgasm is gaining traction. He grabs onto my hips and moves me faster; he thrusts upward in sync with our movements.

"Babe! Babe, I'm gonna come! Oooooh! Yeees!"

"Me too! Don't stop! Yes! Micah, oh God, yeeees!"

My orgasm slams into me, I lose my ability to coordinate my movements. Thankfully, Micah remains in control, and he brings us both to the finish. He buries himself to the hilt, I can feel him pressed against my cervix as his cock swells and his warm cum fills me. I grind on him until I shiver as I fall over next to him. He rolls and ends up on top without letting his cock slip free. He looks into my eyes and smiles.

"That was amazing. I always think it can't possibly get any better, then you show me I'm wrong. I love you Peyton," he says as he stares deep into my eyes.

"I love you too, you're amazing. Want to rinse off in the shower?" I ask.

"Definitely. Here I brought you a towel to clean up," he hands me a hand towel. He's always so thoughtful, no wonder I love him. I place a kiss on his cheek and carefully get up and clean off. We make our way into the shower.

"I almost forgot to ask you about next weekend. Anisa asked us to go to a party with her. It's at a beach mansion, someone her Harley Guy knows owns it. His name is Rev, by the way. It's his street name, he's in a motorcycle club," I roll my eyes, it's so cliché.

"Do you mean road name?"

"Oh, yeah, I guess. I really want to go if you're free, but I won't go without you. I need to let off some steam, between school and the stalker, I'm feeling a little stressed. Some alcohol, dancing, and fun on the beach sounds ideal."

"At this moment I don't know of any reason why we can't go."

After we wash, we return to my bed. The cats are curled up on the blanket and Micah and I climb in around them. Felony gets annoyed and moves to her own bed. The other two just let us manipulate them until we're all comfortable.

I snuggle in with Micah and he spoons me from behind. One hand rests on my hip, and the other comes around my neck. I wrap my hand over his and give it a quick kiss before I close my eyes.

Micah

"She definitely said to wear our swimsuits under our clothes?" I ask.

"I promise we won't be the only ones. How does this look?" Peyton asks.

"Whoa! Babe, I'm not wanting to get into a fight at this party. You look like a Sports Illustrated model. Damn!" I swear I almost swallowed my tongue. Peyton is wearing a ruby red bikini, if you can call it that. It's like a couple of strings and tiny triangles strategically placed over her nipples and lady parts. Her ass is uncovered except for the thong string between her cheeks. She looks like a Playboy centerfold. She has on a little sheer dress over her suit. It has solid heart shapes over her breasts. But her ass is perfectly visible through the dress. I swipe my hand through my hair, then down my face. Okay, I'm not a caveman, I can do this, without a fight with her or any drunken assholes.

She completes her ensemble with fuck me red heels. I take in a few deep breaths and try to remember that she'll be coming home with me. She's really excited about this party. I'm determined to show her a good time. She looks me over, scrutinizing my face closely. I smile at her.

"Are you going to be okay, Radiohead? Anisa convinced me to wear this. I'm trying to be okay with it."

"I'm good, babe. Are you ready to go?"

"Yeah. I locked everything. Fed the cats. Bottle of water," she holds up her water bottle. "I've got lip balm in my phone case. I'm all set."

The party is less than ten minutes from Peyton's house. It's just a little ways up the beach. When we arrive there's a huge iron gate entrance. It's open so I maneuver my SUV through and find a place to park near the exit. It's a tiny bit of a walk to the house, but if there's a traffic backup when we're ready to leave, we'll be happy we had to trek a short distance. When we open our doors, the music hits us. The bass is vibrating all of the cars. It's almost our own concert.

Peyton squeals and grabs my hand. She yanks me toward the house. I scan the rooms and the people as we enter the foyer. There're bikini-clad girls everywhere. The areas I can see are shoulder to shoulder, the room vibrates with the beat from a band on a small raised dais. Most people hold a red cup in their hand while they dance. Everyone is screaming at each other trying to be heard. Peyton drags me through the house and out the back door to a huge patio. The stone pavers are varying shades of gray. They look like aged cobblestones. In reality I'd guess this McMansion to be less than five years old. There're a few plain clothes security guards walking the perimeter of the crowd. A bonfire blazes on the beach surrounded by more drunk partygoers. A speaker blasts the same music across the sand to the water, hell, probably all the way to Texas.

Peyton pulls me to a bar line. She spins around and hugs me. I lean down and kiss her temple, then her lips. She wraps her arm around my neck and puts her lips close to my ear.

"Thank you for doing this. Are you going to have a drink?" she yells into my ear.

"Yeah, I'll have a beer. The line is moving."

She smiles at me, then realizes what I said. She faces forward and moves up behind the guy ahead of us. She turns back to me and gives me a sheepish smile. I enclose her in my arms and hold her, enjoying how she smells, since we can't talk. When I look up, I see the bald guy in front of us looking at Peyton over his shoulder. I promised myself I wouldn't fight with anyone. I've never been jealous or possessive before. With all of my being, I want to mark her in front of everyone, and claim her as mine. It's a

Neanderthal move, but my instincts aren't under my control. I force myself to be rational. She's mine. They'll figure it out. I don't have to protect her from their eyes.

Peyton is oblivious that she's being ogled and the center of a territorial dispute. I slide my hands around her back and down to her ass. I stake my claim without a single blow. Her head falls back and she meets my eyes. Hers narrow as she focuses intently on me. I can see that she knows exactly what I'm doing. Life would be simpler if my girlfriend wasn't so smart or if she didn't know me so well. I smirk at her, busted.

I think she's going to push me away or say something to admonish my behavior. She surprises me and throws her arms around my neck while she swoops in and plants a whopper of a kiss on my mouth. Her tongue presses between my lips. I open my mouth to accept her advance, she sucks on my lower lip. What's she doing to me? Did she forget we're in public? She feels amazing in my arms. I think about bad crime scenes, assholes I've arrested, anything to stop my dick from growing. There we go, my blood is flowing in my brain once again.

She wasn't kidding when she said she needed to let off steam. I haven't seen her so free, ever. I kinda like it. I carefully keep my crotch from rubbing against her. She continues our kiss until the guy behind us whistles. It's loud enough to startle us. We look around and move forward filling the gap.

When she gets up to the bar, I can't hear what she orders. The bartender shakes his head. He hands her a card; she looks it over then points to what she wants. She hands the card to me and I point to a Corona. Once we have our drinks in hand, she leads us to the beach. The music is less intense on the dunes.

Now that we're closer, I can see a big seating area between the bonfire and the water. It's filled with sectional sofas aimed toward the fire and the house. There're bar height tables scattered around the beach. They have a weighted base made to look like natural rocks, which is a cool idea. Peyton stops at a tall table next to a dance floor. The raised platform is at least 30x30, it's huge. It's covered with partiers who're bouncing to the beat. Peyton bounces on her toes and wiggles her hips in time with the music. Thankfully the sand is fairly solid so far, and she's doing okay in her heels.

I hold onto her, following her lead. She takes us to the dance floor. I chug the rest of my beer and place it on a table. Peyton takes a couple gulps of her drink. She makes a sour face and leaves her cup on the table next to mine.

We spent the next hour dancing, she's a good dancer. I just try to keep up doing whatever she does. I'm not hating it. She signals me. The best I can decipher is that she either wants to get a drink or she wants to bid two-hundred-thousand-dollars. She takes my hand and we make our way through the bikini clad bouncing bodies.

We order water at the bar; I get two extra bottles. Mine will be gone in less than thirty seconds. We carry our refreshments to the furthest seat from the speaker broadcasting popular music now. The band must be on a break. She falls onto the light blue fabric. I sit next to her. There's a nice breeze coming off of the water.

She finishes her first bottle of water and says, "Man that was fun! I love the music they're playing. Do you think they have a DJ?"

"Yeah, he was set up in the dining room. Want some more water?"

"Yes. Thanks, Radiohead, you're the best. Always so thoughtful." She smiles at me.

"I'm always thinking of you. It makes it easy to come up with ways to anticipate your every desire," I let a grin lift my cheeks. I plant a kiss on the corner of her mouth and I look into her eyes. I'm seeing some heat in her beautiful blue eyes. It must reflect my own.

"Are you thinking what I'm thinking?" she asks.

"Are you thinking about going back to your place and fucking our brains out?" She laughs, and I join her.

"No. I was thinking about walking down the beach and doing it in the sand." She smiles a large angelic grin as I choke on my water.

She purrs, "But we can go, if that's what you want..."

"Hey! You guys!!" I jolt as I see Anisa barreling towards us. I cough a few more times, and try to slap the disappointment from my face.

"Hi Anisa! I was beginning to think you weren't here. How's everything going?" Peyton asks.

Anisa leans in and hugs her. She whispers something to Peyton. Then Peyton's eyes drift behind Anisa. I see a guy around my height, he has tattoos up and down his arms. He's thicker than me, no matter how much I eat I can't seem to bulk up. There's a tattoo on his neck that I recognize, despite half of it being under his collar. His hair is dark, and he has a dark beard. His baseball cap hides the top of his head but I'm going to guess he's not balding with the mess of hair hanging beneath the brim. Anisa's face is split by a brilliant smile she aims at Peyton. I'm sensing pride. She must be excited for Peyton to meet this guy.

"Peyton, this is Rev. Rev, this is Peyton," her smile doesn't dim. He jerks his chin in acknowledgement at Peyton. Peyton looks down and then her eyes search his.

She grimaces, "Nice to meet you, Rev." She looks to Anisa who smiles with approval.

"I'm so happy you guys are finally meeting. I told him all about how smart you are and how I want to be you when I grow up," she tells Peyton. Then she notices me and forms her own grimace.

"Oh, Micah, sorry. Um, this is Rev. Rev, this is Peyton's boyfriend, Micah." He gives me a chin lift and I return it.

Anisa turns back to Peyton; she leans in to whisper again. Peyton shakes her head and laughs. I smile even though I wasn't privy to the joke. Peyton's smile makes me happy. I look back at *Rev,* and he's leering at my girl. I breathe in a harsh breath. I scan him for weapons out of habit. He's got a gun in a holster at his waist and a knife in his pocket. I can't see it but based on what I can see, he has a knife strapped to his calf. He notices me evaluating him and he throws a hard grin at me. He places his hand on Anisa's hip. She immediately focuses all her attention on Rev.

"Do you want to dance, baby?" she asks him while fluttering her eyelashes.

"Nah, you wore me out. Let's find some food."

Anisa swats at Rev and her face turns red. From what Peyton has told me about her friend, this seems out of character. Maybe she really is into this biker. Anisa turns back to Peyton and says something I can't hear. This music is killing me; the DJ is great but it's too loud. Peyton nods, and Anisa pulls Rev toward the house. We follow them. I let Peyton lead. I hang back and scope out the guests and staff. The people dancing seem much less coordinated than they were an hour and a half ago, and more than likely two or three drinks ago.

We follow Anisa into a room at the end of a hall. The music presses in on us, and it echoes around the marble floors and minimalist décor. When Anisa throws open the door, we enter a room that has sofas around the exterior walls, and a few largish tables and chairs in the middle. There're a few guys sprawled on the u-shaped sectional sofa. One has an almost naked girl writhing in his lap. His hands cover her breasts as she rides his crotch.

Peyton gives me a surprised look. She puts her arm around my waist. I drape mine over her shoulders and place a kiss on her hair. She rubs my belly with her other hand. She turns to me with her mouth open in shock.

"What?" I whisper.

"There's someone going down on that guy in the corner. Holy shit! I've never been to a live porno before. It doesn't bother you?"

I glance at the corner. There's a guy completely reclined with a head bobbing in his lap. His face is slack, his eyes rolled back in ecstasy. He begins thrusting into the person's mouth and his face scrunches.

"It doesn't. I've seen a lot of things, this isn't so bad. I'm assuming everyone is of age, and gave consent. Does it make you uncomfortable or horny?" I offer her a crooked grin.

Her face flushes pink, "Maybe both. Discomfort wins though," she whispers into my ear. There's a lull in the music just as the guy shoots his load into his partner's mouth. We hear his loud groan of satisfaction.

Peyton's mouth drops open. Her eyes are wide and her eyebrows are raised comically high. Her breathing picks up and she begins to pant. I'm lost. I don't understand her reaction. I look around and search for any threats, then my own chin falls to the floor. There, in front of the dude tucking himself away, on his knees, is Peyton's friend, Jake. He wipes his mouth and kisses the guy on the sofa. He stands and straightens his clothes and swipes his fingers through his hair. He notices Peyton as soon as he looks this way. His face lights up and he makes a beeline right to her. He sees me at the last minute and his face is suddenly serious.

He gives me a chin lift, "Hi, how's it going?"

"It's good. Everything's good," I shake his proffered hand, trying not to think about where it may have been.

"Jake? I thought you couldn't come because of a family obligation. What happened?" Peyton sputters.

"He left early because the family had a big blow out. His mom and dad got drunk and started insulting everyone. His cousin got into an argument with his dad. Then his uncle jumped in and it almost became a brawl," Anisa blurts.

"Thanks, Anisa," Jake gives her a placating smile.

"Are you okay?" Peyton asks him. Her lips thin when her eyes narrow and her brows pull down as her head tilts. She inspects his face and stops when she seems satisfied.

"I'm used to it. They all drink, then get self-righteous and judgmental. I leave so they can't attack me or my sexuality. My parents claim they're okay with me being gay. They act like it, most of the time. But sometimes when a family member makes a comment, they join the attack, instead of defending me. It only happens when they drink. I recognize the signs, and I leave. It keeps the peace." He shrugs and seems unaffected by his family drama. Peyton releases me and she hugs Jake tight. He gives me a nervous glance; I chuckle and shake my head.

"It's cool dude, chill. I have no issues with you. Peyton obviously likes you, so I'll give you a chance. Just, don't fuck it up."

Jake visibly relaxes and hugs Peyton back. She lays her head against his chest and then gives him a forceful squeeze before she lets him go and looks over my face, and I smile at her. I can tell she's trying to see if I'm angry or jealous. I'm honestly fine. I'm sure it's not because he's gay, he was on my *okay list* before finding out that piece of information. Yeah, I'd be lying if I said it didn't soothe my jealousy tonight knowing he's not interested in Peyton, though. I sigh at myself. Peyton's eyes shift to mine, and her brows lift. I offer her a grin, she returns it. I love that we know each other so well, but sometimes I wish for a little more mystery. She knows exactly what just went through my head.

Rev stands in front of a large buffet table decked out with cold cuts and vegetables. There're bowls of chips and dips. Some hot items include pizza, pigs in blankets, meatballs in a dark sauce, and chicken wings. I didn't realize I was hungry until seeing the food, my mouth waters. I wonder if Peyton is starving too, we didn't eat much before we left and it was hours ago.

Peyton's face lights up when she spies the food, which answers the question. She doesn't hesitate to get a plate and start piling on food. Jake follows her and does the same. My stomach speaks up and I join them. Anisa stays behind and reserves a spot at a table for us. I would've called this the family room of the house; the tables make it something else. It reminds me of a bistro that's trying to capture the millennial crowd. When we sit with our food, we're all feeding our faces and Anisa just watches us.

"Aren't you hungry?" Peyton asks her.

"Nah, I had a big dinner," she responds and looks away.

Some of my FBI training shoots off a flare. Anisa is exhibiting evasive behavior. She's probably lying. About dinner? That's odd. I scrutinize her face, she looks embarrassed. Her cheeks are pink and she's avoiding eye contact. I glance at Rev, he's oblivious, chewing on one of the tiny hotdogs covered in dough. He looks at me and smirks. I'll be pulling his records when we get out of here.

When I scope out the room again, I'm pretty sure the couple on the couch is having sex. The guy who hooked-up with Jake has left the room. Two more couples have come in, and a lone biker is hanging out by the bar drinking a beer. I catch him sending a hand signal to Rev. It looks like a greeting. I suppose it could be something else. I idly wonder if they're dealing.

At our table, Anisa rejects Peyton's offers of food from her plate. Rev doesn't offer her anything. I continue my observations, I'm happy to be out of the direct blast of music and watching people is a longtime habit. The beat still thumps at the walls when the door is closed, at least we can talk without shouting. Peyton avoids looking at the couples on the sofas. Jake keeps whispering to Peyton and she laughs loud. It's a beautiful clear sound that rings out across the room like a crystal bell. I find myself smiling too.

"Anisa, d'you wanna dance with me?" Peyton asks. Anisa immediately looks to Rev who lowers his brow in a mini-scowl.

"You can go dance if you want. I'm gonna go talk to Tool about tomorrow. I'll be upstairs if you want me," Rev tells Anisa, before he walks off towards the door. Anisa's face falls as she watches him. The biker who was at the bar follows Rev out. I wonder if that was Tool.

"Dance? Anisa?" Peyton points toward the door with her eyebrows raised. When Anisa doesn't answer, Peyton waves her hand in front of her face. Anisa snaps out of her daze and looks at Peyton.

"Oh. No, I don't feel like dancing. Why don't you and Jake go ahead, and Micah. I'm gonna go upstairs and probably take a nap. I don't want to be wiped out for our study group tomorrow. Thanks for coming though. I hope you guys had fun."

"I had a great time. Thanks for the invite. Hopefully I'll have a chance to see Jamal again," Jake smiles at everyone. "I'm going to head home. I'll see you guys tomorrow. Great seeing you all, and Micah." He gives us all a salute. Then he holds out his hand for me to shake, I do. He half-heartedly hugs Anisa, from the side. Then he hugs Peyton and gives her a kiss on her cheek. He meets her eyes with a smile and he leaves.

Peyton looks intently at Anisa and tilts her head. Anisa's chewing on her thumb nail and has a blank look on her face. It makes me wonder if she's on something beyond the drinks being served. Peyton's eyebrows are scrunched in the middle. Her mouth is pulled in at one side. She shrugs at me and I shrug back. I have no clue what's up with her friend. I don't know the chick and so far, I'm not impressed.

"Anisa, do you want to talk?"

"Huh? Oh. Um, yeah sure. What do you want to talk about?"

"I think maybe you need to talk. What's up? You seem kinda lost or upset," Peyton asks.

"Ladies, I'm going to find a restroom. I'll be back in a few. Okay, Eagle?" I ask my girl.

"Yeah, sure. I'll be right here, with Anisa. Safe and sound. I promise not to leave this room." She smiles at me, having correctly addressed my concerns that I wasn't going to voice.

"Sounds good, lovely Eagle," I give her a goofy grin and walk out the door, narrowly missing a smack on my arm. Peyton is spending too much time with Rhett and Paige. She's learning Paige's bad habits of slapping everyone.

The minute I pass the threshold, I'm barraged with an assault of sound waves. My insides vibrate with the bass. My eardrums hum, it's not an enjoyable feeling. The music style has taken a turn and it's not pleasant at all. It sounds like someone mixed rap with country and the rappers came back to whoop ass. The country part of the song is dying an ugly death. I set my coordinates on a restroom and take a guess the line in the hall is for the closest one. I'm not standing in that line. A house this size certainly has more than one.

I walk down a hallway that has too many doors on either side. I try a few and they're locked. When there's a pause in the music, I can hear sex noises behind each door as I pass. I try the next knob and it turns in my hand. Inside is a dim room with multiple doors along the left side wall. There's a bed that hasn't been disturbed and a dresser. I sigh and try the doors inside the room. The décor is dark, adding to the dimming effect of the tiny bit of light shining through the blinds and from the hallway.

After I find a huge walk-in closet behind two doors, the third one is the charm. It's a small, modern restroom. I lock the door behind me and take care of my business. A noise reaches me from the bedroom. A door slams and voices are raised in anger. I flush and wash my hands assuming they'll be alerted to my presence. I can't tell if they're male or female.

A banging noise is followed by a loud male voice, "I said no, Diamond!"

A female voice replies, and it sounds angry too, but I can't make out the words. I'm not going to hide in here, so I step out of the restroom. I see the back of someone as they close the door on their way out of the room. I see dark clothes and dark shaggy hair being wrangled by a cap. The last thing out the door is a large tattooed hand. The left hand has *G-O-O-D*, tattooed across the knuckles and a leather cuff around the wrist. I quickly follow. I want to see who was in this room.

When I burst into the hallway to my right it was empty. To my left are three people. A small purple-haired female wearing a leather dress with lots of skin on display. Her hair is filled with intricate braids and hangs down her back. I can't see her face. With that hair she'll be easy to spot in the crowd, so I focus on the two males with her. One is my height but with a stocky build. He has a mess of dark hair falling out of his hat. From the back, the other guy looks the same. My height, stocky, dark hair. He's also dressed in black and wearing a cap the same color as his companion's. I walk past the trio hoping to see some faces.

"Holy shit!" I don't even hear myself say it out loud until the music has a pause right on the expletive. Both guys turn their heads to me in a move as synchronized as the Rockettes Christmas Show. I'm doubly shocked. It's Rev and...Rev. What the fuck? Okay, my brain comes back online and I grasp that I'm looking at twins.

"Oh, hey man. You're with Anisa's hot friend, right?" Rev says.

"Yeah. Micah, and you're Rev, right? So, you're...?"

He smirks at me and the resemblance is disturbing. I can't tell them apart. I look at their necks and they both carry the Southern Suns mark. I look at Rev's hand where he now holds a cup. Oh, score, he has the letters *G-O-O-D*, across his knuckles. It was Rev in the room with a female. I look at the purple haired girl, and my eyes meet bright blue orbs surrounded by way too much black makeup on her droopy lids. There's a hoop in her eyebrow and her lip. A diamond sparkles from her cheek. She looks to be college age like most everyone here. I wonder if she was the female voice. Since only these three were in the hallway, it seems likely. I catalog everything I see, relieved that I have some things figured out.

"I'm Rev. We met earlier?" He answers like I'm senile.

"I thought you were the guy I met earlier," I say looking back at Rev number one, confused as fuck.

"I'm just fucking with you, dude! I'm Tool, Rev's my brother," he laughs.

"Nice to meet you, Tool," I look for any type of facial differences and find nothing. I give him a chin lift; he returns my man greeting. He raises a cup to his lips, on his knuckles, are the letters, *G-O-O-D*. My eyes bug out of my head. Shit, there goes the one difference between them I thought I spotted. I feel like I'm in the twilight zone.

Coming back to my senses I look at purple hair and say, "Hey, I'm Micah."

"Hi. You can call me Diamond," she aims a sultry look my way.

"Nice to meet all of you. I'm going to find my girlfriend. She's with Anisa." I watch all three of them for any reaction, I get nothing.

I awkwardly added, "See you around." And make my way back to the room where I left Peyton. I'm once again relieved when the music cuts down to a reasonable level as soon as I close the door behind me. Peyton's seated at the table where I left her. Anisa's nowhere to be seen. I place my hand on Peyton's shoulder. I expect her to be startled by the sudden contact, but she just reaches up and wraps her hand in mine. Her eyes lift, and meet my look head on, they dilate a little. I kiss her lips.

"I'm ready to go. This wasn't as fun as I hoped it would be. I thought we'd hang out with Anisa and dance more. She seems pretty obsessed with Rev; he makes me uncomfortable."

I use her hand and lift her from the chair so we can go. I was done when I got hit in the face with the music a few hours ago. It's a huge relief when we close the front door behind us and get further across the front yard.

"What happened to Anisa? I thought she wanted to talk to you," I inquire.

"She said she wanted to talk, but she looked scared. Then she said she had to go and took off. I begged her to stay and tell me what was wrong, but she said she couldn't talk right now and left."

"I found a bathroom off the beaten path. When I was in there, I overheard a guy and a girl. When I came out, I was sure it was Rev."

She freezes and looks at me with her eyes bugged out and her mouth hanging open.

"Oh my God! Please tell me he wasn't screwing some girl!"

"No, they weren't having sex when I overheard them. They were arguing. The weird thing is, there's two of them."

"Two of who?" she asks, giving me a confused look.

"Two Revs, he has a twin brother. They're the most identical twins I've ever seen." Her confusion turns into a look of shock so comical I can't hold in my laugh. Her eyebrows are raised to her hairline and her mouth falls open again.

"Anisa didn't tell me he's a twin. She just asked me if I think he's hot, and do I think they make a cute couple? Would I fuck him if I wasn't with you? That sort of thing, I told her the truth, a big fat no, and he's not my type. She seemed to act more like herself after that, but something was off. I'm hoping to have a few minutes alone with her tomorrow. Did we park this far when we got here?"

"Yeah. The car hasn't moved. It's only been like 50 yards. We might need to get you in shape so you can make it to the car in the future," I chuckle at her.

"I'm just worn out, and these stupid heels aren't helping. It was so hard to hear with the music. I swear my whole body was tense the entire time we were in there and now my ears are ringing."

"I can't argue that, it was rough. Maybe we're too old for that type of party now?" I know I'm pushing it and I stay alert for a swat.

She surprises me, "I think you're right. Not that we're old or anything. I think we may just be too mature and sophisticated for a party this loud. With so many drinks and drunks, it's even more like a sophomore frat party. I think we might be past those."

As if to emphasize her point a loud group of young men, who look like athletes, dare each other on the lawn next us. They end up tackling one another until they're in a pile of wrestling grunts and verbal assaults. She laughs at their stupidity. Two of them are shirtless, the rest are getting their shirts dirty rolling on the ground. We speed up to get out of their way.

Once the car's in sight, I click the key fob and the doors unlock and the interior lights come on. Something's not right, I can't tell what it is from this angle.

"Oh! Micah there's something on your car. Did someone vandalize...it?" Her voice cuts off abruptly. I scan the area; I don't detect any threats. I pull my firearm from its holster to protect Peyton, in case there's something I can't see.

She's oblivious and visibly upset. Her eyes are filled to the rim. Her shoulders are pulled up near her ears. As we get to the front of my dark SUV, I can see there's something on the windshield. There's something on the hood as well. A rancid scent reaches my nose. I take her with me as I circle the vehicle and check it over. The rest of it appears untouched; I evaluate the situation. I'll be able to see through the windshield, though we only have to go a few miles down the beach to reach Peyton's. I make a decision and open the rear passenger door. I double check the interior with the light on, it's clear. I holster my firearm and usher her into the seat. Her lower lip trembles as the tears overflow from her eyes.

"Why does this keep happening? I'm so tired of this. I want to fight back, but I don't know who to fight. I'm sorry they messed with your car."

I lift her chin with my fingers and look into her sad eyes. "Babe, this is not your fault. My car is just a material thing, I don't give a fuck what happens to it, as long as you're safe. I'm going to lock your door and double check that it's sound to drive. We'll go back to your house and then I'll deal with the...situation. I'm not going anywhere, but I'm going to check the tires, the undercarriage, and just make sure we're good to go. If you need me but don't see me, just yell. I'll hear you because I'll be right outside. Okay?"

She sniffles and puts on a brave face as she nods, "Okay. I'm okay. Do what you need to do. Micah?"

"Yeah?"

"Thank you."

"For what?" I tilt my head and examine her watery eyes and shaking hands. I place my palm against her cheek attempting to offer comfort.

"Just for being you, for taking care of me, keeping me safe. I love you so much." A real smile breaks through her tears. I'm relieved, she's still with me and she'll be all right. She's so strong, I'm happy to see she's not letting this push her over the edge.

"Can't help being me, or loving you. I'll do whatever it takes to keep you safe... never doubt it."

"Never. Please don't think I'm crazy, but I feel like we're meant to be together. Like fate had a hand in our paths crossing. Nova once told me that she saw the love of my life, and he's something special. That he'll love me fiercely, protect me with his life, keep me warm with extraordinary passion, and make me laugh when I need it the most. I hope you don't think I'm forcing the title on you, but you're him." She gives me the sweetest smile. I can see her emotions and she's secure in her love for me. I know how much I love her, she's my first thought when I wake, her safety and well-being are paramount, always.

I want her safe, happy, fed, and in my arms, forever. I can feel that my heart is hanging wide open for her to see inside. She gasps and then kisses me, flinging her arms around my neck. I kiss her back, a niggle at the base of my neck makes me end our kiss and look around.

"I love you. Please stay in the car while I check it. If you need me, yell. Okay?"

"Okay." She's smiling now and seems alert and capable. I lock her in the back seat and circle the vehicle again. I scan the ground looking for anything that will give me a clue. There's nothing obvious near the SUV. There're a lot of cars parked in this area, and we're lucky we can get out. I study the surrounding cars and woods. I don't see anything unusual. I still have that feeling of being watched, and it causes a shiver to trace my spine.

I focus on the SUV and check the tires carefully. I shove myself under the engine and use my phone to light up the mechanisms in the drive train, axles, brakes, and the oil pan. I look over everything that's visible. There's plenty of dirt and none of it's disturbed. I take one more look at the hood and decide to take a few photos. I get up close and further away. I snap all sides and the surroundings. When I'm finished, I open the driver's door and climb inside.

"Everything look drivable?"

"Yeah, it looks good. Whatever is on the front seems to be the only thing they did. I'll have us back to your cottage in no time. You'll need to get out through that door so you may as well stay put. Cool?"

"Yep! I'm cool," she giggles softly.

Peyton

"I'm trying as hard as I can not to look at whatever that is on the windshield and hood. Can you see, okay?"

Micah chuckles his deep manly laugh. "I can see well enough to make it to your place. I wouldn't want to go further than these neighborhood roads though. You seem like you're doing better, but are you?" He glances at me in the mirror, I smile trying to portray the reassurance I'm feeling.

"Yeah. I think I'm a bit hormonal. You're lucky I'm pretty low maintenance on that front. Maybe half a day of hormone nonsense and like three days of shark week." I give him a grin.

"Yeah, you are pretty easy going with all that. Melanie used to spend a few days in bed every month. I don't remember my birth mother or my sister ever talking about any of it. Guess I was too young. Poor Melanie, she suffers with endometriosis. She's debating surgery," he elaborates.

"I love how you think of Melanie as your mom. Paige too for that matter. I think it's really sweet how much you love and respect them."

He shrugs, "It's not like anyone else ever did the job. Melanie's an amazing mom and will be the best grandmother. Paige is, well she's Paige. Smart, strong, protective, and loyal. I couldn't ask for a better-chosen family." He smiles at me in the rearview.

"I know. Paige and Rhett are the best. I'm not as close with anyone else at Savage, but I hope to get there eventually."

"You will. They're a welcoming bunch. Plus, since you're Rhett's baby sister, I think you'll get special treatment," he tells me as he maneuvers the car under the house.

There's a bunch of lights on in and outside at Orlando's. I can see him talking to someone. Probably Ax, but his back is to me so I can't say for sure. There're a few guys sitting on the ground around two motorcycles. Looks like they're working on them, which explains all the lights. Orlando notices us and he starts walking towards my place.

"Stay in the car for a minute, okay?" Micah requests.

"Okay. Is something wrong? I mean, something else?"

"No. I just want to check the house real quick and confirm it's safe and clear." He pauses, looks me over, and continues, "Thanks for never giving me a hard time about being careful. Paige was a huge pain in the ass when she was in danger. You're something special."

Warmth swirls in my chest, I squeeze forward between the seat and the door. I'm able to press just enough of my face into the tight gap so he can kiss me. He gives me a big smooch and signals he'll be right back.

As Micah slams the door, Orlando walks over, his eyes are glued to the front of the dark SUV. After he investigates the hood and front window, he looks at me. His head is tilted, sympathy marks his face. I give him a goofy double thumbs-up and giggle at my ridiculously weird behavior. He smiles through the glass next to me. As soon as he turns back toward Micah the grin turns wooden and falls away. Concern fills in the vacancy.

Micah has the same look emblazoned on his handsome countenance. I squint, I can't see what they're doing nor hear what they have to say about this latest situation. A very short time later the passenger door opposite me and pulls open.

"Come on, it's safe upstairs. Let's move you up there, inside. Okay, Eagle?" Micah asks.

I slide across the seat and climb out the door he holds open for me. I accepted his offer of a hand. I clasp his palm to mine and I don't let go once I complete my exit. We make our way up the stairs, I let him lead the way. The front door opens without the key and the alarm isn't screaming for a code.

"I checked everything; nothing is disturbed. The cats didn't even flinch. If you notice anything out of place let me know. I'm going to wait downstairs with Orlando and Ax. I have my phone, so just yell down or call me if you need me. It shouldn't be too long. Do you need anything before I go?"

"Nope. I'm going to take a shower after I play with the cats for a minute. Feel free to join me if I'm not out when you're done," I give him my best attempt at a seductive expression. He places a gentle kiss on my mouth and goes out the door. Well, that was a fail, but I get it.

Felony rubs on me, and I scratch her while I replay our night. I did have fun; it was great dancing with Micah and laughing with Jake. Thinking about the party I have an idea. I noticed security cameras all over the McMansion, maybe...

Me: Hey. Are you busy?

Anisa: Nah, what's up?

Me: Something happened before we left to the car. Will you get the security footage for me? Please?

Anisa: Shit! Are you okay?

Me: totes, just something weird was on the car, like vandalism, I guess? Will you please email whatever you're able to get?

Anisa: yeah. Of course. I have to ask Rev. I'll go ask now and send asap. K?

Me: Thanks, Anisa! See you tomorrow.

Anisa: can't wait Bee-atch

*Me: *bee emoji**

Me: Did you ever notice we sound like cool high schoolers in text?

Anisa: Cool? No. High school girls? Hellz yeah!

Me: Buh-bye, B!

*Anisa: *bee emoji**

I sit on the sofa between Beta and Felony. After I put my phone away, I've got two hands for scratches. Qwerty watches from the cat tree. She thinks I can't tell her eyes follow my every move.

"I'm on to you, Miss Qwerty. I see you acting all uninterested over there. I can see your cute little eyeballs moving young lady. I won't out you, but be less obvious, okay?"

Qwerty responds, *Meow!* I laugh and shake my head. That was a funny coincidence. I swear sometimes they're so convincing, like they understand everything we say when they do stuff like that.

"But if you understood everything I said, and answered appropriately, we would be making millions on YouTube, right?"

Meh! She makes a short little sound and I crack up. She's too funny. I leave the other two staring after me and give Qwerty a good scratch, then a hug.

Addressing all three I announce, "I'm going to take a shower. You kids be good, okay?" I chuckle my way down the hall.

Dressed in fresh clothes and with my hair still damp, I can see Micah in the circle of light surrounding his poor SUV. It's parked close to the bottom of the stairs, and not where I last saw it.

Someone in hooded white coveralls and a mask with gloves is examining whatever was left on the hood. Orlando and Ax stand close by watching with Micah. The lab technician, I'm assuming, is using small metal instruments to poke at whatever it is, gross.

I still can't tell what it might be from up here. I want to get a little closer and hear what's happening. When I circle around behind the guys, Ax notices me first. Orlando is mid-story; he's animated using his hands to illustrate his tale. As I try to focus on the conversation my phone vibrates in my jeans pocket. I drag it out and check the screen.

Anisa: just emailed you the security footage. They wanna know if they need to talk to the cops or anything?

Me: no. We left so that's on us. Where it happened doesn't matter now.

*Anisa: that's what I said *eye roll emoji* but they didn't believe me, thanks! Maybe they'll listen to you.*

Me: thank you! I'll fill you in tomorrow, see you at 9am!

*Anisa: yeah, yeah *bee emoji**

*Me: *angel face emoji**

When there's a pause in Orlando's story, I clear my throat. They all look at me and I grin awkwardly.

"Hi guys. Sorry to interrupt, Anisa just sent me the security video from the party. Do you want me to forward it to you?" I look at Micah, holding out my phone.

"Yeah, perfect. Thanks, Eagle," he wraps his arm around me, pulls me in close, and kisses the top of my head. I love it when he does that.

I forward it, then put my phone away. I can feel Micah's phone vibrate on my hip. I lean into him. Still trying not to look at what the lab tech is doing, I restart the conversation.

"What were you guys talking about before I interrupted?"

Ax speaks up, "Orlando was telling Micah about the time he hit a deer. Roadkill always makes him pull out that story. I've heard it a hundred times," he glares at Orlando. Who looks appalled by Ax's review of his story. His brows are lifted high, and his mouth hangs ajar. Orlando turns to me and smiles like a member of Slytherin House.

"Ax is just jealous because he doesn't have any interesting stories to tell. Right, Sebastian?" Orlando says, confusing me.

"Who's Sebastian?" I ask, completely lost.

"You know him as Ax, that's his road name. Sebastian is his birth label. He hates it when anyone calls him by his fancy name, so you can call him that, anytime you want to annoy him," he chuckles at Ax.

"So uncalled for, dude." Ax stares daggers back.

"Okay, Micah. I'm ready to bag this up. Will you please help me get it in the bag? There're gloves in that open case. Hi Peyton, not sure if you remember me from before," says Micah's lab friend, who helped last time.

"Of course, hi Keiko. Thanks for coming out so late. I hope you don't live too far away."

"I live a bit closer to Ocala, but I was out this way. I always carry my equipment, I have an agency car, and I can be available any time. It was no trouble to come over plus, it's my job. I would've had to come out early tomorrow if I couldn't make it now. This way I'll be able to sleep in." She gives me a brilliant smile and a wink. I like her, she seems really funny and smart, but she's a bit of a rebel too.

Micah stretches on gloves with a snap. He lifts open the bag and Keiko lifts the blob into it. Once they have all the pieces sealed inside, they take off their gloves. Keiko continues and removes all of her biohazard gear. She packs everything neatly into a pouch. She includes Micah's gloves and presses the opening closed. She peels off a strip and pushes down on the tape closure.

"I have a weird hypothesis about the thing on your hood. Want to hear it? Or do you want to wait for my report?" Keiko asks.

"Tell me," Micah replies.

"It's roadkill like your friend said. I think it's a fox or a coyote. Not enough fur left to easily identify for sure, it's pretty squished too."

Ax butts in, "That's your big theory?"

"No, if you let me finish, I'll explain my theory. Okay?" she admonishes.

"Okay. Sorry," sufficiently fileted, Ax gestures for Keiko to continue.

"Anyway, there are no discernible teeth marks anywhere on the corpse. Nothing has chewed on it, yet. This tells me it was killed on a fairly busy road. Despite its extremely flattened state now, I'll make my guess for T.O.D. I say it died early today and has been run over all day long. Here's the part you'll enjoy," she looks at Orlando.

His eyebrows lift and he touches his chest while mouthing, *Me?*

Keiko nods again and continues, "Even though there're no teeth marks, I believe I see two spots with claw marks. There're tears and a couple punctures. Otherwise, I see no other place where the creature has been grabbed. You saw when I picked it up, it held together fine.

"I propose a different scenario than you imagine. A person didn't do this. I believe a bird of prey, possibly an Osprey or an owl, picked this carcass up from the road when the traffic finally slowed. While it was flying with such a large meal, it had difficulty and dropped it on your car. Then something stopped it from retrieving its lost meal. It was probably watching nearby when you drove off," she relaxes and waits for our questions.

Micah stares at his hood, then looks at Keiko, "I don't know what to say. After hearing Orlando's deer story, I can't argue against your hypothesis. I think you could be right. Holy shit, Eagle. Talk about a weird coincidence. Maybe your stalker didn't have anything to do with this, how crazy is that?"

"Wild. So, Keiko, how will you figure it out?" I ask.

"My microscope sees all. I'll be able to tell you what type of creature the body was, what put it on the car, and the approximate size of the culprit. Unless it was a human who wore gloves. Then it's much less certain what we'll find."

With all of our heads spinning and the clock well past the witching hour, we bid farewell to Keiko. All three guys follow me up the steps and into my home. Micah passes out beers to all of us.

"Not that I want you to leave before you share the deer story, but don't you have guests at your house?" I ask Orlando.

He responds, "Nah, those guys are fine on their own. They'll go when they're finished with the bikes. You really want to hear the story?"

"Definitely. Go!" I cheer him on.

He chuckles at me, I'm ridiculous, "This was probably eight years ago. I was riding my old Harley. I was on this little ancient, narrow, two-lane road surrounded by woods. I was enjoying nature. The sun had just risen above the horizon. I came around a curve and there was something in the road up ahead. There were shadows interspersed with bright beams of sunshine. It was difficult to see what it was, it just looked black, and it was moving. I slowed as I got closer. I recognized that it was a bird or birds as I approached. You know how birds are, we get close, they fly away. I wasn't trying to hit one or anything, but I wasn't going to stop either.

"When I got right up to them, they started taking off. Apparently, a big one wanted to take his meal to go. He took off when I was almost on top of him. He ascended with a big old deer leg caught in his talons. When he lifted it away, it was still connected in one spot to the rest of the deer. The entire carcass lifted up into the air for just a moment. It was too heavy and the vulture couldn't lift the whole body. He began to fall back to the ground. To avoid the crash to earth, he let go of the leg at the last possible moment.

"I was going around twenty miles per hour. A deer leg hit me in the face of my open helmet. What was left of the abdomen hit my handlebars. Guts and pieces of deer splattered all over me, it knocked me off the bike. I came to rest in a pile of deer entrails. The skeleton and all that clung to it, was twisted up in my bike, which was on its side in the middle of the road."

"Oh my God! What did you do?" I'm stunned, that's a horrific story.

"I crawled to the stream at the side of the road. It was freezing cold, but just like heaven. I was able to wash off the worst of it. I couldn't get rid of the smell, but being free from the pieces of deer was good enough."

"How'd you get home?" I ask, mesmerized by the story.

"Luck was with me, if you don't count the part where the deer exploded on me. A guy came by in a pickup. He and I were able to get my bike into the bed, and I rode in back with it. He took me to a garage and then brought me home to his house for a shower and breakfast. I was traveling through Tennessee at the time. I had a bag with a change of clothes. The garage was able to fix my bike for four-hundred-bucks. The dude let me sleep on his couch. My bike was ready the next day and I was able to head home. It all worked out from there."

"I thought it was a hot blonde who found you with her pickup truck? Isn't that the story you always tell? This is the first I'm hearing about a dude," Ax laughs. Orlando punches him hard in the biceps and Ax chokes a little. I laugh at their antics, then a huge yawn takes over.

Micah notices and calls it a night, between laughs. We walk them out to say goodnight. Micah engages my alarm when we get inside.

"What did you think about his story? Do you think Keiko is right?" I ask him.

"Yeah, I think Keiko is right. I looked at the security video while you heard the deer story. It looks like it just fell from the sky. It could've been thrown by someone, but I think there'd be at least a glimpse of them on the recording."

"Wow. Show me," I request.

"Let's go in the office so I can show you on my laptop," He leads the way.

In no time we're both glued to his screen waiting for the video to load. We watch as people come and go through the front of the property. The angle isn't the best, but since Micah backed into the spot, we can see the hood from the high position. There, one second the car is fine, the next, splat! The dead body appears as if from nowhere and bounces on the SUV.

"Keiko might be right, I didn't see anyone throw it, the carcass looks like it magically appeared," I voice my thoughts.

"It's crazy, isn't it?" I nod as he continues, "I'm going to let Keiko do her work, but for now, I think we should assume it wasn't your stalker. Seems like just a weird, natural, coincidence." He raises his hands and shrugs.

"That's good news then, right?" I'm standing next to his office chair, where he's seated. He reaches out his arm across my butt and grabs onto my hip. I lean into him and put my arm across his shoulders. I want to focus on him, being in here makes me think about Larue. He hasn't given me any updates this week. I know there's nothing new so he's not bringing it up.

I can't stop myself from asking, "Is there any update on my sister's case?"

"No, not really. I made some formal requests about the DNA. As soon as it's approved, they'll run the DNA with the newest technology we have available. Who knows, maybe we'll get a hit and a new lead. Don't be discouraged, and don't get excited either. It's just another step in this glacial speed investigation. I'm sorry." His face falls a little and his eyes look to the floor. I've gotta stop him from getting so sad, he was fine a minute ago.

"Are you going to take a shower?" I ask.

"Yeah, I was going to take a quick one before bed. Why? You already took one, right?" He asks with his head inclined. I smile a bright happy grin. His cheeks lift and his eyes squint a little with the move. Much better, now I've got my trap set. I'm going in for the kill...eww, poor choice of words.

"Yeah. But you know what I haven't done? Never ever?"

His head slants further, "What?" His pupils dilate. His eyes skim my face like a caress. He might be catching on, he's such a good detective.

I trace my fingers up his neck to his ear where I tickle his lobe as I say, "I haven't tried out the amazing tub that's one of the biggest selling points of this place..." He spins his chair to face me, as he places his hands on each of my hips. I have his full attention. I can see the tent growing in his pants. I put one of my hands on him and slide it up his arm, then I brush his jaw with my fingertips on their way to his chest.

"I was wondering if you wanted to test it out with me? Only if you're not busy or anything," I take my hand from his chest, close my fist, bite on the tip of my thumb in a way I hope is sexy and not goofy. I open my eyes wide and flutter my lashes a little, so he knows I'm trying to be flirty.

He turns me toward the door and places his hands on my shoulders as he guides me to the large and luxurious bathroom. When we cross the threshold, he lifts my shirt by the hem and removes it. Then he removes his own. I giggle. He quickly unhooks his pants then he pulls at mine. Mine slip down my legs and hit the floor. He whips his off and steps out of them. We're both standing in our underwear.

"Shouldn't we start filling the tub? Doesn't it take a long time?" What was I just saying about how smart he is? I giggle again as he jolts and rushes to turn on the water. He holds his hand under it until he's happy with the temperature, then he closes the drain. Once he's satisfied, he returns to me and pulls me to him with a hand on my waist. I look up and kiss him. He immediately shoves his tongue into my mouth. While we make out, he divests me of my lingerie. I gracefully step out of my panties when he gets them to my ankles. I repay the favor and yank his underwear down. Using my foot to avoid breaking our kiss, I push them the rest of the way down his legs.

We continue to kiss while the tub fills. I stop when I remember we'll need products to wash ourselves. I dig around under the sink and hand Micah some body wash, a razor, and some conditioner.

When he deems the tub full enough, he calls it, "Let's try this and see if we need to add more water. I'll get in first since I'll displace the most water."

He steps over the edge of the tub and his erect cock juts out proudly; I appreciate the view. He takes a breath and submerges his package. Then he reclines into the rounded corner of the tub. There's still a generous amount of tub space, so I climb in while he works to keep me from tripping on his legs.

The water is scalding, "Yowza! That's some hot water. Can you add a little cold, please?" I wait for a little cold to mix in, then I dip in and sit.

The water raises as I sink, "Whoa, just made it. For future reference, when we're both in here we fill it to this light," he tells me as he points to the circle.

"It has lights?"

"Yeah, see this panel? It has lights, jets, a waterfall, music, Bluetooth, you name it."

"You sound like you sell them. Did you figure all of that out looking at the panel?"

"No. I looked up how to work it the first time I saw it. I was hoping to join you in here one day," he smirks.

"So, you looked it up before we got together?" I ask, a bit surprised.

His cheeks grow pinker than the hot water caused, "Guilty. I told you how long I've wanted you, so it shouldn't be a shock."

"Actually, it's kind of sweet. I wish I moved here sooner," I smile at him.

"Me too. But you're here now, and I'm so happy about it; all is right in my world. You can't even imagine how much you mean to me."

I can't keep from touching him. I reach out my hands as I slide closer to him. My hands hold his cheeks while I look into his beautiful eyes. They look blue green, but he has gold around his pupils. Together the effect is gorgeous, and I kiss him. He pulls me onto his lap. Then he shocks me when he fills his hand with body wash and begins washing my hair. He washes me all over and I return the favor. After I rinse off, he rubs conditioner into my hair.

He kisses me, and our tongues meet, then our kisses become passionate. His hands travel my body squeezing and rubbing as they go. My own trace his hair and neck, and they fondle his shoulders. I feel the strong muscles in his biceps, and I squeeze him. He pulls me onto his hard cock and my arousal allows him to slip inside me. I move my body up and down and around. There's a vibration in my chest as my heart pounds harder. It's a feeling I've never had before during sex, holy shit! I think it's emotions making me feel this way because I'm overwhelmed with love for him in this moment.

As I begin to pant, our kiss breaks and I focus on the pleasure singing in my veins. I sneak a peek at Micah, his eyes are closed, his mouth is open, and he has a tense look of concentration on his face. I close my eyes again and work my body to bring us both as much pleasure as possible. When he moans, I know I'm doing it right.

My orgasm begins to bloom in my core, and I move faster to capture it. Micah starts to thrust with me as I grind down on him. His hard manhood fits me perfectly, stretching me as I writhe. His hands grasp my breasts, he presses them up and pinches my nipples gently.

"Mmmm, yes..." My voice is husky with adrenaline. When I look back at Micah, his eyes are locked on my face. His pupils are blown, his skin flush, and I can see he's reaching his own finale. I hope I look half as sexy as him. His hands hold tight to my hips. He guides me as my rhythm falters the closer nirvana looms.

"Yes! Oh, Micah!" It hits me hard and my body feels like it's being reborn. I'm like the Phoenix bursting into flames.

"Oh fuuuck! Babe!" His orgasm strikes before mine waivers, my own bliss is renewed with his hard, fast raid on my nervous system. Now I'm the Phoenix taking flight, whole and reborn.

We slow as the intensity lessens. I hold him close and move slowly until his manhood leaves me. I must have closed my eyes again because when I open them, Micah is smiling at me.

"What?" I ask.

"I've never made love to anyone before, so I'm not sure that's what just happened. Whatever you want to call it, that was freaking incredible. I mean, sex with you is always amazing, but this time it was like I could feel my love for you as part of the pleasure. Does that make any sense?"

"It makes perfect sense. Believe it or not, I felt the same way. It was like the warm fuzzy feeling I always have in here for you, burst into a supernova right when the fireworks hit down below." I grin at him and realize I just said Nova. There's a pinch in my heart as I recall that she's gone. I miss that crazy old woman. I'm so glad her namesake is around.

He laughs, "I set off fireworks and a supernova? You know I'm going to have to brag about this right?"

"What? To who, my brother?" I smirk at him.

"Eww! No. I was thinking Thomas, and maybe Orlando," his eyes quickly jumped to mine.

"You like him, don't you?" My eyes squint as I scope out his reaction.

"Yeah. I think our first impressions of him were wrong. I'm not sure why, but I get the feeling he's a good guy and he wants to do good guy things. There's been a few times when I think he wanted to confide in me, but he stopped himself. He doesn't trust me enough yet. Not surprising since he grew up in the club and I'm a cop."

I give him a bright smile, "I agree. Our first impressions, mine especially, were wrong. I think he's a good guy, Ax too. Not sure why I think so, but it's more of a feeling, you know?"

"Yeah, they put off good vibes. The water is getting cold... let's get out of here." He begins to lift me off of his lap. I fall to the side of his knee and release him from my grip.

He looks at me questioningly, "What are you doing?"

"I just need to rinse off a little," I raise my brows.

"Oh. Right. Okay," He stands, steps out, and wraps a towel around himself.

I quickly clean up and pull the plug. He holds a towel out for me. I take it and wrap myself up like a burrito. I place a kiss on his cheek and go to my room to get ready for bed. He follows and so do Qwerty and Beta. Felony is already lounging in the middle of the bed. She's gotten spoiled in just a couple weeks. I shake my head at my pet parenting, for letting that happen.

"Ohhhh," I yawn, "I'm so tired," I fall onto the bed illustrating my statement.

"Me too." He lands next to me.

Micah

“Stop it!” A sleepy voice says from next to me. I stretch and hear it again. Someone’s knocking on the door. I reach for my phone, shit, it’s not there. I look down and I’m barely wearing a towel, nothing else. I remember, we had a long night, but it ended nicely. We were worn out, I guess we passed out when we hit the bed. I get up on my side of the bed and fix my towel as I round the end. The knock sounds again as I exit the room.

I get to the door and raise my voice, “Just a minute.”

“Okay,” A female voice replies. I get back to Peyton’s room and find her getting dressed. She notices me and gives me a sleepy grin.

“I’m sorry. I passed out without setting an alarm. I don’t even know where my phone is right now. Did you let them in?”

“Nope. I think it’s just Anisa so far. I didn’t check but I only saw one shadow through the door. I needed to get up anyway, I’ve got some work to do after last night.”

Three sets of eyes watch me as I drop my towel and pull on some clothes. They follow me down the hall and into the kitchen. I start the coffee and once I feed them, they lose interest in me. I open the door, let Anisa in, and direct her to the living room.

"Peyton will just be a minute," I say as I point at the sofa.

"Thanks." Anisa is subdued as she sips from her large designer travel cup. I make my way back to the kitchen. Peyton comes into the doorway, and she looks more like herself. Her hair is neatly styled, some color is on her lips, and she has a spark in her eye.

"You're the best! Thank you." She fills a coffee cup and heads to the door, another knock beckoning her. I go down the hall to the bathroom.

When I come back out to the living room, everyone's arrived. Anisa, Jake, and Roger all have coffee in some form or other, and they have their eyes pasted on their computers already deep in the legal trenches. Not wanting to interrupt or procrastinate any longer I pour myself a cup and doctor it with sugar and cinnamon. I make myself comfortable in the office, retrieve my bag of Red Vines from the drawer, then start up my own computer and get lost in the FBI.

A few hours later I'm hungry and need more coffee, so I lock my laptop and emerge from my cocoon. When I walk into the living room, Jake notices me and says hello. Everyone looks up and then says hello. Peyton rubs her stomach.

"I'm starving, do you want to break for lunch?" She asks her study buddies. They all nod and start closing up their books and laptops. My ears perk up at the mention of lunch.

"You want to go back to Tres Burritos?" asks Roger.

"Mmm, yes! That place is so good," Anisa responds.

Peyton looks at me, "You hungry?"

"I thought you'd never ask. I'd love to join you," I check my pockets and remember my phone is on the charger in the bedroom.

After we're gathered and have everything we need, we all pile into Jake's SUV. It's pretty big and we all fit comfortably. I need to get my vehicle washed before I can take anyone out in it.

I haven't been to Tres Burritos before. Peyton told me all about it and being friends with the waitress there. Peyton seems to meet people easily, and it's strange she doesn't have more close friends. I guess the way her childhood went, it didn't really lend itself to long term friendship. Mine wasn't any better, probably worse. Maybe that's part of why we connect so well.

When we enter the establishment, I'm hit in the face with the most delicious smells, and my stomach grumbles. Peyton smiles at a smallish woman with dark hair and eyes. She's pretty, but looks a bit run down. She's a little older than us and Peyton did tell me she has two little boys. That's a lot of work on top of a family restaurant. She rushes over and seats us at a large table in a sparsely occupied corner. She says hello to the members of our party she's seen previously.

Before I sit, Peyton introduces me, "Micah, this is Aishwaria, she's the waitress-slash-owner I told you about. Her husband is the chef. Aishwaria, this is my boyfriend, Micah." I offer her a smile and my hand. She shakes it and looks me over. She smiles at Peyton; I must have passed inspection.

"It's a pleasure to meet you; your girlfriend is so kind. Her friends are also nice. My husband will be excited to meet all of you. I told him about Peyton last time," her voice has a musical British lilt, but doesn't bother me at all.

"The pleasure is mine. I've heard everything about you as well. We'd very much like to meet your husband," I smile, not sure what else to say.

Aishwaria hands us menus and waits until we decide. Once she collects our order and the menus, she rushes off to submit our choices. She returns a few moments later with everyone's beverage orders.

In a whisper to Peyton I say, "She's sharp, got all of our drinks right and delivered to the right person. She's nice too, I see why you like her." Peyton smiles at me.

"Okay, your order is in, you have your drinks, and now we can talk more. No-one is allowed to be hungry here," She smiles at me.

"Thank you. I can't wait to try the food. I've heard such good things," I tell her.

"Thank you. Peyton, I was hoping you would stop by, as my husband's family is having a problem with immigration. They need some paperwork and proof of work, but their boss won't give them the proof they need. His uncle and his cousin both work at the same place. He pays them cash and doesn't file any of the taxes, so he refuses to give proof they're employed. If they don't get everything turned in by December 31st, they'll be deported. I'm trying to help, but we really need a lawyer."

"You're in luck since we're all law students, except for Micah. We can't practice law before we're licensed. Well, only under special circumstances. Anyway, we can't directly help. However, since we're students, we know a lot of brilliant attorneys. They're our professors, mostly. Jake's family business is law, and he plans to be an immigration lawyer. Let's exchange contact information and we can talk to your relatives and get them in contact with the right people to help them, okay?" Peyton says and looks at everyone, they're all nodding.

Aishwaria is smiling and the defeat that was riding her hard just moments ago has lifted considerably. For some reason I feel good about that, even though I did absolutely nothing to help. I'm very proud to call Peyton my girlfriend. She's a wonderfully considerate person who always wants to help others.

When Aishwaria brings our food, I don't know where to start. I ordered a variety of a-la-carte items because they all look so appealing. As we make our way through the huge amount of food my stomach is finally happy.

After Aishwaria clears away most of the empty dishes, she returns with a dark-haired man. He's only a few inches taller than her and they make a nice-looking couple. She showed us photos of her boys. After seeing her husband, I notice they look just like him. He has two mini-me's for son. I want a mini-me someday.

"Everyone, this is my husband, Angel Sanchez, the chef." She beams at us.

He reaches his hand out to shake mine first. "Hi, Micah Castleman. This is Peyton Baker, my girlfriend." I gesture toward Peyton next to me. He moves around the table meeting each member of our group. Turns out Roger speaks some Spanish and he uses it to greet Angel.

Anisa abruptly stands up. "It was nice meeting you, but I need to go. Thanks for everything today, Peyton. I think I'll pass the quiz tomorrow because of you." She gathers her things.

"Call me later, okay? Are you walking to the dorm?" Peyton responds off kilter, by Anisa's sudden need to depart.

"Yeah, it's just around the corner. I'll call you later. Thanks guys, it was fun!" Anisa announces as she runs off. Apparently, she took an Uber to Peyton's this morning. I wonder why.

We chatted a few more minutes about how good the food was and how much we enjoyed it. Angel tells us more about his relatives, including his talented uncle who paints the sugar skulls. There're a lot of them around. Peyton and Aishwaria exchange info before we leave. After our goodbyes with the Sanchez family, we climb back into Jake's SUV. Both guys want to continue studying, and Peyton is amenable to their suggestion.

My thoughts wander to the list of things I need to accomplish. I decided my priority will be washing my vehicle. I should've taken care of it this morning. While I mentally continue to plan my schedule, Peyton takes my hand. It makes me smile. I'm about to say something to her when my phone vibrates in my pants. I scoot down in my seat so I can retrieve it from my pocket.

"Oh shit. What the...?" I exclaim after reading the preview on my screen. I opened my email and read the first paragraph. Peyton watches me closely, concern etched on her face. She raises her brows at me.

"I'll tell you when we get back," I whisper, using my eyes to indicate the ears in the front seat. She nods and chews on her bottom lip.

When we pull up at Peyton's I hop out and practically run up the stairs. I go straight to the office and get my computer online. My foot taps with impatience. Peyton enters the office and stands with her arms across her chest and her lip still being gnawed upon.

"You can come look at this. I can't believe it."

She hesitates before joining me behind the desk. She looks me over, then her eyes turn to my screen.

She inhales a ragged breath as she reads:
DNA Match located. Sample #2016-06-2498-777tw-34p3q-1
99.87643...% positive match *with donor*
#93-4581-eDCx-099467-23tS-j4-06 ID: RAMSEY, MARK DAVI-SON
DOB: 03/13/1993
*DOD: 06/24/2017*approximate*
REPORTS ATTACHED-
DNA Verification
DNA Scores
DNA Identifiers
Coroner Report
Agency Reports-Multiple FDLE
COD: Gun Shot, Homicide
-End Notice
"What does it mean? Who's Mark Ramsey?" she asks.

I scroll into the Agency Reports, I find a mugshot and a list of aliases for Mark Ramsey. I highlight them for Peyton.

"Samo? Seriously? Wait, he's dead?"

"According to this he died not that long after Larue. It says he's a match to the DNA found on her body. I'll read the details when you're not with me. I'm sure there won't be anything you'll want to see. It also says it appears to be a *gang style execution that* killed him. Two bullet holes in the back of his head."

"Holy crap! I need to call Rhett," she says as her phone comes out.

She dials and puts it on speaker, "Hi, Pey. What's up?" His voice is filled with laughter, until Peyton replies.

"Rhett. I...I don't even know what to say."

His voice immediately switches to concern, "What's wrong? Did something else happen with your stalker? Are you okay?"

"You're on speaker, and Micah's with me. Nothing with my stalker. Micah got a report from his inquiries into Larue. I'll let him explain, but he found a DNA match. We know who killed her. Shit, Rhett, I can't believe it," Tears enter her eyes. I take over and pass her a tissue from the box on the desk, my touch lingers on her hand in support.

"Hey Rhett. I'm sending you what I have. The summary is Samo, or Saint/Monk killed Larue. He was executed shortly after her body was found. Two to the back of his head," I relay.

"Got it. I'll look it over. I don't know what to say either, I'm stunned. Why don't you guys come over for dinner and we'll go over it." He taps on his phone for a few minutes then says, "Good, I see you copied everyone. I'll extend an invite to them as well. Y'all can come over anytime, okay? Peyton, you okay with that?" He asks.

She sniffles, "Yeah, I have some study buddies here. Once we get them squared away, we'll head over. I love you, Rhett."

"Love you too, Pey. Thanks, Micah. See you in a bit." He disconnects. I pull Peyton into my lap and hold her. She cries softly against my chest. I rub her back and do my best to comfort her. My heart hurts for her. It especially sucks knowing we won't be able to bring her sister's killer to justice. We also won't be able to question him to find out what happened to Larue, or why. I sigh, frustrated for my girl.

When we pull up at Rhett and Paige's place the door flies open, and Rhett comes barreling towards us. He opens Peyton's door, and she jumps into his embrace. They hug and mumble to each other. I go inside, not wanting to disrupt their family moment.

"Mike-yeah!!" A little body slams into my legs, and I catch her before she can bounce off. I lift her up and she squeals in delight.

"Hello, Nova! How are you doing, little munchkin?"

"High, Mike-yeah, up-up!" I comply with the command from her majesty. I lift her up to touch the ceiling and she laughs. That sound just soothes the soul.

"Micah! How are you?" Paige asks with her eyes scrutinizing my face.

"I'm good. Peyton and Rhett are outside. I think they needed a moment. I'm shocked we got a match and that he's dead. I'm not surprised he did it though. I just wish he was alive to answer some questions."

"Up! Up!" The cutest kid I know orders.

"It's crazy to find him after all this time. Okay, Nova, leave Micah alone. He's not here to be bossed around by you, young lady. Down please, ma'am." she puts her hands out to take Nova from me. I set her down on the ground instead. Paige is starting to show, and she doesn't need to carry around a heavy toddler any more than necessary. She gives me an appreciative smile. I return it with understanding.

"How are you feeling?" I ask.

"I'm much better. The morning sickness has been gone for a few weeks, so I think it's really over. With this one," she points at Nova, "it lasted the whole pregnancy. I'm afraid to believe I'm in the clear. He's kicking up a storm too," she laughs.

"What?" I look around for something funny.

"Sorry, I just remembered that our princess told me to stop eating because my tummy is too full. It was so cute. Her eyes got really big, and she tilted her head, like she was lecturing a naughty child. She's so funny sometimes. The things she says, oh man, I'm just thankful she hasn't copied Rhett's colorful vocabulary yet." I chuckle imagining little Nova Larue, with a potty-mouth and Rhett's touch of a southern drawl. She takes my hand and pulls me to the toy box.

"Blocks, Mike-yeah!" She doesn't wait for me; she lifts the box of Legos and dumps them out in a huge pile.

"Okay, what are we building?" I ask my boss.

"Cin-ellwa! Cin-ellwa!" She jumps up and down with excitement. I look at Paige with my brows lifted in confusion.

"She wants Cinderella's Castle."

"Umm, I don't think I have that kind of engineering ability. How about a tower?" I implore my commander and sit on the floor next to the pile of blocks.

"Cin-ellwa. Mike-yeah make Cin-ellwa!" She must have noticed my distress. She places her tiny, and slightly sticky, hand on my cheek. She puts her nose right up to mine and looks into my eyes.

"You can try, Mike-yeah," she tells me with her eyes wide and her head tilted. Oh my God! Paige wasn't kidding, she's too adorable!

I smile, "Okay, Boss Lady, you got it. One Cinderella Castle coming up." She nods at me, and I share a snicker with Paige.

"Told you. I think she learned it to get anything she wants from Rhett. I mean, how can you say no to that?" She gestures toward Nova with her hand flat, palm up. She looks like a TV spokes model demonstrating her wares. I shake my head, chuckle, and get busy snapping together a castle before I get in trouble with the boss.

"You want a beer, Micah?" Rhett asks as he and a red-eyed Peyton enter the room. She gives me a little smile. Her cheeks are pink and her hair a little disheveled. I return her grin and send soothing thoughts her way.

"Sounds good," I answered.

"Are you all right, sweetie?" Paige asks.

"I'm okay. It's just a shock after all this time. I'm disappointed none of my questions will be answered. How does that work? Will you close the case now?" Peyton directs her question at me.

"No. It won't be closed because we don't know for certain that he did it. He could've had accomplices, he could've been the one who dumped her body, but not the one who did it. It'll remain open, with a notation that the primary suspect is deceased," I try to censor my answer for little ears.

"Here you go," Rhett hands me a beer, Peyton a cup, and then sits with his own beer. Paige already had a cup of something, probably lemonade. It's been the theme for both pregnancies.

"Thanks, man. You doing, okay?" I question Rhett.

"Yeah. Me and Pey'll be fine. It's just a shock. I haven't looked at any of the reports or information in a long time, reading through it again was a little rough."

The front door opens and in walks the rest of our motley crew. Thomas is in jeans and a t-shirt, Ace is in khakis and a button shirt, Samson walks in behind them. I didn't realize Rhett meant Samson too. He aims right for me and shakes my hand as everyone greets everyone else.

"Don't get up, that looks like important work. Don't want you getting into trouble with the Queen," He gives me a big cheesy grin.

"Yeah, we don't want that. It's good to see you, I feel like it's been forever. How's everything going with Melissa?" I ask him. I've been so wrapped up in Peyton and her stalker I haven't kept in touch with them like I usually do. A wave of guilt passes through my chest and I divert my eyes from his sharp sight. He pats my shoulder and smiles at me.

"She's good, son. I have strict instructions to invite you and Peyton for dinner as soon as your schedules will allow. What do you think, Peyton?"

"Oh. Um, I think we can swing something next weekend, if that's alright? We don't have any plans Friday night." She looks to me for confirmation. I nod in agreement. She smiles at Samson.

"Great, I'll send you both a calendar invite. How're you doing with this news?" He directs that question to Rhett. I tune out since I've heard it already.

Thomas plops down next to me and starts snapping blocks together, "What're we building?"

"Cinderella Castle." I inspect my work and find it severely lacking. Nova has moved over to her mother, and is holding Paige's leg, watching everyone. She's not shy, she knows all these guys, but it's overwhelming when so many adults show up at once. I've noticed she heads for her parents when a lot of people come around at the same time. I've never been around a little kid before, so it's interesting watching how she reacts to things.

Ace leaves the room and comes back with a beer for each of the new arrivals. He takes a seat next to Peyton and for a brief second, my hackles rise in jealousy. I talk myself down and it passes.

We spent a pleasant afternoon and evening laughing and telling stories. Eventually the five guys break off and go out back to BBQ some burgers and dogs. We discuss the details of the case and what'll happen next. I want to locate Zombie and find out what he knows, I'm not finished with Larue's case. I won't be satisfied until I've followed every lead and questioned every witness and suspect myself.

"Is Peyton recovered from your crazy night?" Samson asks. My eyes shoot to Rhett. I didn't tell him about the dead animal on my SUV. He looks at me with a tense frown.

"What crazy night?" Ace and Thomas stop their ridiculous debate about which is better, charcoal or gas for barbecuing. They watch me patiently.

"She's fine. Thankfully it was nothing so she got over it quickly. Did Keiko tell you about it?" I ask Samson.

"No, I read your report. I get a copy of every report. I don't read them all, but when it is from you I at least glance at it. When I saw it involved you personally, I read it all."

"Ah. I'll fill in the rest of you," I proceed to explain what happened.

"I've never heard of anything like that," Samson says.

"Like what?" Rhett asks, visibly tense.

"She said she thought an animal had dropped it on my car. Her guess was a bird of prey like an Osprey or an owl. I watched the security footage and the carcass literally looks like it just fell from the sky. Crazy right?"

"That's bizarre. I've never heard of anything like that," Rhett agrees.

"I've seen it before. I was driving through a nature preserve, and some vultures were working on a big animal, deer, I think. One tried to fly off with a big piece and dropped it on my moving car. It hit the roof. Luckily, it rained before I got where I was going so the car was cleaned off. It freaked me out, but I don't think it's that uncommon," Thomas shares.

Ace laughs, "Of course it happened to you. Do you realize every time anyone says they had some crazy thing happen, you pipe up with a story of when it happened to you, too?"

"That's not true!" Thomas defends.

"No, man, it's true. Ace is right, you're the King of weird stories," Rhett teases.

"Fuck you!" We all laugh. I love my family, the crazy bunch of weirdos.

Our dinner is ready, and we carry everything inside and rejoin the girls. Nova's in her pajamas with damp hair, she apparently had her dinner. She kisses and hugs everyone goodnight and Rhett takes her to bed. We all dig in and have a great meal in spite of its simplicity. Good company and good food make for a pleasant evening. After we say goodbye to everyone and reconfirm our dinner plans with Samson, we head to Peyton's.

Peyton

It's been about ten days since we found out who killed Larue. I think I'm finally starting to accept it. It's been like grieving for her all over again. I've been through all of the stages. Today's the first day I feel like maybe I'm accepting what happened and what'll never happen. I sigh.

"What's wrong?" Anisa asks.

"Nothing, just some family stuff. No big deal," I force a smile.

"If you say so. Every time we've talked, you've been weird since the party. You say you're fine, then I say I'm fine too. We aren't really talking or listening."

"Sorry. Just family drama, settling into law school, you know...life. I think I'm better today. How're things with Rev?" She's always quick to talk about her life and her problems or brag about her success. I haven't wanted to share about Larue, it's too painful to rehash. Hopefully she'll take the bait and change the subject.

"We're still good, mostly. I'm not sure what he's looking for in a relationship. He's sooo good in bed. I love sleeping with him. It's the rest of the stuff that's hard. He's rough around the edges, you know?"

"Isn't he in a biker gang? Didn't you expect him to be rough? Isn't that the appeal of a bad boy?" I ask her, it's out of character for me to be so blunt and inconsiderate. Maybe I'm not doing better today, afterall.

"Geez, Peyton, that's not helpful. Yes, he's in a motorcycle *club*, not a gang. His bad boy ways are appealing, I'm just not used to being in a relationship. I usually get what I want and move on. I don't think he's ever been in a relationship either. We're having some differences of opinion, that's all."

"I'm sorry. What type of differences?" I ask, trying to be more under-standing and friendly.

"He ghosts me sometimes. He says it's his responsibilities in the club that keep him busy. But I wonder if he's seeing other women. I tried asking him some questions, wanting details, and he got so pissed he left. We made up later, but I need to figure out how to relax and quit worrying about what he's doing when I'm not there. I don't want to nag him, but I can't stop. Do you nag Micah?"

"I don't think so? I mean we've known each other a long time and I trust him implicitly. I don't question where he goes or who he's with, he tells me if he's allowed, but some of his work is confidential. Maybe you guys just need some time, get to know each other better, and build trust. Has he done anything that makes you suspect he's been with someone else?" I ask her.

"Not exactly, it's more of a feeling. Ugh! I'm probably being ridiculous like he says." She reaches up and runs her fingers through her hair. When she lifts her hand, her sleeve falls up her forearm. There're bruises all around her wrist. Some look like fingerprints, some are bigger.

I gasp and grab her hand, "Anisa, what happened?"

Her formerly open expression collapses in an instant. She tugs her hand away from my grip and pulls her sleeve back down to cover the marks. At the same time her eyes widen and dart back and forth between mine. Her cheeks turn red, she pulls in on herself, her shoulders are bunched up to her ears, and her face is tight. She holds her sleeve over the bruises with her other hand. She folds her hands into her chest; a common self-soothing move.

She forces out a tight chuckle, "Oh, I'm so dumb, I hurt it at the gym. You should always follow the instructions on how to use the equipment, right?"

She starts packing up her things. She still has more than half of her lunch in front of her and she won't meet my eye. As soon as her things are packed, she stands, looking anywhere except at me.

"I just remembered I need to see my advisor. I'll see you tomorrow, okay?" she says as she starts inching away from me.

I touch her arm gently, not wanting to hurt her injuries, "What's going on? Do you need help?"

She fake laughs like I'm being ridiculous and this has come up out of the blue. "Help with what? Don't be silly. I told you I screwed up at the gym. It's fine. I'll see you tomorrow," She shows me a big fake grin.

"I'm not nagging you. I'm genuinely concerned. I've seen the signs before. I have a degree in psychology, remember? I want to work with trafficking survivors. Please, tell me what's going on," I calmly tell her.

"Fuck, Peyton! I told you what happened, and it's not my problem if you don't believe me. You may not nag Micah, but you're sure as shit nagging me, and I don't like it. I have to go," she stomps off leaving me with my mouth hanging open. The rest of my classes are hazy, I can't stop thinking about Anisa and her strange reaction; she was so defensive. I'm worried about her and the situation she seems to be in.

After dinner I'm studying for a quiz, then my text alert sounds. I frown when I see it's Anisa.

"Why the frowny face, Eagle?" Micah asks me.

"Oh, um, it's Anisa. We had a bit of a disagreement today. I'm going to try to make up with her. I'll go out to the living room in case she calls." I'm out the door before he can reply.

Anisa: I'm sorry. I'm hormonal and I may have overreacted to your concern. Forgive me?

Me: of course! I'm sorry too. I shouldn't have assumed anything. Are you okay?

Anisa: I'm okay- mad at myself for getting annoyed with you and lashing out. I know you were just worried. I promise you I'm fine.

Me: OK I won't bring it up again, just know I'm here if you want to talk.

Anisa: Have you seen the weather? Us Katrina babies have to stick together! At least the school is a shelter and my dorm room doesn't require evacuation if this storm comes.

Me: First I'm hearing about it. I'll definitely have to evacuate. Luckily my brother is far enough inland.

Anisa: that's definitely lucky. Are you ready for the Halloween party?
Me: yeah
Anisa: why won't you tell me what you and Micah are going to be?
Me: told you it's a surprise.
Anisa: we're doing my idea of Dracula and Mina from Bram Stoker. Tool is going as Lestat. I love Halloween!
Me: I do too. See you tomorrow
Anisa: okay. □ TTYL

"Hey Radiohead," I call out as I make my way back into the office. "Have you heard about a storm?"

"Yeah. But it's really far away and if it comes here, which they never do, you can stay with me or Rhett. You'll be fine. Felony is welcome at both places, so you have nothing to worry about. The track doesn't even go past Naples yet."

"Okay. I forgot to tell you I got the last piece of our costumes on my way home today," I tell him with a smile.

"Oh yeah? So, we're all set?"

"Yep, I can't wait." I leer at him as I picture him in his costume. He's going to make a seriously attractive pirate. I'm mixing two different Disney movies for our characters. I tried on my costume the other day and I'm hoping he'll have trouble keeping his hands off me. It makes my boobs look amazing, like they're fake perfection.

"Do you want to tell me what happened with Anisa?" he asks, all signs of playing around gone from his face.

"We had an argument. It's just a feeling so please don't say anything. Because of my experience working with domestic violence survivors, I asked about some bruises, and she flipped out."

"I remember. You started calling me almost every day during that time. You needed to vent about the denial those victims experience. Do you think Rev is abusing her?" he asks, concerned.

"I don't know, but I think she's in denial about her relationship with him. It feels like one sided affection when he's around. He never seems to care what her needs might be at any given moment. He also strikes me as a fairly violent person. I don't know much about him or his background, so I could be wrong..." I ponder the circumstances.

"I know some things. I ran a background on him and his brother. Looks like their childhood was pretty messed up, in and out of foster care. But look at my background, it doesn't mean anything now. They do have a few juvie arrests that're sealed. I didn't see any reason to request them. They have a shared GTA, and Tool has three dismissed possession charges, marijuana twice and ecstasy once. The GTA was from when they were 18, and they were still in high school and extended foster care. It was with two other boys, but the keys were left in a running car." He raises his brows waiting for more questions from me.

"None of that sounds violent or particularly concerning. I guess I'm just going to watch everything like a hawk and see what happens." I shrug my shoulders. I'm not thrilled with this option. I can't do anything about it, even if Rev has a record of violence against women, if Anisa won't listen.

"Don't you mean, like an Eagle?" he smirks.

"Why? Oh! Funny. I think I'm ready to hit the hay. Ha. My dad used to say that. Yep, I'm tired. Weird rambling has begun, you've been warned." I lean over him and give him a kiss on the side of his head. I walk to my bedroom with a small furry parade. All three cats follow me. They must be tired too.

Anisa and I hug it out when we meet for breakfast, "I'm sorry."

"I'm sorry," We both say it simultaneously. We laugh and try again.

"No more arguments," I say while she says the same.

"No fighting. My hormones are better today," she says while I speak. We laugh again. We both wrap our arms around each other until our laughter dies off.

"No more saying the same thing as me. You won't believe what happened last night. You can't tell anyone okay? Not even, Micah," she says, her lips pursed, and her eyes squinted. She looks as stern as my elementary school principal.

"Cross my heart. Go for it," I take a huge bite of my breakfast burrito.

"I haven't spent very much time with Tool, even though I'm dating Rev. He's around sometimes and we say a few words, but I barely know him. Last night, I was at Revs and Tool came home. We were all drinking and telling stories. Well, Tool tells this story about him and Rev being with the same girl." She looks at me like she's waiting for something.

"Oh my God! You mean at the same time?"

She nods dripping in smugness, "Exactly. Then Tool asks me what I think about that. I said it's on my bucket list. You know, cuz, holy fuck. Who wouldn't want two gorgeous guys doing everything they like?" She hugs herself then slides her palms down the tops of her thighs, over her jeans.

"You mean...you...both of them?" My eyes must be enormous, they feel like they're about to pop out of my head in shock.

She nods again and her smug smile is bigger than I've ever seen. She leans back in her seat and crosses her arms. I feel like I can't breathe. It helps if you remember to inhale. I take in a bigger than usual breath and the air feels good in my lungs. Geez, how long did I forget to breathe? I enjoy a few more deep breaths then I sigh and settle back waiting to hear more. I completely forgot we're in public too. I take a quick nervous glance at the neighboring tables. Thankfully, nobody seems to be paying attention to our NSFW conversation.

"He said he couldn't screw up my bucket list. Then Rev agreed, and before I knew it, they were roasting me. It was Ah-maze-ing!" She laughs.

"Wait, what? What's that mean? Oh, never mind, I think I got it," I awkwardly gesture like there's a dick in my mouth, then sort of wave at my crotch. I can feel how red my face is getting, it must be glowing.

"It was better than that!" She waves her arm at me and leans in close.

She whispers, "Rev got all excited and was like proud or something that his brother wanted me. He started kissing me and we all started undressing. They both put their hands on me. Then I was going down on Rev and Tool got behind me, and..." Her eyebrows lift comically high and then she bounces them up and down.

I sort of make a choking sound and clear my throat, "Wow, I don't think I could do that. Especially with my boyfriend's brother. I mean won't it be uncomfortable now when you have to see him?" I ask, doing my best to be tactful and avoid another disagreement.

"No. We're closer now. If he wants to do it again, I'd be down, pun intended. It was so hot. When we all came the final time, holy shit, Peyton. You just don't understand how incredible it is to have your mouth and your cooch filled by fine bad boy cock!"

"I don't see it happening and it's not on my bucket list. I only want Micah. I don't think about anyone else. I notice if someone is good looking, but it doesn't go beyond that. If I think about sex, I see Micah." I punctuate my thoughts by lifting my shoulders.

She chuckles at me, "You're such a prude sometimes. If you're happy with your vanilla love life, good for you. I want rocky-road with hot fudge and sprinkles! I want to enjoy my sex life while I'm young and flexible," she ends so seriously I burst into big guffaws. Now everyone at the surrounding tables is eyeing us. I'm glad it's time for class. I cram one last bite into my mouth, chug the last of my latte, and I'm ready to go.

"You ready for class?" she asks.

"Yep, let's hit it." I thank the guy manning the table of food. It seems a perk of attending law school is that all of the law firms and organizations trying to woo us for our futures, make their first move by feeding us. There's always food in the big hall. Since the weather's nice today, they were able to set up buffet tables outside. Under the big oak trees is my favorite eating spot.

When we enter our class, there's a commotion at the bulletin board. We see Jake and squeeze between a few people to join him. Everyone is looking at a paper pinned on the board. A girl with a huge, long red ponytail bursts into tears and runs out of the room. I have second thoughts about looking at the paper hanging there.

"Hey Jake, what's going on?"

"Trial Team."

"I'm going to go sit down. I don't want to know." I turn away from them. Someone grabs my shirt and keeps me from leaving.

"Oh no you don't, you have to find out with us," Anisa taunts. The group of guys who'd been blocking the notice step away. Jake steps up and moves his finger down the names listed. At the second name he looks at me.

"You're in, Baker."

His finger continues, next he looks at Anisa, "You got it."

"Whoop!" Her large hand pumps into the air, then she hugs me. I watch Jake's finger and read along the names. He stops in the 'S' section.

"Roger Stanley, made it, where is he?" Jake takes a quick look around then returns to his meticulous work. He gets a huge smile on his face.

"Yes!" He fists pumps the air, like Anisa did. He turns and looks at me, then Anisa drags us all away from the list so the others can see. Jake is grinning like the Grinch when his heart grows three sizes. Anisa looks like she won the lottery. I must look like a happy idiot too. We hug, and jump up and down. I'm thrilled. My practical side is already working on alterations to my study schedule.

We're going to have to discontinue our weeknight study groups, unless we can still do Wednesdays. We've been studying at home on Wednesdays, but we spoke just yesterday about meeting at the library next week. I know Professor Jameson holds practice Tuesday and Thursday nights. I don't know beyond that. I think they're weekend tournaments; this'll be so interesting. When I sit down, I send a quick text to Micah. If he's at Savage, he can tell Paige and Rhett.

There's a loud bang at the front of the room, everyone looks to the front to see what happened. A tall guy with brown hair stomps over to the professor who doesn't look up.

"I want to speak with you, professor. My father's going to be furious about this, you know that right?" The guy threatens Professor Jameson.

"Mr. Strauss, if you have a grievance, you need to adhere to my office rules and schedule. We don't discuss personal matters during class. Now, please be seated." Mr. Strauss, stomps to his seat grumbling curses under his breath. I almost feel bad for him, seeing his attitude towards our professor keeps it from sticking. What an asshat.

Anisa whispers to me, "He's cute, too bad he's such a dick." She grins with a superior attitude.

"Don't you have a boyfriend?" I ask her, whispering back.

"Yeah, I guess. But I can look, just no touching. I can notice a nice-looking person. I just hope..."

"All right class let's get settled. I'm going to review some cases with you. You can follow along on the live stream. This lecture will remain in the student portal until after midterms next week.

"The first case is Stanwyck vs Kentucky, you'll notice this case went to a jury trial and then worked its way up to the Supreme Court..."

I zone out at that point. Always a risk when there's a live lecture that I can watch later. I look at Jake and he's completely focused on the professor. I still can't believe I saw him giving some guy head. He's not the least bit embarrassed. He said that his *date* gets off on public sex and he doesn't mind it, if he's not the one who's naked. I really like Jake; he's been a good friend. I hope he finds happiness with someone, and if it's the public sex hottie, that's okay. I just want him to be as happy as me. I look at Anisa; she's got on long sleeves again. While she types on her tablet, I see fresh bruises peeking from her cuff on her opposite wrist.

"Huh!" I gasp and her attention snaps to me. I force a smile, her eyes squint and she twists her head to the side. Shrugging I smile bigger, trying to avert her suspicion away from my thoughts. I shake my head at myself, I'm never going to be a good investigator, I'm too obvious. I'm going to have to work on my poker face. Maybe we need to host a card game so I can practice. I work hard to tune back in to Professor Jameson and pay attention to the lecture.

Micah

When I get to Peyton's she's not there yet. I let myself inside and turned off the alarm. Three furry faces watch my every move. Felony is the only one who's impatient. She meows until I put a dish of food down for her. My cats wait quietly for their dinners. Not that it's Peyton's fault, but her cat is a brat, she's very demanding.

I'm not much of a cook beyond microwave snacks. I have no clue if Peyton is planning to cook something, but it's after 5:30, and I decide to order some food. I use my favorite delivery app and order Chinese. I take the opportunity to set up in the office and file the updates I got today on Larue's case. Nothing new or surprising, just more evidence that Samo was her killer.

His murder is without any evidence at all. They found his body near some warehouses and determined it was murder. The bullets were collected along with lots of DNA samples. Nothing matches any known persons. There are no suspects and no witnesses. The only thing I didn't know before is that he's survived by his mother and a younger sister.

His mother identified his body, and he was cremated and buried. The record doesn't mention a father. There are some photos of Southern Suns as his known associates. One of them is the MIA biker, Zombie. I'd like to find him and question him as my next step. I begin typing his known names and monikers into our search portal when a weather alert flashes on the screen.

I click on it and it takes me to the NOAA and National Weather Service forecast. The storm is rounding the western end of Cuba and the track is still too far from us for accuracy. The spaghetti models are showing it turning into the gulf coast of Florida. Right now, the *cone of death and uncertainty,* shows a swath from Tampa to Tallahassee as the possible landfall zone. We don't have any watches or warnings on mainland Florida yet, and only The Keys have a watch right now. They'll have some wind and storm surge no matter what path the storm takes. It's a slow-moving storm which can be bad. It helps them strengthen and dump more rain wherever they hit.

I hear the front door close and I pause what I'm doing to greet Peyton and keep her from cooking. I didn't realize Beta and Qwerty joined me in the office, but there's no sign of Felony.

"Okay, okay! I can hear you cutie. You don't need to be so loud. I know Micah didn't neglect you and not feed your poor starving belly." Peyton is scratching Felony's ears while she presses her face into Peyton's hand as she makes a growling meowing sound. When I enter the room with my cats following, she immediately begins to purr. I have no clue what all that was about.

"Hi Eagle, how was your day?"

"Did you get my text?" she asks me.

"Text? No." I pull out my phone and check it for texts from my girl, but there's nothing. I held it up so she could see I didn't get her text.

"Crap! Let me see…" She retrieves her phone from a pocket and begins scrolling on it.

"Shoot!" My text alert sounds, I open it, then I grab her and hug her hard.

"Congratulations! Eagle, that's fantastic news! I'm so proud of you, I knew you'd get on the team."

"I'm so excited. They're emailing our schedule this weekend. I think our first competition is in two weeks. We're going to have practice in class and after class. I'll be coming home late on Tuesday and Thursday now. Today we just had a quick orientation and finalized the practices. Our first tournament will be against Tampa College of Law." She smiles so brightly. I think this is the happiest I've seen her lately, since we found out about Larue.

"I ordered some Chinese. I didn't know what you planned and it was late, I hope that's okay."

"It's great. Thanks so much, it's a huge help, you're the best. I love you." She hugs me and plants a smooch on my lips. I kiss her and hold her, but she can't be still.

"I'm going to change, too. I'm hot for some reason. You can follow me, if you're not busy." She looks me over, and I shrug to indicate my availability. I follow her.

I get distracted when she lifts her button top over her head. Her black lace bra captures all my attention. When she steps out of her slacks I gulp. Her G-string panties are also black lace and teeny-tiny. I'm not sure who to thank for inventing mainstream G-string undergarments. Dude, whoever you are, thanks-a-million! She pays no attention as I ogle her soft, tan, body.

She rifles through her drawer and pulls out shorts and a t-shirt while she continues, "Professor Jameson, who runs the team, posted the list on his bulletin board. Jake was checking to see which of us made the team. Only twelve people made it, and four alternates. This one guy, he got so pissed he actually threatened our professor. My friends all made it, and our whole study group is on the team. Oh." She looks at the ground and her finger rubs her chin.

"What's wrong? Why do you look worried now?" I question. She pulls her shirt over her head. Her shorts were pulled into place while she told me about her class, somehow, I still heard what she said.

"Roger wasn't in class today. I thought he lived with Jake, but Jake seemed surprised Roger wasn't there. He's never missed a class before."

"Maybe he's sick. Why don't you call him and see if he needs anything?" I ask as the doorbell chimes.

"Yeah. Let's eat before the food gets cold. I'll text him." All three cats watch us as we walk around gathering everything we need on the table. When I'm fork deep in my orange chicken, her text alert finally sounds.

"Is that Roger?"

"No, it's Jake. He says he's getting worried. He doesn't think Roger came home last night. His car was gone when Jake left this morning." Her fingers tremble as she types a reply. She eats a few more bites of her lo mien, her movements are mechanical and forced. Her chopsticks stop midair when her text alert chimes again. She drops her utensils into the white box and lifts her phone.

She drags in a sharp breath, "Oh no. Shit. Jake called the police. They just called him back. Roger's car was found parked at Scallop Park, but no sign of Roger. No surveillance. Some fishermen said his car was there when they arrived before dawn this morning." She sniffles.

"What can I do to help?" I'm asking how involved she wants me to get. Boyfriend of distraught friend involved, or FBI Agent involved. The tears crest and fall from her lids when she looks at me, her bottom lip quivers. I move in to hug her, pulling her into my lap. She gratefully entwines her arms around my neck and I rub her back hoping to comfort her. She sniffles a few more times and I hand her a napkin.

Ahem. "Sorry. It sounds like something must have happened to him." She startles when her text tone chirps again. She looks at the screen then swipes her eyes with the napkin. She holds the phone close to her face then stretches her arm out.

"My eyes are blurry. Will you please read it?"

"Sure. *I'm talking with Roger's family. They want to set up a search party at dawn, I'll send you details. I'm announcing it on student chat. I think he's seeing someone, since he's stayed out a few nights in the last few weeks. He wouldn't say who or how serious, but he was really happy yesterday. I'll keep you posted, but put your phone on the charger.* That's it. Do you want me to reply?"

"Yeah. Hit the icon for talk to text please." I do as she asks and she voices her response.

"Thanks Jake. Hang in there. Call me if you need anything at any time." She nods and I touch the send icon.

I wait for her to wipe her eyes, nose, and focus back on me. She looks a bit better. Maybe having a plan of action helped.

"What would you like me to do?" I asked her again.

"Can you call the Mystic Cross Police and find out if there's any more information? That's probably not ethical, never mind. What d'you suggest?" she sighs out a frustrated sound.

"I can call them. It would only be unethical if I share confidential information. I can also file a companion report if I have contact with them, which will allow me to assist later if they ask. Are you okay if I step into the office to call?"

"Yeah, I'm okay. I'm going to step out onto the porch. I need some air and less ceiling. Thank you." She lifts off me and I hold her hips until she's steady. She gives me a small smile. I watch her step through the door, then walk to the office and dial the local department.

When I get transferred to the right person he answers with distraction, "Detective Morales?"

"Good evening. Special Agent Micah Castleman, FBI. I'm calling about the missing college student, Roger Stanley."

"What about him?" Still distracted. I hear him saying something to someone else, and I can't make out what he says.

"I'm working on another case that may be related to your missing student. I don't want to step on your toes, I'd just like to be kept in the loop. If you want my assistance, I'll be happy to give it, just let me know," I told him.

"All right Agent, Castleman, was it? Email me your information and credentials, I'll loop you in."

"Yes sir. SA Castleman, I'll email you now. Thank you, Detective Morales, have a good night."

"Thanks, you too," he disconnects. I quickly send an email and walk to the front porch. When I step outside Peyton is leaning over the railing and Orlando is on the grass below.

"So now they're having a search party in the morning. I'm not super close to him, but he's a nice guy from a good family. I'd definitely call him a friend."

Orlando says, "I'm free in the morning. I'll help, and I can ask Ax too. Will you send me the details? Hey, Micah."

"Hey. Thanks for helping, I'll be there too. Maybe we can carpool, but we can figure it out in the morning," I tell them.

"That's a good idea. Orlando, it's going to be before dawn, is that okay? I'm thinking at Scallop Park, where they found his car," Peyton says.

"Yeah, no problem. We'll talk in the morning. I'm going to bed so I can get up. Good night, guys," Orlando replies.

Peyton and I both say goodnight and go inside. One set of eyes watches us from the back of the chair in the living room as we pass. When we enter the bedroom, four more eyes carefully watch us. My own eyes follow Peyton as she kicks off her shorts, folds them, and places them on the dresser. I argue with my dick that now isn't the time, she's upset. My eyes follow her perfect ass as she leaves for the bathroom. I squeeze my dick through my pants and try to think about awful things. I'm left with a semi as I remove my work slacks and shirt. I toss them into my duffle and crawl onto the bed.

When Peyton joins me, she has me spoon her from behind and I work hard to keep my semi from bothering her. After she falls asleep, I get out of bed, use the restroom, and brush my teeth. Next, I settle behind my desk and file that report on Roger Stanley. Detective Morales has already forwarded his file on Roger. After I read through it, I looked into him. He's never been in trouble. His family has a good reputation and no criminal history. Then, I start at Scallop Park and find as many cameras as I can. I spiral out until I find his car on screen.

There it is, a white, two door, BMW, M8 F92, 2020, Florida tag: SNSLAW4. I watch it drive to the park on multiple cameras. I copy all the videos and put them in a new file. I followed him all the way back to his place. I watch the videos closer to the park a few more times. I check out each car that's not his and make note of them. Some of the camera footage is high end and clear. I'm able to get most of the license plates and a couple partials. My eyes get droopy, it's a good place to stop so I log off and go back to bed.

Peyton is breathing soft and even, she's curled into a ball. I slip under the covers and touch her. She rolls and stretches, then leans against me. I spoon her like before and try to shut off my thoughts about where she's touching me and her gorgeous ass.

I open my eyes to find Peyton dressed and holding out a cup of coffee towards me. I'd prefer an energy drink, but in a pinch, I'll drink coffee with plenty of sugar.

"Are you awake?" she asks.

"If I wasn't would I answer you?"

"Ha-ha, you're so funny. Here, drink this coffee and get up. We have to go soon. Ax can't come, we're taking Orlando with us and meeting Jake there. Okay?"

"You've been busy," I accept the cup and take a sip.

"Did I get it right," she asks.

"Yeah, good job. Got it in one."

"I'm going to finish getting ready. I have some bug spray for mosquitoes, and a couple flashlights. Anything else I should pack?" she asks.

"We should bring a cooler of water and some snacks. Probably sunscreen for when the sun comes up. Sun glasses and hats too," I reply.

"Okay. Can you get the cooler, drinks, and snacks? I'll dig up the other stuff and meet you at the door in ten." She doesn't wait for me to answer. I shrug and get moving. I can tell she's wound up tight. Her face looks tense, and she almost has dimples when she's like this. I'm going to work hard not to add to her stress. But God help me, she's cute with dimples. I rush through my morning routine and gather the requested items. Our paths crossed once and I asked to borrow a hat.

As I set the cooler on the mat by the door she rushed out from the hall with a big tote bag suitable for the beach. My stuff is in a small backpack. It has a built-in holster for one of my firearms. I have another at my back. I used to think firearms were stupid and I didn't want to learn to shoot. It's one of the main causes of the delay in my rise to Special Agent. I lucked out and had an excellent teacher. Paige is the best sharpshooter I know, and that's saying something when I'm in the FBI.

"I fed the cats, you have the drinks and food, I've got sunscreen, bug spray, hats for both of us, and flashlights. Am I forgetting anything?"

"Do you have your phone? Sunglasses? I've got chargers in the car...I think we're good. Let's hit it." She feels her pockets and nods as I ask.

"Thank you. I know I'm being a bitch. I'm trying not to be, I'm just upset. I'm sorry, please know it's not you. You're the best, and I love you so much."

"I love you too. You're not a bitch and I understand you're worried. Don't apologize babe," I reply as I pull her close and place light kisses across her head.

When we get down the stairs Orlando is waiting for us with a small backpack. I can tell he's carrying as well. He has a permit. I wouldn't say anything if he didn't... for today. I don't want to say anything to Peyton, but we may be looking for a victim and the killer. The more people who can defend my girl, the better.

Our greetings are subdued. Peyton climbs into the front seat and Orlando sits behind her. It helps me relax. I trust him, so far, but I would definitely be uncomfortable with him at my back. He shoots me a knowing grin and I return a grateful smile.

Peyton guides me to the park using a map app. I've heard of the park but haven't been there before. Orlando says he was there once, years ago. When we pull into the lot there's at least ten cars. A line of five more cars is pulling in behind us. There's a table at the far end of the lot where people are gathered.

"There's Jake's car. He must be over there with everyone," Peyton points out.

"I forgot to tell you Ax's brother is coming. I guess he overhead me when I was on the phone with Ax. Anyway, he wanted to help. Said he would take Ax's spot," Orlando informs us.

"Connor?"

"Yeah, I forgot you met him at the shelter, right? He had to work at 10 so he wanted to drive himself. But he said he'll stay until the very last minute if he can."

"That's great. I'm really thankful to all of you for helping. It's still surreal that he's missing," Peyton says.

As we climb out, two Mystic Cross Police cars pull up to the table. Two uniformed officers exit the vehicles followed by a plainclothes officer. I'm assuming that's Detective Morales. His clothes are disheveled, his hair uncombed, his face hasn't had a shave. He aims right for the coffee and pours himself a generous cup. Peyton grasps my hand. I meet her eyes and she looks a little desperate, like she's trying to keep from crying. I head for the coffee pot with her in tow.

We lost Orlando. I spot him with Connor right when Peyton spots Jake. She drags me over to him, drops my hand and hugs Jake. They both have tears on their faces when they separate. I hand each of them a tissue. Jake looks like hasn't slept either. Honestly, I don't know how much sleep Peyton managed.

I notice an older couple just beyond Jake. The woman is sniffling, her eyes are red and watery. The man is dressed in expensive pants and a golf shirt. His face is tight, his eyes are red. The woman has a lot of sparkle on her wrist and fingers as she dabs at her eyes with a tissue. Jake quickly turns back to them like he just remembered they're here. They come closer and Jake introduces us. Connor and Orlando join us and there's more introductions all around. Once we've all met, the man I pegged as the detective asks for everyone's attention.

"Thank you all for being here this morning. If you saw Roger Stanley any time over the last few days, I have a questionnaire for you to complete before you leave. We're going to form into groups of four. Because of the terrain, a line of searchers won't work. I'm going to hand out whistles, if your group finds something, blow the whistle and tag it with the tags I give you. Please go slow, watch where you step, and be careful. Not just for evidence preservation, but for your own safety as well. If you don't have a flashlight there're some at the far end of the table. Are there any questions?"

I ask, to clarify for the civilians, "Will you assign us a direction to go? Should we spread out or stay close together?"

"What's your name?" he asks me.

"Micah Castleman."

His face lights with recognition, "Thanks for asking, Micah. Yes, when you get your tags and whistle, I'll also give you a map with your area marked on it. Thank Officer Davison, he's a wiz on the computer." One of the uniformed officer's waves. "I want you to stay within eyesight of others as much as possible, and definitely within whistle distance. Anything else?" He searches the crowd. When no one speaks up he directs us to line up for our gear. Orlando and Connor will team with us and Jake will team with Mr. And Mrs. Stanley. We all stick together in line.

"Hey guys, sorry I'm late. What're we doing?" Anisa asks. After some more introductions and explanations, she joins the team with Jake and the Stanley's. After we get our maps, we walk to the edge of our zone. Jake's zone is next to ours. As we were walking to the starting point Anisa was glued to Peyton. When Connor tripped over a root, Jake kept him from falling, and they've been talking ever since. When we're ready to begin Connor and Anisa trade groups.

I'm really glad they told us to wear jeans and boots or at least sneakers. There's a lot of sand. Palmettos have overtaken a large amount of the area between the pine trees. When we reach orange trees, that's the far end of our zone. The next property is an old orange grove where the oranges continue to flourish in the wild. We form a line of sorts with me on one end and Orlando on the other. We could probably touch hands if we held our arms out. The sun is coming up and I don't think we need flashlights anymore.

"Everyone ready?" I ask.

"Yeah."

"Yep."

"Uh huh."

We begin moving at a snail's pace with our eyes glued to the ground. When we run into palmettos blocking our path, we have to adjust our trajectory. We sweep everything even below the stiff, prickly branches.

Anisa lets out a squeal, "Aaahhh! What the fuck is that?" There's a crash up ahead. Four deer flee, their white tails bouncing in the gray light of dawn. Anisa holds her hand over her heart and breathes heavily.

"Shit, that scared me," Peyton commiserates.

"I know. My heart is ready to bust out of my chest. Fuck!" She jumps and runs to the side. I see an armadillo waddle across the path we're following, and I chuckle. Anisa shoots me a fierce look and I cough into my hand to wipe off my grin. Peyton eyes me.

"Sorry. He was so little and not interested in us. It made me laugh," I defend.

"Little? He was huge and came right at me!" Anisa adds.

"Aren't you from Louisiana? I thought they had lots of wildlife there?" I ask.

"New Orleans. I'm a city girl, I hate the woods."

"You're from New Orleans?" Orlando asks, lost in thought.

"Yeah. Why?" she retorts. She looks ready to pounce.

"Oh, I lived out there for a little while, when I was a teenager. What area did you live in?"

"My family has a home in the Garden District," she answers.

"We stayed in St. Bernard Parish," Orlando replies.

"Oh." That's all Anisa verbalizes, her face says plenty more. She raises her chin and thins her lips. She gives Orlando the coldest shoulder I've seen since my last visit to the morgue. We regroup and get back to our line. Anisa is closer to Peyton now. Orlando is laser focused on the ground.

"Everyone good?" I ask.

They all agree and we begin. When we reach the orange trees the sun is above the horizon. We line up on the next area over to make our way back to the start. Peyton hands me the hat and a few gulps of water. Everyone takes a few sips and we get back to searching.

After ten minutes of silence, we hear a whistle blow and almost out of sight, we can see past Jake's section. A man in a red shirt waves his arms. We all stand still waiting to know what he found, silently praying it's not a body. A uniformed officer tells us it was just a piece of evidence, or maybe it's just trash. Then he directs us to get back to searching, all through a megaphone.

When we get back to our starting point, we wait for Jake's group to return. Jake and Connor are still chatting. The Stanley's look ready to drop. We check back in at the table. Everyone drinks and grabs a snack and we apply sunscreen.

"Can I join your group?" Jake asks Peyton.

"Yeah, of course. What's up with yours? Are the Stanley's okay?"

"No. They haven't slept and walking the rough trails in the sun isn't helping, and they're older. Connor doesn't have time for another round. So, it's just me."

"Of course, you can join us. Let's go find out from Detective Morales what's next," I interject. Jake and I leave Peyton and Anisa to get a new assignment.

"Micah. You can call me Raul. I didn't expect you to be here. I thought you just wanted to be in the loop," Detective, *Raul* Morales, admonishes me.

"The missing man is a friend of my girlfriend. I'm here to support her and help, nothing official. We came to get another assignment. We'll be a team of five now, we're adding Jake," I point at him and he salutes the detective. The detective, or *Raul*, nods at him. He still gives me a bit of side eye, but nothing too extreme. I ignore it as locals get weird about the FBI. I meant what I told him. I don't have any interest in taking over. I'm hoping it's not related to anything I'm working on, and we find Roger hungover at some chick's house.

When we get back to the others Anisa isn't there. Orlando jerks his head towards the restroom, and I nod. Peyton is talking quietly with the Stanley's. They're seated in camp chairs. They refuse to leave despite needing to rest. I touch Peyton's arm to let her know I'm back. She looks relieved to see me. She quickly says goodbye to the Stanley's.

She decides to use the restroom too before we head out again. Orlando is quiet, and his eyes are sharp as he watches everyone. Groups are coming and going back out. Other people are leaving for work or school. One of Peyton's professors is here helping. Most of Peyton's class is here as well. Jake was able to get approval for class to be postponed. It's not like they can afford a scandal at Wellington. One of the top school officials was arrested in the operation that preceded Paige's kidnapping a couple years ago. I push my cynicism down and refocus.

"You doing, okay?" I ask Orlando. He seems off.

"It's weird, I feel like I've met Anisa before."

"Didn't you meet her when Peyton was in the hospital?"

"Yeah, but that's not it. When she mentioned New Orleans, something clicked. But that's all I've got. I definitely would remember meeting someone named Anisa though. Never heard that name before..." Orlando cuts off his thought and moves his eyes over my shoulder.

"She probably just looks like someone you've met. Maybe she has a doppelganger," I offer.

"Yeah, maybe."

"You guys ready?" Peyton asks.

"Yeah, let's go." I take Peyton's hand into mine and guide us so Orlando is on my side and Anisa is on Peyton's. Jake chooses to be on the outside, next to Orlando.

The sun is up in full force. Even though it's not a particularly warm day, it's probably about eighty degrees. In the sunlight it feels hotter and we're all sweating. I stop often on this round and make everyone drink water. Nobody complains since we're all feeling hot and tired at this point. After we make the turn to head back toward the parking area, a flock of birds startle us when they take flight. After the noise it causes dies down, we can hear distant screaming. Fuck! That can't be good.

"Let's finish our track until they tell us differently, okay, Jake?"

He snaps his eyes to mine and I see fear, as he says, "Yeah. Okay." His words are sharp and rough, he looks miserable. Peyton doesn't look much better when she nods in agreement. Orlando also nods, his face stoic. Anisa nods and she can't hold back her tears. They fall down her cheeks and she turns away from us as she wipes her eyes. I can hear a commotion toward the water, I can't see the beach at all, just the water of the Gulf. We're higher up on sand dunes that go from hard to soft sand and slope up and down. When we have traction because of the weeds and brush, the little green stems are covered in spiked burrs that painfully stick to our pants and shoes. This is dismal terrain. My calf muscles burn with the strain of trudging through soft sand. I'm sure our entire group feels the same way, but no one voices the slightest complaint.

When a siren goes off, we stop and look towards the sound. A uniformed officer I haven't seen before is using the siren function on the megaphone to get our attention. It works. While we wait to find out what he has to tell us I see multiple officers in uniforms, lab techs with gear, and plain clothes officers walking past him towards the water.

"Folks! We have an update on the search, please carefully make your way back to the staging area. Follow your zone back. If you have any evidence to mark right now, please raise your hands," I can't see more than a couple people from our spot, nobody raises anything.

"Okay, please make your way back now. Thank you!" He finishes and we move as fast as we can through the difficult landscape.

Jake seems to be mumbling to himself. I can't make out the words but it sounds like he's saying, *Oh God,* over and over. It's muddled into a chant of despair. Peyton is holding his hand now instead of mine. Her face is pinched, eyes narrow, lips thin lines pressed together. Orlando and I sigh simultaneously when we reach the parking lot.

Things have changed dramatically since our last stop here just under two hours ago. There's an official police tent set up with Detective Morales and two other plainclothes officers seated beneath its shade. There're various police vehicles lining the exit road from Mystic Cross and Rebel County. A coroner's van and crime scene investigation unit round out the official transportation.

Unfortunately, there's a news van setting up. The mobile communication tower on the roof is raised, and a reporter in a tight suit is preening her sprayed stiff hair, while a guy in a t-shirt and jeans attaches a microphone to her lapel.

The Stanley's are nowhere to be seen. Anisa goes to the restroom, presumably to get herself together. Peyton won't let go of Jake, which seems to be keeping him from freaking out.

"Can I grab your keys?" Orlando asks. He returns a moment later with two chairs and our cooler. He sets them up behind the original staging table next to the chairs the Stanley's used earlier. He passes me the keys and walks off to the restroom.

"Eagle, are you okay if I go talk to Morales?" I ask.

"Yeah, do whatever you need to. I'm going to stick with Jake since he's alone."

"Good. Orlando set up a couple chairs and our cooler next to where the Stanley's were sitting before, if you want to take Jake over there," I reply. She kisses me and mouths, *thank you.* I offer her a consolation filled smile. I make my way to Detective Morales and wait for him to notice me. The last thing I want to do is interrupt or step in, I plan to be polite and helpful.

"Micah. We're heading to the beach, want to join?" Morales barks at me.

"Yes sir. Thank you," I look for Peyton. She's engrossed in quiet conversation with Jake. Anisa isn't back yet. Orlando's leaning against a tree nearby watching everything. He gives me a chin lift and points at Peyton, then gives me a thumbs up. I take this to mean he's going to watch over Peyton while I go do police stuff. I nod in return, hoping I'm conveying my gratitude.

I hustle and get in step with the plainclothes officers. I stay back and let them lead, I still don't know what's happening and I'm assuming the worst. That thought causes my gut to clench. If Roger had an accident, it'll be horrible. If he was harmed by someone else, the damage to his friends, school, and family could be catastrophic. I steel myself for what's to come.

"Micah Castleman is a Special Agent with the FBI. Micah, this is Detective Dave Larson with Mystic Cross Police," he indicates the shorter dark-haired man.

He points to the taller guy with reddish brown hair, "This guy is Detective Lane Warren, he's with Rebel County." Both men give me a barely audible greeting.

"Nice to meet you. Unfortunate circumstances though," I reply, "I came to support my girlfriend today. She's a friend of the missing guy. I'm not here officially, but if I can help, please let me know." Both men perk up noticeably with my words. We're all seasoned enough to not shake hands, when you're at a crime scene you keep your hands to yourself, even if it would be rude in any other situation.

When we get to the beach there's yellow tape marking off an area further up the sand. There are a bunch of rocks along the beach and into the water, some of them are huge. I've no clue if they were brought in for erosion control or if Mother Nature decorated the shore.

Detective Warren speaks up, "He's not missing anymore. Body washed up on the rocks. Can't tell if it was an accident or something else. We'll have to wait for the coroner's report."

"Shit. That sucks, I was hoping for a much better outcome," I reply. Everyone agrees with my assertion.

We make our way closer and I see the Stanley's. Mrs. Stanley is on a stretcher sobbing. Mr. Stanley is trying to comfort her, without much success. EMTs are trying to check her out and she's not cooperating, but they don't push. I can tell by the looks on their faces they're being very gentle with her. They're squatting on either side of her while they speak in soothing tones as if they're speaking to a child.

The forensic techs are still collecting evidence so they have a sheet up to block the view of the body. I've seen enough of them that it doesn't bother me, it never really bothered me. If I had any interest in it, I could've been a surgeon or a mortician without a second thought. Morales speaks to one of the techs, but I can't hear their conversation.

I take the time to look around. It's getting close to noon, and the sun beams from high above. The water is flat. The Gulf rarely gets swells of note unless there's a storm. There're seagulls and pelicans bobbing on the tiny waves. Two dolphins play where the water gets darker. If not for the dead body of Peyton's friend, it'd be a perfect beach day. She's going to be so upset, and poor Jake. I scan the rocks; I can see the edge of the sand that meets the sea grass further from the water.

When I spot something blue peeking from the grass. I move closer. I watch where I step and make sure there isn't anything like footprints that could be destroyed before I place each foot. When I get close enough to see what the blue thing is, I stop. I bend down for a closer look. It looks like a rubber glove, like the kind from a hospital. The same kind we use in the FBI for evidence collection. I wonder if someone here dropped it or if it may be evidence. I still have the tags in my pocket from our search so I attach one to the grass swaying above the glove.

"Micah! Can you come over here?" Detective Morales yells from over behind the screen. I walked over to a uniformed officer and let him know about the rubber glove. He thanks me and I meet Detective Morales.

"Yes sir. How can I help?" I ask him.

He approaches and leans in to speak softly, "I'm sorry to do this to you, but would you mind looking at the body and confirming the ID? I don't want the parents to see him until he's been cleaned up. You said you know him, right?"

"I've met him. No problem, happy to help." He gestures behind the screen, and I walk around the edge. I'm expecting something truly horrible. There on some rocks lies the body of Roger Stanley. He's blue, his eyes are half open. He's laying at an odd angle that would be terribly uncomfortable if he were alive. His face is scraped a bit, yet still very recognizable. His hair is wet and some sand is mixed into his dark strands. He's wearing a t-shirt with what looks like the name of a bar across the chest. It looks like it says, *Boondocks* in large black letters across a beach scene with turtles and palm trees. Then the word *Florida* is scrawled beneath the image. His jeans are dark with salt water. There's no shoes or socks on his blue feet. One hand is twisted out of sight beneath him. The other is stretched out palm up. More scrapes mark his hand. It's almost as if he's reaching out for help, the irony is not lost on me. A twinge of sadness tightens my chest. His poor family and friends, my poor girl, she'll be distraught I'm afraid. His mother's already inconsolable and continues to sob on her stretcher. As tiny waves curl onto the shore, they rock his swollen body. Other than the few scratches I don't see any other injuries.

I turn and walk back beyond the barrier, "Yes, it's him," I quietly inform Detective Morales. He nods and thanks me. After letting him know the positive identification I go back to the staging area. I need to hug my girl. I'm already aching for her and the pain she'll endure.

When she sees me, she runs at me and hugs me, "Micah, he's gone, isn't he? They found his body..." Her tears overtake her before she can finish. I hug her close and murmur how sorry I am. She manages to nod in acknowledgement. Orlando nods at me too, letting me know he's got the scoop.

Jake comes running from the direction of the restrooms. He sees Peyton crying and his face twists into a terrible grimace before his own tears begin to fall in earnest. He falls to his knees and sobs like a child. Peyton pulls away from me and looks into my face. She's visibly in pain, it breaks my heart, there's nothing I can do to fix this.

She places an open mouth kiss on my lips and then she kneels in front of Jake engulfing him in her arms and holds him. The other people milling around have taken notice of Jake's state and they make the assumption that something awful has been found. Many of them have tears falling from their eyes.

A uniformed officer sees the situation spiraling, he grabs the megaphone, "Folks, our situation has changed. Unfortunately, we have located a deceased person who seems to match the description of Roger Stanley. We still need your information on the questionnaire if you saw him in the last few days. We're still investigating what happened. We don't know if he had an accident or if foul play was involved. Please don't ask questions about the case. We don't have any answers yet. Please also give his family and close friends some privacy as they cope with the unfortunate outcome. They wanted us to thank all of you for coming out and helping. If you need a questionnaire, please see me; if you've completed your questionnaire, please place it in the tray and you may leave. Again, thank you for your help." A few people approach him and he hands them the papers to fill out. Peyton and Jake are on their knees hugging each other, oblivious to their surroundings.

I don't see Anisa anywhere and I wonder if she left. Maybe Orlando knows. I don't want to leave Peyton so I look at Orlando and gesture for him to join me. He rolls off the tree he was leaning against and walks over. His eyebrows raise in question.

"You doing okay?"

"Yep. You?"

"Yeah. Where did Anisa go? We can't lose track of anyone," I declare.

"She went towards the beach when you went. You didn't see her over there?"

"No. I was distracted, I guess I missed her. Do you mind looking for her?"

His face is impassive, "I don't mind. I'll be back in a few."

"Thanks man."

"You're welcome." After he walks off, I refocus on Peyton and Jake. They're both sitting on the ground now holding hands and speaking softly. I wonder if Jake had feelings for Roger or if he was just a close friend. Peyton told me Roger was straight, but that doesn't mean Jake didn't have feelings he wasn't acting upon. Man, this sucks. He seemed like a nice guy. Nobody deserves this, and I hope it wasn't a homicide. Peyton looks at me and she gestures with her fingers for me to come closer.

When I squat down next to her, she says into my ear, "I don't want to leave Jake alone. What do you think about inviting him back to my place?"

"Whatever you want is fine with me. Just tell me what you need, and I'm on it. Do you want some water?"

"Yeah. Thank you. I love you." Her tears fill up and overflow again.

"I love you too." I kiss her cheek.

I bring her and Jake each a bottle of water, they both thank me. Jake looks a little better, but Peyton is holding it together. I see Orlando approaching with Anisa in tow. She stops where the officer is handing out forms and begins to fill one out. Orlando continues to where Peyton and I wait with Jake.

"We're going to head out. I might need you to drive my car back. Jake's coming with us and I'm not sure he or Peyton should drive right now. You can drive my car and I'll drive his. Is that cool?"

"Sure, whatever you need. Would you mind if I stopped for food? I'm starving. Chips and granola bars aren't cutting it."

"Yeah, go for it. Here," I hand him a few bills and my keys. "Grab enough for everyone, okay?"

"Okay."

"Oh my God, you guys, I can't believe this. Are you okay, Peyton? Jake?" Anisa asks.

Jake speaks up, "Yeah. I'll be okay. It's just a shock. I mean, I was probably one of the last people to see him. He's been my best friend for over a year. Oh. Shit."

"What is it?" Peyton asks, still holding his hand.

"His stuff is all over my place. His room is full of his things. I can't ask his parents about it right now. I don't want to go there either. Shit."

"We've got you covered. I'm going to drive you and Peyton to her place," I insert.

"If you're okay with it, I'd like you to stay over tonight, or as long as you need," Peyton adds.

"Come on, let's get out of here. This is getting more depressing by the minute, and I'm not good with emotional stuff," Anisa adds her thoughts to the mix.

"I guess I can check in with the Stanley's by phone. God, I feel like I'm trying to walk through water. Everything is blurry and it's hard to move," Jake continues.

"You'll get through it and we're going to help," Peyton reassures him.

We all walk to the lot. Orlando loads the chairs into the back of my SUV, and I place the cooler next to them. We say farewell and take our separate cars. Anisa is also coming over, but not spending the night. She leaves in her car. Orlando takes off in mine. I accept Jake's keys and drive us to Peyton's house.

Peyton

When my eyes open, I stretch like a cat in my bed. It feels good, I'm sore from yesterday. Shit. Yesterday. Roger is dead. It all floods back, the emotions, the sadness, my pain for Jake and Roger's family. Micah was so wonderful; he took care of all of us. God, I love that man. Wanting to hug him I reach out and find my bed cold and missing my boyfriend. I sit up and look around, noticing the sun is up. I glance at my phone and see that it's 9. I'm late for class. I smell coffee, I'll worry about class after I have a cup. I stumble to the bathroom and take care of my morning routine. Then let my nose lead me.

"Good morning, beautiful!" Jake jokes. It's good to see him able to smile.

"Hi. Where's Micah?"

"I'm here. Just checking in with the office. Want coffee?" I nod and take a seat. He fills a cup and adds some sugar and cream.

"Are you hungry? I got some breakfast. Jake and I already ate but we saved you some."

"Yeah. Not eating yesterday has caught up with me." My stomach lets out a loud growl to punctuate my statement. I wrap my hands around my middle embarrassed.

Jake chuckles, "Hurry Micah! Her stomach sounds like it's going to come after us. Did you sleep okay?" he asks.

"I guess so... I passed out. Yesterday was exhausting. My legs are sore from trudging through all that sand. How did you sleep? I'm sorry I only have a couch to offer."

"No, don't apologize. I passed out too and slept good despite everything. I can't thank you guys enough for letting me stay over. I couldn't handle the thought of going home alone. The cops called and they're searching the house. I can't go home yet, anyway."

"Geez. I'm so sorry Jake. Why're they searching your place?"

He looks at Micah, "You want to explain?"

Micah nods and elaborates, "The autopsy is finished. Cause of death is drowning, a homicide. They found ketamine in his bloodstream. They're saying he was drugged and then drowned by force. Jake has to go to the station for questioning at eleven." My eyes grow large with shock.

"Why? They don't think you did it do they?" I sip on the coffee, unable to take a bite of the breakfast sandwich Micah placed in front of me.

"I don't know what they think. My dad is flying in this morning with his criminal team to make sure I'm covered. I was one of the last people to see him alive. I'm not surprised they want to interview me. I don't know if they have any suspects."

Micah speaks up, "I don't know either, but they would always interview a roommate no matter what. The search of their place'll look for evidence of ketamine, blood, anything left behind from visiting that park. Also, since Jake thinks he was seeing someone, they'll check his electronics to try to figure out who, and if, they're involved."

"I don't mean to sound like an ass, but what about school? We're already late," I ask.

"We're excused for the rest of this week. All the classes Roger was in are excused, plus any of his friends are excused. They'll give us an extra online assignment to make up for it. You probably have emails about all of it. I only looked at the one from the Dean," Jake answers.

"Okay. What do you need? How can we help you?" I ask Jake.

"You guys are doing it. I just need friends, support, maybe some clothes," he looks at Micah.

"You're welcome to borrow anything. I don't have much here though. I also think my stuff will be long on you but help yourself. We could go to the store or my place and find something, if you want. We've got a couple hours." There's a knock at the door. I jump at the sound. I'm on edge. ketamine. That's the same thing I was drugged with, is this related to my stalker. Is it my fault Roger was exposed to the...killer?

Micah lets Orlando and Ax in and offers them coffee.

Ax speaks first, "Hey guys, sorry I couldn't make it yesterday. I'm sorry about the outcome for your friend. Orlando and I wanted to see if you need anything."

Jake responds, "Hi, thanks. I think we're kind of lost on what we need. How's Connor? Have you told him what happened?"

"He's okay. Yeah, I told him. He said to tell you all how sorry he is about your loss. He asked me to get your number, Jake. I guess he has yours, Peyton, at his work?" Ax answers. I nod in agreement. I look over Orlando and realize he and Jake have similar builds. Maybe he would be willing to loan Jake an outfit. I clear my throat, and everyone looks at me, my stomach growls again. My cheeks have to be turning red, they feel hot with embarrassment.

"Hi guys, do you think you could lend Jake something to wear? He can't go home and he has to be at the police station at eleven, for an interview," I ask looking pointedly at Orlando.

"Hey, yeah. No problem. Jake, you can come over and pick out whatever you want. I even have brand new boxers I haven't worn yet."

"Thanks man," Jake sighs and seems to relax when his shoulders ease down from his ears.

"Babe, please try to eat a few bites. Then we can get ready and take Jake to the police station. I might be able to find out more information if I go in person. Okay?"

"Yeah. Okay." I force myself to take a bite. What looks like a delicious breakfast sandwich tastes like cardboard in my mouth. I zone out while I mechanically force feed my angry stomach. Felony climbs into my lap and rubs against me. I sneak her a few bites of my breakfast and hope Micah won't notice. She purrs, all too happy to help.

My brain won't stop going over the things that the stalker has done so far. Why would he target Roger? I'm probably being ridiculous. It's got to be a coincidence that he had ketamine in his system. That's probably a fairly easy drug to get, poor guy. He was really sweet. Poor Anisa. I know they weren't dating, but she kind of had that brief thing with him. I know I would be more upset if I was in that position, and we were all friends. Maybe I better check on her. I push away my empty plate and leave the room to get my phone.

Me: Hey girl. How're you holding up?

I pull on some jeans and a t-shirt while I wait for her to reply. As I tie my sneakers, my text alert chimes.

Anisa: I'm okay. Passed out last night. Yesterday was exhausting. My legs are sore from dredging through all that sand. Any updates? How r u? How's Jake?

Me: we're okay. Just upset-the autopsy showed ketamine in his system and they said it was homicide.

Anisa: WTF!! I figured it was an accident. Holy fuck! There's a murderer around?

Me: I know. I'm freaked out too. It's the same drug from when my stalker drugged me.

Anisa: Dude! That's fucking scary!

Me: I guess we have the week off. Jake has to go be interviewed by the police at 11

Anisa: they think he did it? WTH?

Me: IDK but he's a witness for sure. They're searching his house. He can't go home. His parents are coming in from Texas.

Anisa: Shit. What can I do?

Me: nothing right now. I'll keep you posted. I'm still in shock.

Anisa: me too. You let me know asap if you need anything. I'm just going to get caught up on my projects while we're off. I have to keep busy.

Me: I'm caught up. Thankfully, bc I can't focus.

Anisa: I'm going to try. Hugs girl

Me: You too, stay safe. Like don't go out alone, okay?

Anisa: I promise

Me: ttyl

*Anisa: cool *bee emoji*

I scratch Felony while I think everything over again. She rubs her face against my hand. I lift her to my chest and hug her there. I don't know what to think. I guess I'll have to wait it out. I hear the front door close and Micah walks into the room and assesses me. Felony squirms out of my arms and I try to give him a smile, it probably looks like I'm in pain. He takes my hand and lifts me to standing and then coils his arms around me. I hold him close and listen to the soothing beat of his heart.

"Thank you. You're always here for me, my support, my rock. I love you so much," I tell him. I know I say *I love you* often, I do it with purpose because you never know when you could lose someone. I want the people I love to know it, without a doubt, if something ever happens to me or them.

"I love you too. Can I do anything to help you feel better?" He looks at me with such empathy, I know he's hurting with me.

"No. It's just going to take time. Besides, everything you've been doing has been perfect. I appreciate how kind you're being to Jake."

"He's a good guy. I like him. I'm glad you're friends with him. Especially now, I think he's going to need some good friends to get through this."

I lean back and look up at him, "I think you're right. I'm glad you like him, and you're right, he's a good guy. Where is he?" I look behind him.

"He went to Orlando's to borrow clothes. They said they'll come back later after we get back from the police department. I'm thinking we're going to have to help Jake get some stuff from his house or maybe even pack up Roger's stuff. We'll have to see what he wants to do, but he's going to need clothes."

"Yeah. You're right. We'll talk to him after the police. Oh Micah, I'm scared it's my fault." My face crumples, tears fill my eyes, and my lip quivers.

"What? How can you think that, baby?" he asks, his face tense with worry.

"Well, you said he was drugged with ketamine. What if it was my stalker? Then it would be me who caused their paths to cross. That means it's my fault," my voice is thick as the tears fall to my cheeks.

"Eagle, babe, there's no way in hell any of this is your fault. Even if it was your stalker, that's on him. Not you! Come on, you can't think shit like that. The stalker is not your fault. Roger is not your fault. You didn't ask to be stalked. ketamine is a fairly common drug. It's probably just a coincidence anyway. Please don't do that to yourself."

He bends down so his eyes are level with mine and looks at me intently. I smile through my tears. I can't help it, his face is so serious, like he's ready to kick my ass because I feel guilty. He won't even let *me* hurt me.

I throw my arms around his neck and kiss him hard. My tongue finds its way into his mouth. I kiss him passionately hoping he feels how much I love him. He pulls me against him, and we kiss and hold each other. It's what I need. I feel his love flowing through my veins and it fortifies me. When we break apart, he's out of breath and I'm panting.

The front door slams, "Hey you guys, oh, sorry." Jake turns to leave.

"No, Jake, don't go. It's okay, we're just talking. Did you find something to wear?" I blurt.

"It looked like talking," he winks. "Seriously, yeah. I think Orlando's stuff will fit pretty well. His shirts are a size bigger than I wear, but the pants are my size. I should be good. I'm going to grab a shower and then we can go. Okay?"

"Yeah, of course. There're more towels in the closet if you put the one from last night in the hamper."

"Nah, it's on the hook on the back of the door. Doing my own laundry has taught me a lot of things, like washing towels after each use is a waste." He smiles at me. Micah chuckles. I smile and we all have a goofy laugh. It relieves some of the tension.

When we pull up to the police station, Jake looks nervous. My own stomach feels tight. Micah looks fine, he always looks fine. No wonder he's a great agent, nothing ever rattles him. When we exit the car I grab Micah's hand in my right hand, my left hand finds Jake's. He gives me a brave smile. When we approach the building a man in a very expensive suit steps out from the lobby. He's a nice-looking, older version of Jake. He has silver around his ears and a few lines on his face are deeper than Jake's. Otherwise, they're almost carbon copies.

Jake dropped my hand and outstretched his hand to shake with his father. Mr. Waverly pulls Jake into a hug. Then he holds him at arm's length and looks him over as if to see if he has any injuries. Then he pulls him back in for a second hug. Mr. Waverly looks relieved to see Jake is alive and well.

"Thank God you're safe. Your mother is beside herself. Can we have a quick chat before we go inside?"

Jake clears his throat. I can see he's emotional and that his father's not normally affectionate with him. He's told me quite a bit about his parents. He'd been thinking about starting a firm with Roger in Florida and not returning to Texas because of the strain in his relationship with his parents.

"Sure. Um, this is Peyton Baker, my friend and classmate."

"Pleased to meet you Mr. Waverly. This is my boyfriend, Micah Castleman," I reach out my hand to shake his. He shakes my hand firmly and looks at Micah.

"I'm pleased to meet you both. Jake has told me about both of you. Thank you for helping him through this. Please, call me Jacob." He firmly shakes Micah's hand.

"Nice to meet you sir, *Jacob*," Micah responds.

"Where did you want to speak, dad?" Jake asks his father.

"Let's step under that tree." He gestures to the huge oak in front of the station. The shade from the tree covers the sidewalk. Micah and I go inside the building to give them privacy. We find seats in the lobby and wait. There're two men wearing expensive suits with fancy leather bags. I wonder if they're more lawyers Jake's dad brought.

Jake storms in through the door, his face red and twisted in anger. He stomps over to us grumbling under his breath. I stand up and touch his arm. His eyes snap to mine and his anger eases a bit. He takes a couple deep breaths calming further. His father comes through the door, the man looks miserable. His eyes are watery, his face is red, and his mouth pulled into a tight grimace.

"Jake, I'm sorry," he pleads.

"Just drop it, and let's get this over with," Jake dismisses his father and takes my hand in both of his. I search his eyes trying to determine what's up.

"Are you okay?" I ask Jake quietly.

"I'm fine. The asshole just asked me if I was sleeping with Roger. He knows Roger was straight. What the fuck?"

"I'm sorry. He just doesn't understand. He's thinking like a lawyer, and he needs to know the nature of your relationship. Try not to be too angry with him. You know he loves you and he's trying," I offer in hopes of smoothing things over a bit. He looks at me and physically shakes it off, almost like a dog.

"You're right. I just…he just…ugh! It doesn't matter. You're right, thanks." Not sure what else to say, I hugged him. Then I pat his arm.

"You've got this. We'll be here when you're done. Listen to your dad, and remember he's a good lawyer, okay?"

"Okay. Thanks," he turns to his father and joins him next to the other two lawyers. They all follow Detective Morales into the back. The detective didn't acknowledge us. I guess we're all suspects until he learns differently. I sigh. Micah reaches out and pulls me to the chair next to him. I hold his hand and try to keep my thoughts from going too dark.

When it's been almost two hours, I have to use the restroom. Micah went about a half hour ago. I'm fidgeting. I need to move more than I need to pee, but it's a good excuse to get up and walk around. When I come back out of the bathroom Jake is chatting with Micah. His father and the other lawyers aren't there.

"Hey, how'd it go? Where's your dad?" I ask.

"He's still talking to Morales. I was done and didn't want to stay in there any longer than necessary. It was how you would imagine. I had to tell them everything I did the last few days and then what I could remember about what Roger was doing. They really want to know who he was seeing. I guess they didn't find any evidence about who it was," he shrugs.

"Do you think you're a suspect?" I query.

"I don't know. I think I'm on the list, but probably near the bottom. They're checking known criminals, and asking everyone who knew him where they were, when they saw him, and so on. You filled out that questionnaire at the search, I don't think they need to talk to you because you answered those questions," he tells me.

"I guess that's good. Are we ready to go? Or do you need to wait?"

"They said I can go. I think I need to wait for my dad though. Oh shit," he exclaims.

"What?" I ask as I turn to look where his eyes are locked. The Stanley's are making their way to the door. Mrs. Stanley is dressed in black and she has tissues to her nose. Mr. Stanley is dressed in a dark suit and he looks like he's aged a decade since yesterday.

Jake greets them at the door. They both hug him and Mrs. Stanley holds onto his arm and won't let him go. Micah stands and I follow his action. I twist my hands together dreading feeling their sorrow. We approach them, and they recognize us from yesterday. Mr. Stanley shakes both of our hands.

"Dear, it's good to see you. You're taking care of Jake, aren't you?" Mrs. Stanley says as she hugs me.

She reaches out and pats Micah's arm while she holds onto me with her other hand. He pats her hand and smiles at her.

"Thank you, Micah. I can tell you're taking care of both of these sweet kids," she says as she touches him.

"I'm trying my best, ma'am," Micah replies to her.

Jake's father and his entourage join us in the lobby. There're greetings, introductions, and hugs. Detective Morales waits and watches silently on the periphery of our group. I eye him warily; I hope he doesn't want to speak to me. Eventually he makes eye contact with Micah and gestures with his head for Micah to step aside with him. They speak quietly in the corner while the rest of us try to arrange where we're going from here.

I learn that Jake is allowed to go home now, but he doesn't want to. Roger's parents want to collect his things whenever Jake allows. He's happy to let them go any time. We come to the decision to let the Stanley's visit Jake's and collect Roger's things tomorrow. Jake wants to swing by and get some clothes, but he doesn't want to stay there.

"Are you sure you're okay with me staying over again?" Jake asks me.

"Of course. I'm sorry it's on the couch, but you're welcome for as long as you want." I smile at him in encouragement. I want him to know I really mean it.

"Thanks so much. You're a good friend, Micah too. I really appreciate it."

"Jake, it's seriously our pleasure. You're our friend and we're happy to help. Oh, I think your dad's ready to go."

Jake pastes a small smile on his face and approaches his father. Micah rejoins me, and I ask with my eyes if everything's okay. He gives me a brusque nod. Hmm, not sure what to make of that. We finally made it out of the building. Everyone says their goodbyes and goes on their way. We're going to Jake's.

Micah

I'm happy to be back at Peyton's. Both she and Jake are actually holding up well despite how hard it was going to Jake's. He has a suitcase filled with everything he needs for at least a week. The police were not considerate with their search. Everything had been rifled through, or disturbed in some way, and I mean everything. It was a mess. Jake didn't want to look at Roger's room.

I looked, and his bed sheets were missing. His computer was gone. His desk had everything removed and scattered on top or on the floor. I don't know what they took as evidence, but there was a lot left behind on the carpet. His trophies from baseball and swimming were still on a shelf. There were ribbons from trivia nights lining his mirror. His school books were stacked on his desk. A few posters with girls in bikinis were still on the walls. It looked very much like a single, male college student's room.

Overall, their apartment is modern and masculine. They have dark leather furniture, and a huge TV takes up the main wall in the shared living area. As is typical with many guys, a gaming system is set up beneath the massive screen. Everything looks like it was clean and organized before the cops made their visit. They each have their own bathroom, which is ideal in a roommate situation. I think Jake is going to have a hard time going back to staying there. I don't mind having him around and I think he and Peyton are helping each other cope.

"I just got a text from Mr. Stanley. Roger's funeral is going to be in two weeks. He says they want to give everyone time to make travel arrangements. It's being held in Tallahassee," Jake updates us. Peyton looks at me, "I guess we'll have to plan a trip. I've never been to Tallahassee, beyond driving through on I-10. Jake, do you want to make arrangements with us and go together?"

"Yeah, probably. I'll have to see if my parents are going, but I'd rather stay with you guys than them."

"Are you guys hungry?" Peyton asks.

"I could eat," I told her.

"Me too. How is it only four o'clock? I feel like it should be midnight," Jake answers.

"Are you guys cool with pizza? I want some cheesy, yummy, comfort food. What do you like on yours, Jake?" Peyton asks.

"I like anything but olives. I'm going to change into my own clothes. Can I use your washer and dryer? I want to wash Orlando's stuff before I return it."

"Yeah. I have a few dark things I could throw in too. Micah, do you need anything washed?" They both look at me.

"Actually, yeah. Thanks. Why don't you get changed and then I'll help you get the laundry going while Peyton orders the food." I say.

"Thanks, Radiohead." Peyton plants a kiss on my cheek and walks to the kitchen, presumably to find the pizza menus she has there.

Jake follows me down the hall dragging his suitcase. I continue on to the bedroom. I gather the few dark things I have that need washing. Then I fish out the dark stuff from Peyton's hamper. The gigantic bathroom contains a closet with a washer and dryer stacked unit. It can hold a surprisingly big load of clothes. When Jake finishes changing, I show him the units and the soap and we get the wash going.

When we rejoin Peyton, Ax and Orlando are over and she informs us she's invited them to stay for pizza. I excuse myself and go to the office. I send off the emails I need to deliver with the reports attached. I read over what Morales sent me.

I haven't told Peyton yet that we're officially considering the possibility that her stalker's involved. In spite of ketamine being a commonly available drug on the street and in clinical settings, there are specific chemical signatures to each batch. One sample can be compared to another for similarities. They can be matched chemically and it can be proven that two samples came from the same source and batch.

Unfortunately, the sample from Peyton's poisoning is a chemical match to the sample from Roger's autopsy. She's going to be very upset. Maybe I'll tell her in front of everyone so they can help me convince her she's not to blame. I just need to decide if that's manipulation or consideration.

While we're seated at the table scarfing down pizza, we tell Ax and Orlando all the details we know. I decided it's a good time to share about my official involvement. Orlando and I are well past him being in an MC and me in the FBI. Peyton will have support from all four of us when she learns the truth. She's also on her second piece of pizza, so even if it ruins her appetite, at least I know she ate something.

"I got another update. I haven't had a chance to tell you yet. Detective Morales sent some information that shows the ketamine found in Roger's lab work is associated with the samples from when you were drugged. I'm officially assigned to investigate Roger's murder. They're officially linking his case with your stalker case." I see her face fall, "Please, remember what I said this morning, it's not in any way, your fault. Don't think because you knew Roger you somehow led the killer to him. It's unlikely, because you weren't close to Roger and it could be a coincidence that their paths crossed. It's a small town anda small school, it could be as simple as him grabbing a coffee and meeting the killer. It has nothing to do with you, Eagle," I plead.

"Yeah, absolutely nothing to do with you. Even if it's your stalker, that doesn't mean anything. You're one of the best people I know. Roger thought you were great. He would be devastated if he knew you tried to blame yourself, so don't, okay?" Jake adds.

"I know it's not my fault directly. I just can't help thinking if it wasn't for me, my stalker wouldn't have met him... and killed him." Peyton purses her lips trying not to cry.

"It's not like you asked to have a stalker. Seriously, you can't accept any responsibility for what happened to your friend. The blame lies one-hundred percent with the guy doing this, none of it rests at your door," Ax eloquently declares.

Orlando contributes his two-cents, "Yeah, Peyton, just because some asshole is going around hurting people and he seems to have a thing for you, doesn't mean that's the case. Maybe he was after Roger before and it just worked out for him to hurt Roger in the middle of him trying to hurt you. You need to be aware of your surroundings at all times, not go out alone, and trust no one. Forget about blame. We need your boyfriend to catch this fucker and lock him up."

"I know you're right. I'll try to quit blaming myself. It's hard, but I do agree with all of you. I'll be fine. I also promise to continue to be very careful. Okay?"

Everyone confirms their approval of her statement. Our gathering breaks up after that. We're all tired. Orlando and Ax are going out of town for a few days and we agree to keep an eye on Orlando's place, and thank them profusely for all of their help. Jake returns Orlando's clean clothing; he declines the boxers and gifts them to Jake. I get it. There's just something sacred about having your boys in your own underwear, and never in someone else's.

Peyton and Jake want to watch a movie. I have work to do so I leave them to it. Beta joins me in the office. I guess Qwerty and Felony are with Peyton. They must be so confused about where they live. I'm getting tired of dragging stuff back and forth. I wonder if Peyton would consider moving in together. I'll have to talk to her about it. I'll have to check with my landlord about my lease too.

I make a note on my phone to speak to them and a reminder to grab some cat food at the pet store. We probably need kitty litter too. I'll have to check. Okay, enough procrastination. I dig into work. I have more reports to read and file.

"Micah?" Peyton sticks her head into the office, "I'm going to bed and Jake is, um, heading to sofa? Are you going to be finished soon?"

"Shit. I didn't realize the time. Sorry I bailed on you guys. Yeah, I'll be right there. Just need to finish this last bit."

"Okay, see you in a few." Beta follows her out. He must be ready for bed too. When I enter the bedroom Peyton is lying on her side scratching Qwerty, who is coiled up against her. Felony is in her own bed and Beta is on the foot of the bed watching me.

"We need cat food. Do you know if we need kitty litter?" I ask.

"Yeah, we need everything, some groceries too. I'll take Jake and get what we need tomorrow. I know you have work and you've already missed a lot. Jake and I are excused from school, so we'll handle it."

"Can I talk to you about Jake?" She cringes and sits up straighter. I smile reassuringly at her, sitting on the edge of the bed next to her, I take her hand in mine.

"How bad is this going to be?" she asks.

"Nothing bad. I was wondering if you think he's going to want to get a different place. Then I was thinking that I would love to live with you, here or at my place. It occurred to me, maybe Jake would want to take whichever place we move out of, thoughts?"

"Oh. Hmm, I would love to live with you. The thought of sleeping alone hurts my head and my heart. I feel bad you're always living out of a bag and the poor cats being dragged back and forth must be confusing for them." She looks at me like it's my turn to talk. Realizing I've been holding my breath, I take in a deep breath of air.

"Is that a...yes? You'll move in with me? Or I'll move in with you?"

"Yes! Sorry, thought I said that. We'll have to figure out which place makes more sense. But I have to say, I think I want to stay here. What do you want?"

"That sounds good to me. I like this place. Let's think about it and talk about it some more tomorrow. We need to talk to our landlords and Jake too. Has he said anything about what he wants to do about his apartment?" I ask.

"Yeah, he doesn't want to stay there. He was talking about looking for a place. and this might work out great." She yawns and looks worn out. She seemed restless last night, and I don't think she slept well. Hopefully tonight will go better.

I climb into bed and pull her close. She snuggles into me and rests her cheek on my chest. My tension eases, knowing she's safe in my arms is just about the only thing that makes me completely calm these days. I'm trying not to be worried about the stalker. I'm not successful, but I'm trying. I wonder how Rhett is holding up. I had a hard time keeping him from charging over here and dragging Peyton to move into his house. I sigh as her breathing evens out. Man, I love this girl. I've got to keep her from harm.

Peyton

After our talk this morning, Micah went into the office to work. Jake wants to take Micah's apartment. We'll all have to speak with our landlords, then there'll be a weekend of moving. We settled on Jake staying with us at my place until after the funeral. Now we're at the pet shop to pick up what I need for the cats.

"It smells weird in here," Jake states. I laugh at him.

"Haven't you ever been in a pet shop before?"

"Actually, no, I haven't." He smirks at me.

"How is that possible? You've never had a pet? Or at least been curious?" My eyes are wide with shock.

"Nope. My mother never allowed any animals in the house. I grew up in the city. I never had any interest. I went to the zoo once on a school field trip, does that count?" he asks with a goofy grin.

"No. You seem okay with the cats; they don't bother you?"

"They're pretty cute. The black one, I mean Felony, was laying on top of me when I woke up this morning. When I looked at her, she started purring, and it was cool. I suppose I like pets okay... I just don't want to have to clean up after them. So, I think visiting your cats is about my limit." He smiles a big toothy grin.

"As long as you're good with our cats, you're still my friend," I chuckle, and he realizes what I said.

"Hey! Not nice, Eagle Head." Now my jaw falls open in offense.

I stop. "There's the dry food I need." I point to the top shelf too far out of my reach. He's not as tall as Micah, but he can reach it and places it in the cart. We had a few cases of canned food in the cart already. Now I just need the litter. They keep it at the back of the store.

As we walk to the back, I reprimand him, "You aren't allowed to call me Eagle. That is Micah's and *only* Micah's nickname for me."

"I didn't, I called you Eagle Head. Get it right, Miss Baker!"

"Oh, you! That's it!" I lunge at him and tickle him. He chases after me and right when I get to the last aisle, my cart smacks into another cart.

"Ow!" I blurt as the jolt vibrates through me like when you hit your funny bone.

"Shit! Peyton, I'm sorry. Are you okay?" Jake questions.

I shake out my hands and look at the stranger I just crashed into. He looks familiar.

"Oh my God, I'm so sorry. Are you alright?" I ask him.

"Peyton?" The stranger asks.

"Yeah?"

"Hi, I'm Tristan. Remember, we met when you were moving into your place? Me and Jason helped you bring your stuff upstairs, then we all had lunch?" The tall, light-haired guy says.

"Oh yeah. Are you okay?"

"I'm fine. Is this your boyfriend?" he asked me.

"No. This is my friend, Jake," I look at Jake. "This is Tristan. He helped me move in when he came to move out some furniture for my landlord. He and his friend, Jason, took me to lunch since I was new to the area and clueless about where to find good food."

Jake is stiff and eyeing Tristan hard, "Hey."

"Nice to meet you," Tristan says, holding out his hand for Jake. He shakes it reluctantly. He's wound up and in protective mode. He reminds me of Rhett.

"I guess you got a cat since you moved in. I have two, they're so spoiled," Tristan says as he looks over the cat food in my cart. I look at the litter in his cart, and nod.

"Yeah, the Renault's are really sweet. They had no issue with me getting a cat. I rescued her from Furry Paws."

"I love that place. They're so nice. I take my two guys to Dr. Ree. Have you met her yet?"

"Yes, I love her too. She's our vet now, she's a gem."

Jake stands silent, watching us chat. He's making me uncomfortable, so I wrap up our conversation.

"It was nice seeing you. We have more errands to run. We better get to it. Take care."

"Yeah, good seeing you. Take care. Maybe we'll cross paths again, at Dr. Ree's office," he chuckles, and I join in.

"Maybe. Bye, Tristan."

"Bye Peyton, Jake." He nods and rounds the corner.

I stop in front of the litter I want, and Jake helps me put two huge bags on the shelf beneath the cart. He's quiet, I wonder if he's missing Roger.

"Are you okay?"

"Fine. Do you need anything else?"

"I usually get a cat toy when I shop here. The toys at home are worn out. Do you mind visiting the toy aisle?"

"No, I don't mind." He waits for me to lead the way. I don't want to shine a spotlight on whatever is bothering him, so I let it go.

After all the groceries are put away and the cats get their toys, we put on a movie while we wait for our dinner to cook. I picked up some ready to cook chicken cordon bleu and au Gratin potatoes, with a pre-made Cesar salad. I'm a great ready-made chef. Micah's still working, and I'm worn out. The emotional toll has been exhausting all week.

Jake's text goes off and he texts back and forth with someone. I try to stay focused on Legally Blonde. It's funnier when you're a law student. I chuckle to myself when she shows up at the party in her bunny costume. That reminds me, the Halloween party is next Tuesday. I don't think I feel like going anymore. But I really want to see Micah in that costume. I'll have to talk it over with Jake and Micah.

Jake is smiling a huge grin. His cheeks are red and his eyes sparkle. I wonder who he's chatting with, I can't decide if it's rude to ask. When he finishes, he chuckles a little and notices I'm staring at him.

"That was Connor. He was checking in to see how we're all holding up. I invited him to the Halloween party. Is that okay?"

I swallow hard, surprised. "Yeah, of course. I wasn't sure if we would be up to going. But if you want to go, we'll go with you. Do you have a costume?"

"I do, but I didn't bring it with me. I'll need to go by my place over the weekend to grab it before Tuesday night."

"Micah and I'll go with you, don't worry. My brother and his wife are coming over Saturday for lunch, but any other time, I'm there."

We settle back into the movie until I can't keep from asking him. "So, you like Connor, huh?"

His face turns pink again, "I kinda do. He's really smart, and very kind. I always seem to hook up with the wrong guys. I'm thinking it might be better to try dating a nice guy for a change. What do you think?"

"I think you should go for it. Connor's really nice. He works at a cat rescue and shows up to help strangers. I think he's awesome. But what about that guy you hooked up with at that party? You're not involved with him?"

His face falls a bit, "No. Case in point, he ghosted me after he got what he wanted that night. I think I'm done with bad boys." I reach my arm around him and hug him. I rest my head on his shoulder, and we finish watching the movie.

Peyton

When we wake up Saturday morning, I clean a little in preparation for Rhett's visit. Jake works on all the laundry. Micah had to run some errands, pick up some stuff from his place, and go by the bank. When Jake's phone rings he gives me a weird look after he checks who's calling. I raise my brows at him.

"Hello, Mrs. Stanley, what can I do for you?"

Now I understand. He hates talking to them, their grief is painful for all of us. They act like Jake is another son, and it makes him really uncomfortable. I get it, well I understand, I can't imagine the terrible loss they're feeling.

"Oh, okay. Yeah, sure. I can do that."

He looks unhappy. They must want him to do something with them, and that's the most difficult. His own parents went home the day after his police interview. The Stanley's haven't left. I think they're avoiding going home without their son.

"I can probably be there in twenty minutes...It's fine, really. Okay...Okay...See you then."

He rolls his eyes. "They want me to meet them at the apartment. They packed up his room, but they don't know what's mine and what's his in the rest of the house. They want me to meet them while the movers are still there. Are you going to be okay if I leave?"

"Yeah, I'm fine. My brother's coming in a couple hours. Go do what you need to do. Don't forget to grab your Halloween costume, okay?"

"All right, I better get going. They're waiting on me."

"Okay. Don't let them keep you too long. I know they make you uncomfortable, you don't have to fill the void of their loss. Protect yourself, please."

"Yes ma'am. Thanks Eagle Head," he runs away so I can't smack him.

"Dick!" We both laugh. It breaks the tension from his call.

I keep cleaning after he leaves. I dust everything, vacuum every room, and scrub the bathroom. When I'm ready to start on the kitchen the doorbell rings. I check the time, crap, they're early. I haven't even showered yet. Oh well, it's not like they care. I shove the cleaning supplies into the hall closet.

I fling the door open with a huge smile on my face, "You guys are early! Oh." I'm completely shocked. Tristan, mover-slash-pet shop guy, is standing there.

"Hi, I guess you were expecting someone else. Am I interrupting?"

"Uh, no, my brother's coming over soon. I was just cleaning. What're you doing here?" I'm confused to see him.

"I'm really sorry to stop by unannounced. May I come in? I wanted to talk to you."

"Sure, I guess. What's up?" I close the door behind him and follow him into the living room. We sit, him on the chair and me on the sofa.

"I didn't have your number, but I remembered where you live. That's why I stopped by, instead of calling first," he says looking a little chagrined.

"It's okay. What did you want?" I ask.

"When you were moving in, you said you didn't have a boyfriend. When I saw you at the pet shop, I thought Jake was your boyfriend. But you said he wasn't. I thought you were beautiful when I first saw you, but I was shy about asking you out. I can't believe you don't have a boyfriend. I wanted to know if you'd like to go out to dinner with me sometime?" He smiles earnestly waiting for my answer. Ugh, awkward. I swallow hard.

"Oh. Tristan, I'm sorry. Jake isn't my boyfriend, but I do have one. His name's Micah. He's actually moving in with me, I didn't mean to mislead you."

"Oh. Of course. It was wishful thinking that you'd be available, I guess. Or maybe you just aren't interested in dating a lowly moving man? Is that it?" His face is getting red and his fists clench. He's making me very nervous. Why the hell did I let him in? Shit!

He continues and my discomfort grows, "You could just be honest you know, I'm not stupid. If you don't want to go out with me, just say so. You don't have to make up a boyfriend." I stand and back away from him, I want to run but I'm not sure which way to go.

"You know, I'm really sick of stuck-up bitches lying to me. Why can't you just tell me the truth? Huh?" His eyes narrow, his mouth is a tight line.

"I'd like for you to go now, please," I do my best to sound stern and strong, but I'm terrified. I'm shaking and breathing hard. He stands, but he comes towards me instead of going towards the door. I step back until I'm against the wall but he follows.

"You know, if you gave me a chance you might like me. I can be nice. I'm not ugly. I don't get it. Why? Answer that and I'll go."

"Tristan, I wasn't lying. I'm sure you're very nice. You aren't ugly, but I really do have a boyfriend."

He boxes me in and I try to disappear into the wall. He places a hand next to my head and uses his other hand to touch my face. I twist my face away from him. He bares his teeth and I think he growls at me. He puts his hand on my throat, thankfully not crushing it, though I can't move. I try not to look at him, if I do, I'm going to cry and look even weaker. His other hand brushes through my hair and I cringe. He looks into my eyes, I look away. I'm desperately trying to think of something to say that will de-escalate the situation.

"Look, I have a boyfriend. But if you want to be friends, I'm okay with that," I try.

"I don't believe you, pretty girl. I think if you let me, I could show you a good time," he puts his lips to my ear and tightens his grip on my throat ever so slightly, "I could make you feel so good," he whispers and my skin crawls. Using his free hand he drags the tips of his fingers down my cheek, my neck, and to my chest. Tears fall without my consent. His fingers brush my breast and softly circle my nipple.

"P-please...stop. Please d-don't..." I'm shaking so hard. My insides are twisting in revolt. I unfreeze enough that my hand finds his wrist and I try to remove him from my throat. He doesn't budge. I wiggle and try to slip away to the side. His other hand grabs my breast in a painful grip. I freeze again, in the grip of a fear like I've never felt before.

"Hold still. I don't want to hurt you. I just want to make you feel good." His hand releases my breast and he fumbles at my waist, oh God, he's trying to unfasten my shorts. I kick at him and hit anything I can reach, scratching at his face. He growls at me again and presses his body against mine, holding me in place. His hands get ahold of mine and he locks my wrists in his strong grip. His hip presses into my belly and his knee tries to pry between my legs.

"Don't fight me. I mean it, you're going to get hurt. Just let me touch you. You'll see, I can make it so good."

When I feel his hand touch the skin on my stomach something snaps inside me. With a burst of strength, I throw my arms up and rip my body to the side, taking him by surprise. I wish I could kick him where it counts like Rhett taught me. But in that brief instant I'm able to break free, I take the opportunity, I scream and run to my bedroom. He's right behind me. I keep screaming, now that I've found my voice, it won't stop. I slam my door and lean hard against it, engaging the lock. I quickly use my back and shove the tall dresser in front of the door. I lean there gasping for breath.

The dresser rattles as he bangs against the door. I take that moment and check my pockets for my phone. It's not there, I recall it's on the kitchen counter, where I placed it while I cleaned. He bangs against the door again. It sounds like he's using his whole body to slam against the door. The dresser moves, slanting momentarily away from the door then it falls flat, back on its feet. I frantically search the room for a weapon to protect myself. Micah has his back-up gun here. Thankfully, it's locked in a safe otherwise I might be tempted to try to use it. I would probably end up shooting my own foot or something. I'm clueless about using a firearm.

He bangs against the door and I hear a terrible crack. Backing up, I watch the door while I try to figure out if I should hide. Maybe I should climb out a window. I rush to the closest one and lift it open. The screen prevents me from looking straight down. The ground I can see looks painfully far away. I have a slight fear of heights, jumping from a second story window qualifies as part of my phobia.

I fall to the ground and look under the bed, I'm not sure I could fit under there. He'd probably look there first if he gets in. The closet is probably the best option. I use the chair I have in the corner to pop out the window screen and I throw one of my shoes out the window. Then I crawl behind the longer clothes at the back of the closet and stack some things in front of me. The door cracks louder with what must be his whole body slamming into it and the dresser almost falls over. It's come away from the door by a few inches now.

On his next attempt he breaks the door and the dresser moves further allowing him to push against it. Oh God, he's going to get in here any minute. I'm trying to steady my breathing so I don't give myself away. I take off my other shoe and pull my legs up beneath me. I think I'm out of sight. I pray he thinks I went out the window. I know it's silly, but I can't look. I close my eyes and just concentrate on breathing as quietly as possible. When there's a terrible loud sound my eyes snap open.

His next strike sends the dresser at least a foot from the door, it teeters precariously before landing upright again. The door crashes inward in pieces, and I slam my eyes shut. I have to force my lungs to take in a breath. If I don't stay focused I'll become lightheaded from holding my breath. I hear things falling and a loud scraping noise as the dresser is moved across the floor. It crashes into the bed and breaks the frame.

"Where are you?" He sing-songs, "Come on out. I'm not going any-where. I'm going to show you what I can do whether you want it or not."

It's amazing how your hearing can zero in on the smallest sounds when you're frozen in terror. I can hear his footsteps move away from me. The window sill rasps as he leans on it. I imagine he's looking at my shoe below and trying to determine if I'm gone. His steps come closer and stop at the closet door. They're a few steps away from the closet before they stop again. The pop of a knee protesting reaches me. In my mind I see him squatting down to look under the broken bed.

A soft scuff of a shoe sounds even further from the closet. Then a crunch of wood as if someone has stepped on a broken piece of the door. He must be going out to see if I'm on the ground beneath the house. My muscles relax ever so slightly. My mind spins with what I should do next. I need to get to my phone, or the alarm panic button by the front door. In the throes of fear, I forgot it was there. I strain my ears and try to hear any sound he makes. The front door opens. It's a distinct squeak and the pressure in the house changes. A breeze flows through the room from the open window now that it has an exit path.

As quiet as a mouse, I uncoil my body and move the things I stacked in front of me. I noiselessly crawl from under the clothes and stand. My foot is asleep from sitting on it. I shake it out and the pins and needles come alive all the way to my calf. I press my weight onto it a few times until the feeling returns and the red ants retreat.

I pad softly across the room and assess the damage. I pick my way through the splinters of wood littered on the floor. Squeezing behind the fallen dresser I peek out into the hallway, leaning just far enough to see the front door is open. I press my body against the wall and tip toe toward the kitchen on the hunt for my phone. I recognize a feeling in my bladder that makes me debate a pit stop. I threaten my bladder to remain intact and pass the door of the bathroom. Feeling a little more secure, I speed up.

Pain flashes across my body as an elephant hits me from behind. My breath gushes from my lungs leaving me with none. My feet lift from the floor, my hands raise to protect my face from impact with the wall or the floor. Octopus arms wrap around me and squeeze. I fall forward with the weight of the hunter on my back. His growls rumble in my ear. His nails dig into my middle like talons of a great beast. At the last moment his weight shifts and we turn enough that he protects me from hitting the ground at full speed. I land most of my body on his. My knee is the only thing that hits the floor, a stinging scrape burns around it. I take in a huge breath as soon as my lungs allow and scream bloody murder. As my brain engages, I understand he found me. At the same time, my mind rejects that possibility.

I become a wild thing. My head twisting back and forth like the exorcist. Arms and legs flail independently trying to strike or scratch the enemy. Whatever harm I can cause, I will. I scream like a screech owl that's mixed with a fire-breathing dragon. No words, just extreme terror and retaliation pour from my open maw. I push away from him and the floor as hard as I can. Surprisingly I'm able to escape him and stumble to an upright, if not natural, posture. Still screaming, I ignore the pain traveling my leg, and step over him, towards freedom. When I'm just five feet from the border between certain death and possible escape, a dark figure blocks my way. Not willing to stop, I barrel past the tall, dark shadow. Near the porch stairs stands a much smaller figure, it has two heads and a round middle. I skid to a stop.

When my terrorized mind comes back online, I'm able to compute the scene before me. My gorgeous sister-in-law stands there, on my porch, holding my beautiful niece. I quickly close in on them and wrap myself around them. I carefully guide them down the stairs. I look at her in question, she hands me the key-fob. I depress the button and open the back door for her. She places Nova in her car seat inside the rear door. She quickly fastens Nova's harness and climbs past her. Then I close the door, open the front door and climb in. I jump into the driver's seat as I lock the doors. Paige and I look at the stairs for any sign of life.

Paige takes out her phone and calls Micah, "Get to Peyton's NOW! She's okay, but we have a situation. How long? We're locked in my car. Get upstairs and help Rhett as fast as you can. We're safe. Okay, love you."

She meets my eyes and her pretty orbs assess me. Without realizing, I look down in guilt. When I grasp what I just did, my face snaps to Paige. It's not my fault. How many assault victims have I said that to? It doesn't matter if I let him in, or dressed provocatively, or even encouraged his advances, which I definitely did not. When I said no, it should have ended.

She waits patiently for me to tell her what happened. "A mover who helped me when I got here... I bumped into him yesterday and he misunderstood when I said Jake wasn't my boyfriend. He knocked on the door wanting to talk to me. I didn't think so I let him in. When I explained about Micah, he attacked me." Her face is tight, there's no judgment. She just looks pissed off.

She takes a deep breath, "Are you injured?"

"No. Not really. Some scrapes and bruises."

She looks at her phone then dials, "I need fire rescue at 77 Sand Dollar Lane. Yes, ma'am. She was attacked, not sure. Nothing appears broken. Yes. Peyton, are you hurting anywhere specific?"

"My knee and my chest."

"Her knee and chest. I don't know, the authorities are on their way. Yes, ma'am. FBI. SA Micah Castleman. Thank you."

"Aunt Pey?" A small voice calls out, I forgot she was here. I guess the stress rendered her silent.

"Yes, button?"

"Okay? You got bonks?" Her sweet little face scrunches up in empathy.

"Just a little bonk. When we can go, you can kiss it for me okay?"

"Kay." She smiles her little gap tooth grin and instantly returns her attention to the truck in her hand.

"Wow, I wish I could change my thoughts so easily," I state.

"I know, me too. It's a little person gift." Micah's SUV slides to a stop behind us. He glances our way, not slowing. He runs up the steps and disappears from our view.

A siren rises in the distance. When the fire rescue truck pulls up, Rhett comes down the stairs. His hair is mussed and the middle of his lip is split, otherwise he looks okay. Despite her large baby-bump, Paige hops out of the truck and runs to him. He bends down and catches her as she flings herself at him. I can see her speaking into his ear but I don't hear anything. I'm so thankful he's okay. Now, where's Micah?

"Pey, I want daddy," A sweet little voice breaks the silence.

"Sure, thing button, just a minute, okay? Mommy and daddy will tell us when we can get out," I smile, trying to make everything seem normal. Her blue eyes assess me, and I swear she can tell everything is not okay. She's very bright, like her namesake, and she often leaves me flabbergasted the same way.

Paige and Rhett make their way over to us. The EMTs ask them where the victim is located. My brother asks them for a moment to help me exit the SUV. I take that as a signal it's safe for us to climb out. I twist through the front seats and help Nova out of her carseat. When Rhett opens the door, she jumps into his arms. His eyes are locked on me.

"Is Micah all right?" My voice waivers.

"He's fine. Are you?"

"Yeah, I think so," I fight back tears.

"Who the fu...fudge, is that guy?"

"He's a mover. He was one of the guys who helped move my stuff when I moved in here. I ran into him at the pet shop, he was always nice. When he knocked on the door, I wasn't thinking, and I let him inside. This is all my fault." The tears start to fall. Rhett shifts Nova on his hip and hugs me tight. Paige takes Nova and he hugs me full on.

"Don't be ridiculous, you know it's not your fault. You should be able to trust people you know. Come on, let's see the EMTs."

He guides me to their truck. They open the back and ask me to come inside, Rhett helps me climb up. My knee is swollen and stiff. I didn't notice how much it hurt until now. Adrenaline is the best pain medication around. Rhett climbs in after me since he's not willing to leave me alone. Another SUV pulls up and I can just see a sliver of Samson getting out of it. Rhett doesn't even look in that direction, all of his attention on me.

The EMT checks my vitals which are fine. He puts an icepack on my knee. Then he cleans off my scrapes, which sting. Rhett turns away so the EMT can look at my chest. My breast is bruised and there're some scratches there and my belly. Nothing serious, my knee is just bruised. The EMT suggests I see my doctor if it's not feeling better tomorrow. I have to stay off of it and ice it the rest of today. It doesn't escape me how much worse things could've been and I'm grateful things ended like they did. Finally, Micah enters the rescue truck. He grasps my hand and kisses it.

"Can I hug him?" I ask the EMT.

"Yeah, I'm finished with you. Be careful climbing out, and keep it iced as much as you can, take Tylenol for pain. Any questions?"

I shake my head in reply, completely focused on Micah. He pulls me up into his arms and I relax at last. He kisses my face and my lips in between looking me over. I look him over too. He appears uninjured.

"Are you hurt?" I ask him.

"No. Rhett had him restrained when I got here. I just cuffed him and searched him. He told me he knows you, and you invited him inside. He tried to play it off like he wasn't doing anything wrong. Please, tell me what happened."

"I do know him and I did let him in, I didn't invite him exactly... He's one of the movers from when I first got here. Remember, they helped me get my trailer unloaded and took me to lunch?"

"Yeah, I remember. Why was he here today?" I explain what happened starting with the pet shop and ending with the EMTs.

"Fuck. I'm so sorry I wasn't here. Please forgive me," he pleads.

"Forgive you? Are you crazy? How's this your fault? I'm the idiot who let him inside. I wasn't thinking. He seemed so nice the two times I've seen him. It didn't occur to me he could be a complete psychopath. I'm the one who's sorry. Look at all this, it's my fault," I babble and wave my hand to indicate the collection of responders who came to my rescue.

"Okay, let's put the blame where it belongs, on him. It's definitely not your fault, I'll accept it's not mine either, okay?"

I hug him, my arms squeeze his middle tight, "Yeah, okay. Are you arresting him? Or are you calling the police to do it?"

"I'm taking care of it. Please don't panic, but his phone had your photo as the screensaver."

My eyes pop wide, my mouth drops open in shock. I can't believe it. Why would he have a picture of me, how would he have a picture of me? Holy crap, this just got scary. I try to remain calm like Micah asked me to.

"Did you ask him why?"

"Yeah, he's not talking. He asked for a lawyer and hasn't said a word. Samson is sitting with him until we're done. I need to finish going through his phone. His record says he's done this sort of thing before. He stalked two other women and assaulted them."

I gasp and cover my mouth in shock. I'm so lucky I got away without more injuries. My God, I could be seriously injured right now. Oh, what if he's my stalker? Is that possible? I mean, I couldn't have two stalkers. Holy shit, this is crazy.

"Do you think he's my stalker?"

"I don't know, maybe. He's not saying anything, so I'll have to investigate and see if we can figure that out. I didn't want to be away from you for another minute, so I came to check on you. Now that I know you're safe, I can get to work. Samson is going to transport him. I already requested a search warrant for his house, but it may take 24 hours according to the court clerk. I need to get it before Mr. Price can get out on bail and get rid of any evidence. He lives in Oakdale and if he gets out on bail, there'll be a restraining order to keep him away from you."

"That's good. Thankfully, you're going to be on the case. That makes me feel much better. Oh, there's Jake."

Jake gets out of his car with a look of fear on his face. Paige intercepts him, he relaxes so I assume she explained that I'm safe. I don't want to see Tristan again. I wonder how we're going to handle the logistics. I need to call the Renault's and tell them what happened before a neighbor calls and scares them. We get out of the fire rescue truck and make our way to Rhett's family.

"You're coming to our house," Rhett demands. Paige elbows him, "If you want to." He gives me his stern big brother face. I smile at him and look at Micah, he's nodding.

"That's a great idea. You go to Rhett's and take the cats. I'll get busy with investigating and hopefully exercising some search warrants. Jake can stay at my place, and if it's okay, I'll join you when I can. Will that be alright Rhett? Jake?"

Paige speaks up, answering on Rhett's behalf, "Yes of course. Peyton will come with us and the cats. You join her whenever you're free and we'll make sure she's safe. Nova will love having Aunt Peyton visit."

Right on cue, "Aunt Pey! Aunt Pey!" She reaches her tiny hands out to me.

I take her little hands and kiss them, "Is it okay if I come stay at your house, Nova?"

"Yes! Yes! Yay!" She bounces in Rhett's arms.

"I'm going to need to pack some things. I don't want to go inside with him here though. What're we going to do?"

"You go with Paige and Nova to our house. We'll pack everything and I'll drive your car over when we're done here. Micah will know what you need, right?"

Jake answers, "Yeah, Micah and I'll be able to handle it. We'll pack up you and the cats in no time. I'm fine with staying at Micah's place."

"Jake, you're welcome to come too. We have more than one guest room," Paige interjects.

"Thanks, that's really nice of you to offer, but I need to work on being able to stay on my own. I'll be happy to accept invitations to hang out though," he grins. I give him an appreciative hug.

"You're invited any time," Paige offers him a brilliant smile. I'm so glad she likes Jake. Rhett is still on the fence, though I think he's beginning to lean toward Jake's side.

Once the decision is made and I'm finished giving my statement, Paige and I are in the car with Nova heading to their house in no time. Micah brought my phone and purse downstairs. Everything else will be brought by Rhett later.

Not wanting to say details out loud in front of Nova, but desperately needing to vent, I text Anisa and fill her in on what happened. She wants to know if Tristan is good looking. I roll my eyes every time she replies. Eventually she gives me the proper amount of sympathy for my circumstances. I finish up with her as we pull up in front of Paige's house. I let out a sigh and the tension eases from me. I feel safe here, it feels good.

Micah

Tristan Price is a registered sex offender. He's stalked and attacked two women that we know about. Both women have blonde hair, blue eyes, and are similarly built to Peyton. Her photos are on his phone. There's one in a place I don't recognize and I suspect it's Baton Rouge. The others are from here, in Florida. Some are at her house. A couple at a restaurant, and a few more at the pet shop.

We looked into his car through the windows, on the front seat, sitting in plain view is a length of rope, a pair of gloves, some zip ties, and a small brown bottle. It looks like he had plans no matter what she said or did today. I'm really glad Rhett beat the shit out of him. I wish it could've been me, but my case'd be blown if it was me.

I've arranged for repairs of the damage to Peyton's house, again. I'm continuing to search Tristan's background while waiting for the contractor to show up for the repair. I contacted Peyton's landlords myself. I wanted to know how they found Tristan Price as a mover. They have no clue who he is since they hired a guy from an app who was listed as a handyman/jack of all trades, with hundreds of good reviews, Jason Treadmore. When I finally track him down, he claims he met Tristan that morning of the move, at a big box store. His usual helper was a no-show, and when he was complaining about it on the phone, Tristan overheard, spoke-up, and offered to help for $100. I'm not sure I believe him since it doesn't fit with the facts I know to be true. Jason Treadmore is a drug addict with an extensive record. I don't see any reason to trust him. I'm frustrated with the lack of answers.

Rhett left about a half hour ago with Peyton's car loaded up with our things and the cats. Jake headed out right before Rhett. My landlord is cool with Jake staying at my place for a while. As long as the rent is paid and the apartment is maintained, she's agreeable to just about anything. I wish at least one of the cats was here, it's too quiet.

Rhett helped me reinstall the screen in Peyton's window. I cleaned up the mess too. The only thing left to do is replace the door and her bed frame. I check the time again; the contractor should be here with the new door and bed frame soon. The search warrant shouldn't be much longer either. Thankfully Samson knows everyone and he was able to get a hold of a different judge and get the warrant expedited. We just have to wait for this judge to finish his golf game, must be nice.

My phone rings and I dive on it, "Castleman?"

"Good afternoon, this is the clerk of court Bethany Braxton. I have your warrant in hand sir. I'm sending it electronically now and it'll be at your crime scene in 20 minutes," the woman's voice tells me.

"Perfect. Thank you." I check the time again. I'm debating calling the contractor to reschedule when there's a knock at the door. Standing on the porch, is a big guy in a white t-shirt and jeans with a tool belt slung around his waist, holding a new door.

"Hey, how's it going? There's an extra hundred in it for you if you can be done in twenty minutes or less," I greet him.

His smile grows, "Yes sir! I'm on it."

I show him to the bedroom, and he gets to work like he has a fire lit beneath his feet. I love people who understand urgency. I decided to check in with Samson and Peyton while I wait.

"I'm good, I promise. Felony is enamored with Rio. The two of them are chasing each other all over the house, it's so cute. Qwerty and Beta are hanging out with Bingo and Nacho. It's like a cat retreat over here," Peyton reports.

"I'm glad everyone's getting along. Did I pack everything you need?"

"I haven't really gone through everything yet. But with the quick check I did, it seems like it. How're you doing over there all alone?"

"The door repair man is here, and my warrants are on their way. I should be finished here fairly soon. Then I'll be heading over to Oakdale to search Price's home. I'll keep you posted. I wish I was there with you. I miss you and I want to hold you," I whine.

"I miss you too. But I'm safe, don't worry about me. Do what you need to do and put that asshole away for a long time so he can't hurt anyone else. I'll be right here when you're finished," she reassures me.

"I love you."

"I love you, too. Good luck! May your searches be fruitful, and may the odds be ever in your favor," she chuckles.

"Thanks, Eagle."

"Thank you, Radiohead. I'll see you later, bye."

"Bye, beautiful." I dial Samson next. I'm smiling and I feel more relaxed. I love that woman so much. Knowing she's with the other man who loves her as much as I do helps. I know she's safe at Rhett's.

"Hey, Micah," Samson greets me.

"Hey, the warrant is on the way. I called for the tow truck, I'll run an inventory on the car. His house will be next. I'll let you know when I'm ready for the team to meet me there. They can go over the car at the impound."

"Sounds good. He's still not talking, and his lawyer is on the way. He won't be arraigned until Monday. We'll have him until then at least. Is Peyton, okay?"

"Yeah, she's settling in at Rhett's. She says the cats are all getting along, but she sounds good."

"Glad to hear it, but I'm going to have Dr. Newman call her. It won't hurt for her to have a phone consultation with the trauma specialist. If she needs a follow up, she'll have a starting point. If she doesn't, no harm, no foul," Samson explains.

"Thanks. We appreciate it. The repair man seems to be finishing up, I'll check in with updates."

"Same. Micah?"

"Yeah?"

"I'm proud of you, son," Samson surprises me with his praise.

"Thank you, sir. That means a lot. I'll talk to you later," I try to keep the emotion from my voice, but I'm not very successful.

"Okay. Sounds good." We disconnect. The door is fixed, it took only eighteen minutes, the bed frame just came apart but he snapped it back together. I happily pay the man, and hand over an extra hundred-and-twenty-bucks bonus. He's thrilled. As he leaves, he offers to work for me any time, any place.

When his truck vanishes around the corner, a small blue car comes into focus. A little man wearing an ID from the court's courier service, hands me a hard copy of the search warrants for the perpetrator's car and home, specifying all electronics, and any structures on the premises that can be attributed to our suspect. I sign his paperwork and thank him. I have the keys for the car and residence. They were in his pocket.

I collect some evidence bags, and gloves from the back of my SUV. Peyton's security footage will document what I'm doing overall. I use my phone to document up close.

I unlock the car and film everything inside before I collect the items. After I have all the things from his front seat bagged and tagged, I open the glove box. It's mostly paperwork related to the car, his owner manual and insurance information. There're a few court documents showing he's a registered sex offender. He also has information about his therapist and treatment program ordered under court supervision. I film each document and place them into an evidence bag. His car is surprisingly clean. I didn't find any trash under the seats. In the center console is a box of condoms. I bag it and try to keep my anger under control.

In the trunk I find a shovel and trash bags, along with an unopened tarp. What the fuck was this asshole planning? Combined with the little brown bottle, which I suspect is chloroform, there's enough circumstantial evidence to paint a disturbing picture. Possession of chloroform is illegal, in the hands of a sex offender, it's terrifying.

When I'm finished and I have all of the evidence in my trunk, I text Peyton and Samson to let them know I'm headed to his residence now. Samson confirms he's sending the lab techs, and the tow truck is on its way for the car. Thankfully, I don't have to wait for it. I double check the alarm and make sure the locks are engaged before I leave.

I pull up to a squat building containing four units. Number eighty-four is listed as the landlord's address. I want to start there. Apparently, this guy is also a registered sex offender, as are all the tenants here. I'm not sure if it's good or bad to have them gathered in one spot. It keeps them away from neighborhoods and meets the 1000 feet requirements for distance from playgrounds, schools, and daycares. However, it just allows them to fraternize with other offenders, which is up for debate as to how dangerous it is to have them learning from each other. Some offenders are prohibited from contact with other offenders. Usually, those are the ones who traffic or distribute children and child porn.

I knock on his door, and a bald, sweaty man reluctantly answers. "Are you here for Tristan's place?"

"Yes sir. I have a warrant. Are there any outbuildings or storage facilities on the premises for Mr. Price?" I handed him a copy of the warrant.

"Yeah. He has storage room three. Here's a key. Just return it before you leave. Do you need a key for his unit?" He asks as if he is bored to death.

"No sir, I have a key. Does Mr. Price have any pets?"

"No pets allowed," he snaps.

"Thank you. I'll return the key when I'm finished." He slams the door in my face. What a pleasant guy.

When I reach his unit, the lab team arrives. They're suited up. I pull paper booties over my shoes, and I film as they enter with the key. The place is immaculate. It smells clean. We look through everything, every drawer, every book, every container, and find absolutely nothing. Brighton Hughes is the lead tech today, and he's meticulous. When he lifts the mattress, he finds a couple magazines with centerfolds. He collects them. He also collects some hair from the bathroom for DNA testing. I bag and tag his laptop. That's it, there's nothing else.

We make our way to storage unit number three. It's like a closet more than anything else. It's also incredibly neat and clean. The shelves contain mostly memorabilia. Old yearbooks, photo albums, trophies, a few base-balls and a glove. On the top shelf is a shoe box. When Brighton opens it, he freezes.

"Micah, you better look at this."

I aim my phone at him and the box. Inside, it's filled with images of Peyton. There're photos from Baton Rouge and Florida. There's a small prescription bottle without a label. Inside are small vials of a clear liquid. Brighton bags it. I bag the photographs still inside the shoe box.

"I'll check this right away. I'll let you know immediately if it matches," he assures me.

"Thanks."

We finish up, finding nothing else in the storage closet. I returned the key to the 'friendly' landlord. It's getting late and I'm tired, despite the way my brain is spinning with all the possibilities. Brighton leaves for the lab, freshly loaded with the evidence from my trunk and the residence.

I text Peyton that I'm on my way and call Samson with an update. I'm still having a hard time making all the pieces fit together. Price was a resident of Florida when Peyton was in Baton Rouge. It doesn't mean he didn't travel there and stalk her without reporting his whereabouts to Florida law enforcement, or Louisiana for that matter. I can't piece together how he started stalking Peyton or why. It makes no sense. I'm missing something.

I let it go when I pulled up at Rhett's. My beautiful girl comes running out to greet me and I don't care about anything else. I catch her in my arms and kiss her hard. She presses her tongue into my mouth, and we kiss like we've been separated for months.

"I'm so happy you're here!" She glows with elation.

Peyton

After Micah eats, we turn in. It's been a long day and I can see how tired he is, and something else is weighing him down.

Once we're showered and snuggled in bed, I ask, "I can tell something is on your mind. Can you talk about it? Or do you want to?"

He lets out a big sigh, "I can talk to you about it, though I probably shouldn't. Maybe you can help me figure it out."

"What did you find?"

"Nothing good. I promise you're safe from him. He's locked up, and if that changes, we'll all keep you safe. You know that, right?"

"Of course. I know you and Rhett would kill to protect me. I guess I can't leave Paige out either." My chuckle is a nervous burst.

"I found some disturbing things. First of all, this guy is a registered sex offender. He's stalked and assaulted at least two women." He looks at me intensely, inspecting my face. I gasped when he said *sex offender*, as I thought the guy was nice. I really need to stop being so naïve and trusting.

Satisfied, he continues, "He had some things in his car that seemed to indicate nefarious intentions. We're lucky Rhett showed up when he did.

I may have been too late. That won't happen again." He looks at the floor and I meet his intense gaze, nodding. I know he'll beat himself up about not being there. I certainly don't blame him for anything. That blame rests firmly on me, though I'm trying not to unfairly abuse myself over it. I'm not having much luck so far.

"I know. What else did you find?"

"It's weird. His place was immaculate, and he must have OCD. There wasn't anything in his apartment. He also had a storage unit. It was neat and clean as well... disturbingly so. There was a shoe box on the top shelf with pictures of you. They're pictures from here and Baton Rouge." My mouth opens in surprise. Big ugly moths take flight in my belly and I feel a chill crawling uncomfortably across my skin.

I voice my thoughts. "How's that possible? I never saw him before the day I moved here. Wait, the first note said he was going to find out where I went, like he didn't know. How did he show up here, at my house, so fast?"

"Exactly. I don't understand it. I'm missing something. He's been around the block, so he asked for his lawyer and remained silent. I can't ask him if he was in Louisiana. I'm going to have to dig, old fashioned detective style, and see what I can find out about where he's been."

"Wow, I'm totally shocked. I'm pretty good with faces and I have a good memory. I would have recognized him if I'd seen him before. Unless he wore a disguise or something. Do you think that's a possibility?"

"Anything's possible. We didn't find anything resembling a disguise in his apartment or his car. I don't know. I need to look at everything fresh tomorrow. You must be exhausted."

I snuggle into him. Beta is on the foot of the bed. Felony and Rio have become best friends in only a few hours. I don't know where they are, but presumably together. Qwerty is sleeping curled on the chair in the corner.

"Yeah, I'm pretty tired. My thoughts are spinning though. Would it be okay with you if I invite Jake and Anisa over tomorrow? I think we need some time together to refocus on school before we head back to class."

Tomorrow is Sunday, then it's back to school. I have some reading to finish, otherwise I'm caught up. Our study group isn't ready to gather without Roger. I may ask them over here to socialize and see if we can get some semblance of normalcy established before we return to class.

He hugs me close, "Of course, babe. Whatever you need. I'll work while you hang out with them. I'm sure Paige and Rhett won't mind. I think it'll be good for you and Jake, especially."

I rest my temple on his chest again and settle in. I try to relax and not think about the crazy negative stuff. I'm really tired. I forget what I was about to say and his breathing evens out before I remember. I force myself to think positive thoughts, and my sweet little niece comes to mind. She was so excited when we got here. She asked me twenty times if I was going to sleep here. Her adorable little face lighting up is the best thing for my troubled mind. She told me if I stay at her house, I have to read her a story before bed, and she held me to it. I read *Goodnight, Moon* twice before she fell asleep.

My next conscious thought is that I'm incredibly warm and comfortable. Light is visible behind my eyelids as my lashes flutter open. There's a small puddle of drool on Micah's shirt. Oops. My eyes shoot to his face in embarrassment. His beautiful eyes are watching me and he smiles.

"Oh my God, I'm so sorry," I desperately swipe at the damp spot.

"It's fine. You're so cute when you sleep. You were making little noises and smiling. I was enjoying the show," he smirks at me.

My face must be red and my cheeks feel hot. I sit up and stretch. He watches my every move. I checked the time and can't believe it's almost nine.

Once we're up and have eaten breakfast, I reach out to Jake and Anisa. Nova is playing with a doll. She's feeding it in the corner. Paige and Rhett are busy in the kitchen. Micah went to work in Rhett's office.

Me: Hi guys. Do you want to come to my brother's house and hang out a while today?

Anisa: Is his pool heated?

Me: Yeah, you want to swim?

Jake: I'm down, what time?

Anisa: Definitely, I need to work on my tan before it gets any colder.

Jake: it's like 75 dude

*Anisa: I know, *eye roll emoji*, but the water is too cold at the beach, or unheated pool*

Me: Pool party it is, what do you guys want for lunch?

Anisa: salad, I'm trying low carbs

Jake: Whatever's easy is fine, can I bring something?

Anisa: hard lemonade!
Me: Sure, anything that sounds good to you. What time can you come?
Anisa: 11ish
Jake: that works
Me: K see ya

I make our bed and get dressed in a swimsuit while entertaining Nova. She wants to swim too. I need to ask Paige before I tell her yes. Once I'm ready, I scoop her up and carry her to the kitchen. Rhett's making something on the stove top that smells delicious.

"Oooh, what are you making?"

"Eventually it'll be French onion soup. Right now, it's just onions and some beef. What's up with you? Are you going swimming?" Rhett asks.

"Is that okay?"

"Pey, I told you, treat it like it's your house. Do whatever you want. All we ask is that you keep little ears and eyes in mind," he smirks at me. As if I was considering a Playboy Mansion style party.

Paige smacks his arm, "Don't tease her!" She turns to me, "Do whatever you want. We trust you to manage little eyes and ears. Are your friends able to come over?" She comes closer, her growing belly prevents her from leaning against the island comfortably.

"Swim! I want to swim, Mama!" Nova tells her mom.

"Is it okay if she swims with us? I didn't want to say yes without asking you first," I interjected.

"I think it'll be okay. But you have to listen to Aunt Pey. When she says it's time to get out, that's it. You have nap time."

"Yaaaaay!" Nova squeals and wiggles so I'll put her down. She takes my hand and drags me towards her room.

I help her get dressed in a bathing suit. She has a little two-piece, and it's adorable. She's potty training and Paige said getting her out of a one-piece when she has to go is a nightmare. She has a little unicorn cover-up that I slip over her head.

"Let's use the potty before we go back to the kitchen." I used to ask her if she wanted to use the potty, but Paige pointed out my mistake in giving her the choice. I sit her on her little plastic seat that attaches over the regular seat. She pees and we have a celebration, then she adds a star to today on her little potty chart. She gets a prize for every five stars.

"Mama! I went pee-pee on the potty! I got four stars!" Paige praises her, then takes her to play in the other room while I wait for Jake and Anisa.

I find Micah in the office and fill him in on the plan.

"Good, I'm glad they're able to come. I think the three of you need a day of normal together."

"I couldn't agree more. Nova's going to swim for a little while before her nap. Maybe you can join us for a swim? Or at least lunch?"

"I can definitely do lunch. Ask me about swimming when you're ready to swim. I'm spiraling down a black hole trying to follow the movements of Price. He doesn't use credit cards. He doesn't have friends that I can find. I haven't been able to find any family except a cousin in Texas. It's getting frustrating."

"That's weird. You said he's a registered offender, are there records about his movements there?"

"Not really. He's only required to check in every six months. It's up to him. Nobody checks up on him unless he misses more than one check in. But he can check in by phone from anywhere. If he leaves the county for more than 24 hours he's supposed to call in, but nobody would know if he didn't."

"That seems so unfair to his victims. How can they ever feel safe if he's not really being monitored?"

"One of them's in Pennsylvania. The other one got married and changed her name, then she moved to Oregon. I imagine the distance helps."

"That would help." I chew on my lip thinking over how I'm going to feel if he gets out. More likely, when he gets out.

The doorbell rings and I check the time, it's ten-fifty-eight. I kiss Micah and promise to keep him posted before walking to the front door. Rhett opens the door to Jake and they greet each other kindly. I think Rhett is past his negative feelings for Jake, now that he knows Jake is a good guy.

"Hi, I'm happy you were available." I hugged him.

"Not like I had anywhere else I wanted to be. Roger's parents left town. They packed or gifted all of his things. I'm avoiding going to the apartment to get my stuff. Maybe next weekend we can all swap around."

"Yeah, that should work. Our landlords are great. I'm happy they both agreed easily. You don't mind being further from campus?"

"Nah, it's not that far. The place is great and my new landlord is really nice. I like that she's close by and communicates easily, it's helpful. I have to pay rent at my old place until new tenants take over. They have an ad up and they said there's been a few people interested. Hopefully, I won't have to pay past next month at the most."

"I hope so. Micah is working, but he may join us later. Maybe we can finalize a plan for next weekend."

He opens his mouth as his text notification chimes. He pauses and pulls his phone from his pocket. His face lights up with a huge smile as he reads the message. He quickly types a reply and shoves his phone back into his pocket. When he looks at me his cheeks turn pink.

"Okay, I have to know. Who was that? Your face just lit up," I question already knowing the answer.

The pink on his cheeks deepens to red. "Oh, um, it was just Connor."

"Just Connor? Dude! Your whole face broke into a huge smile, that's not just anyone. Have you been sexting? Does he talk about kissing you like Prince Charming? Mwah!"

"Stop teasing! I don't want to jinx it." He looks down embarrassed.

"I get that. Don't be embarrassed. I guess you guys are talking regularly, huh?"

"Yeah. We talked for hours last night. I like him."

I hugged him. "That's awesome! I really like him too. I think you'll be great together. Come on, let's quit standing in the entry. You can put your bag down. We can put the refreshments in the kitchen."

He follows me. He places the twelve-pack of hard lemonade in the fridge. We each fill a glass with ice water, then I lead him to the living room where we join everyone, except Micah. Nova charges Jake, now his new best friend since she met him yesterday. She accepts people quickly if she likes them.

"Hi, Jake! Come play blocks, now." She takes his finger in her tiny hand and pulls him to the pile of blocks on the floor.

"Nova Larue! You don't boss people around... you ask them nicely. Try, *hi Jake, will you please play blocks*? Okay?" Paige admonishes.

Nova stops and looks up at Jake, "Hi Jake, you play blocks, pwease?"

He chuckles, "I would love to play blocks with you. Thank you for asking, Nova." She smirks at her mother. Nova looks just like my smartass brother at that moment. He knows it too, as he tries to hide the grin on his face. Paige misses nothing. She gives Rhett an exasperated look. The doorbell rings the second Jake's butt hits the floor.

"I'll get it. Should be Anisa." I make my way to the door and look out the peephole. Yep, it's her, I open the door. Her hair is braided and perfect. Her make-up is flawless. She looks nightclub ready, not poolside casual. I smile to greet her.

"Oh my God, I had to stop for gas and some dickhead tried to pick me up. He wouldn't take no for an answer. He was cute, and normally I would be down, but I have a boyfriend. Why isn't that a good enough reason to leave a girl alone?" She bitches. I open my mouth to say hi, she's not finished.

"Do I look okay? I wasn't sure if these braids look right on me. A girl that hangs out with Tool did them. I figured it would keep me from frizz city after the pool, but I usually don't like my hair up. What do you think?"

"Hello. I think you look fantastic. I love the braids. Everyone is in here." I directed her to the living room. Rhett isn't here. He must be back in the kitchen.

"Do you want something to drink?" I ask her.

After she greets everyone, she asks, "Can we go out to the pool? I'll take a hard lemonade."

Paige comes with us to keep an eye on Nova. Not that she doesn't trust me, she explains Nova's been very bossy and we're suckers for the two-year-old's demands. She has a point; I can't say no to the girl. Once I'm in the warm water, Nova jumps at me completely fearless, and she swims over to me. Paige has been working with her. She's a little mermaid.

When Nova leaves for her nap, I ask Paige to let Micah know we're going to have lunch within a half hour. Anisa is lounging on a pool float, working on her tan. Jake and I play a game with two paddles and a small foam ball, similar to ping pong.

When I beat him for the second time in a row he declares, "This is for all the marbles. Whoever wins this round is the champion."

"What does the champion get?" I ask.

"The loser has to serve the champion lunch."

"Okay, game on." We battle it out alternating who's in the lead. When we get to the game point, it's my serve.

"Eleven, eleven, this is it," I call out and hit the ball. He hits it back. I have to dive for it and I successfully return it. He jumps up and spikes it hard. I rush to reach it, but I miss it.

"Yes! I win! You have to serve me lunch," he gloats.

"I'm getting out," I pretended to pout. I can't hide my smile, and his smirk tells me he knows I'm playing.

"Let's all get out, I'm hungry." He lifts himself onto the side of the pool. Anisa paddles to the stairs and rinses off before climbing out. I dry off and tell them to sit at the table.

Once I'm dry enough, I enter the house. My teeth chatter in the freezing air-conditioning. In the kitchen Rhett has a platter of hotdogs ready. There're small cups with condiments and a divided bowl with three kinds of chips.

"Thanks Rhett, you're the best." I offer him a big smile. Paige went to take a nap when Nova went for hers.

"It's no big deal. Took me five minutes. Do you need anything else?"

"No, this is perfect. Thanks so much. Do you want to eat with us?"

"Nah, I ate a couple dogs already. I'm going to take a nap with Paige. If you need anything else, help yourself." He gives me a quick hug as he heads off toward his bedroom.

"Will you please tell Micah to come out for lunch, on your way?" I ask.

"No need," Micah says when he enters the room.

"Hey, glad you made it." I give him a kiss.

"What can I carry?" he asks. I pick up the bowl of chips and the stack of plates and silverware. Micah carries the platter of hotdogs and condiments.

When we reach the patio table, I fill a plate with two hotdogs and chips and place it in front of Jake. "Your majesty."

"Thank you, kind loser," he laughs.

"What did I miss?" Micah asks.

Jake speaks up, "Allow me, I beat your girlfriend in a game of paddle ball. The loser had to serve lunch to the winner. Peyton is the loser." He smirks at me, then grins brilliantly at Micah. He and Micah crack up.

"It's not funny. I beat you every game, and we were tied until you scored that one point. Don't act like you're really a champion," I grumble.

"I wasn't really paying attention, but she definitely beat you more than you beat her," Anisa adds.

Jake makes a face at me and we all laugh. I'm having such a good time I almost forgot what happened to me just yesterday. Now that I've thought about it, my mood dampens a bit and I get quiet. Thankfully, Anisa is happy to talk.

"Are you coming to the Halloween party Jake? I'm so excited about it. Rev's going to be Dracula, and I'm going to be his girlfriend, Mina. My costume is so pretty and it fits me perfectly. What're you going to be?"

"I haven't thought much about it. I did get a costume, just with everything happening, I can't think about going to the party. I really want to go, but then I wonder if that's wrong," Jake answers.

"You've got to come! It's going to be so much fun. We need a party to get past everything that's happened. It won't be the same if you don't go," Anisa whines. "Tell him to come, Peyton."

"Oh, I'm not sure I'm up for a party myself," I inform her.

"What? You guys have to come to the party. It'll be good for us to get out from under this dark cloud. I won't have fun if you guys aren't there, pleeeease," she begs. I look at Micah and he shrugs. It's up to me, I guess.

"I'm not sure I'm ready to deal with a crowd and blaring music. School tomorrow is daunting enough. How about we discuss it tomorrow? It'll give me some time to see how I feel."

"Yeah, let's see how we feel after class tomorrow. We can meet for a study session, how does the library sound?" Jake asks.

Anisa puts on a pouty face. "Fine. We'll meet after our last class."

"That sounds good. I'll have a better idea if I can deal with a crowd after going to class. I'll be there."

"What's your costume Jake? Peyton won't tell me what she and Micah are going to be." Anisa glares at me, before she turns back to Jake.

"I got a Batman costume. I always wanted to be the Dark Knight. Hey, we should watch a Batman movie," Jake suggests.

"I'm up for that," Micah agrees.

"Ugh! No thanks. I guess I'll go if you guys are going to watch a guy movie," Anisa counters.

"Don't go, it'll be fun. I'll make popcorn," I offer.

"I can't eat popcorn. Diet, remember?" She's so high maintenance. I wonder how Rev puts up with her sometimes.

I notice her plate still contains the bun from her hot dog. She never took any chips; all she ate was a hot dog and mustard. I'm not sure what to think. She doesn't need to lose weight in my opinion. I don't think saying that to her will go over well.

"Please stay, I'll make anything you want," I try.

"I'm going to go. You'll see me tomorrow. We can meet for lunch, okay?"

"Okay. I'll walk you out," I offer.

I'm not sure what part of the movie inspired it, but we find ourselves in a discussion about superheroes fighting. I think Paige is the first to mention self-defense. Jake has no interest and takes off. Before I know it, Paige is teaching me some basic self-defense over her pregnant belly. We end up in the gym with Rhett and Paige showing me the most important moves.

"What about that movie? Where the FBI agent demonstrates self-defense, she says to remember to S.I.N.G. Did you see that one?" I ask.

"I love that movie. She's so funny, and she's not wrong. I just wouldn't go for the instep unless you have on good shoes and your attacker doesn't. The solar plexus, nose, and groin are excellent choices. Always remember your elbow is a great weapon, and hitting someone in the nose can be extremely painful. The throat is another good spot," Paige says.

Rhett jumps in, "I know you said you froze a little when that asshole attacked you. It's hard to get past that. You need to practice so that you just respond without thinking. You also need to keep going until you can get away. Hit their nose, throat, eyes, and balls. Hit hard and repeatedly until they stop restraining you. Then you want to get away as far and as fast as you can. Your main goal is to get away. You don't want to be trapped in a building or a car if you can help it."

Micah asks, "You said something snapped and you went crazy on him, which helped you get away, right? How can we help you tap into whatever that was every time you need it?"

"I think I thought about you. I thought about Larue, and how she never got to be happy and fall in love. I love you, and I didn't want to miss out on my life with you. I snapped and fought like a wild animal until I broke free. Then I ran," I replied with a shrug.

"That's perfect. You need to think about Micah and how much you love each other. Use it to fuel your fight. Think about how much you want to get back to him. Let's see what you've got. I'm going to grab you from behind and you fight me off, okay?" Rhett tells me.

He grabs me around the neck and I hit him in his gut with my elbow, afraid to hurt him, so I don't hit very hard. He wraps his arms around my body, trapping my arms and pulls me to the floor and pins me.

"Okay. I suck at this," I whine, discouraged.

"No, you don't. You were holding back. Don't do that, Rhett can take it. I beat him up all the time when we spar. Give it your all, go again," Paige directs. I stand up again and Rhett tries to grab me from behind. I elbow his middle again and then I spin and kick at his knee. I punch toward his nose and then try to hit his groin with my knee. He blocks everything and I feel like a loser.

"That was much better! Go again," Rhett orders. I already feel worn out. Maybe I need to start working out, I'm so out of shape for a young person. It's embarrassing that I'm out of breath and Rhett looks perfect. We set up and go again.

"Good job, babe! You almost got him that time," Micah encourages. He's exaggerating. I wasn't even close. I appreciate his enthusiasm though. I love these people.

Micah

I left for work before Peyton left for school this morning. I rode to Savage with Rhett. I'm going to work in their office for the day. Paige had a checkup this morning, but she'll be here later, and Nova went to preschool. Rhett and I dropped her off and I walked her in when Rhett got stuck on a call. She held my hand and led me to her class. Her teacher was surprised, but Nova was a little boss and told her I'm staying at her house now with Aunt Pey. It was so cute, and her teacher asked for clarification while Nova went to tell some kids what to build with the blocks. They listened. I think she's going to be a leader like her parents. Her poor little brother better be able to stick up for himself.

Once I dig into my search for information, I'm able to tune out my surroundings. I'm down the rabbit hole looking for more information about Tristan Price. I've gone through his arrest records and court transcripts. I've read all of his reports from probation and every law enforcement check-in. I'm putting together a list of known associates and former employers and former addresses. I haven't found any connection with Baton Rouge. He lived in Texas for six months and Arkansas for twelve. Otherwise, he's been in Florida. All of his arrests have been here, except for one possession charge in Arkansas that was dismissed, when he was nineteen. I can't find any history in Louisiana.

His phone was a dead end. Even though he had some pictures of Peyton, there was nothing else. The pictures looked like he snuck a few shots of her during the move. The one picture on his phone from Baton Rouge looked like a picture of a picture. There's a glare on the image that makes it look like a photograph. His computer's still being analyzed by our system.

Frustrated, I opt for a lunch break. Checking the time, I realize Peyton should be at lunch too.

Me: Hey Eagle, how's your day going?

Eagle: Class has been good. I'm at lunch with Anisa. She's really pushing for the Halloween party. What do you think about going?

Me: Whatever you want to do is fine with me. I do think she's right, that you'll have fun. Doing normal things always helps get past difficult situations.

Eagle: Yeah, you're right. I think I'm going to say yes so she'll quit bugging me. Jake already agreed. He's bringing Connor! I'm so excited for him.

Me: That's great. I like them both, they'll make a good couple.

Eagle: I know! So cute.

Me: Are we still working out after you're through?

Eagle: Definitely. I'm meeting Jake and Anisa at the library for a one-hour study session. Then I'll meet you in Rhett's gym.

Me: It's a date. Love you, Eagle

Eagle: Love you, Radiohead

My sandwich is lackluster. I force it down anyway since I can't skip meals. I finish lunch with a Kitkat bar. Gotta have some sugar to make it through the rest of this day.

Paige joins me, "Hi, how's it going?"

"Not great. I'm not getting anywhere with his background. I can't find any connection to Louisiana so far, and it's frustrating. How was your check-up?"

"The baby's good. He's facing down and all his vitals and mine are perfect. The doctor thinks he's going to be big so they want me to have another ultrasound in a few weeks," she replies.

"How big was Nova?"

"She was seven pounds and seven ounces. Hopefully this guy won't be too much bigger," she says, patting her round stomach.

"Is that big? Sorry, I don't know much about babies."

"Not too big, it's about average. I know someone who had a nine pounder. That's getting pretty large, I'm hoping he stays under nine pounds or comes a few weeks early. Do you want some help with your case?"

"Yeah, maybe fresh eyes will find something I missed. Finish your lunch and I'll show you what I've found." Paige eats her bowl of chicken and rice while I tell her about the dead ends of my search.

When we get back to the war room, I show her everything I have, which is just about nothing. She sets up next to me, we both dive into the web and search for more. When I'm ready to give up for the day, Paige grabs my arm.

"I found something. Look at this. He was in foster care from age twelve to fourteen. Look at the address of his caregiver, it's in New Orleans."

Leaning over, I read her screen. "He lived with a non-relative caregiver through the Florida foster system. Interesting. Send me that file. I'll start there tomorrow, maybe I can find some more connections to Louisiana through this record. Are you ready to go? I promised Peyton I'd work out with her."

"Yeah, let's check in with Rhett," she answers. Paige ended up leaving a couple minutes before us, to pick up Nova. When Rhett and I get to his house Peyton is at the breakfast table with Felony.

"Hi Eagle, what's up?"

She looks up and accepts my kiss on her lips, "Hi Radiohead. The AirTags I ordered for the cats showed up. I got the ones for Beta and Qwerty on without any trouble. This one keeps on making a chirpy bird noise." She waves at Felony. She was nervous about having the cats away from home and we decided to order AirTags to track them if they somehow got outside. They're little GPS devices that attach to anything, in this case the cat collars. You can track the tag on your phone. She was able to get them sent overnight to Rhett's house.

"Let me see your phone. Oh, it's locked," I aimed the screen at her.

"My password is your birthday," she smiles at me. I type in my birthday and the screen unlocks. I look at the app and I don't see anything wrong with the settings. All three cats look the same on the app, only their photos and names are different.

"I'll add the app to my phone and see if I can figure it out. Where are the others?"

"They took off when Felony's tag started making that noise. I feel bad. She keeps looking at me like she's begging me to fix it. It stops for a few minutes, then it starts again."

I downloaded the app and set up an account. When I look at her, she's watching me. I smile and her face lights up. She's so gorgeous. I sigh. I still can't believe she loves me.

"What?" she asks.

"Nothing, are we going to work out? You should go change and get ready. I think Rhett went to change."

"Oh, okay, I'll be back in a minute." She kisses my cheek and saunters toward the bedroom. I watch her perfect ass as she goes. Felony makes a small meowing sound with a growl on the end.

"Okay, okay, don't get impatient with me. It's your fault you need the tag on your collar. If you didn't escape three times from home and refuse to come back inside, you wouldn't need this thing." I point at the little gadget around her neck. She gives me a dirty look.

Once I get the app on my phone connected to all three cats, it seems to be working fine. I scratch Felony in the spot she likes behind her fluffy black ear. She rubs against my hand and begins to purr.

"See, now you like me, huh? I think you're free to go. It doesn't seem to be making the noise anymore. I'll keep scratching until my hand gets tired, as long as you don't bite me, okay?"

She ignores me and keeps purring with her eyes closed. She's a mysteriously beautiful feline. She makes me think of magical witches and dark nights with a full moon. The contrast of her bright eyes against her dark fur presents a mystifying picture. A door slams down the hall and she startles and takes off.

Peyton's dressed in yoga pants and a sports bra when she returns. She's been complaining about being out of shape, but she looks like a fitness model, minus the cut muscles, and she has soft smooth skin. I'm mesmerized by her as she walks towards me. I have a quick mental chat with my growing dick... *now is not the time.*

"Are you ready? Were you able to get the tag to work without making that noise?"

"Yes, and yes," I grin at her. I follow her to the gym. Rhett's already on the treadmill warming up. She pulls on some sparring gloves and begins punching the hanging bag. I stretch by reaching my hands up and bending from side to side, then I touch my toes and repeat.

"I'll be done in five minutes," Rhett tells us.

Once Rhett is ready to work with Peyton, I hop on the treadmill. I warm up by walking. I'm not much of an exercise fan, I do what I need to stay in good enough shape to pass the FBI requirements and not pass out if I have to chase a suspect. I can't hear what Rhett is telling Peyton. She turns her back to him and he pretends to attack her. She uses her elbow, her fist, and her heel to fight him off. She does a good job, and I can tell she's been thinking about this, maybe even practicing on her own. She's already notably improved since yesterday.

We work out and practice for more than an hour, Paige joins us after she gets home with Nova. There's a Nova workout playpen in the corner. She plays with her toys in there. It's old hat for her. When Nova gets tired of being locked in her designated space, we call it quits.

Rhett had something in the crock pot, so dinner is ready after we all take turns showering. I wanted to join Peyton, but somehow, I got volunteered to watch Nova while everyone else showered first. Rhett either planned it to keep me from fucking his sister in his house while he's awake, or so he could shower with Paige. I understand either motivation, but that doesn't stop me from being cranky about it.

"I need to do some reading for school. Will that be okay?" Peyton asks me.

"Yeah, of course. I want to watch the weather. I got a notification that the hurricane shifted its track and I want to double check we're still in the clear."

"Oh yeah, they were talking about it at the office, I didn't get a chance to look at it yet either. I'll watch with you," Rhett adds.

"Well, if anyone wants to know, I'll be giving her majesty a bath and reading bedtime stories," Paige throws out.

Rhett chuckles, "I'll be in for a story. Are you feeling, okay?"

"Yep, perfectly fine," Paige responds. Rhett leans down and kisses her head on his way by. Paige starts helping Nova out of her booster seat. She's singing something to herself. Sounds like a song about sharks. She's always singing and smiling. She's the happiest kid I've ever seen. I give Peyton a kiss on her cheek and place an affectionate pat on Nova's head. Paige gets a smile that she quickly returns, before I join Rhett in front of the giant flat screen.

The storm spins over and over on a loop as it drifts across the Gulf waters. They show the past twenty-four hours as it jumps much further east than they expected. The whole track has now shifted so that we're in the *Cone of Death*. We're on the edge and even though we have a hurricane watch for our area, the spaghetti models still show it making landfall quite a bit west of here. Somewhere between the panhandle of Florida and the line for Louisiana. No reason to panic. Not that we'd panic anyway. Rhett has two natural gas generators that come online automatically if power's lost. He also has an emergency pantry stuffed to the gills with non-perishable food. When they found out they were having Nova, he spared no expense prepping for any conceivable emergency. Rhett's house has been my emergency shelter for the last few years.

"What's the name of that weather guy you like?" he asks.

"Ryan Hall. His YouTube channel is *Ryan Hall Y'all*. His forecasts are the most accurate I've found," Rhett tunes the channel to YouTube when I answer. Thankfully, my favorite weather guy has a new video posted. He thinks it'll make landfall at the furthest east side of the track, closer to Tallahassee than Louisiana.

"As you can see, this cold front will be coming into play sooner than originally predicted. That'll push the hurricane further east and the clash between the cold air and the tropical system will lead to a tornado out-break in Texas, Oklahoma, and possibly Arkansas." He points at the offending air mass. If he's right, we could get the strong side of the storm awfully close to us. We'll be lucky that it won't strengthen much because of the cooler air that kills hurricanes. It should be a declining category two or maybe a one. The amount of damage from a two to a one is considerably less.

"I'm going to send a group text to Ace and Thomas, we need to keep on top of this. We have a case this side of Tallahassee, and we won't be able to go in if there's a storm. Have you talked to Samson about it?" Rhett asks.

"Nah, I guess I'll send him a message, too. Make sure we're all on the same page. I know he gets NOAA alerts through work, but they seem to be behind in their assessment if we believe Ryan, which I've no reason not to. The guy is usually right."

"His explanation makes sense," Rhett adds, reinforcing my argument.

After I send off my message, I help Rhett cleanup the kitchen. I'm tired, it was a long day, and very frustrating. I'm hopeful the information Paige found will be the key. After I say goodnight to Paige and Rhett, I join Peyton in the bedroom. She has her laptop on her lap, back leaned against some pillows, and legs out in front of her. I quietly remove my clothes and crawl into bed next to her in my boxer briefs. I lean back against my own pillows with my arms crossed above my head.

Peyton glances my way and does a double take. She types something and closes her laptop, then sets it on the nightstand next to her phone. She rolls toward me and lifts her knee over my hips placing it on my other side so she's straddling me. Her hands rest on the front of my shoulders. She stares into my eyes and a devilish grin curves her lips.

"Hi. How's it going?" she asks me while keeping eye contact.

"Hard," I answer completely serious. I make my hard dick twitch beneath her hot center. She wiggles and presses against me.

"You don't say. What can I do to remedy that?" she asks, without looking away.

"I think you're doing it," I can't keep a smile from curving my own lips in a mirror of her fiendish grin.

"What if I did this?" She leans closer and kisses me.

"And this?" She pushes her tongue between my lips and moves her tongue against mine.

Pulling back enough to speak she adds, "Or this?" She grinds her heated pussy over my hard dick. She dives back into kissing me while she rubs herself against me.

"Mmmm hmmm," my response is just a moan.

She sits up and lifts her shirt over her head. She wasn't wearing a bra and her perfect tits rest beautifully on her frame. My hands find them and squeeze. Her pupils are blown, her face is pink, her mouth is open slightly as she pants. Her hips continue to move as she rubs against my ready cock. I slide my hands to her hips and my fingers under the straps of her thong. I pull it down slowly. She lifts to accommodate the removal of her panties. I get impatient and yank on them, tearing them off.

"Shit! You're eager tonight. I like it." She puts her fingers under the waistband of my underwear and moves to stand on the bed with one foot on each side of my hips. She bends and slides my damp boxer briefs down while I lift my ass off the bed. My view is spectacular as she stands again. She got my garment to my knees, with a quick maneuver I'm able to get them down low enough that I can kick them off. My eyes never leave her assets.

She smirks at me and does a little sexy dance move without moving her feet. Her hands reach up to balance on the ceiling. Her fingertips just touch enough for her to gain balance. She moves a little more now that she's steady. My hands trace up the outside of her legs from her calves to her hips. Her beautiful pink pussy glistens with arousal. Her breasts bounce with her movements and her nipples are peaked. She's a vision.

"Bring me that beautiful pussy," I growl. "Sit right on my face."

She carefully steps up closer to my shoulders, using the ceiling to balance. Slowly, she lowers herself to my face. She watches as her pussy makes contact with my tongue. I grasp her hips helping to steady her and aim my tongue right where I want it. She holds onto the headboard and grinds onto my face. My tongue laps at her as I lick the arousal from her opening. Then pointing my tongue, I find the spot that makes her jolt. She presses against my tongue as I flatten it out and work it against her. Her hips twist in small circles as she pleasures herself against me. I alternate my speed and actions finding what she reacts to the most. She tenses and her head flings back as she speeds up her movements. I increase the speed of my tongue and help her hips move with my hands.

"Yes! Yes! Oh God, Micah!"

Moisture floods my tongue and I lick up every drop of her release. I slow my movements with her and flatten my tongue against her clit. She trembles and slows to look at me. Her hair is wild, her cheeks glow, and her eyes are bright. She smiles a knockout grin of satisfaction. She lifts her leg over me and then twists her body around until she's facing the other way. Now there's a knee by each of my ears. Her pussy is in my face once again, I pull her hips closer. Wet warmth envelopes my cock and her tongue swirls around the tip before she presses it into her throat. Oh, fuck! I'm seeing stars.

"Shit! Babe..." I mumble against her pink flesh. She grinds against my face as she bobs her head up and down my hard shaft. She always swirls her tongue just right, between that and pushing the tip as far as she can take it down her throat, this isn't going to take long. I want to be inside her. I smack her on the ass to get her attention.

"Mmm, what's up," she mumbles against my skin.

"I want to be inside you, spin around. Slide that perfect pussy on my cock, baby," I instruct.

She makes one more deep thrust onto my cock with her mouth, then she turns around. When she's in position above my dick, she moves so the head finds her opening. She's so wet and she slides onto me without resistance. We both groan as she seats herself onto me as far as she can. She pauses for a minute. I squeeze her hips. I need her to move.

"Yeeeessss, like that babe," my voice is gravel.

"Mmhmm, yes, that's so good," she moans her words, lost in the sensations, same as me.

My hands lift her hips and I thrust up into her as she lifts herself at the same time, then falls onto me, slapping our skin together. Before long we begin to falter, our rhythm erratic. We pound against each other harder and harder. I feel her tighten around me, the sensations increase as jolts of electricity travel down my spine and into my balls. She starts to make a noise, and I have to take over most of the movements as she's unable to control her body. My balls tighten, and I feel the explosion building.

"Fuuuck! Yes! I'm coming, baby," I try not to be too loud; I simultaneously realize I can't tell what volume I'm yelling out.

"Yes! Me, too!" We both give one last ditch effort to make it the best orgasm ever. Then as cum spurts out of me and into her, I lose all ability to control my moves or control what comes out of my mouth.

She falls onto me, and I wrap my arms around her waist as I slowly move in and out of her. Shivers pass through me as the last drop of cum leaves my body. She kisses my cheek and my mouth, tasting herself on my lips, then rests her chin on my shoulder. She completely relaxes. I could stay like this forever.

"I love you," she says quietly by my ear. Her breath tickles me, sending another shiver down my spine.

"I love you, too. So much," I reply as I hug her close, at peace.

Peyton

I don't remember falling asleep as I'm jolted awake by my phone. Checking the time, I answer, "What's up, everything okay?"

"You tell me. You're not at the hospital, are you?" Orlando asks, concern obvious in his voice.

I chuckle, "Nope, no drugs this time. One of the guys who helped me move in decided to attack me."

"Holy shit! Are you okay? Are you at the hospital?"

"No hospital. I'm fine, just shaken up, mostly. He might be the stalker."

"What the fuck? I leave town for a couple days and you get attacked by *maybe* the stalker? You're like a walking bullseye or something. Damn, I'm glad you're okay. What can I do? Do you need anything?"

I wander out of the bedroom in search of Micah while I answer, "I'm staying at my brother's house, Micah too. Jake is staying at Micah's place. There's some damage at my place. Plus, I didn't want to be there so soon after..." My voice cracks and I feel the heat of tears trying to form.

"I'm really sorry I wasn't here. Are you sure you're alright?"

"I am, I promise. It's just the thought of what could've happened. The guy has a record of stalking women, and um, assaulting them. I just need a little time. I love that house and I'm not letting some asshole scare me off." Micah jerks his head in my direction from his spot leaning on the kitchen island. His eyes are narrowed as he looks me over. I point at the phone and mouth, "It's Orlando." Micah nods and relaxes.

"That's good. You definitely can't let some sick mother fu...*jackass* chase you away. So, they caught him this time? He's in jail?"

"Yeah. Micah's here, he can probably fill you in better than I can. Want to talk to him?"

"Yeah, if he's not busy. Please let me know if you need anything. I'm right next door if you need anything at the house. I'm glad you're okay."

"Thanks, I'll let you know. Here's Micah." I handed him the phone.

"Hey, how was your trip?" Micah asks as he walks toward the hallway.

"Cool." His voice is slowly getting further away. "I'm not sure..." When I can't hear him anymore, I turn to Rhett. He's at the stove cooking some bacon which smells incredible. My mouth waters and I have to lick my lips to avoid drool dripping out.

"Good morning. Whatever you're cooking, I'm in!" I announce.

"Of course, you are. You, little sister, are in luck. I'm familiar with your ability to make bacon disappear. I shopped accordingly." He chuckles at my expense. As I close in, I see eggs, home fries, and gravy on the stove. There's a pan of fresh biscuits cooling on the counter.

"Wow! What's the occasion? You made so much food."

"Did you forget what day it is? Since there's going to be candy for dinner, I figured we should at least have a good breakfast."

"I completely forgot. Micah and I have that party tonight. Where are you taking Nova to trick-or-treat?" I ask the world's best brother.

"There's a trunk-or-treat at Suwanee Park, from 5-8 p.m. Paige wants to go there. They have a petting zoo, hay rides, and kid friendly games. It's cute. We went last year but she didn't understand the concept of trick-or-treating. She got the first piece of candy and a toy and wasn't interested in anything else after that."

"What's a trunk-or-treat?" I ask, clueless.

"It's great, it's like a giant tailgate party, only everyone hands out candy and toys. It's a lot of reward crammed into one manageable location. Great for little legs who insist they can walk like a big girl and pregnant women who won't admit when they're tired," he smiles.

"I heard that!" Paige calls out as she chases a *big girl* dressed in black, into the kitchen. Rhett's face is comical when he realizes Paige heard him. His eyes enlarge and his mouth falls open in exaggerated shock.

"Uh oh, I'm in trouble. I love you, Turner. You're the most beautiful pregnant woman I've ever seen." He places his palms together and begs forgiveness with his eyes.

"Yeah, yeah, I've got your number, big guy. Telling your sister things behind my back." She looks at me.

"I'm not the stubborn one in this family. Don't listen to him." She kisses his cheek and slaps his ass, before she lifts Nova to her booster seat.

"Daddy gets spanks! Bad daddy! Bacon!" Nova yells and then bursts into giggles. I wish I was that happy first thing in the morning.

"Are you a witch?" I ask Nova.

"Scary witch! I scare John-Sebs-John! I say *boo!*" She cracks up. I look to her mother for clarification.

Paige explains, "She means John-Sebastion, a boy in her class. They're best friends. It's so cute. He scared her when he told her he was going to be a monster for Halloween. She's been obsessed with scaring him back. No fairy princess costumes for her. She wanted something scary. She says witches are the scariest. I didn't have the energy to argue, so here we are, she's a witch with plans to scare her friend."

"I agree with you Nova, you can't let boys get away with that. You scare him good, okay?" I told her.

"I scare John-Sebs-John. I sneak up and scare him and say, *boo!*" She smiles at me proud of her plan. This kid... she's so freaking cute.

I hold up my fist for a fist bump. "That's right!"

Four of the six cats currently in the house, precede Micah when he returns to the kitchen. He hands me my phone and we make our way to join Nova at the table. Rhett carries over a platter of meat and eggs. We all dig in and fill our plates. Nova happily munches on bacon, while Paige is busy spreading jam on toast.

"Do you know when the painters will be done?" I ask Micah.

"They're coming out this morning and should be done this afternoon. Do you need something?" he asks.

"No. I want to get ready at home for the party tonight. Our costumes are there, and all my makeup is in the bathroom, except for the couple things I always wear. It would be easier to get ready there. I need to face it sooner than later."

Through a mouth full of breakfast Rhett voices his opinion, "You don't have to go there Pey. We can get your stuff and bring everything over here."

"I know. I just need to do this. If I don't get right back on the horse, so to speak, I might never be able to do it."

"Yay! Horsey! Can I wide it?" Nova exclaims. She takes a long drink of milk while she waits for an answer.

"There's no horse. Aunt Pey was talking about a pretend horse," Paige rationalizes. She takes a big bite of red jam on toast.

"Play pee-ten horsey!"

"*Pre*-tend," Rhett corrects automatically.

"Pee-tend horsey! I want to wide it!"

"Told 'ya she didn't understand our pretend talk," Paige gloats.

"Sorry sweetie, I don't have a real horse. But I promise to take you to see one this weekend. Okay?" I ask Nova.

"Okay!" Nova agrees quickly and shoves another strip of bacon into her tiny mouth. Somehow, I feel manipulated by a two-year old. I look at Rhett, and he's holding in a chuckle. Paige is grinning, Micah has his hand over his mouth to hold in the laugh.

"Don't feel bad, she does it to all of us. Only her mom has been able to thwart her abilities," Micah chuckles. I shrug and get back to my breakfast.

As we finish up, Rhett asks, "What was the verdict? Are you going home after school?"

I look at Micah. "I'll meet you there if that's what you want to do," he answers my unasked question.

Looking back to Rhett, I answer, "Yeah. We're going to the party tonight, but I'll call you if I decide I can't sleep there. Okay?"

"Okay. You can come any time day or night, if you change your mind. Please be careful," he tells me in his dad voice, the same one he uses with Nova.

"Yes sir. Oh, shoot, can the cats stay one more night?" As the words leave my mouth Felony jumps into my lap and meows loudly. I guess she objects to the plan.

"I can get them before I meet you at the house," Micah offers.

Without thinking, I blurted, "That's why I love you Radiohead!" When I realize what I just did, my eyes shoot to Rhett. At the same time, I squeeze myself down as my shoulders raise. My eyes are large as I wait for him to freak out.

He laughs at my fear. He smiles and I feel it in my chest. Holy shit! My big brother, who hates everyone, is happy. He approves. Tears well up in my eyes as I realize how much his approval means to me. A warmth spreads through me and my heart flutters with love, for Micah, Rhett, and my family. Yep, there go the tears. I rush to Rhett and hug him as hard as I can. He knows exactly why I'm reacting this way. He holds me tight and brushes his hand down my hair. He mumbles something soothing. I sniffle and lift my gaze. He kisses my forehead and squeezes my shoulders. I relax my hold on him and lean back a little.

"I love Micah, and I love you, of course I approve. I'm happy you found love; it couldn't be with a better guy. Love you, kiddo." He squeezes one more time and let's go, I release him. Smiling through my tears, I consider my brother. I can see a bit of our father. Not much of our sister, who favored our mother. He and I look the most alike from our immediate family.

"Thanks. For everything. You're the best brother a girl could ever ask for."

With tears streaming down her face, Paige, her voice gravel with emotion, yells, "That's it! Don't you know you can't get emotional in front of a pregnant woman? Stop. Now. Everybody loves everyone, we're done!" She swipes at her cheeks and takes Nova to brush her teeth. Even the cats watch her storm off.

"That's my cue. Be safe you guys. Don't forget to engage the alarm," Rhett says as he walks away. Micah and I look at each other. I wipe my face again and he hands me a napkin. We clean up the kitchen in quiet contemplation. Once we're ready to leave, Micah walks me to my car. I'm still quiet, but not tearful. He hugs me and kisses my lips. He brushes the hair from my eyes and looks into them, seemingly satisfied, and he kisses me again.

"I'm okay. I'll text you when I leave school and meet you at the house. Thank you..." I tilt my head and shrug a bit, "...for being you and supporting me. I love you, see you later," I tell him.

"Okay, Eagle. I'll see you later. I love you too." He places one last kiss on my lips, we climb into our cars, and drive away.

Anisa's waiting for me when I park my car. She's all bouncy, but it's too early in the morning for bounce. Usually, it's Jake who has too much cheer before noon. She looks excited, happy, and really cute in her long wool skirt. I roll my eyes at myself. I never care about how people are dressed until she's around.

"It's about time! You're almost late," she berates me.

"I think you just said I'm on time. Why are you so bouncy? Did you have espresso or something?"

"Yes, but that's not why. It's Halloween! It's my favorite holiday. Tonight's going to be amazing!" She can't stop grinning at me, and her face must hurt.

"Look, I got my nails done to match my costume!" she keeps yelling. I put my free hand over my ear.

"Please stop yelling. I'm right here, I can hear you," I reply at a reasonable volume.

"I can't help it. Tonight is going to be epic! You're definitely coming right?"

"Yeah. I'm excited too. Micah looks incredible in his costume. No, I'm not telling you. I can't wait to get some cute pics of us. Plus, I need to dance out some anxiety. We're going to sleep at the house tonight," I rush to get everything out before she starts talking again.

"Good. You need to face it and get past it. That's how I have to deal with stuff. Just attack it head on," she clears her throat and looks away. I wonder what memory she's reliving.

By the time we reach our afternoon class, Jake, Anisa, and I can barely stop talking about Halloween. We're as excited as eight-year-olds preparing to collect candy from strangers. Recognizing the futility of teaching anything, our professor dismisses class early. When I get home, Micah's waiting at the foot of the stairs. He offers me a tight smile. I kiss his cheek.

"How does it look?" I ask.

"Like nothing ever happened. New doors, paint, bed, everything's all good." He watches me carefully evaluating my every move.

I have a hard time meeting his eyes under the scrutiny. I pass him and climb the steps. I take a few deep breaths as I ascend. The door's unlocked. Felony greets me with a rub against my legs. Beta and Qwerty watch from the furniture. It smells clean with an undertone of fresh paint, and there's no more mess from the struggle. I glance into the living room, but it feels okay.

I look over the kitchen, no bad feelings. The dread that's pressing against me is like a drunk friend at the end of the night. I'm afraid there'll be a fall, jail, or vomit. It tightens its grip as I make my way down the hall.

The new door looks brighter, otherwise it's the same. The new bedding is the same as the old sheets. The bed was the landlord's. I ended up replacing it with the same thing. It's a good mattress. Before I can step a foot in the room, three cats come barreling past me. They sniff everything in sight. Felony is particularly interested in the bed. Everything looks the same, but better, I know it's new and that makes a big difference. I let out a gush of air I hadn't realized I was holding in.

I spin and hug Micah, "Thanks for making sure everything got done. I wouldn't have been able to walk in here otherwise."

He squeezes me then looks me in the eye. "I wouldn't have been able to sleep here either. We lucked out with the repairman's schedule." He smiles sweetly. I have a feeling he had to make a sacrifice to get everything done so quickly.

"Let's get ready for the party. I want to watch Nova trick-or-treat before we go."

I have two choices of shoes to wear with my costume. One is a sexy pair of heels that are higher than I like. They hurt my feet pretty quickly. The other pair are boots with a much lower heel, and less effort required not to fall on my face. I want to look like a fantasy for Micah. He plays a lot of videogames, and the girls are always in heels and not much else. He's mentioned in the past how hot he thinks this one or that one is. I want him to see me and think I'm his hot warrior fairy princess.

Micah showers while I gather everything for our costumes. Once I have everything together, I watch a tutorial about how to do my makeup. It looks amazing when it's done, and it's easier than I thought. I'm pretty sure I can do it. Micah comes in wearing his costume pants with socks and nothing else. He looks pretty hot and sexy himself. *Sigh*. We don't have time to fool around if I want to see Nova. I pull my shirt from my stomach and flap it, hoping a cool breeze will lower the heat oozing from my skin.

Micah smirks, he knows what's going on with me, he always knows. I scrunch my nose at him. His shirt is flung over his shoulder, and he has the bag of accessories in his hand. I gather what I need and go to the bathroom for my shower. While I shampoo, I think about everything that's going on and I wonder what's happening with the hurricane. I'll have to ask Micah. I blow-dry my hair so I can get it styled faster, it hangs in long blonde waves. Too bad I'm wearing it in a bun, I have a special clip that's a hair-hack to get my locks into the right style.

When I rejoin Felony in the bedroom to get dressed, Micah isn't in the room. I'm wearing neon green lingerie, it's lacey and racy. I smile at my stupid rhyme. I really need to relax tonight. I sit on the edge of the bed and roll on neon green fishnet stockings. As I attach the garter belts I lean down and notice Felony is playing with something.

"Hey, young lady, that better be a toy," she ignores me. My fingernail gets caught in my fishnets. I don't have a spare. I can't let them rip. I twist my finger until I get my nail unhooked. My jagged talon needs a file before I have any more mishaps. Once the crisis is averted, I get into my costume, put my hair up, and apply a lot of makeup. The dreaded shoe choice is upon me. Hmm, look hot and strap on torture devices or look cute and be pain free. Nope, it just doesn't look right without high heels, my man deserves the full fantasy. I crush my feet into the gorgeous shoes and turn around in front of the new mirror.

My boobs are pushed up so I have shocking cleavage. My ass cheeks are half in the costume and the half that's not, looks mighty fine. I'm still thankful the skirt hides it for the most part. The heels make my legs look amazingly long. The fishnets and garters make them tight and smooth; it looks good. I clip the fluffy white balls onto my shoes, they're cute. Next, I slip on my small wings. I wanted bigger ones but I didn't think it would work well at a party. I put my phone in the pocket of my skirt and collect my wand. One last glimpse in the mirror, I approve.

"Micah?" I called out.

"In here," he replies from the office.

"What're you..." all thought leaves my head, and my brain stops functioning enough to allow speech.

"Holy, fuck!" His eyes are bugged out of his head, his cheeks are red. His mouth hangs open after his exclamation.

"What, what, are y-you doing?" I force my brain to focus.

"What're you wearing? Holy fuck, babe, I'm about to come in my pirate pants!"

"I told you I was going to be Tinker Bell, Captain Sparrow. Do you like it?" I pose like a movie star, one hand on my hip, one toe pointed down, wings up straight.

He shakes his head like a dog, "Babe, you have to know how sexy you look. And like it? I'm going to need you to wear it at least once a week."

His eyes shine bright, and he keeps forcing them from my cleavage. I continue to admire the view, until I remember that I came in here looking for him, we have to go.

I place a kiss on his lips and slip from his grasp, "Come on Radiohead, we have to go. We don't have time for sex right now so get your mind out of the gutter. I don't want to miss Nova. I promise you can pry this off of me after the party."

"I was checking the weather. The storm hasn't made that turn yet. The new update will hopefully show the turn, but it's already later than expected. I have a bad feeling about it. Our weather might begin to deteriorate in the morning. Should we bring an umbrella?"

"If you want, I just need to grab my Chapstick. I'm so excited I have pockets; you won't have to carry my phone in yours. I'll be right back."

I hurry to my room and grab my Chapstick from the nightstand. Felony's still playing with something, it's small and now I'm worried she's going to choke on it. I try to grab it and she picks it up in her mouth and jumps into the middle of the bed.

"All right, troublemaker, hand it over," I lean over the bed and remove it from her clutches. I avoid her teeth, but she growls at me. I look at what she gave up by force. I'm not sure what it is, I turn on the light to have a closer look.

"Is this from your collar? You bad girl, come here young lady," she avoids my fingers and shoots under the bed.

I get down on my hands and knees and try to coax her out. Lying flat on my belly I stretch out one arm and try to reach her. My wing gets stuck on the bed frame, and I come up short.

"Please come to mama, Felony, come on sweetie, spspspsp..." She's looking into my eyes and begins to creep towards me. I hold my breath, willing her to keep coming.

"Eagle!"

"Ow!" I smack my head when Micah startles me.

"Rhett called, they're almost ready to go! We're gonna miss it!"

As I rub my head, I see that Felony has moved as far from me as possible. I pull myself up from the floor, giving up. When I look at my hair in the mirror, my perfect Tinker Bell updo is askew.

"Oh, shoot. I'll be right there!" I yell back to Micah as I quickly fix my hair. Once it's good enough I turn off the light.

As I make my way through the door, I call out, "I'll deal with you later, Miss Felony!"

We make it just in time and we get to watch little Nova ask for, *'tricks and treeks, pwease!'* She loves the green rhinestones on my costume. She didn't even recognize Micah at first. He hasn't shaved for his costume, and he has a fake mustache and fake braids making his hair hang past his shoulders. He looks like a much taller and more handsome version of Captain Jack Sparrow from the Pirates of the Caribbean movies.

When she realizes it's Micah, she gets really excited because she thinks he's a zombie. She's under the impression that witches control zombies. I need to ask what my brother is watching with Nova around. It takes all of us to convince her that she can't boss a pirate around, even if she is a witch. Paige and Nova poop-out at the same time. We help Rhett get them into the minivan and we're on our way to the party before 9 pm.

"How's my hair holding up?"

"I'm not sure what you're asking, Eagle. It looks good, if that's what you're trying to find out. How's my hair?" Micah playfully flips his hair over his shoulder.

Giggling, I reply, "Oh Captain Jack, it's magical!" He laughs with me. I think Tinker Bell should've made a cameo in one of the Pirates of the Caribbean movies. We make a great pair and I'm not as moody as the tiny pixie.

When we pull up to what I've been told is the twins' house, I'm surprised by its size and condition. It looks like every other mansion along the beach. How do those bikers have money for something like this? Other than Orlando, I've never heard of a biker who gives a crap about their house to this degree. Before we get to the door the music is already pounding against my insides.

"I know, we need to pass through and head out back as fast as possible," he grins like the Cheshire Cat.

"How did you know what I was thinking?"

"You really have to ask? We've been friends for, what? Four years? I know every thought you have, my beautiful Eagle."

"Oh yeah? What am I thinking now?" I place my hands on my hips.

"That your boyfriend is so hot you want to rip his pants off right here. But your legs and arms are sore from training and your shoes are hurting your feet. Before you can focus on taking his pants off, you need to get out of your heels?" My mouth falls open. I need to work on not being so predictable. For my first attempt, I grab a handful of his ass and plant a wet kiss on his mouth. I end it quickly and enter the house. The music blasts into us the moment the door opens.

I aim for the kitchen, following a few people who look determined. When we reach the kitchen there're liquor bottles all over the island and counters. A big metal tub holds ice and bottles of water. There's a keg at the far end of the island. Several guys are working on the keg. I opt for some vodka in cranberry juice. Micah is able to get a cup of beer from the keg guys. I don't know how he does that. I was afraid to approach them, and now he has five new friends.

After we each have a drink in hand we pass through the crowd and go out the French doors at the back of the house. A beautiful pool and stone deck lay beyond the double doors. There are a few people in the heated pool in their costumes. Two girls in mermaid tails swim back and forth. Weren't there mermaids in Peter Pan? I think about this as we make our way down the steps and into the yard.

The moment my heels hit sand they sink in. I kick them off and place them next to the last step. Micah smiles at me with his knowing grin. I take a move from Paige's book and sock him in the gut, and he folds over.

"Oh, shit! Micah, I'm so sorry! I didn't mean to actually hurt you. Are you okay?" Placing my hand on his back I lean down to look at his face, it's scrunched in a grimace.

"I'm okay. Damn, Eagle, you learn fast. That hurts. I don't have any pads and you don't have gloves on. You're a little dangerous. I like it. Makes me feel better about your safety." He stretches his back and rubs his stomach.

I kiss his cheek, "I'm really sorry. I wasn't thinking. Are you sure you're, okay?"

"Yeah. I'm fine. Did you bring your Chapstick? My lips are dry."

I reach in my pocket and pull out something round. It's difficult to see what it is in the dark. I hold it up so the patio lights illuminate it. Oh, no, it's Felony's AirTag. I must've shoved it in my pocket in my rush to get out of the house in time to see Nova trick or treat. I hand him the Chapstick and as I'm about to tell him what a dummy he has for a girlfriend, someone tackles me from behind, wrapping their arms around me. Lucky for her, I don't react with a punch like I'm now trained to do.

"Holy fuck, Peyton! You look amazing! Thank you so much for coming. Now we can have some fun. What are you drinking?" Anisa yells at warp speed. She must have been lying in wait for me out here.

I regain my composure and take a sip of my drink. "It's cranberry and vodka. You look gorgeous! Wow! Where's Rev?"

"He just went to see some guy that just got here, he'll be back in a few minutes. Look there's Tool, doesn't he look great?"

I look where she points and I see a gorgeous man in an old-style suit, with a top hat, ascot, and long hair. He does look great; his teeth are long and pointy. I can see them as he speaks to some chick. She looks familiar, and I remember I saw her at another party.

"Who's he talking to?"

Anisa looks closer at Tool, "That's his friend from the club, Diamond. Isn't her costume adorable?"

"Yeah, she looks like an old-fashioned little girl, who is she? A nursery rhyme character? Or anime?"

Micah pipes up, "Isn't she the girl vampire from the Interview with a Vampire movie? Celeste?"

"Claudia, she can never grow up and she goes crazy," Anisa explains.

"Oh yeah. It's been a long time since I saw that movie and I've never seen Dracula, just bits and pieces," I remarked.

"What? No way! We have to do a vampire movie night! Bram Stoker's Dracula is the ultimate love story. It's so romantic." Anisa flutters her lashes and fans herself.

"Really? I remember previews showing so much blood. It's a romance, not a horror story?" I ask, surprised.

"Oh, it's definitely a gory horror flick, but underneath the blood, it's a romantic love story. Dracula's love for Mina is so beautiful. That's why I wanted Rev to be Dracula and me to be Mina. I'm planning for some fun tonight. I love yours and Micah's costumes, by the way. You look incredible, so sexy. He looks better than Johnny Depp. I love your mash up!"

"You look incredible. Is your dress custom made? It fits you perfectly. I don't know if you look like Mina, but you definitely look like a gorgeous gothic Victorian supermodel," I chuckle at the thought of Victorian supermodels. My brain quits working except for schoolwork.

"It's made from an authentic pattern from Victorian times. I had three fittings to make sure it was perfect. Plus, I've lost like twenty pounds."

"Really? Well, I always thought you were beautiful, no matter what you weigh. You have a gorgeous figure, and your boobs look amazing! And I love your hair up like that with all the ringlets hanging down, it looks incredible. It must have taken all day."

"Nah, just a couple hours. I went to the salon and had them do it. It probably would've taken me all day. Here comes Rev," she lifts her chin in his direction. Micah and I both look over to see a tall guy heading towards us. He's wearing a top hat, ascot, and fancy old coat just like what Tool was wearing. They just have different color coats and Rev has some facial hair and little purple glasses, otherwise they look exactly the same.

"Hey, babe." He hugs Anisa to his chest and kisses her temple.

"Hey, you remember Peyton and Micah, right?" she asks him.

"Yeah. Hey how'sss it going?" He lifts his chin at me and speaks towards Micah, his 'S' lingering from his long fangs.

He answers for both of us, "We're good, all things considered. Cool costume."

"You too. Captain Sssparrow, right?"

"Yep. Peyton is Tinker Bell."

He grasps the back of Anisa's neck in a way that makes me uncomfortable. It seems forceful. She holds a tight smile on her face.

Clearing my throat I ask Anisa, "Want to go get fresh drinks? Mine's just a little melted ice at this point. Do you need a new one, Micah?"

"Yeah okay," Anisa responds, stepping out of Rev's hold.

"Nah, I'm good. I'll hang out here with Rev."

I smile at Micah, grateful he knows what I'm thinking and that he knew I was trying to get Anisa away from Rev for a minute. Anisa leads the way inside and I brace for the musical assault as she opens the door. She really looks incredible in that dress. She's so tall and her figure is proportionally perfect. She has that hourglass figure that Marilyn Monroe had, and the dress accents her assets.

When we reach the kitchen, I ask loudly, "Which way is the restroom? Will you pour me a cranberry and very little vodka, please?"

She points, "Down that hall. Yes, I'll pour you the perfect drink."

"Thanks, I'll be right back." Seeing far too many magical creatures crammed into the hallway she pointed out I try a different hallway and find an unlocked door. Luck is on my side, there's an attached bath and nobody's in this room. I quickly take care of business, then check to see how my face looks. My makeup has held up well. A little water has my hair smoothed back into place. I find Anisa in the kitchen with Diamond. She's got a drink in each hand.

I greet Diamond, "Hi, I'm Peyton. I think we met briefly before. Is that my drink?" I point at the cup in Anisa's left hand.

"Yeah, here you go, I made it with just a splash of vodka." She hands me the cup. I tasted it, she did it just right. I take a big gulp and smile my approval.

Diamond is using a straw to avoid messing up the bloody makeup dripping in trails from her mouth. Her hair has a big bow on top and hangs in blonde curls down her back.

"Hi, yeah, I remember you. How's everything going?"

"Great, I'm happy to be here," I yell.

"Let's go outside again, this music makes it too hard to hear!"

A group of guys at the breakfast table yell as their team wins whatever drinking game they're playing. About six guys are chugging red cups of beer while the others taunt them. I point at my ear and nod. I'm tired of yelling. Anisa leads us through the crowd back towards the French doors and outside. As soon as the door closes behind us it's a huge relief. There's music on the patio, but it's just one little speaker and easy enough to talk over. I sigh, as my ears continue to ring from the assault.

"Where's Rev?" I ask Micah when we get back down to the sand.

"He went to look for Tool."

"I think he's busy. I saw him go into a bedroom with some chick," Diamond informs us.

"How crazy was it in there?" Micah asks.

"It's ridiculous. There's a bunch of jocks in the kitchen playing drinking games, and they were louder than the music. When Rev comes back, I'm going to ask him to move them somewhere that's not in everyone's way," Anisa offers.

"Oh, I see a dude I need to talk to. I'll catch up with you guys later." Diamond disappears into the crowd.

"Oh, I love this song! Dance with me Peyton!" Anisa starts to dance and grabs my free hand with hers to encourage me. I lean into her enthusiasm and dance with her. Her face lights up with a brilliant smile. We shake our hips in a synchronized movement. I'm so glad I was able to shed my shoes at the bottom of the stairs again. The short trip inside made me quickly remember how much they pinch my feet. I keep wiggling my ass and I smile at Micah as he supervises.

A loud noise makes us all turn towards the back door. I can see some people running out of the door screaming. Their faces are pale masks of fear. We all freeze and watch as more people come storming out of the door.

BANG! BANG-BANG!

"He has a gun!"

"Go!" Micah jolts into action. I'm terrified something will happen to him, but I remind myself that he's a well-trained FBI agent.

"Stay right here. If anything happens out here, run! Don't look back, just go. I'm armed. I'll be fine. Don't worry." He kisses my lips and I watch as he disappears into the crowd, just like Diamond a few minutes ago.

I realize I'm holding onto Anisa's arm. I slide my hand to hers and clasp her fingers with mine. She squeezes my hand in return. We just stand there watching for our men to return.

BANG!

"Shit! I don't know where Rev is, if he went inside to look for Tool, where is he? He has to know I'm freaking out. He's not answering my messages. I need to find him," her voice raises higher and higher as she presses the letters on her phone screen. We're both shaking as we press against each other.

More people come running from the house and we're getting pushed off to the side. I pull Anisa to the edge of the crowd with me. She's focused on her phone, so I guide us to a safe spot, out of the way. Some girls are crying, and a few guys are trying to calm them down. I hear the words *gun* and *crazy,* a few times from different people in the crowd. I hope Micah's okay. I know Micah is okay, I have to stay positive.

I point to a guy with blood dripping from a gash on his forehead. I watch him stumble along holding onto another guy's arm. Things are getting out of control.

"Do you see that guy? Do you think he was shot?"

"Oh my God! I'm freaking out! What should we do? I want to know where Rev and Tool are, and where's Jake? Isn't he supposed to be here? Why isn't Micah back? Peyton, what do we do? How are you so calm?" Anisa is hyperventilating.

"I'm not calm, I'm just hiding it better than you. I feel really lightheaded. Ugh, I think I need to sit down."

"Okay. Okay, relax. There's a bench right inside these woods by the Zen Garden. Come on, I'll show you where. We can sit and get out of this crowd." Anisa leads me into the edge of the trees. Thankfully there's enough moonlight that we can see the path. We walk carefully since I'm without shoes but quickly reach a round area that's filled with white and gray stones. There's a pagoda in the swirling design of rocks. We make our way to a bench and sit down hard. Once I'm seated everything stops spinning. I get out my phone and text Micah. I doubt he can answer or even hear the alert. But this way if he can't find me, he'll know where I am when he checks his phone.

A strong gust of wind bends the pine trees surrounding us and I feel a bit dizzy again. The movement of the trees is making me feel like I'm rocking on a boat. The edges of my vision are blurry. I must be having an anxiety attack. I feel like it's difficult to breathe. Anisa looks into my eyes and assesses my condition.

"You look a little green around the gills. Do you want to lie down? You can use my lap as a pillow. Here, I can bunch up the skirt of my dress to make a cushion. You should probably lie on your side and try taking some deep breaths," she suggests.

I do as instructed, smashing her skirt to make it comfortable. I take some deep breaths and count slowly trying to calm my breathing and my heartbeat. I feel a little bit better. I can't believe what's happening. I want Micah.

"Have you heard back from Rev?" I ask.

"Yeah, he's looking for Tool. He says some guy is wasted and having a paranoid meltdown. He won't let anyone near him, but he hasn't shot anyone. He says Micah's trying to talk the guy down. He shot at the ceiling and the TV so far. Rev says he's not pointing the gun at anyone. I feel much better knowing they're all right. How are you doing?"

She leans over me and examines my face. She doesn't look impressed by my appearance. At least my green gills match my green costume. I chuckle at my ridiculous thought.

"What's funny?"

"Nothing, I'm a little loopy. My thoughts are absurd. Can you see anyone?"

She looks back the way we came and shakes her head, "No, I don't see anyone. It seems quiet though. Maybe they went back inside, and everything is okay now."

I try to sit up and my whole world tilts left in a swift move that leaves me reeling. "Whoah!" I quickly lie back down and put my arms out to steady myself against the moving bench.

Anisa lifts my head a bit, "Let me up. I'm going to take a couple steps back the way we came and see if I can find anyone helpful. Don't move. Don't try to get up without me or you'll probably fall on your face." With my eyes closed against the spinning, I nod and make a noise, so she knows I understand.

She slides out from beneath me and gently places my head on the bench. Without her lap, I'm forced to lie on my back. The spinning speeds up and I'm feeling nauseous.

"I'm right here, Peyton. Just taking a few steps. To see down the path. I see a few people walking past, no one I recognize. No one coming this way."

I can hear her footsteps on the gravel path fading as she gets further away. I try to open my eyes and see nothing but the faintest glow in a field of blackness. The spinning alternates with a wavy boat feeling. Oh boy, I really feel sick now.

"Anisa?"

"Yeah?" She's further than I expected. I guess I lost track of her footsteps for a minute.

"I really don't feel well. Can you please try to call Micah? I think I need to go home."

Her footsteps approach again. They sound very loud, like she's wearing army boots and clomping towards me. I hold out my phone to her and continue to inhale slowly and exhale while I count to ten for each breath. She takes my phone and I expect her to ask me the code to open it.

I'm suddenly lifted from the bench and up into the air. I open my eyes, but I can't focus them. The person holding me smells like cigarettes and alcohol. There's a faint smell of cologne. It's definitely not Micah.

"Anisa!" I struggle in his arms, it's useless, I'm barely able to move. My voice comes out as a soft, incoherent mumble.

"Hurry up! You have to get out of here. Be sure to ditch her phone."

My eyes won't open at all, I can't move to fight, and blackness closes in.

Micah

“Dude, you don’t want to hurt anyone, including yourself. Come on, put down the gun. Let’s walk outside and get some air.”

“No, nobody’ll listen to me if I put it down. Nobody cares about me. Why did she dump me? What did I do wrong?”

“Come on Neil, that’s not true. I know people care about you. Your friends are right outside scared to death that you’re going to hurt yourself. Maybe she made a mistake, don’t you want to go outside and find her and ask her?”

Oh shit. I can see flashing lights reflecting through the front windows. The cops are here. If he sees them he’s going to freak out again. I’m about ready to tackle him.

“I want to call her. I’ll give you the gun if you let me call her.”

“Sure, Neil, whatever you want. Give me the gun and we can step outside and call her. Just put it on the ground.”

I can’t believe it. He hands me the butt of the revolver like it’s nothing. As soon as I have it, I shove it into my pocket. My own firearm is in my shoulder holster. I haven’t needed it since we’ve been talking. He reaches into his own pocket for his phone and I rest my palm on his revolver. He lifts out a cellphone and begins dialing or texting, I can't tell which. Chaos ensues when the cops burst in through the door. They tackle Neil to the ground and have him handcuffed in no time.

"I'm FBI, I'm going to reach under my shirt for my badge," I say with my hands in the air.

"Hey Micah.Yeah, he's FBI, guys. What happened here?"

"Detective Warren, nice to see you again. I think he drank too much and his girlfriend dumped him. He didn't hurt anyone, but he was waving this revolver around and fired off a few rounds." I hand Detective Lane Warren the butt of the revolver.

He snaps open the cylinder and dumps out the bullets and casings into his hand. Only one left, that's what I thought. Whew! I'm so glad he didn't hurt anyone. I need to find Peyton; she must be worried.

"I'm going to go find my girlfriend. I'll be right back to answer your questions and fill out any paperwork you need, okay?"

"Yeah. Go ahead, I'll be here. I'm going to read him his rights and see if he'll talk. I can smell the alcohol from here," he shakes his head and turns to focus on Neil, who's on the floor, sobbing. He's going to have one hell of a headache in the morning, and a mountain of regret to deal with.

Thankfully, someone shut off the music during the panic. I make my way through the mostly empty house and out the French doors. I see a few girls with their makeup running like they've been crying with friends or boyfriends trying to console them. The people milling around on the patio look like zombies. Some of them may be in shock, I suppose. Mostly, I think they're drunk.

When I get to the spot where I left Peyton, she's not there and she's nowhere in sight. I look at everyone in search of her bright green costume. There's no sign of her. If she had to move to a different spot, she probably texted me. I check my phone. Ah, yep, there's a message from her.

Eagle: I had to move. I don't feel. Well. I'm with An is a.in Zen. I won't move from there with out tel long yoo. Path LOve

WTF? What is she talking about? I need to find her, now. I called her phone. Dammit! Voicemail.

"Peyton, where are you babe? Please text or call me so I can find you," I leave her a message.

I look around and I spot a path leading into the woods. Not far in, there's a huge area of arranged white and gray stones with a pagoda in the middle. There's a seated Buddha statue at the far end of the cleared section. Maybe this is what she meant by Zen. There's nobody here. I look around and find a couple cups next to the bench, nothing else. Alarm bells ring in my head. I try to quash them and continue my search. I carefully assess every person I see trying to determine if I've seen them before and if they may know Peyton.

Fuck it, I start asking everyone I pass. "Have you seen Tinker Bell? Did you see a blonde in a green Tinker Bell costume?" Everyone I ask says no or just shakes their head. I go back into the house once I've checked with everyone outside. I scan the faces inside. I finally see someone I know.

"Thank God. Jake! Hi, I can't find Peyton."

"What happened here?"

"A guy had a meltdown after too much alcohol. Everyone is fine and he's in custody. I had to leave Peyton outside with Anisa, to come in here and talk him down. But now I can't find her."

"Anisa and Rev just went upstairs. Maybe they know where she is," Connor speaks up next to him. He's wearing a Robin costume that matches Jake's Batman. Jake has his mask in his hand. Connor's still wearing the black mask around his eyes. I take off up the stairs climbing two at a time. I listen for voices or movement and I hear something in a room on my left. I knock on the door.

It opens and Anisa's standing there. She looks surprisingly calm considering a gunman shot up her boyfriend's house. Her makeup is still pristine, though her dress is a bit wrinkled and her hair is disheveled.

"Micah. What's up? Do the cops need us back down there?"

"Where's Peyton? I can't find her?"

"She was with me for a little while, then she saw Jake and took off to catch up with him. She's probably still with him."

"She's not. I just saw him. He hasn't seen her."

"Really? That's weird. Hang on a sec, and we'll come help you look."

Directing my question to Rev, I ask, "Do you have a computer I can use?"

"Yeah, it's downstairs. Let me grab my phone. I had it up here on the charger. Come on, I'll show you."

I follow Rev to a small office. It has a few bookcases against the wall and a laptop on the desk. He fires it up for me. I pound on the keyboard, quickly accessing my FBI portal and I enter Peyton's phone information. I attempt to triangulate between the closest cell towers to pinpoint the location of her phone. After a few painful minutes it marks the approximate location of her phone. It's out back, somewhere further down the beach. I call it again, straight to voicemail. I send a text.

Me: Babe, please stay where you are. I'm coming to find you. Call me if you get this. I love you.

"Thanks," I close out from my portal and closed the laptop.

I keep checking my phone, but there's no reply and no call from my Eagle. Frustrated, I stomp down to the cops in the living room.

"Detective, I can't find my girlfriend. I did a search on her phone and I'm about to go out back and look for her. Can you spare anyone to help? She wasn't feeling well, apparently, and I'm worried."

"Shit. Isn't she the one who has a stalker?"

"Yes. We caught him, I'm more worried about a medical emergency right now."

"What's wrong with Peyton? Where is she?" Jake joins us.

"I can't find her. She left me a text saying she wasn't feeling well and she would wait for me. She wasn't where she said. Did you see her at all since you got here?"

"No, we just got here when we spotted you. We'll help you look though. Where do you think she might be?" Jake asks.

"We'll help too," Anisa offers.

"I can bring two uniforms and we'll look too. Which way?" Detective Warren asks.

"The GPS locator pinged a little way down the beach. There's a wooded area with a Zen Garden, that's where I thought she was, based on her last text. There was no sign of her there. Come on," I lead them across the patio and down the steps.

"Wait! Those are her heels. They were hurting her feet. She definitely didn't go back into the house without them. This way." I direct everyone down the beach. Jake and Connor check the woods. Detective Warren and the uniformed officers follow close to the tree line. We spread out with Anisa and Rev checking the beach. Once we've gone almost twice as far as the GPS locator pinned her location, without any sign of her, we turn back. Panic has a tight grip on my throat. Where is she?

"Hey! I found something!" Connor yells out from the woods. I take off running towards the sound of his voice. When I find him, he and Jake are guarding a spot on the ground. When I get close enough, I see a cellphone on the ground. It looks stepped on. I squat down and use a stick to poke at it. Flipping it over so I can see the screen, I see there's a big crack right down the center that spiderwebs off from there. It's still working though. Detective Warren joins me. He removes a glove from his pocket, once he has it stretched on his hand, he lifts the phone.

Aiming the screen my way he asks, "Is this her phone?"

"Yeah. I need to make some calls. Get some more guys out here, and some dogs please."

"On it. Everyone! Please be careful what you step on and be meticulous. Start searching here and spread out. If you find something, shout out until we hear you, but *don't* touch anything. Go!" Detective Warren orders. Anisa bursts into tears and Rev is soothing her with soft words, his hand is rubbing her back.

"H-how can she just be gone? We should've stayed with her! I'll never forgive myself if she's hurt." Anisa turns into Rev's chest and she's inconsolable. Her back heaves with her sobs. I step away. I don't want to deal with her hysteria. I also need to call Samson and, oh God, Rhett. When I'm done calling in the Calvary, I begin searching. When I catch up with Detective Warren, he's directing four more uniformed officers.

When he takes a breath I ask, "Where's her phone? I need to see if I can find anything helpful in it."

He hands me an evidence bag containing Peyton's phone. I pocket it and continue my search. I know Jake and Connor are searching in the woods. Anisa and Rev were following an access path towards the road. When I reach the bench at the Zen Garden again, I sit and put on some gloves. Using her password, I access her phone. Her text to me was the last outgoing message. She has a text from Jake explaining he was running late for the party. Apparently, Jake and Connor couldn't keep their hands off each other. TMI for me.

There's nothing from a stranger or anyone that would concern me. Her last photos are of us in our costumes, and one of Anisa and Rev in theirs. Her last search was a makeup tutorial for Tinker Bell. Without my computer, there's nothing else I can search on her phone.

"Micah! Where are you?" Orlando yells out to me.

"I'm over here!" I holler back, "Hey, thanks for coming," my voice shakes a bit as they come into view. He and Ax crunch along the gravel path and join me.

"What happened? How did you get so many cops out here so fast?" Ax questions.

"There was an incident with a gunman," I began.

"What the fuck?" Orlando interjects.

I fill them in and finish with, "We found her phone."

"God dammit! What can we do? How can we help?" Orlando exclaims.

"I don't really know. There're a few uniformed cops looking and Jake and Connor are here searching in the woods somewhere. Anisa and Rev went to follow an access path to the road. I guess just pick a direction and start looking. She was wearing a Tinker Bell costume and no shoes. Her hair is up on her head. Oh, here's a picture of her costume," I aim Peyton's phone at them. I realize I should be disseminating this photo of her. I send it to myself and then I open a group text and send it to everyone I know, including Detective Warren. Both of their phone's ping with an alert from my text. They check their screens.

"Got it," Ax says.

Orlando adds, "Me too. Come on Ax, let's try this direction." He points and they walk that way.

"Thanks guys," I say to their retreating forms. They sort of nod and wave as they focus on the ground.

I think about what my next steps should be. I'm trying so hard not to have a meltdown of my own. My chest hurts and my heart is pounding so hard against my ribcage. I'm sweating and shaking with adrenaline. My thoughts are spinning, I'm trying to picture her smiling face from the last time I saw her. I don't want to picture her gorgeous face on a dead body. I've seen so many, and it's really difficult not to put Peyton's face on their broken bodies. That's not going to happen.

Trying to outrun my fears, I quickly jog back to the house. I run up the steps, across the patio, and into the house. The front door slams open when I arrive. Rhett, Ace, and Thomas storm inside, closely followed by Samson and Keiko.

Rhett looks furious, his face a tight mask of fear and anger. Ace and Thomas look so worried, they seem ready to burst with emotion. Samson looks grim and calm. I'm not sure why he brought Keiko, of all people, but I'll accept all the help I can get. I approach them and start telling them exactly what happened. After repeating myself for the third or fourth time, I'm frustrated with the male character of my story. Why does he leave the beautiful pixie alone? I'm also frustrated with the beautiful fairy who seems to wander off every time I tell the tale. Shit. Am I referring to myself in the third person? Fourth? Fifth?

Samson takes over when he sees that I'm in no condition to lead this search. He's called in some search dogs and they begin to arrive as we head outside.

"Thank you all for coming. Time is of the essence. We need to find Peyton Baker, immediately. She reported not feeling well in her last message. We have to assume she's sick or injured. You all have your assignments. Please let the dogs go first when we get to the starting point. She was last seen near the Zen Garden entrance. Are there any questions? All right, head out!"

Rhett holds my arm as he walks next to me, "Listen, we're going to find her. You look awful, I get it, but you need to stay focused. We won't give up until we find her. Okay?"

"Yeah. I won't stop until she's found. I'm trying not to lose it. I'm struggling. If you see me losing it, punch me or something." He nods.

When we arrive at the entrance to the path, Jake and Connor join us. I don't know where Orlando, Anisa, or any of them went. Three search and rescue dogs are here with their handlers. Samson gives them guidance and the dogs sniff her phone, shoes, and the bench before they take off with their noses to the ground. Each handler keeps their dog away from the others. One dog is very interested in the cups left on the ground. A uniformed officer collects both cups in an evidence bag. Another uniformed officer takes his place following the dogs.

Keiko dons some gloves and follows as well. The rest of us stay back and follow at a distance. This is making me crazy. I want to move faster. I want to find her right now. Up ahead one of the handlers asks his dog to sit. I see Ax and Orlando come through the trees. They join us and after everyone greets each other, then we all fall back into our spots.

"Did you guys find Anisa and Rev?" I ask Ax.

"Yeah. They said they were working their way back to the house. Anisa's a mess. He was having a hard time with her."

"I'm not surprised. First her boyfriend's house gets shot up, then her best friend disappears. I'd be hysterical too if I didn't need to be focused to find her."

"Who's her boyfriend?" Ax asks.

"Rev. You know him, don't you? From your MC? He was with Anisa, wasn't he?"

"Yeah. I'm just confused. This isn't his house. I have no idea whose house it is, but it definitely doesn't belong to Rev. He and Tool have a mobile home on a few acres, east of Highway 19."

"Oh. I thought this was his house for some reason. Hmmm." That's so strange, why did I think the party was at Rev's house? Peyton thought so too. I'm positive we talked about it when we arrived. Fuck. That seems like forever ago. Where's my girl? I want her in my arms so desperately. The pain in my chest stabs anew. It feels like a chain is getting pulled tighter around my ribs with a spike sticking out of my heart.

One of the dogs sits and lets out a short bark. Everyone perks up and watches the dog and her handler. The handler gives her a command in another language. It sounds like Dutch. I'm not great with foreign accents and dialects. The dog barks again and remains seated. One of the other dogs is circling behind the sitting dog, nose to the ground. The third dog is sitting at his handler's command. We all watch and wait in silence.

Finally, the handler for the sitting and barking dog speaks to us. "Dottie says she's reached the end of the trail. Miss Baker went this way, then she stopped leaving a trail right about here," the short man points to the ground.

As we watch, the circling dog sits and lets out a short bark. His handler gives him some commands that sound like English, but they don't make sense. I would expect, *find* or *search*. Not, *eat some popcorn*. The dog barks again and doesn't budge. The handler gives him a ragged looking toy to hold and pats his head.

Then she speaks to us, "Justice agrees with Dottie. Her trail stops here."

Rhett asks, "What does that mean? She vanished into thin air?"

The man with the third dog speaks up, "I'm sorry Mr. Baker. Rogue says the same thing. In our experience, it usually means the person got picked up in a vehicle. It's the fastest and most complete way to cut off a scent trail."

Now what? I finally looked around and saw that we came out to the main road via a beach access path. There's no parking area but there's evidence that people occasionally park here. The grass is missing in two trails of dirt, suggesting that cars pull off and park here. I look closely at the dirt for any specific tire marks, footprints, anything at all. The sand is just a lumpy mess of tracks that're wholly unidentifiable.

Jake walks to the road and looks both ways. His face looks haunted and his eyes are watery. He's not holding up well either. We've got to snap out of this and concentrate on finding her. We can be miserable after we find her. That didn't make sense. Frustrated, I shake my head to dispel the negative thoughts.

"Jake, when you came into the house, how far did you get before you had to stop? Had the guy started shooting yet?" I ask.

"I, we, didn't get far at all. The cops stopped us in the driveway and said we couldn't go inside. We waited until they gave us permission and that's when we saw Anisa going up the stairs. Then you came in from the back. Why? Did we miss something important?"

"I'm not sure yet. How about you, Connor. What did you see?"

Connor clears his throat before responding, "I stayed in the car while Jake spoke to the cops. When it finally seemed like people were going in and out freely, we asked if we could go inside and they allowed us in. I didn't see Anisa. I didn't see anyone I know, until I saw you come in."

"What about her costume? Did you see anyone in a green costume? A Tinker Bell costume?" I ask him.

He grabs his chin and with his Robin costume he looks very super-hero-side-kick-like. If I wasn't so upset, I would find it funny. Now, it annoys me because it's a distraction.

"No. I didn't see anyone in green or Tinker Bell. There was a guy wearing a giant pickle suit, with green beach balls," he shakes his head. Then he clears his throat again, "It looked just how it sounds. But it was dark pickle green. That's the only green costume I saw all night."

Alarm bells are going off in my head. I have that familiar feeling that I'm missing something. I made a note on my phone to remind myself of what everyone said. I notice Keiko is recording what each person says. Why didn't I think of it? That video will be invaluable as we investigate.

"Micah, did you have any more questions?" Samson asks.

"Not yet," I replied.

"Okay. Let's each partner up and take separate routes back. Handlers, please have the dogs take different paths and see if they pick up anything. Everybody ready? Let's move."

I walk next to Rhett. We're both silent, lost in our thoughts about Peyton. Shit! Poor Rhett, he's lost one sister and Peyton is the only one left in his family. We have to find her. My chest throbs until it's become a constant dull ache. I need to get in front of my computer. I need to be looking at video surveillance from the area. I'm strongest behind a keyboard, and I better be strong enough to find her. When we get back to the mansion without any new information and not a single clue, I can't take it anymore.

"I need to get behind my keyboard. I do my best work there. I can start pouring through surveillance footage and checking any images from the party. I need to be hunting her down in cyberspace. Are you staying here?" I ask Samson, while Rhett, Ace, and Thomas, listen intently.

"I'm not leaving here until we're certain we've searched every possible inch of this area and we've exhausted every possibility. Go do what you need to. I'll check in with you. I know how focused you get, even more so now. I'll have as many personnel as you need ready at a moment's notice. Paige is online from home too, right Rhett?"

"Yeah, she said she was starting with gas stations in the area. Micah, she wants to hear from you when you get online so you can coordinate and not duplicate efforts," Rhett says. I nod at him and the rest of the guys, then I start walking towards the door.

"Micah, what should we do? Do you want us to stay here, or go with you, someplace else? We'll do anything you need," Jake follows me and asks.

"Oh. Why don't you two come to Peyton's. You guys can help with communication and updates between everyone. Get everyone's contact info you don't already have before you head out, okay?"

"Yeah. Okay. Great. We're on it," Jake replies.

Connor adds, "We're going to find her. She's also very smart and re-sourceful, don't forget that. Stay strong." He pats my shoulder. I give him a forced smile, with real gratitude. I don't know if Jake and Connor will stay together, but they're both good guys. I'm glad they're friends with me and Peyton. Same with Orlando and Ax. They already left to drive around and check more locations in the area. They'll be at Peyton's or Orlando's later. I'm not waiting to see what Rhett and the guys are doing. I'm out the door and in my car before anyone else can stop me.

Peyton

My head's pounding, I have no clue where I am and I don't know what happened. I remember being at the Halloween party with Micah and Anisa. Then I remember dancing, but nothing else. Why can't I see anything? I can't figure out if my eyes won't open or if something's covering them. I try using my hand to feel my eyes. My hand won't do what I ask, I can't move at all. Maybe my eyes just won't open.

I take stock of my body and I can't feel my hands or feet. There's a random tingle every now and then, so I know they're still attached. The throbbing in my head is sharpest between my eyes, but it radiates out all the way around my skull and into my neck. I want to squeeze my temples and massage away the pain.

There's an unpleasant smell, like old cigarettes and bleach. It reminds me of the women's shelter I volunteered with in Baton Rouge. It's the scent of desperation and despair. Not discouraged, I try to wriggle my body. I can move a bit, though it's not really under my control so I stop trying, to conserve energy.

I'm a little cold overall and I seem to be on a hard surface, on my back. Listening I try to isolate every sound, a mechanical hum behind me, and a dripping sound splashes on something metal every time I count to four, on my left.

A door squeaks and closes softly. It's in the room with me. Footsteps come close, then continue past me. I want to call out, but not knowing what's going on has me frozen. What if I make a noise and they kill me? What if I'm in a medical facility and they're waiting for me to wake up? The person in this room is moving some things around that sound metallic. There's a tearing paper sound and I can't take it anymore.

"Hello?" My voice is barely a whisper and gruff gravel.

"Oh! You're not supposed to wake up yet. Naughty, naughty. I'll be right back, don't go anywhere," she laughs.

"Wait..." the door opens and closes. What was so funny? I try to move again and I'm able to flex my toes a little. I try my fingers and they wiggle but continue not to do what I ask.

The door opens, "Okay. You might or might not feel a pinch. Good night." There's a bee sting feeling on my arm.

"Ow!" I can't say another word, my mouth stops working. The female voice is still talking. I can't understand what she says. I hear a mumble like it's from underwater, and then nothing.

I have no concept of how much time passed. My head is throbbing, and I can't see anything. Am I dreaming? Somehow, I'm having déjà vu. It's like I've already done this, or dreamed it... I don't know. My head hurts so much and I can't seem to move or feel my extremities. I have that stiff feeling like I've been in this position for a very long time. I try to wriggle my body and it doesn't do what I want.

I definitely remember this happening before, but I'm not sure if it was in a dream. There was a woman who hurt my arm in my dream, or before I can't remember clearly. A wave of nausea hits me hard and I have to swallow fast to keep from vomiting. Oh, that was close. I'll do anything to avoid vomiting. I hate it so much. *Okay, quit thinking about vomit!*

I flex my fingers and they move when I try. I still can't bring them to my face. I flex my toes, they respond. Taking a few deep breaths to ease the nausea helps me figure out I can feel my torso. My middle is all pins and needles. I must be getting the feeling back. I try to open my eyes again. Still completely dark, so pitch black if I could move my hand, I still wouldn't see it right in front of my face.

A door squeaks open, and I can make out at least two sets of footsteps. I'm pretty sure the female who hurt my arm was real and I don't want to alert anyone that I'm awake. I hold still and keep my breathing as even as possible.

"Ah, ah, no touching. We said you could only look. What d'you think?" the same female voice asks.

"You weren't lying. She's quite spectacular. Did you dress her up for me?" A male voice answers. His voice is deep and has a slight accent. Not anything I'm used to hearing, maybe Russian or from that region.

A different male chuckles, "No. She happened to be wearing the costume when she got here. If you don't like it, we can put her in something else."

"I find it intriguing. What is she supposed to be?" the man with the accent asks.

"It's a Disney character from Peter Pan, she's a fairy. She's very healthy and well nourished, don't you think? We've gotten quite a few responses to the images we sent out. If you're interested you need to make a decision quickly," the female says. I think I recognize her voice. She sounds a lot like Tool's friend, Diamond. What the fuck?

Neither of the males' sound like Tool, or Rev for that matter. Both men sound older, not like some dickhead biker in his early twenties. I'm breathing harder as I get worked up about who may have me. I try to slow my breathing. I crack one eye open a little, bright light stabs my aching head through a gap in the dark cloth covering my eyes. Definitely blindfolded. That can't be a good sign. They're all on my left, so I only open my right eye. Hopefully they won't notice.

"Yes, I would like to make an offer. I want just a few hours to start. What are the rules about damage to the product?"

"Well, Mr. Fedorov, we really have only one rule. *You break it, you buy it.*"

The man with an accent, Mr. Fedorov, I suppose, laughs. I can hear movement very close to my face. Then there's a long inhaling sound. I get a whiff of faint cologne, mint, and cigarettes. Is he smelling me? Oh my God, that's so not okay. It's taking every survival instinct I have not to move. I want to fight and scream in protest. If this is what I think it is, fighting right now will only get me injured. I need to be smart, pay attention, and wait for the right opportunity. I suspect my hands and feet are secured in some fashion. I'm not going to get away right now no matter how hard I fight.

"Let's discuss it in my office. Babe, check her vitals, will ya?" the voice without a foreign accent commands.

The door opens and the noisier footsteps fade away. Soft footsteps move around the room. A cold hand wraps something around my arm. It tightens and a cold piece of metal presses beneath the band crushing my arm. *Blood pressure cuff,* I recognize it from my recent hospital stay, I woke up so many times with my arm being crushed just like this while I was there. The cold metal rests on my breast next. *Stethoscope.* The cold hand wraps around my wrist, awkwardly. I feel something restraining my wrist, it's a little tight.

The longer she touches me the more difficult it becomes to hold still. The cloth over my eyes moves and comes off. I don't react, making my eyes roll back as if I were asleep… I hope. The cold fingers pry my left eye open, and I do my best to keep it rolled back. I'm trying to look at my brain so hard it hurts my aching head.

"Oh, Peyton, you can't fool me. I know you're awake. You need to drink some water. The drugs will wear off faster if you have some fluids to wash them out. You can open your eyes," she admonishes.

I debate my options, which are roughly, none at this moment. I'm extremely thirsty, it feels like an old sponge curled up in my mouth and soaked up all the moisture. I decided it won't make anything worse to open my eyes.

When I peel them open, using more force than is usually required, I can't focus. Everything is a blur and the light stabs repeatedly at my brain. It's like those little green army men are poking my brain with their bayonets. Squinting, I try to see more clearly and limit access of the lightsaber Darth Vader is plunging into my painful blue orbs.

When I'm able to focus enough to see it is indeed Diamond standing over me, I'm disgusted by her. Her hair is once again purple, and her blonde wig from the party is nowhere in sight. She no longer has theater blood dripping from her fangless mouth. But she's no less of a blood sucker than she was in her costume. What kind of woman helps men kidnap another woman?

"I can see you remember me. I'll be taking care of you while you're with us. I'll be the one to give you food and water. I'll take care of any medical needs you may have as your time here progresses. I suggest you be kind to the hand that'll feed you, or I won't be kind in return. Got it?"

"Yep," I grit through teeth clenched in anger. "What's wrong with you? Why would you help kidnappers?"

"I don't think you're in any position to hate on me. Remember, the hand that'll feed you? Are you hungry now? Your stomach is growling up a storm." She's right. My stomach is growling in protest. I must've been here for quite a while. I'm so thirsty, her offer of water sounds heavenly, I don't want to ask for a drink though.

"Here," she cracks open a bottle of water. "Take small sips or you'll get sick." She presses the bottle to my lips and my thirst takes over and I gulp a few small swallows. She pulls it away before I'm finished. I flash a dirty look her way before I can stop it. She laughs and pats my lips with a paper napkin.

"That's enough. You can have more in a few minutes if that stays down."

Ugh! Why does she keep saying things? My body is reacting to what she says like it's an order. A wave of nausea overwhelms me for a minute and I have to pant to keep from vomiting. Once I'm past the crisis, I take a quick look at my surroundings. It looks like a warehouse with a tall ceiling of metal and exposed steel beams. There're some industrial lights hanging from long rods in the ceiling. There's a sink across the room to my left. Under the sink is a wood cabinet and a long counter lines the wall as far as I can see. There're no windows and just one door in my view.

A large commercial refrigerator is on my right, and next to it looks like a deep freezer. They both continue to emit their mechanical humming sounds. I'm strapped to some kind of table. I can't see what it's made of, whatever it is has no consideration for comfort. There are some big green and red tanks marked with hazardous warning labels. I don't know what all the symbols mean, but one says, *explosive,* right on the bright orange label.

"Hey, I need your help in here really quick. I don't give a fuck… I need you now. Get over it!" Diamond puts her phone back in her pocket. She sees me watching her phone and gives me an evil look shaking her head. I hate being so transparent.

"Can I please have another sip of water?" I ask, doing my best to keep the sarcasm from my voice.

"Okay." She unscrews the lid and places it to my lips again. I take a few cautious sips this time and stop before she pulls it away.

"You learn fast. That'll help you while you're here."

"Where's here?" I asked.

"This is our home. Yours too, for now. I don't know yet how long you'll be with us." I don't miss how she keeps phrasing my time here like I'll no longer be around. Does she mean no longer *alive*? A chill runs down my spine and I shiver.

"Are you cold?"

"Yeah, and I need to pee."

"I know. You can go as soon as I have some help." As if on cue, the door opens more forcefully than the previous times. Tool walks in with a pissed off look on his face. At least I'm assuming it's Tool. I don't actually know, it's just about impossible to tell him and Rev apart.

"What do you need help with?" he growls at her.

"I definitely don't need your attitude. You wanted to do this, so suck it up, buttercup. Help me get her up; she needs to use the restroom."

"You're the nurse. I thought you're supposed to handle that shit," he grumbles.

"Nope, just pee," she responds sarcastically. His face scrunches in anger. She gives him a lifted eyebrow and he sighs, frustrated. He takes a knife from his pocket and approaches my wrist with the sharp looking blade. I try to jerk away but I can't because I'm cuffed in place. He uses his terrifyingly sharp blade, and my hand pulls free. I bring it to my chest, feeling the pain from the restraint fully. He cuts the other hand free and moves to my feet. Once I'm free, Diamond takes my arm to help me down.

Tool takes my other arm, thankfully they both hold me up while I steady myself. My legs don't want to bear my weight, and I'm weak and stiff. After a moment I'm fairly stable, but they both keep a hand at my elbow. My knees wobble and I'm glad for them, I think. They lead me out the door and down the hall. There are two doors I can see. The hallway is wide, and one side is stacked with boxes and crates, and some are covered with tarps. We enter what looks like an apartment. They take me to a small bathroom that has a single sink with barely any countertop. There's a plastic walled shower that might not even fit a guy Micah or Rhett's size. The toilet is old and dingy, but looks clean. Tool waits outside the door.

Diamond leads me to the white porcelain throne. I realize I'm in my costume and I'm going to have to remove it to pee. I reach under my arm where the zipper holds the bodice closed. I slide it down and refuse to look at her to see how closely she's watching me. When I slide it down, she lets out a whistle.

"Wow! I'm not into chicks, but you look damn fine in that green lingerie. Did Micah pick it out?"

"No," I growl my answer very annoyed that she feels like we're friends or something, and she can talk to me about my boyfriend. My disgust is renewed tenfold.

I take care of my business and keep my eyes to the ground. I've never in my life been so happy to wear a costume, as I am once I'm back in the snug and somewhat skimpy, faerie garb. I wash my hands and as I dry them. I see that Tool's standing in the open doorway. Shit! How long was he watching? My stomach turns at the thought.

They lead us back through the shabby but clean apartment. I'm able to walk without assistance now and I hope they won't drug me again. My head is better. I think the water did help, but there's still a dull ache in my temples. When we're closed back in the room with the table, I take another look around. It's very clinical, but not as well equipped as a doctor's office. The table is metal and reminds me of a coroner's table from every cop show I've ever seen. It's a disturbing thought and I banish it.

"Hop back up on the table. Tool, will you just cuff her feet to the table? I want to leave her hands free for a few minutes. The plastic restraints are damaging her wrists. Even better, just cuff her wrists together but loose enough it doesn't cut into her skin, okay?"

"Yeah, okay." He works quickly to restrain my feet, then my hands. It's more comfortable and I hate to admit I'm thankful for the relief.

When he's done, he asks, "Anything else?"

"No, we're good. Thanks, and quit being a jackass."

"Fuck you. I'm out." He slams the door on his way through.

"Geez! Who pissed in his beer? He's new to this and he's not thrilled that I outrank him here," she tells me. Then she seems to realize we aren't friends. It's probably because I'm staring daggers at her.

"Anyway, do you need another sip of water before I go?"

"Yes."

I drink sensibly when she brings the bottle to my mouth. When I'm finished, she puts the bottle in the fridge and looks me over. She opens a cabinet and pulls out a worn blanket, at least it looks clean. She covers my feet then she wraps it around me, tucking it in as she goes. I instantly feel better, and less exposed.

"Okay, I'll be back to check on you. Don't do anything stupid or I'll have to drug you again. I don't have anything to entertain you, so I recommend a nap. I have a suspicion you're in for a long night."

With that ominous remark she exits the room, closing the door softly, and leaving me in darkness. My thoughts are a chaotic mess of escape plans, self-defense moves Paige taught me, and Micah. Poor Micah, he must be worried sick. Oh God, Rhett! He must be devastated after we've already lost Larue. Shit, I'm in a similar situation. What are the odds of two sisters meeting the same fate years apart in different states? When you factor in that it seems to be at the hands of the Southern Suns, again, it must be astronomical.

I want Micah. I want Paige, Nova, and Rhett. I want Jake, Connor, and Anisa. I want all of my extended family at Savage. I need to shake this off. Falling into despair isn't going to help me live. Oh, and Orlando! From what he's told Micah he's trying to reform his MC. I'm sure he doesn't know anything about this.

Okay, come on Peyton. Focus. I assess my cuffs and find my feet are cuffed more loosely than before. My hands are cuffed together with a decent amount of wiggle room. I twist them around in an attempt to get them free, it's futile. They're still tight enough that I can't escape them.

My hands are only fastened together, and my feet keep me trapped on this stupid table, with each one attached to it separately. I sit up and try wrenching my foot to break the strap. Using my hands, I pull the opposite direction while my foot pulls the other way. I swear I saw a movie where a guy was able to break these plastic things. I think he said there's a certain angle that if you hit it just right, they'll snap. Aggravated, I go crazy jerking my hands and feet in every direction.

"Rrrraaaaahh!" I shout in frustration, falling back onto the table with a bang. Sweat beads on my brow and I'm breathing hard. My hair is falling from its up do and I blow a few strands out of my face. Lying still and breath heaving, I stare up at the ceiling. The barest glimmer of dull gray light seeps in around the eaves. There's a glow up there. I look around letting my eyes adjust. I can see hulking gray outlines of the largest items in the room. The sweat on my forehead cools my still slightly throbbing head as it evaporates. The blanket Diamond had wrapped around me is now in a clump at my waist and half hanging off the table.

I take a few deep breaths again and try to clear my mind. What are my options here? Obviously, I'm not strong enough to break loose despite my very recent exercising. I can't overpower Tool, but maybe I could gain an advantage over Diamond. When the lights were on, I noticed a cabinet that looks like it holds medical supplies based on the contents of the countertop there. Maybe if I can get away from her, just a few steps, I can find a weapon in there.

Next, I picture the path we took through this building. We went left from this room. The hallway in that direction has two doors. One to the apartment, but I don't know what's behind the other. When we came back to this room, I could see the other side of the hall ended in a wall where you had to choose to go right or left when you reached that point. I'll need to guess my way to an exit. The floor is concrete and it has dirt embedded in it, stained from many shoes walking on its surface. I think I'll be able to see the most often used path in its gray patina.

I go over the self-defense moves that Paige and Rhett taught me. In my mind I picture each action and how I need to defend each type of attack. From there my thoughts begin to wander over my family, and the people I love. I imagine what they're doing right now. I know Micah... he's on his laptop scouring the town for clues. Rhett is probably ready to rip someone's head off. His go-to emotion when his loved ones are at risk, is anger. Thankfully, despite his anger, he's usually able to channel it in constructive ways. Nova should be asleep, or at school depending on the time. Shit! School. I'm missing classes, again. I'm going to have to retake the entire semester at this rate.

Micah

F elony charges me as soon as I walk through the door.

Meeeow! She wails.

"Okay, come on, let's get you some food." With the mention of a meal the other two cats come running. Beta rubs against me aggressively. Once I have them fed, I'm ready to jump on my laptop. Felony is staring at me. Her late-night snack remains untouched.

"What is it?" I ask.

Mewow, wow-wow! She tilts her head, like she's waiting for an answer.

"Are you looking for your mom? Trust me, I wish I knew where she was, come on. You can hang out with me while I look." She follows right next to me as we set up in the office. Once everything is turned on and warmed up, I'm logged in and using my skills to scan for cameras at the party house and every surrounding house. I call Paige on speaker.

Paige starts talking the moment we're connected, "I didn't find anything at any gas stations... there's no sign of her. I'm scanning for cars that passed both directions tonight on the main roads. What do you have?"

"Nothing yet. I'm checking the houses in the area. I have her phone; I'm going to hook that up in a minute. Can you grab whatever videos are on the socials? I want to see if there's anyone that looks familiar or especially interested in Peyton. It sucks that everyone is in costume. It's going to be a chore to identify every partygoer."

"We can just mark them as whatever their costume is and if we have anyone interesting, we'll identify them."

"Yeah, okay. I'm connecting her phone now. My Persona4 Program is searching through it."

"Good, it'll do the job, it's my favorite scanner. Thanks for sharing it with me. I've got two different cars that went both ways so far and I've confirmed with multiple businesses. I'll send you pictures as I isolate more. I'm working on their tags. I wish Florida required front tags. It sure would make LEO's work and mine a lot easier."

"Yeah, I've often thought the same. I'm sending you images from her phone with identifying information. The people she took pictures of, I actually know. I'm going to call in Darren Reiss from my office. I'll pass you anything he finds. We need more eyes on this, I want to check every person in every image and I need his detail-oriented approach for that. Plus, he's cool with me and my methods."

"Sounds like a good idea. Go do that and check back with me. We're going to find her. Remember that she's fierce and smart. I love you, Micah."

"Love you too, *mom*." Whoa, my emotions are raw. Not sure if I've ever called her that out loud before. Don't have time to dwell on it now. I shake it off and get Darren up to speed. I sent him the party house stuff so he can continue matching and identifying people. Once I have him working on the people, I concentrate on the houses around the party house.

As I'm working, random windows pop up with information from Peyton's phone. Felony's sitting on my desk watching me. She must feel my anxiety. I'm not finding anything useful, and I'm getting frustrated. I'm pounding on my keyboard so hard I'm surprised it's still working. Felony startles when I burst out of my chair and storm from the room. I need a breather.

I grab a Red Bull from the fridge and a pack of Oreos then walk out the front door. Leaning on the railing I look to the sky. The clouds are whipping past the moon, gray and angry. The trees are bent to the east as the outer bands of Hurricane Isaac make themselves known. I haven't checked the storm, but it can't come here when Peyton is out there, alone. *God, please let her be okay. Please help me find her,* I think towards the heavens. I don't know why I reach out to God. He's never helped when I needed Him in the past.

Headlights come up the road and pull in below me. I crunch the Oreo in my mouth so I can speak when Jake and Connor come up here. Jake has bags in his hands, the plastic grocery kind. Connor is carrying a duffle over his shoulder and a twelve-pack of canned refreshments. They stomp up the steps.

"I'm just saying I wouldn't bring that up," Connor is telling Jake. When Jake gets to the top of the steps it takes him a moment to notice me.

"Oh. Hey, Micah. How're you holding up?"

"I'm frustrated, and a little pissed off. Trying to get a breath of fresh air to get past it."

Connor speaks up, "We have more stuff in the car. In case the storm comes closer. Should we leave it there or bring it up?"

"Leave it there. If the storm actually hits here, we'll have to move our headquarters. We can't stay this close to the beach if we're getting hurricane winds and storm surge."

"My weather app says it still hasn't turned enough. Pretty soon we're going to run out of time, and it'll be here before it turns," Jake says ominously. Orlando and Ax pull up next door, seeing us, they come right over. Both of them look overwrought, and disheveled.

"Hey guys, what's up?" Connor greets them. Jake and I nod our greetings. They nod in return, faces grim.

"What?" I ask Orlando.

"We went to the clubhouse and the bar, we asked around the guys. Nobody said anything specific enough to be helpful, yet. It seems the trafficking ring that you guys busted up a while back, is low-key still around. Buzzard's running it while he hides. I'm sorry, man. We didn't know."

"What the fuck? If he's hiding, he can't be doing it alone."

"He's not. Seems he has an old lady now. He's also using some of the younger guys and prospects. Some of the prospects have disappeared, but I just figured they took off. Guys do that. Rumor is some of them talked about what Buzzard's up to, and they weren't seen again after that. Nobody's talking now, out of fear. We lucked out and ran into two fringe guys who were drunk as skunks and they told us what they know. They helped Buzzard with a disposal project," Ax says.

I look between them. This is bad. Buzzard is bad news and we thought he left the area after what happened to Paige. He hasn't been spotted anywhere. I have face recognition software searching for him and a couple other most wanted criminals. I know these guys wouldn't be sharing club business, especially with me, if they weren't worried for Peyton's life. My heart twinges in my chest. *God, thanks for this connection, please keep her safe!* Okay, maybe He helps, sometimes.

"Are you going to keep trying to find out more?" I ask them.

Orlando answers, "Yeah. We just came here to get the hurricane shutters up and gather some stuff to take with us. What can we do to help you? Does this place have shutters?"

"No. The landlords live in Ohio and they're terrified of hurricanes. They installed storm windows guaranteed up to a strong category three. Thanks though. Is it coming this way?"

"I don't know. One guy says yes, one says maybe. I just want to be prepared. It takes 15 minutes to pull them down. Best decision I ever made when installing those roll out shutters. I figure if we cover the windows I won't be worried about the place while we're out." He doesn't say *searching*, though we all know it was there at the end of his thought.

"All right. I'm going to get back to work. Thanks."

"You doing okay, bro?" Ax questions Connor. I didn't hear his answer. I bring my snack with me to the office. Felony follows me and perches back in her spot on the desk. I plunge back into my screens, newly focused, and I check out a few ideas.

I don't know how much time has passed. Jake and Connor are cleaning. They said they couldn't sit still and I told them they could do anything they wanted, and to consider it their home. Then the vacuum started. Peyton and I keep the place neat and clean, but three cats leave a mess without even trying. I'm watching the Doppler of Isaac; it still hasn't turned. The strongest band yet, is poised to hit us in about a half hour. Even if it does turn now, that band is coming. The surge shouldn't be an issue unless we get the eye.

I'm trying to focus on the images I found on the video systems for the houses near the party house. One house has a camera that aims towards the beach access path we found. There's a car at the entrance on one clip.

I can't see much detail because the camera is really far away. It looks like a black blob, but there's a quick moment where a person loads something in the trunk and pulls off. It could be a fisherman, but I need to be sure. The timeframe is suspiciously close to when Peyton went missing.

Every few seconds there's a pop-up on my screen from Peyton's phone. I'm getting annoyed, it's disrupting what I'm doing, and I'm about to disconnect her phone so it'll stop. I freeze when I finally read what the message says. It's from Felony's AirTag.

Alert: Out of Range\ \ tag ID: FELONY

I look at the cat. She's still on the desk, curled up now. She can't be out of range, since she's right in front of me. I check her collar; the tag is missing from its silicone casing. I look back at the screen, how is it out of range? I opened the app on Peyton's phone. She has all the alerts set up for all the cats. She set up a home range and common locations, Rhett's house, and mine. She has the distance set at three-thousand feet. If any of the cats gets more than three-thousand feet from the center of the set location, her phone gets an alert.

I get up and run into the bedroom looking for the other two. Both Beta and Qwerty are in the bedroom, she's on the chair and he's on the bed. I quickly check their collars and now they're as freaked out as me. I ran back into the office. Connor sees me run across the hall and he quickly comes to stand in the doorway. I opened the mapping on the app. Qwerty and Beta both show as *HOME,* on the map. Felony is *OUT OF RANGE* and her tag shows up as a feline silhouette blinking about three miles away. I locate the spot on my FBI software. It's a warehouse. *What the fuck?* Peyton must have Felony's tag with her for some reason.

"Holy fuck! I think I found her!"

"Oh my God! Jake! Jake! Come quick!" Connor yells.

"What happened?"

"I think I found her. I'm sounding the alarm for all hands-on deck. I need you guys to get on the phone. I'm texting you the address. Send it to Orlando and Ax and Detective Warren. Then if you guys could pack up the cats and take them to Rhett's that would be awesome. Stay there. The storm hasn't turned. It's drifting a bit, so they're hoping it'll turn now. Either way, it's not going to be safe to stay here much longer. Got all that? I'm heading out." I walk past them, carrying my laptop in its case, into the bedroom not waiting for a response. They follow me.

"Their crates are in the laundry room. Don't worry about anything else. They have food and stuff over there. If you have a chance to throw a couple things in a bag for me and Peyton and take it with you that might be good. Don't stay here long though. These roads could be under water with one good rain and a little storm surge."

"We're on it. Don't worry about anything. We'll make sure the cats are safe. What about locking the door? Or the alarm or anything?"

"It's automatic, since it's a keypad lock. It'll lock and set itself. Just don't lock yourselves out, actually, I'll text you the code in case. Thanks guys." I pull on my jacket, double check my holster. Put my ankle holster on, load extra clips in my pockets, collect my laptop, and walk out. I grab another Red Bull, the keys, and I'm through the front door.

The trees are whipping around as the wind is howling. It blows my hair and rain into my face. I don't even notice; all my attention is on a flashing cat on my phone. I sent out a blast text and email message to everyone who needs to know where to meet me. There's another set of warehouses in front of the one we're heading to. We're going to meet at the far end of those and then coordinate our rescue. Samson would have choppers already there if it weren't for the storm. He can't bring a mobile command center either. Once the winds reach a certain speed our resources dwindle. I don't give a shit. We're going old school and that's fine with me. I can't believe she's been so close this whole time.

It's almost 7 a.m. The sky is still dark because of the storm. We arrived in various vehicles and Samson was somehow able to gain access to the warehouse we're parked near, so we can get out of the weather. He's a miracle worker sometimes. Rhett's pacing like a caged beast. I would be too if I didn't need to be on my computer. Darren is helping coordinate our rescue, he's also still analyzing megabytes of data from the party.

"All right guys, everyone understands the plan?" Samson yells above the wind. He brought gear for all of us, and we're decked out in tactical rain protection, helmets, and vests. We have night vision and we're ready to head into the darkness like soldiers in combat. Everyone nods and mumbles their acknowledgement.

"Then let's move, teams, head out!"

I'm with Rhett, Thomas, and Ace. Darren's at our office monitoring and guiding us. We have earpieces for communication. There are two FBI teams of six each, in addition to the four of us. We're all approaching from different sides.

My earpiece crackles, "BASE, I see smoke. FD is enroute, proceed with caution. OVER."

"Fuck that!" Rhett beats me to the punchline. I'm right with him as we run to the warehouse throwing caution to the wind. We quickly evaluate the area and then breach the door.

Peyton

I jolt awake when the light turns on. There's a sound outside. Maybe wind howling? It takes a second before I remember I'm a prisoner. I must have fallen asleep while I was plotting. Before I can go over all my plans in my mind, a man walks into the room. I've never seen him before. He's probably around forty, under six feet tall, and on the thin side. He looks like a professional, maybe a doctor or lawyer. He has dark hair and eyes while a friendly smile graces his lips. There's a wealthy air about him.

My skin crawls with goosebumps. A cold and slimy creature curls in my stomach. It feels like an alien has taken up residence in my gut. I watch as he carries a wood chair next to where I'm held. He places it softly and then sits down with his back ramrod straight, his fingertips pressed together and resting beneath his chin. His eyes rove my face and my body, and the alien does a somersault.

"I'm told your name is Peyton. What a lovely name, for a beautiful woman."

I stare daggers at him. His eyes are bright with mischief and it scares the crap out of me. I've never had such strong warning bells ringing in my head.

Every once in a while, you come across a person that is so cold and evil that it radiates from their skin like perfume. All of my senses are on high alert.

"I'm told you're a student. What do you study?" His accented voice sets my teeth on edge. I stare blankly at him, angry, I'm not going to play his game. He smiles and stands up.

"Are you thirsty? There's supposed to be some water in the refrigerator. Would you like some?"

My throat clenched in thirst and my mouth just got so much drier. I refuse to engage with him. My mouth wants me to say yes, so much, but I won't and I clench my teeth to keep from speaking.

"I will just put it here. You can tell me if you would like some cold water, yes?" He waves it in front of me and places it on the counter within my line of sight. My eyes rest on the bottle and I watch as condensation forms on the plastic. I unconsciously lick my lips. I realize what I just did, and my eyes snap to the man. He's watching me with an evil grin. He looks like a predator who just spotted his next meal. My stomach flips again. At this rate it's going to be tied in knots.

His hand reaches out and removes the blanket that wasn't covering much, but covering everything at the same time. I feel completely exposed now. I shiver, I think it's a combination of fear and disgust. I'm cringed away from him as much as possible, he leans over me slightly.

"Your eyes are quite beautiful. I have never seen such a shade of blue." He stands back up straight and his eyes drift from my face to my chest and then down slowly, to my feet. I turn my face away from him. I can't keep him from looking at me, but I don't want to look at him. My stomach is still twisting, my fight or flight reflex is on high alert, pressing against my chest, wanting me to flee.

"We are going to have some fun. You see, I have very particular tastes. I cannot indulge them with my wife. I like to find women who are captive participants in my...activities. I can afford to fulfill my every desire. What do you think, Peyton?" He says my name with emphasis in a strange place. It sounds like *pay-TON* on his vile tongue. I keep my face turned away and stay silent. My heart is pounding hard in my chest and adrenaline from fear has me shivering with goosebumps across my skin. When my teeth chatter, he laughs. This causes me to look at him. His face is wearing a smug grin, satisfied he got me to look his way. My eyes roll automatically. His mouth stretches into a thin line as his eyes narrow.

"I don't like that, Pay-TON. Don't do it again, my wife does that and it makes me angry. You will not like my anger. Do you understand?" I remain silent.

"You will answer me when I ask you a question from now on. Do. You. Understand?" Once again, I remain silent.

SMACK!

A sting burns across my cheek as my head snaps to the side. The evil asshole slapped me! Leaning my head down I touch my face with the back of my hand, my mouth hangs open in shock. Tears fill up my eyes involuntarily as I gasp a breath.

"Now do you understand? You will answer me when I ask a question, yes?"

"Y-yes." My eyes fall to the ground in shame, my lip trembles. The tears overflow my lids and roll down my cheeks. He reaches out a finger and scoops a tear from my burning face. He sucks my shame from his fingertip and closes his eyes in pleasure. The reality of just how much trouble I'm in, hits me hard, right in the chest, like a cannonball. The trembling spreads to my whole body. I can't seem to stop the tears either, they continue to stream from my eyes.

"Delicious. Your tears are beautiful. Tell me, do you have a boyfriend?"

I open my mouth to speak, a quiet sob escapes without my permission. Unable to say anything, I nod. I cringe in fear that he won't accept my response. He smiles at me. That creepy, evil grin. I watch him closely, waiting to see what he'll do next. He moves over to the cabinet that I guessed contains medical supplies. He opens a drawer and I hear things being moved around and clinking together. He places everything he gathered onto a tray. Then he places the tray on a small table with wheels and brings it beside the table where I'm being held.

He placed a paper towel over the items on the tray. I'm glad. I don't think I want to know what he has planned. My stomach churns and the alien in there wants to come out. He begins to hum under his breath. It's a happy tune, he's perfectly at ease.

"My name is Levin, but you may call me *Mr. Lev*. I'm getting ready to begin. I will need to remove part of your, coz-TOOM. You will need to hold very still. If you move, you will be hurt. Do you understand?"

"Yes, Mr. Lev," I mumble without emotion, barely a whisper.

He removes his jacket and tie. He unbuttons the top two buttons of his shirt. He unbuttons his cuffs next, then rolls up his sleeves. His forearms are covered in greenish navy-blue tattoos. Some look like words in another language. Some are symbols and there's a skull with barbed wire twisted through it and a bleeding rose. It's the only splash of color. The rest look like they're gang tattoos that were done at home or in jail. His sleek business façade is gone. He looks like a dangerous criminal now. I have no clue if he's a gang member or mafia leader, but it doesn't matter to me. The only thing that matters are the various sharp things on the tray he just uncovered.

Fear takes hold of my throat and I feel like I can't breathe. I bring my hands to my mouth and try to make myself as small as possible. I wish I could pull my legs up to my chest for protection. I still feel far too exposed. He watches me and his grin grows with my terror.

He plays with some of the items, snapping them open and closed or touching a sharp point to his fingertip until a spot of blood blooms there. Smiling in satisfaction, he turns to me and examines my costume.

"How does it open?"

"W-what?"

"Your coz-TOOM, how does it open?"

"There's a z-zipper. Here," I twist a bit and gesture under my arm with my hands. I don't want him to touch me, but I don't see any way to avoid it. My tears begin to flow more heavily. I feel like I'm down a tunnel and everything's closing in on me. I realize I'm breathing hard and a cold sweat has appeared on my forehead. I've never been this scared in my entire life. Even when that psycho stalker attacked me, I wasn't this afraid. This is the first time I can clearly see my life coming to an end. I feel frozen, my brain is stuck, and leaving the rest of me without hope.

"Sit up. Here, take my hand. I will help." I ignore his offer and sit up on my own. My tears have matured into soft sobs with an occasional hiccup.

He walks around the table and stands on my right. "Lift your arm. Let me reach the zeeper." I mechanically lift my arms as instructed. My mind may be breaking, it's as if I'm completely disconnected from my current reality. It's like my spirit has floated up out of my body and I'm hovering above myself.

There's a loud noise from outside, and it rattles the metal wall. I picture Thor's Hammer smacking into the building. The storm must be raging.

I have that thought somewhere in the back of my mind. It's a mist of consciousness that isn't floating up here with me.

"It's not really your consciousness, sweetie. You're just so scared it feels that way. Peyton, you need to pull it together. You're strong. You're a smart girl. Get it together young lady, you need to fight back. You're going to have one chance to escape. You need to be focused, and not let the opportunity slip away," Original Nova's voice rattles through my wandering thoughts. Of all the things I could do to cope, why am I imagining Original Nova?

"Listen, you don't have time to argue. You aren't imagining me. I'm here to help you. I'm new to this guardian angel stuff so you can't hesitate. I don't want to screw up. You have to snap out of it. Think about Felony and Micah. My adorable namesake, your niece Nova. Oh, and of course my sweet Paige and Rhett. Come on Peyton, you'll know what to do. Just do it! Hey, do you think I could be the voice on a Nike commercial?"

"What're you talking about?" I say out loud.

"I did not say anything. But I cannot get this zeeper to open!" Mr. Lev growls.

"No, I wasn't talking to you."

"I'm the only one here, my pet. Who else would you be talking to? Dammit!" I realize two things, first he can't get the zipper open and he's jerking on it, and I'm being jolted from his efforts. Secondly, I either manifested Original Nova or she really paid me a visit to encourage me. Either way, her little pep talk has me focused and feeling present in my body at the moment. I take a couple deep breaths and think about what I can do to help myself.

"It will not open, I'm going to cut it off. If you move, I will cut you." He holds up a scalpel, "This is very sharp. You understand?"

"Yes, Mr. Lev."

He reaches for the front of the costume, right at the center of my cleavage. He holds the costume with his left hand, his disgusting fingers touch my skin, and cuts into the fabric with the scalpel in his right hand. I hold my breath and remain very still. When he gets past my breasts, the fabric is close to my ribs. The scalpel nicks my skin and I jump a bit. My movement causes the scalpel to catch my skin again.

I bite my lip to keep from screaming out. When he cuts to my belly button, he places the scalpel back on the tray. He takes the fabric from each side in his hands and rips it. It rips to my crotch. I can see my underwear.

My strapless bra is the only thing keeping my chest covered now. He's staring at the small drops of blood leaking from the cuts he inflicted. He seems hypnotized by the red liquid of my life dripping in a slow flow.

"Mmm, you are so beautiful, my pet. I like your pale skin. It is the perfect backdrop to your bright blood. I need to see more."

Without warning, he grasps the scalpel again and draws it lightly across my ribs. The sting from the injury follows a moment later. Before I can stop myself, I suck a deep breath through my teeth. His eyes close for a moment as he savors my pain. I'm beginning to figure him out. He gets off on inflicting pain, he's a violent sadist. I let the pain sharpen my senses.

"Yes! Perfection. You are stunning, my pet. I wish you could see how glorious this looks." He rubs the blood and looks at his red finger. Then I almost vomit when he licks my blood from his hand.

"My pet, I think I would like to have you strapped down. Lie back."

I do as he asks. Watching him carefully, I see he has a long plastic strap. It looks the same as the one holding my hands together. He pulls my hands to the side and uses the strap to tie down my right wrist to the table. The strap still holds both of my hands together. He uses the scalpel to cut the restraint from around my wrists. My right hand is now connected to the table. My left hand is...free.

"Mr. Lev? I'd like some water now, please," I say and clear my throat for emphasis. He meets my eyes and that hideous grin forms on his lips again.

"Yes, okay." He collects the bottle and twists the cap, breaking the seal. He hands it to me, since I have a free hand. After just a sip, he takes it away. I open my mouth to ask for more and he gives me a look. A look that says, *don't ask*. I close my mouth. I lean my head back onto the table. Looking at the ceiling, I recall what Original Nova said. I need to pay attention and take the chance when it's presented.

I place my left hand on the table as if it is strapped down. He's watching the blood again. I think I can distract him.

"Ooooh, it hurts. Please, can you put something on it to stop the pain? It hurts so much. Oooow!" His face breaks into a huge smile. His cheeks are pink. Oh God, when I look him over, I can see his pants are tented. Disgusting!

"Ahhh, my pet. I can't do that right now. But I will give you some of my vodka if you like," he lifts his jacket from the counter and removes a flask from his jacket pocket. The last thing I want to do is drink alcohol out of

Satan's chalice. But I have an idea, if it works it'll be worth touching his disgusting property. I nod.

"Good girl." He unscrews the cap and leans over me to bring it to my lips. I barely lift my head, when I get a mouthful of vodka, I sputter and choke. I quickly sat up, coughing and spit vodka in his face with a big cough.

"Arrrrgh!" He swipes at his face with his hands. He stumbles over to the sink and splashes some water on his face, especially his eyes. Then he pats at his face with a paper towel.

While he's busy, I stretch my free hand to the tray. I have to lean almost off the table. I strain against the straps on my feet and my other hand. The plastic strap around my arm cuts into the delicate skin on the inside of my wrist. I quickly wrap my fingers around a sharp medical implement. I don't have time to look at exactly what I was able to grab, I hide it under my left palm flat against the table. I try to look casual when he turns back around. I remember that I was just choking, and I forced a cough.

"I'm so sorry, Mr. Lev. I don't usually drink very much."

"I see. Even so, I cannot let this go unpunished. I will make some small marks; you will not move. Do you understand?"

"No. I don't understand. Why? What marks?"

"My pet, I want to paint you with your life's blood. I will only do a little at a time so our play can go on for a very long time. You are nearly perfect. With my help to enhance your beauty, you will be complete perfection. I must punish you for spitting the vodka in my face. You do not ever do that, not even by accident, and you never waste good vodka, you must be punished. Now, lie back and concentrate. If you make a sound, I will continue longer. Do you understand now?"

NO! Asshole!

"Yes, Mr. Lev."

I lean back and take a few deep breaths. I focus on his movements and location. I think about the sharp weapon under my hand, and everything Paige showed me. I think about the practices with Rhett and Micah. With my loved ones firmly in my mind I prepare for a fight.

"This is just beautiful. I think I will mark this side now. I will make them match." His sadistic grin is back. His pants remain tented, and as he leans on me, I can feel his erection on my arm. I cringe but hold my ground.

He leans over me with the scalpel in his fingers. He looks carefully at his earlier handiwork. It's finally stopped burning, but I think it's still seeping blood. While he's comparing my ribs, I look at the points I want to hit from what I've been taught. His throat, his nose, and his groin are within reach. I debate poking his groin with my weapon. The thought of it turns my stomach, though it seems like the best way to incapacitate him. I feel like a man with a puncture wound to the groin will focus on that, not me.

When he slices into my skin, it takes a moment for the pain to hit me. Scalpels are so sharp that it's hard to tell you've been cut at first. The copper smell of blood in the room reaches my nostrils as the nerve endings he's cutting begin to flare in agony. When the harm he inflicts reaches the pain receptors in my brain, I lose my focus. The burning sting swells like the crescendo of an orchestra. Without my conscious consent, my hand thrusts my curved scalpel into his neck. The tiny scythe aims true and cuts into his carotid artery, I continue to push it into his flesh with all my strength.

I roar with my assault, "Grrroaaaaaah!"

Hot blood spurts down my arm and falls onto my torso from the deadly injury. His eyes go wide, for a moment he seems ready to speak, then confused. Ultimately, he only makes a gurgling sound. He drops his scalpel onto my belly. I don't feel any further injury, but adrenaline is flooding my system, and I may just be numb. He crumples into a pile on the floor, like a discarded dress, at the end of a long day.

I hear a loud gasping sob, it keeps repeating. Eventually, I realize I'm making the sound. I hope anyone else that can hear me thinks I'm being harmed by him, not the other way around. I concentrate on calming my breathing.

When I get the gasping sobs to stop, I'm vaguely aware that I begin repeating, "Holy, shit! Holy, shit..." Over and over again.

To stop from mumbling, I start talking to myself, "Okay. That wasn't so hard. He's probably not getting up. Focus, Peyton. What now?" More deep breaths ease some of the adrenaline rushing through my veins. I look around and feel my stomach with my bloody hand. When my fingers find the scalpel dropped by Mr. Levin Federov the evil sadist, it pokes into my middle finger. I yank my hand away; this motion causes the scalpel to slip from my belly. It slides down my right side, and lands next to my cuffed hand. I hold my breath waiting for the sting of a new cut. Thankfully, there are none. I take a couple more deep breaths.

"Brilliant Peyton! Come on, focus. Okay. Okay, I got this. I just need to...stretch a little...owwww! Relax. Come on, it's going to hurt for a second, you can do this. Ahhh! Yes! Oh, be quiet. First, cut off your wrist cuff. Hold on. You're shaking too much. Deep breath. That's better, now be careful, you don't need anymore, in-jur-ees. Hey! Good job. Oh, that feels so much better." I rub my wrist; it hurts from when I pulled against it. The cuff was tighter than I thought. I look at my feet, afraid to look over the edge of the table. I stretch forward and my ribs burn. I can feel the red liquid dripping across my skin. I'm able to quickly release my feet.

"Oh my God! I'm free! Celebrate later, you need to bandage your wounds. Some of them seem like they'll need stitches. Be gentle, you're going to be stiff. Remember your first steps to the bathroom. There you go, just breathe for a moment." I sit on the edge of the table. The corpse is behind me and out of view. The medical cabinet is to my right now. I look it over and see he left the door open on one side. I can see a variety of medical ER type supplies. Tape and bandages, antiseptic creams and liquids, and jackpot!

There're some navy-blue doctor clothes. I started talking myself through the plan. "Scrubs! That's what they're called. Move slowly down from the table. Carefully put weight on your feet. Good. Hold on, oh shoot! Pins and needles, ow-ow-ow. Slow and steady wins the race. You're doing great, Peyton. Stay strong. Oh, yeah! Paper towels, yes. I don't think you're Bounty but thank you for soaking up so much blood. Much better. Mr. Rubbing alcohol you can rinse off my arms. Shit! Shit! Cut on my finger, ouch!"

After I clean his blood from my skin the best I can, I let my shredded costume fall to the ground. I quickly selected a top and pants. They're too big and hang loosely from my frame. I can't stand to be undressed another minute. I gathered some bandages, an antiseptic spray with numbing lidocaine, scissors, and tape. I rip open the packages and get everything ready. I spray my cuts, then bite my hand to keep from screaming. Once the pain subsides, I cover the cuts the best I can and tape down the bandages. My breasts are blocking my view and I have to feel my way.

I finally get everything covered and steel myself to face my attacker. I'm determined to get past him as quickly as possible and get out of here. I'm staring at the door and nothing else, eyes on the prize, as I make my way around the table.

"Whoa!" I slip on his blood. I fall back, my feet sliding out from underneath me. I slam onto my butt, hard. A sharp pain shoots right up my spine when my tailbone meets the concrete.

The breath is knocked from my lungs. I gasp until fresh air finally fills my chest. As I recover on the floor, doing my best not to look at the bloody mess in front of me. I notice the tanks of explosive substances. It dawns on me... I need to destroy this place. If they're hurting girls here, it needs to burn.

Once I've reorganized myself, I carefully extract my body from the vicinity of the corpse. I clean off his blood again, avoiding the cut on my finger. I change into clean scrubs and then I read the warning labels on the tanks. I try to lift one. They're up to my waist, and when I try to lift it, my ribs scream in displeasure. I try rolling it by twisting it around on its base. I make slow progress and only track it through the edge of the blood. The pattern created by the tank through the spreading blood, is like a beautiful piece of art. The circles swirl around each other. It reminds me of the pattern left by figure skaters on the ice after some of their intricate tricks. I haven't been to an ice rink in years.

I'm not fooling myself, thinking of random things to avoid my current reality. Once I got the tank to the door, I started digging through every cabinet and drawer. Then I searched through the corpse's jacket. I found a card wallet and a money clip. Both are expensive looking and there's a stack of hundred-dollar bills in his clip. I check the rest of the pockets and find a pack of cigarettes and a handkerchief. Nothing more. Not finding what I want, I take a minute to think. Oh no.

"No. No, no, no, no...Oh God. Look, you can do this. Remember you just stabbed that sadistic asshole. This'll be easy. Be calm. Don't look at his face. Just look at the pockets. Nothing else."

I lay my soiled scrubs, from earlier, over some of his blood. I squat down next to his chest. I keep my eyes below his middle. I don't want to touch him. I pull his right pocket out and try to see if there's anything inside. I can't see anything. Holding my breath, I shove my hand into the unknown. I try to feel only the contents. I close my fingers around the items and remove my hand as though I've just removed Excalibur from its stony prison. I quickly stand and looking away from the corpse, I make my way to the counter that contains his jacket. I drop the items onto the flat surface. They clang when they land. There's a gold key with a white gemstone embedded on each side. I know nothing about geology, but I would guess it's a diamond. Huh, Diamond.

"Ha. I forgot about that evil witch. Yes! Exactly what I need, a gold engraved cigarette lighter sparkles like El Dorado the mythical city of gold. Thank you, God! Think Peyton, what else do you need? You've got the tank, a lighter, a couple weapons. Do you need anything else? Oh, maybe some alcohol, it's flammable. I need a bag to carry some of this stuff. Oh, you dope! You need a drink of water. Maaaybeee...I know, I'll use a shirt."

Drinking a few sips from a water bottle, I finish cutting the arm hole. It looks pretty good. I shove a few bandages, a bottle of water, and a couple bottles of alcohol into my makeshift bag. I pull it up over my shoulder and carry it like a purse. Who knew a few waist ties and a scalpel could make a satchel from a shirt?

I very quietly open the door and peer outside. The hallway is empty. I don't hear any movement. I began rolling the tank towards the apartment where I used the restroom. I carefully and quietly wedge the tank under the doorknob. I'm thankful it's the perfect height, I like the added security of blocking their door.

Hearing nothing, I kneel down and glance down one direction in the hallway then the other. I don't see anyone. I grin when I see the dirty path on the concrete. It'll lead me straight to the exit. I rush back to the room where the corpse remains. I quickly roll another tank down the hall and leave it next to the exit door. One last trip to the corpse room. Without pause I roll another tank near the door but still leave it inside the corpse's room. I pour some alcohol on what remains of the monster, without meeting his dead eyes.

I shove what's left of the bottle into my bag. I open each tank by cranking the handle until I hear it hiss, and I move towards the exit. When I reach the end of the hall, I light one bottle of rubbing alcohol on fire and nearly burn my face off. I toss it away immediately. It doesn't reach the tanks, but it flings more alcohol around, spraying the boxes and crates and I have faith it will eventually ignite. When I open the door to the outside, the wind almost rips it from my hand. It's raining sideways and the wind is blowing fast. Back inside I reach for the last tank and roll it through the door. I wedge it under the handle as I hunch against the beating rain. My hair whips into my face and I'm already getting soaked. I place the second bottle of alcohol on top of the hissing tank, with a strip of fabric in the opening. I don't know how this'll work in the rain.

I light the alcohol-soaked fabric protruding from the bottle, it combusts fiercely and oblivious to the wind. I spend five final seconds before I run, saying my own sort of prayer.

"Rest in pieces you evil assholes! May God have mercy on your souls, because I sure won't."

Then I take off running. Even though I have no clue where I am, this building seems to be at the back of a warehouse area and I'm at the rear of the structure. I want to find an actual road so I can try to figure out which way to go. Once I'm past the other buildings there're fields to my left, and woods to my right. I can see a road up ahead. It's a curved road and meets this one at an angle. Because of the fields I can see a pretty good distance down the road. There're blurry headlights heading this way.

"Come on legs! We need to get to the woods before any cars see us. What if they're more bad guys coming here, or even worse bad guys than the ones inside? Hurry!" I realize talking to myself again while running, and it's wasting energy and oxygen. I immediately close my mouth and aim for a gap in the trees.

I make it far enough into the woods, so they can't possibly see me. Breathing a little easier, I slow my pace enough to keep from passing out and I stay near the edge. When I reach the main road, I look around three-hundred-sixty degrees. Across from me are more trees as far as I can see in either direction. On my left is a very large empty field. When I turn back and look at this side of the road on my right, there's a small building. It's a little shack, like a storage shed. On the side facing me and traffic, is a faded, old, painted sign. It has an arrow pointing up. Next to it reads, *Paxton's Olde Country Store, two miles ahead.*

I know where I am. I dart across the road, even though it's wet, it hurts my feet. I run just inside the line of trees so I can dive for cover if I need to.

BOOM! I flinch in fear, ducking down until what happened registers. The ground trembles beneath my feet. A flash of orange lights up everything for a moment, and a rumble rolls towards my ears. My eyes hurt from the bright burst of light. Once the orange flaming clouds float high enough, they become black billowing smoke. I can't waste time waiting to see what happens. I may have just killed three or more people. Orange mushrooms keep flashing in my eyes as my rods and cones recover.

"Ouch!" I hop to a stop. Resting my shoulder on a tree for balance, I lift my foot and look for an injury. There're three tiny spots of blood. I bring out some bandages. I cover the bottom of my foot and wrap it with tape. Then I do the same to the other foot. The makeshift shoes work well. Only the sharpest rocks register at all.

I'm moving much slower regardless of the improvised shoes. I'm running out of steam and the whipping wind and rain's exhausting. I'm completely soaked to the point I may as well be swimming. Without any clue how far I've gone, I don't know how much farther it is to my house. Though it can't be very far, I'm cutting through the woods. I drive by that Country Store sign at least twice a day.

I stop to rest, leaning against a tree. My ribs are stinging. I must be sweating on the cuts, or it's the rain. The wind howls through the woods. All of the trees bend like they're bowing to a Queen. It's mesmerizing, like a dance of thin green ballerinas. The next big gust pushes them farther than I've seen yet. There's a loud cracking sound as a very tall tree succumbs to the vigorous workout. I watch as it gracefully crashes to the ground. I feel the impact reverberate throughout my body, luckily it went the opposite direction from me.

The weather seems to be getting more chaotic. I make my feet move. I need to get home before it gets any worse. I keep my head down to avoid being pelted in the eyes by piercing raindrops and flying debris. When I get to a crossroad, I slow momentarily and look in all directions. I'm not protected at all from the weather at this intersection. I couldn't care less, I'm two and a half blocks from home. I cover my eyes like I'm shielding them from the sun and I start running again.

Micah

Rhett takes charge as usual and uses hand signals. We enter through a metal door into a wide-open space. There's a wall ahead of us with another door in the middle. Some boxes are stacked in a corner along with the telltale silhouette of a motorcycle under a cover. There's a tall garage door to our right, near the motorcycle. I don't see anything else in the pale-yellow light falling from a couple industrial fixtures.

Rhett signals that we're clear to move forward. He tries the knob on the door, and it opens inwards. Rhett peers inside. He turns and looks in both directions, as smoke floats out from the doorway.

He startles, then yells, "Run!"

We don't hesitate, all four of us bolt for the door we just entered. Ace makes it first and then Thomas rushes through. When I step over the threshold, a force propels me out. I slam on the ground and then something heavy lands on top of me. Simultaneously a bright flash of light momentarily blinds me, and a loud boom steals my hearing briefly. I lose my breath from the heavy thing crushing me. I try to inhale and clear my vision. I can't move or draw a breath.

The weight is lifted from my body and I'm once again able to circulate oxygen into my lungs. I cough a few times as my respiratory system tries to remember how to function. Someone blocks my view.

"An oo ear ee? Rrr oo kay?" Ace isn't making any sense, and he sounds like he's down a very long tunnel, whispering. His face is pinched in concern. I shake my head, like a dog. Somehow it seems like the right thing to do, and sound floods my ears. My back and my knee ache from the impact of my body slamming into the ground. The storm rages on, drops of rain pelt my exposed face. As my vision clears, I survey my surroundings. Rhett is on his back next to me. He looks similarly confused. I lift up onto my hands and knees then fall back onto my ass. Thomas is speaking to Rhett.

"Are you hurt?" Ace asks.

"No. What happened?"

"Explosion."

I shoot up to my feet and turn back towards the building. There's a very large cloud of smoke billowing from what used to be the roof. I run towards the door ignoring the pain in my knee. I don't give a fuck, nothing can stop me, I need to find Peyton. A hand reaches out and grasps my arm, stopping me in my tracks. "Hold on, son. You can't go inside yet. The fire department needs to make sure it's safe first," Samson warns.

"Fuck that!" Rhett yells and fights against Ace and Thomas as they try to keep him from running into a burning building.

I look into Samson's eyes, "Respectfully sir, there's nothing you can say to stop me. I understand the risks. I'm going to find Peyton. I don't care if the building falls on my head. I have to get her out now."

"I know, son. I just wanted to give the fire department a minute to extinguish some flames." He releases my arm and nods towards the building. I take off and Rhett joins me as I reach the door. Some smoke is floating out from the top of the door.

A firefighter tries to tell us to get back, but we ignore him and bend low, entering the burning warehouse. There are emergency lights glowing in the darkness of the main open section of the building. We beeline to the door that's hanging open and blackened. I enter first, and everything looks dark and smoky. There're more emergency lights giving a pale glow to the scorched hall. I follow the path to another hall. The outside is visible from where I stand. Most of the back of the building is missing.

It looks like a hurricane has already been here and left devastation in its wake. There's twisted metal, burning debris, and smoke everywhere I look. I gaze into what appears to be a blackened shell of a former room. The frame of the door hangs twisted from a piece of metal. I don't see how it can be hanging there, it defies physics and gravity. I carefully pass it and enter the room.

There's a soot covered metal table with some burning debris on top of it. On the floor is a black, twisted, burning pile that looks and smells like a body. I can tell right away it's too big to be Peyton. I search the rest of the room and burn my elbow on a hot piece of metal. While I'm checking the damage, a piece of green fabric on the floor catches my eye. I move closer and pinch it between my fingertips, black burnt pieces of the building or its contents, fall away as I lift the stained garment. It's definitely her costume, destroyed in my hand. I carefully scan the room again, there's no sign of her.

I hear some yelling in the hallway, and I turn to investigate. I'm holding my breath in case they found another body. I can't even think of the possibility that Peyton might be dead. I exit the foul-smelling room and observe Rhett carrying some type of tank, like an oxygen tank towards the open outdoors. A firefighter is yelling at him to stop. Rhett takes the tank outside. When he returns, we approach a door that's still intact though, worse for wear.

Now Rhett yells at the firefighters to get out. They wave their arms in exasperation. He and I each stand on opposite sides of the door. He knocks, nothing happens, he tries the knob, and it opens. A huge cloud of black smoke wafts out into our faces and we cough, as we cautiously enter what appears to be an apartment. We have our night vision pulled on so we can see in the dark. We survey the first room and don't find anyone. We check every possible hiding space as we work our way systematically through all the rooms. When we reach the final door in the hallway, Rhett signals me to go in low. He opens the door and I enter crouched low. Another huge cloud of black smoke billows out of the bedroom.

We spot two bodies on the bed. They appear to be intact and not blackened. I approach and look at them closely. They seem to be asleep, except that their faces have a slightly grayish-blue hue. It's fucking Buzzard and tangled in his arms is none other than, Diamond, the twins' purple-haired friend. What the fuck?

Rhett voices my confusion, "What the fuck? He's been staying right here all this time?" I reach out and take off my glove. I grasp her wrist, there's a faint pulse but I'm not seeing her chest rise and fall. I check him, and his pulse is faint and erratic.

"Medic! Medic!" Rhett yells back towards the hallway. I continue to search the room and find no one else. Where the fuck is she? I turn from them and return to the hallway. I point the firefighters towards the patients. If I didn't want Buzzard to tell me where Peyton was, I might think about not helping him.

I retrace my steps, following the hall in another direction, and begin searching for any sign of my girl. I don't know where Rhett or anyone else went. I'm compelled to search the whole building. As I'm looking into what appears to be another much smaller residence, only in almost unrecognizable condition, I see movement. I quickly rush in to assist and see if it's my Eagle.

The body is badly burnt but moving around. It looks like a male based on the size and the masculine frame. I can't identify who it might be. He's trapped under a beam that seems to have fallen from the roof. The part of him exposed towards me is blackened and bloody. He wails in agony and I have pity. I set down my firearm, out of his reach and evaluate if I can pull him free or lift the beam.

The beam doesn't budge at all when I try to lever it upwards. Next, I try to remove him without hurting him. He screams and I stop. His eyes open and he pleads with me incoherently.

I speak in a soft tone, "I'm going to get help, stay calm. Is there a young woman here? Please, tell me where she is," I pleaded right back.

"In the exam room," his voice barely whispered. "Please help me."

"Does the exam room have a table? A metal table?" I beg for an answer.

"Yes," is the last word I hear from him. I pick up his hand to check for a pulse. His knuckles are tattooed with the word *EVIL*. Oh shit! I drop his hand. This is one of the twins. If he makes it, nobody will ever get them confused again. I shake my head from side to side as I exit this last room. Why is a twin here? Did he take Peyton? I make my way to the first firefighter I can find, and explain where there's another survivor in need of urgent help and medical care. I wander back outside, this time through another opening. When I realize I'm not out in front of the warehouse, I begin to search in a circle around the outside.

When I get to the front, I walk right past everyone out there and back to the warehouse where my computer is waiting. It dawns on me that I should check in and tell someone where I am, so they don't waste resources looking for me. I try my comms, and nothing happens. Either the explosion, or my subsequent fall, must have damaged the unit. I shoot a text to Darren and let him know. He can relay it to the others. The cat remains flashing on the map. The tracking app still shows Peyton inside the blown-up building. I personally searched every inch and didn't find her.

"Where are you babe?" I voice my thoughts out loud.

"I'm right here handsome," Orlando is in the doorway with a smirk on his face. Seeing I'm not in a joking mood, his face turns serious.

"Any luck?"

"No. She's not here. I'm glad she wasn't in the building, since it blew-up, but the tracker still says she's there. I'm trying to refresh the data and see if I can pinpoint her better now that I'm closer. Where's Ax?"

"He's outside. He knows a couple of the firefighters. He's pumping them for information."

"Good. What the hell? Come on!" I rush out with my laptop in my hand. The map is flashing Peyton's exact location, and it's definitely inside the warehouse. When I approach, Rhett and the guys join me.

"Follow us, the tracker says she's definitely still here."

We're all focused, searching with our eyes as we make our way back to the apartment where we found Buzzard. When we enter, Buzzard is on a stretcher in the living room area. He has an oxygen mask over his face, an IV in his arm, and cuffs on his wrists. Three of Samson's guys are surrounding the stretcher and EMTs, with firearms in their hands.

I led us past them and into the bathroom. It's a small room, and there's no place for her to hide in here. I step into the shower, physically verifying that she's not here. I want to throw my laptop into a wall. Or walk out there and punch Buzzard in the face. I close the laptop and stop to think over everything and the possibilities. I notice something shiny on the floor when one of the guys waves his flashlight around.

I bend down and look closer. There it is, Felony's tracker. I pick it up and look it over. She was here. The tracker must have been in her pocket. She probably used the restroom and it fell out of her pocket. I hold up the small silver circle. That means she could be anywhere. We have no idea when she was here, but she's been missing at least eight hours now.

"I need to check out the parking lot," I announce as I pocket the AirTag.

"We'll go with you, tell us what you need." Rhett says. The other guy's nod and they all follow me out.

I began searching each license plate on my FBI portal. When I get to a glossy black Maserati Sedan, I ask the guys to get it open. A name I recognize is on some paperwork in the center console. *Levin Federov,* a Mafia lynchpin. I've seen his handiwork, and he's a twisted bastard. My stomach does a flip and falls out on the ground while my heart clenches painfully in my chest. Why is he here? Where is he? Where the fuck is my girl?

The rain had slowed, now it picks back up with a vengeance and a strong gust of wind. I've collected information from all of the cars in this lot. I need to get my laptop out of this weather. The plastic I have wrapped around me is barely hanging on in the wind. When we make our way back to the building we're using as a base, we pass two occupied body bags. One must be the dead blob in the exam room. The other...I guess the twin didn't make it. It's a shame he won't face justice for whatever he did to Peyton.

"Spill it, what did you find?" Rhett orders.

I look at Orlando and Ax. Deciding I don't care if they know, and knowing they won't repeat it, I explain whose car I found and some of his past. Unfortunately, the bikers are familiar with him too.

"We had to hire extra security at the MCs strip club because of that guy. He likes to leave marks, permanent marks."

"What the fuck? He has Peyton?" Rhett yells. Ace puts his hand on Rhett's arm and tries to calm him.

"We're going to find her. She needs you to be calm and focused, okay?" Ace asks.

Thomas is texting. He's able to listen to the room around him while he works on his phone or computer. It used to startle me when he would speak suddenly after seeming uninterested in the conversation and offer a brilliant thought right on point.

"The building next door to the explosion has a CCTV security camera on all sides of the building. I just got through to the company. They're going to send you the videos for the last 12 hours. They should have footage of the front and back sides of the building," Thomas says without looking up from his screen. Rhett hugs him. It surprises him and he almost drops his phone. I want to hug him too as my phone vibrates with an email notification.

I quickly unwrap my damp laptop and wait for it to connect to Wi-Fi. A moment later I'm forwarding the email to Darren and Paige. Then I unzip the file it takes a few seconds to upload. I fast forward to the time of the explosion. It's easy to spot the big flash, the entire screen goes white momentarily, then black. I rewind from there and we see the flash again. Then I go two times the speed to rewind, everyone is circled around me, watching.

I start with the front camera. It's pointed at the front of the destroyed warehouse. We watch the twin exit, go to a car, collect something small and re-enter the building. A long time goes by and then Buzzard enters with a man, I keep rewinding until we can see where they came from. The black Maserati pulls up, Buzzard exits the building, he greets Levin Federov and they enter the warehouse. He never leaves or returns to his car.

"I think Federov is the crispy dead guy from the exam room," I say flatly.

"If he's dead, that's a win for everyone," Ax speaks up.

I begin rewinding the video from the back of the warehouse. Not long before the explosion, Peyton comes out the door with a big tank like the one Rhett got rid of earlier. She wedges it under the door handle. She lights a bottle on fire and then runs into the woods. She's wearing a shirt and pants. I rewind it and play it again.

Ace gets on his phone and begins barking orders. Thomas is typing at lightning speed on his. Rhett and I look at each other, we both give the barest nod and take off out the door. Orlando and Ax follow. When we get to the firefighters still hosing things off, Ax runs to the guy who appears to be in charge. He's waving his arms around pointing towards the woods. The man he's talking to begins yelling into a radio, while I run towards Samson.

"I'll tell him, just go!" Orlando yells at me and heads for my boss. Rhett and I run around to the back of the building. We're oblivious to the cold rain that feels like a thousand nails pelting us. From the back door we run straight into the woods. He follows a path to my right, just a few feet away.

He begins yelling, "Peyton! Peyton! It's Rhett! Peyton, it's safe! Come out!"

I have my eyes glued to the ground. She may be hurt and unable to respond. I look for any dark spots that could be the clothes she had on when we saw her on video, or any hiding spots that she could fit inside. I look for footprints or any sign of her that'll guide us. We keep searching and yelling without any sign of her.

We circle back when we reach the road, spreading out further. We both yell and search without finding anything at all. With the weather whistling through the trees, the constant rain, we have no chance of her hearing us. When we yell, the wind blows it right back at us. The trees are bending so far, the tops almost touch the ground, and we passed a few that looked newly fallen. We looked them over carefully. They'd make great hiding spots and shelter from the weather.

When we leave the woods, the rain is heavier. The trees were blocking a lot of the wind too. It hits us hard as soon as we make it out of the tree line. Samson is directing some officers with dogs. Everyone else is out searching. The dogs are sniffing around the door at the back of the decimated warehouse.

I run inside the warehouse where my computer is set up. Rhett stayed with Samson. He should be able to get an update on who's where, so he doesn't try an area that's already covered. I check my computer and the weather looks bad. Isaac didn't make his predicted turn in time. He's headed right for us. We need to find her, *fuck.*

I'm having the strongest urge to go to Peyton's house. It's a feeling like I forgot something, like if you left the oven on. I can't think of a single reason why I'd have that feeling. I ran out and left Jake and Connor in charge. Paige let me know they made it to her safely with all the cats. Peyton has some things at the house that have sentimental value. Some pictures with her deceased family, some college stuff, like her Bachelor's diploma. Maybe I should go grab some stuff and I can just check that she's not there or somewhere close by along the way. I can't shake this feeling and I need to go. As I'm exiting with my wrapped computer, I almost slam into Rhett.

"Hey, Samson says the dogs have a scent and they're heading into the woods. The handlers said it may take a lot longer with the weather. They've never worked in a hurricane before, and it didn't turn in time to miss us. He's got three FBI teams and local P.D. sent two guys, but with the storm they couldn't really spare them. Ace called in everyone. Thomas made some calls too. We're going to comb this area until we find her. I'm heading back out. What're you doing?"

"I'm going to Peyton's. I need to make sure she's not there. It's not completely out of the realm of possibility. Plus, with the storm, I should grab a few of her important things. I'll call you if I see anything. We'll find her."

"We will." We sort of awkwardly pat each other on the arm and go our separate ways.

When I start the car, a strong gust takes a big piece from the top of the blown-up building. It lifts straight up and then begins flipping around and it speeds off out of my sight. My car shakes a little from the force of the wind as it howls along the roof rack

Peyton

The closer I get to the house the more water is on the road. It's almost knee deep when I finally reach the stairs, I can barely see a foot in front of me between the rain and the wind blurring my vision. My teeth chatter in the cold rain pelting against me like a dart board.

Tree branches snap with a crack and fall with each gust of wind. Random debris flies past me, leaving me puzzled about its former purpose. I'm soaked to the bone, my fingers are pruned, I'm hunched down low trying to keep my head and face out of the worst of it. I'm lucky two neighbors' houses have a fence. I used them to keep me steady and on track to make it home. I knew I made it when I spotted the ridiculous manatee mailbox sticking up like a siren calling to me from the waves of windblown rain and storm surge.

My feet ache and the rest of me is numb. My hands are shoved under my crossed arms to shield my body and my injured ribs. I let go to grasp the railing for my steps. I end up using both hands on one side. The higher I get from the ground, the worse the weather. The wind is howling on the porch, it's a baleful sound. Our porch furniture isn't here. It either blew away or someone put it inside. I suppose the answer will find me the minute I open the door.

What I wouldn't give to find Micah inside. My hands are shaking so hard I can't get the code entered. I stick my hands in my armpits trying to warm them and convince them to stop shaking. I bounce from foot to foot desperately trying to warm up enough to open the door. Thankfully the door lock beeps and lights up green, then the door opens when I depress the handle.

"Peyton? Oh my God! Do you know everyone's looking for you? How did you get here? What happened? They said, *'Possibly kidnapped'* on the news. WTF? Are you okay?" Anisa grills me as fast as an auctioneer. She looks me over and makes a face.

As always, and despite the hurricane, she looks beautiful. Her gorgeous auburn hair is up. Her face appears devoid of make-up and her pale skin, smooth and creamy. She's wearing a raincoat with the hood up. She has galoshes on her feet, with little ducks on them. The most interesting thing is the backpack clinging to her like a chimp with its mother. It's a fairly large pack, not *'I live in the woods,'* big, but probably the biggest school backpack size. Her pack is black and wrapped in plastic film.

Spinning to hug her, I choke out, "Thank God you're here! Come inside, I'm freezing!" I push us both inside. The power is out and it's dark and still. The wind howls again and I feel the house wobble in the gust. I inventory my surroundings and decide someone was here to pack up the cats. I don't know if it was Micah or someone else, but the porch furniture looks to be stacked in the corner. The rain is loud, pounding on the exterior walls and the roof, it feels like we're in for forty days of rain. Something hits the roof with a thud. Then it scrapes across the shingles as it gets blown off.

Another unknown object slams against the wall outside, just past the porch. The windows rattle with each new blast of wind. The many small taps and knocks make me imagine a bunch of little creatures tapping on the wall looking for a way inside. Like giant chickens or maybe dinosaurs pecking at the walls. I can picture those creepy little dinosaurs from Jurassic Park scurrying around the roof.

"We need to get you into a hot shower, you're almost blue and your teeth are about to snap off from chattering so hard. Come on, you can tell me while we get you in there." She leads me to the bathroom where she turns on the hot water and waits with her hand beneath the stream. I've never been so grateful for gas appliances. When she's happy with the temperature, she focuses on me.

"Come here, let's get those wet clothes off. What on earth are you wearing? Lift your arms." Not feeling free to ignore her demands, I lift my arms. She peels off my soaking shirt and then unhooks my soaking wet strapless bra. She drops my top into the tub and does the same with my bra. I instinctively cover my breasts. She yanks my wet pants and panties down my legs. The air on my wet skin causes a full body shiver. They land in the tub with a wet splat!

"Get in there! Don't just stand here! Go on!" she orders.

I step into the shower and turn my back on her. I lift my face and close my eyes enjoying the warmth. The water hits my cuts with a sting, my makeshift bandages long since washed away. I eventually fill my hand with shampoo and scrub it through my hair. Then I apply conditioner and begin soaping my body. Anisa is seated on the countertop watching me.

"Why are you staring at me?"

"Just trying to figure out where you've been and make sure you don't collapse in there. Are you going to tell me what happened?"

"I'm not completely sure what happened. I was kidnapped. I woke up in a warehouse. This weird guy wanted to play with my blood. He cut me. I probably need some stitches. Oh, God, I have to call Micah! He must be out of his mind." I'm not sure why I didn't tell her about Diamond and Tool. I guess if Tool's involved, the chances of Rev being involved are pretty good. I don't want to upset her. Once Micah is here, I can have him talk to her about everything in an official way. Then the bad news won't come from me.

"He's definitely out of his mind with worry, I already texted him. He's on his way with the entire Justice League. He'll have an ambulance or fire rescue with him, someone'll be able to check your wounds."

"Good. It was so crazy. It was like he thought he owned me or something. He had a very weird kink with blood and causing pain."

Her head tilts and her eyes narrow, "A sadist? Those aren't very common. What do you want to wear? I'll go get some clothes for you."

"No bra, just a pair of thick yoga pants and any t-shirt should be fine, and maybe a sweater. Thanks!"

I finish washing and feel refreshed enough to get dressed and face the questions that'll be coming at me. I dry off carefully patting my cut ribs. I take a look in the mirror, and it looks rough. They're angry red cuts in my skin. Some are barely a scratch, but some continue to ooze blood. The deep ones are especially difficult to look at. You never know how seeing your own body injured will feel. It feels bad, and a wave of nausea spreads from my stomach to my throat. I cough and clear my throat, swallowing hard.

Anisa returns with the items I requested and the first aid kit, "I'm sorry, I can't look at that, I'll pass out. You're going to have to take care of it yourself. I'll wait outside the door."

I begin to clean the wounds with an antiseptic liquid. It burns and I make a strange, garbled sound of agony. Blowing out a few breaths, I wait for the sting to subside. Then I spray it with an antiseptic numbing spray which brings an abrupt end to the sting. Next, I examine the wounds and decide the couple that are oozing need something to close them up, so they stop bleeding. I carefully apply a few steri-strips to close them until a professional can do it right. I get dressed and sigh in relief.

"Okay. I'm all done. I'm so glad you're here. I was terrified when I got out of the warehouse. This was the only place I could think to come. It would've sucked to be here alone in the dark."

"I can't believe I found you here. I hope Micah hurries, the storm is getting really bad. Do you hear that?"

I listen, the wind is roaring against the house. It's like a horror movie sound effect. I've been through it before, but there's nothing else like that sound, it sends a chill through me, and I shudder.

"Wow, it's really raging out there. How did you get here in this weather? The water was really coming up when I was slogging through it."

"I know, I didn't think I would make it here. I just had to check. My SUV is all wheel drive and it's fairly high up. But we need to get out of here pretty soon or I won't be able to drive it through the streets. Tell me how you got here."

I shuffle to the kitchen, and she follows. I open the fridge and no light greets me. I take out a bottle of water, I'm really thirsty. I think whatever drugs they gave me cause dry mouth. I take several gulps before I offer some to Anisa.

"No, thanks. Come on, tell me how you got away and ended up here."

I give her a few more details as the wind whips the little house and objects continue to smack into the walls. The house trembles with the shifting winds. The windows rattle but hold strong. Even though we don't have shutters over them I can't see a thing outside. It's very dark and the rain is blowing sideways, blurring the view. Occasionally a tree branch flies by, and I can see that with perfect clarity for only a split second before it disappears back into the chaos of Isaac. She puts on a kettle to make us hot tea. I can't seem to get warm enough, and tea sounds perfect. I have my ear out for sirens, but I don't hear anything. Why isn't Micah here yet?

"Did Micah respond to your text?"

"Yeah, he said he's on his way. Do you want me to text him again?"

"Actually, can I just borrow your phone to call him?"

"It won't go through; I tried that first. I don't know why the text worked."

The kettle whistles and she hops up to fix our cups. I'm confused why a text would work but not a call. I guess it's something to do with how a call is sent versus a text. But I remember my last hurricane in Louisiana. Everything worked or nothing worked. I watch her as she pours hot water into two mugs and floats two tea bags in each. She's mostly dry. She left her raincoat and rain boots at my door with her backpack. I turn to look at her stuff, and there's a puddle around it on the wood floor of the entry.

I get some towels from the linen closet and start wiping up the puddle. I hear a buzzing in her backpack. I place my hand over the pocket the noise is coming from, and it vibrates and feels like a cell phone. I thought her phone was on her. I remove the plastic wrap, unzip the pocket, and pull out a black iPhone. On the screen is a missed call from someone named *Big Man*. Gross. I try to open the phone but it's locked. I don't know what compels me, I have the urge to look in the pack. I unzip the main compartment and look inside. There's a black case, some rope, duct tape and what looks like the butt of a gun. I freeze.

A gasp sounds behind me, "What are you doing?"

"Why do you have this stuff?"

"It's my emergency pack, it has all kinds of things to help in any emergency situation."

"You have a missed call. Maybe I can try calling Micah on this phone?"

"Yeah, I totally forgot about my emergency phone. Here, let me open it," she places both cups on the coffee table and reaches her hand out. I hand it over and she starts typing. She hands it back with the dial screen ready. When I hit the green button, a loud screeching noise blares from the speaker. The call doesn't go through.

"Dammit. I'm getting worried, what if he can't get through? How will we get out of here?" As if to emphasize my point something big slams into the roof. It startles both of us.

"Shit! Now I'm freaked out. Let's sit and have our tea. We can try both of my phones and see if we get through."

Without any better ideas I join her on the sofa. The warm cup feels good in my hands and helps with the chill in my bones. I sip my tea, savoring the warmth and slight twang of it. While I sip, she dials her phone and gets that same terrible sound. She sends a few text messages, and nothing goes through.

"I think we need to see how high the water is now. Can I borrow your raincoat?"

"I'll go. You've been out in it enough."

She gulps her tea and suits up in her galoshes and raincoat. She pulls the hood up over her auburn locks. When she opens the door, it rips from her hand and slams against the wall. Wind and rain swirl in through the open door. The floor collects a new puddle as she slams the door shut. I wipe it up with one of the towels. A minute later the door opens and the sounds of the storm whip through the house in a blast of air and rain. She throws herself into the house and slams the door on the storm. She drips all over the floor.

Micah

I have the wipers cranked, my bright lights and fog lights on, everything is set to optimize my difficult trip. It's so dark and with the wind whipping the rain sideways it's hard to see more than a foot in front of me. It's loud even though the windows are up, the rain roars as it pelts the car. I make it to the main road but it's slow going. Visibility is about zero and there's debris all over the road, random objects occasionally fly past me. The truck shakes in the force of the wind. I'm going four miles an hour.

When I make it around the curve, there's a tree across the road. Luckily the wind slowed long enough for me to see it before I crashed. Looking it over I decide to go off the road around the top of the tree. It's pretty bumpy but I make it without issue. Back on the road, there are more and more puddles. The water is lapping at the edges of the road the closer I get to Peyton's the higher the water.

When I reach the little bridge over the stream just about halfway to Peyton's. The water is rushing over the bridge. On the far side of the bridge, I can see white caps on the waves over the pavement, reflecting in my headlights. I'm fucked. My gut clenches, my heart pounds, my head swims a bit. How are we going to find her in this? I'm going to need a fucking boat.

I dial Samson, he answers with, "What do you need?"

Peyton

"Sorry! Holy fuck! It's blowing so hard. I think I'm soaked despite the rain gear. The water is about halfway up the steps. I don't think we can get out," she says, swiping her wet hair from her face. Her makeup runs beneath her eyes. I guess she was wearing mascara after all.

My stomach falls at her words. All I want right now is to be safe in Micah's arms. He's my home harbor where nothing can hurt me. My ribs ache and there's still a dull throbbing in my head.

"What are we going to do? Maybe I can get a message out through my laptop. Why don't you go dry off. You can borrow some of my clothes if you want. Help yourself," I offer as I leave the room. My fingers twist together, my nerves needing an escape.

Of course, my laptop isn't here, someone must've packed it with the cats. My old tablet comes to life when I dig it out of the drawer and open it. The battery is fully charged, I've kept it plugged in just in case I needed it for something. I began an email to Micah, Paige, Rhett, and Jake. I explain that I'm okay and at my house, but we're trapped. As I read it over, Anisa joins me, she reads over my shoulder.

"What do you think? Is there anything else I should tell them?"

"No. I don't think you should send it at all."

"What? Why?" When I turn to look at her, she's pointing her gun at me. I reach out to push the barrel away, thinking she's playing a really stupid joke. She takes a step back and continues to aim her deadly weapon at me.

I laugh, "Come on Anisa, what are you doing? We need to send this and get some help."

"I don't think so. I was hoping to avoid this, but if that goes through you could wreck my plans. Step away from the desk." She gestures with the gun. My mouth falls open, she's not joking. Her face is serious.

"I don't understand. Why don't you want to be rescued? Water may end up coming into the house. Do you understand that we're trapped? We could drown."

"Look, I kinda like you, but you're my ticket to revenge and escape. I'm not going to give that up, so move it. Now."

Raising my hands, I move away from the desk and leave the office. She follows me with the gun pointed at my back. I'm so confused. What the hell is happening? Am I still drugged and dreaming? Did I never really get away from the man who cut me? I feel sick at the thought. When I get to the living room, I stop and wait for her to tell me where she wants me to go. When I turn towards her to inquire, she has the gun raised up above her and I see it coming down at my head. I try to move out of the way but she catches me in the temple. With a loud crack, I see stars, and everything goes black before I feel the pain of the blow. My knees buckle and...

"Wake up, sweetie. Come on, you've got to wake up right now. Peyton! Peeeyton! Please wake up! She's going to come back any minute. You need to be ready. Pleeease wake up. Come on pretty girl."

"What? Ow! Oh, my head hurts. What happened?"

"We don't have time for explanations, you need to wake up. Listen to me. You need to be ready when she comes back. She's getting the ropes to tie you up. She has bad plans for you. You need to be alert and ready to fight. You do as I say and fight hard. Remember what Paige and the boys taught you. Don't stop fighting no matter what. Your life depends on it. Shit, here she comes."

"Nova?" I crack my eyes open and see the ceiling. No sign of my dead friend whose voice woke me, and still echoes in my head. I must be hallucinating. *Ow,* my head hurts, and there's a sharp throbbing pain in my temple. When I touch it, bright lights shoot into my eyes like sharp blades.

I can hear footsteps coming my way. I lie still and pretend I'm still knocked out. I breathe slowly and try to look relaxed and unconscious.

Some things land on the table next to me with a thud. Cold hands touch my ankles as Anisa wraps rope around them. I feel both her hands, so she can't be holding the gun. I take a chance and open my eyes while I kick my leg where I imagine her head to be. I kick as hard as I can. My foot connects with her shoulder, it knocks her back. I look at my feet and see a rope loosely wrapped around one leg. She's pissed, her eyes are narrowed, and her mouth is a tight line. Her face is red, she scowls and reaches to the back of her waistband.

I kick at her again and jump on her. She falls back flat onto the floor with me on top of her.

"Get off me bitch!" She shoves at me, but I don't move until she rolls us towards the sofa. Not wanting to end up beneath her, I push myself up and look for a weapon. She punches me in the nose and the stars return to my vision as I feel my nose burst and begin gushing blood. It drips onto my lips. We both struggle to our feet and she's reaching for the back of her pants again. I shake my head and try to brush off the sting in my nose and focus my eyes. Before she can tug her weapon free of her waistband, I use my body to shove her as hard as I can. She falls again and takes me down with her.

Her head smacks hard on the carpet and I can see she looks a bit dazed. I untangle myself from her and stand again. With a quick look around, I don't see anything to use against her. As she pulls herself together and begins to rise, I kick at her again. I aim for her throat and catch her chin. But it's just a graze as she moves out of the way. She growls at me like a bear, lunges upwards at me, tackles me and rips at my hair. My scalp burns with her yanking on my tangled strands. I fall into the sofa at an odd angle and painfully twist my ankle. My elbow hits the table sending sharp nerve pains up through my shoulder and neck.

"No! Stop!" I yell at her, uselessly.

"Fuck you! You're going to die, bitch!" She straddles my waist and holds me down. Her knee is on my arm. She presses a hand onto my throat. Her other hand finally pulls the gun from behind her. She presses the barrel to my forehead. I freeze.

She's panting and spits blood onto my floor. The blood from my nose continues to drip down my lips and chin. I lie back and gasp in gulps of air trying to catch my breath.

"Why are you doing this?" I ask.

"I didn't know you had this much fight in you. I always see you whining to Micah and he comes to the rescue. You're stronger than I thought. Now you're going to do exactly what I say. Got it?"

"You have a gun to my head, what choice do I have?"

"Now you're catching on. When I get up, you're going to sit on the sofa with your hands on your knees. You will not move unless I tell you to. Got it?"

"Yep." She removes herself from my hips and stands with her gun aimed at me. I sit up, then slowly lift myself to the sofa. I sit with my hands on my knees exactly as instructed. My face aches. My elbow throbs. My ankle is numb, that's probably a bad sign. My scalp still tingles in an unpleasant way. I watch her and wait silently for her next instructions. She hands me a plastic zip tie looped already.

"Put your wrists in there. Okay, let me pull the tab. Good. Now, stay there. I'm going to get a drink. I have my gun trained on you so don't move."

She pulls the tab hard, until the circulation in my hands feels cut off. The plastic cuts into my skin. It digs into the raw places on my skin left from the warehouse. She gets up and walks to the kitchen. I don't move, keeping my hands on my lap. She keeps the gun pointed at me while she removes a bottle of water from the dark fridge. She drinks and then uses a paper towel to wipe her face, especially around her eyes and mouth. She rips a few more towels from the roll and gives them to me.

"Wipe up your face. You have to look pretty on the video."

I cock my head in confusion, but I take the towels and dab at my mouth and nose. My nose hurts when I touch it, and sharp pains shoot into my skull. I close my eyes for a moment and recenter myself. I take a deep breath and let it out in a sigh. Nova's words come back to me. *Fight as hard as you can, and don't stop.* With her armed, I can't exactly fight with my fists. I'm going to have to be smart and talk my way out of this.

She sits on Felony's favorite chair and faces it towards me. I watch her every move cataloging everything and searching for weakness. I wish I knew what's happening and why.

"I don't understand why you're tying me up and pointing a gun at me. Will you tell me why?"

"I guess I can tell you. It's not like you're going to have a chance to tell anyone. Do you remember the guy that your sister used to go out with, Saint?"

"Yeah. What does that have to do with anything?"

"That guy was my brother."

"How? Isn't his name Mark Ramsey? You're Anisa Griffin. Was he your half-brother or something?" I'm so confused. What does any of that have to do with me, even if he was her brother?

"You're looking at Denise Ramsey, full sister to Mark Ramsey. He's dead because of your brother. I promised him that I'd get revenge. I'm going to hurt your brother as much as he hurt me."

"Now I'm really confused. What on earth could my brother have done to cause anything to happen to your brother?"

"He stuck his big nose where it didn't belong. He got my brother killed with his inquiries about your slutty sister. She was supposed to be brought into the Sun's club; she just didn't realize it was as a commodity. She ended up changing her mind and when she disappeared, they blamed Mark. They killed him like a dog, because your brother asked the wrong people about your sister and Mark. They blamed him and killed him. I hate your family. I hate your brother and I hate you!" She waves the gun around in anger. For the first time I'm very afraid she's actually going to shoot me.

"So, you just pretended to be my friend? Just to get close enough to kill me?"

"I didn't want to kill you. I wanted to hurt you in the worst ways. I wanted your brother broken, alone, and devastated. I wanted him to know you suffered because of his actions."

"But he won't be alone, he's got a ton of friends and his family," I regret the words as soon as they leave my mouth. Did I just throw Paige and Nova under a bus?

"Don't worry, I've got plans for his girls. You were close in Baton Rouge, so I started with you. Plus, they're better protected, but I have some ideas now that I've been in their home, and they trust me as your friend. I'll be so helpful when you're missing permanently."

"I still don't understand. Hurt me how?"

"I had made arrangements to sell you into a human trafficking ring that the Sun's run. I set it up so you'd be used and abused by the most despicable scum. By the time your brother found you, you'd be dead or so used up you'd wish you were dead. But somehow you escaped. I was shocked to see you here. I came to plant some evidence, and low and behold there you were looking like a drowned rat."

"Why would you plant evidence? Wait. You're the reason I was drugged and kidnapped?"

She chuckles, "Yep. It was all me. All of your little misfortunes have been me. You're such a victim, it was so easy to scare and torment you."

Tears fill my eyes, proving her right, and I hate it. But I can't help it. I just remembered that Roger was killed, and I've held the strong belief it had something to do with my stalker or me or both. Does this mean she killed Roger? No, she couldn't have, she can't possibly be capable of murder. Can she? I sniffle and try to stop my tears from getting any worse. I need to remember to fight. I can't collapse into a sniveling pile of fear. I take a deep breath and fortify myself to deal with whatever she throws at me next.

"I still don't get how my sister and brother were responsible for your brother's death. I'm sure my sister only wanted to survive. Rhett only wanted to find her. How is it his fault that your brother was murdered?"

"Your brother asked around about your sister and the wrong people found out she was dead. Mark sent a replacement, and they didn't realize it wasn't her until your brother went poking his nose where it didn't belong. When they learned she was dead, they were furious because Mark had promised them a specific beautiful girl and when he didn't deliver, they killed him. They came after me too, you know. They grabbed me and threatened to sell me to make up for the loss of your sister. I was seventeen and I was terrified. I had to make a deal with them. I had to make payments until I could replace your sister. If I couldn't pay, I'd have to work it off. You're going to kill two birds with one stone by paying the debt and destroying your brother."

"How so?" I need to keep her talking while I think of a way out of this. If she told the truth and the water is halfway up the stairs, I'm not sure how I can get away from her. The gun in her hand doesn't help either.

"By making you suffer, I'll repay your asshole brother and by handing you over to them, they'll cancel my brother's debt. Which has become mine since he's dead. They were going to send a top man to try you out. Did you see a Russian guy before you escaped? I haven't been able to get a hold of Tool to find out what's going on over there."

"A Russian guy? No. I didn't see any Russian guys. Tool is involved? I didn't see him either. Just a crazy biker." I decide to lie and keep her confused. I don't want her to know what happened to the Russian guy, and maybe to Tool. No reason to upset her.

"Mhmm. You didn't see anyone else?"

"Nope. I was out of it though because they drugged me. Someone else could've been there. I woke up because he was cutting me."

"How did you get away?"

"Pure luck. He didn't realize he left a blade by my leg. When he left the room, I cut off my restraints and escaped. When I recognized where I was, I made my way here through some woods. The storm wasn't too bad when I left the warehouse, but by the time I got here it was in full swing."

"Huh."

"How're we going to get out of here?"

"Rev was supposed to meet me at my place. When I'm not there I'm sure he'll find a way to come and look for me. Until then, we wait."

"What about Micah? Are you going to shoot him when he gets here?" A sob escapes me, and I take a few deep breaths to strengthen my resolve.

"He's not coming. I never messaged him, or anyone. It's just you and me," she says with a wicked grin. I dab at my nose and watch her. She looks lost in thought. Probably planning how she'll act surprised when they find my dead body. When I think about all of the things my stalker did to me, I can't believe it was my friend who tortured me all along. I feel so stupid for not seeing through her act. She could win an academy award for her performance.

An outline of a plan comes to me and I make a face to implement it. I sigh. She doesn't even glance my way. I cross my legs. Then I cross them the opposite way. I uncross them and I tap my foot. My ankle lets me know that's not going to work as I wince and switch feet. I tap away. I sigh again and she turns her eyes towards me.

"What?"

"I have to pee. Is it okay if I use the bathroom?"

"Yeah, come on." She gestures with the gun again. It's not necessary, I won't forget she's armed. I hobble to the bathroom on my swollen ankle. It's not numb anymore. The pain in my ankle throbs up my leg. I refuse to complain. She follows me to the door where she leans on the frame. I sit and watch her. She's not really looking at me, though she still seems preoccupied with her thoughts. When I stand to flush, I take the scissors from the first aid kit that's still open on the countertop and shove them into my pocket. I wash my hands and we head back down the hall. I veer towards the kitchen hoping for some water.

"Nope, I don't want you near anything in the kitchen. Stop there."

"I'm thirsty, I just want a drink of water. Please," I implore.

"You stay there, I'll get it. Don't move."

"I won't." She opens a bottle of water and hands it to me. Using my two hands I gulp a few swallows. She gestures towards the sofa.

"Back you go."

"Okay." I limp carefully to the sofa and have a seat.

"What now?" she asks.

"How did you know I was going to say something?"

"The look on your face gives you away. You must suck at poker."

"I haven't played it much. You're right. I didn't do well. My face hurts. Could I please have an aspirin?" I beg.

"Where do you keep them?"

"The medicine cabinet in the bathroom."

"Why didn't you ask while we were in there?"

"I'm sorry. I was thirsty and that's what I was thinking about. I can get it," I begin to stand.

"No. You sit. Don't move from that spot. I'll get it. You keep talking, so I can hear what you're doing while I'm gone."

"What am I supposed to say?"

"Uh, recite the Bill of Rights, that'll work."

"Okay. Congress shall make no law respecting an establishment of religion, or prohibiting the free exercise thereof, or abridging the freedom of speech, or of the press, or the right of the people to peaceably assemble, and to petition the Government for a redress of grievances. Should I keep going?"

"Nope, here you go," she hands me two Advil tablets. I swallow them with a gulp of water. I need to wait for the meds to kick in before I take the next step in my plan. I admire my handiwork. The cut I was able to make in the plastic cuff should let me snap the cuffs off when the time is right.

Micah

I check the time again. The water continues to rise while I sit in my truck and all I can do is watch it get higher over the bridge. The whole truck shakes every time the wind gusts. I'm about ready to jump in and swim. She could be stuck somewhere, getting further and further under the water.

I'm sweating. I had to pull off the road and I turned off the truck. I can't take it anymore and I restart the truck. The air feels good against my hot skin. I'm so keyed up I feel like I'm cooking in my tactical gear.

Finally! I can hear an engine. I look around for the coming vehicle. There's flashing red and blue lights on more than one vehicle. The best thing I've seen is a tactical hummer pulling a rescue boat on a trailer. They flash their headlights at me. I turn off the truck and run full speed to the Hummer. The back door pops open as I approach, I jump in and slam the door. Someone hands me a towel and I remove my helmet to dry off. Then an automatic life jacket gets shoved at me and I fasten it around myself.

At the same time Samson says, "Ramirez and Harper are going with you. We're going back to the warehouse. It's our base of operations for now, while the storm is on top of us. They can launch this Orca right on the bridge and drive it straight to Peyton's. Here, take this radio and give me your keys. I'll take your truck back to the warehouse so you guys can use this to bring the boat back. Do you need anything else?"

"Just my girl."

"Okay. Go get her. Be safe, I'll see you back at base." He pats my arm and leaves.

"Thanks," I yell into the storm.

Turning to the two guys in the Hummer, I nod at them and say, "Harper. Ramirez. Thanks for coming." Harper turns the Hummer around and backs the boat trailer into the water.

"Just doing our jobs, Micah. But I know if my wife was out there, you'd be the first one here to help," Ramirez tells me as he extends his fist for a bump.

Once the boat is in the water deep enough, Ramirez says, "Lets hit it!" He opens his door and disappears into the beast of a storm.

"I'll meet you out there," Harper says as I exit into the wind.

Peyton

I'm tired of waiting here with my tormentor. The storm has gotten worse. I wonder if it's a Category 2 or even 3. The wind is howling like wolves baying at the moon, and it's eerie. It's as dark as night, so we're sitting in shadows. Which is the one thing I don't mind. The longer I sit here the angrier I get. I'm glad I can't see the features of her evil face in the dark.

I'm primed and ready for an opportunity to take the next step. I just need her to move and be focused on something else. Tree branches and who knows what else, continue to bang against the house. It sounds like giants are hitting it with sledgehammers. The throbbing in my face and my ankle have faded to a dull ache. I'm as ready as I'll ever be.

Something big hits the back of the house and it shudders hard. I can't imagine what it could be. There's a loud sound. It's like a train barreling towards us. I stand and Anisa, or *Denise*, joins me.

"What's that?"

"I don't know, but it sounds like it's coming from the back of the house. Let's go see," I shout to be heard over all the noise.

"You go first. I'll be right behind you," she threatens.

I make my way down the hall and into my bedroom. The room is darker than the rest of the house. I know where things are so I make my way inside. The window looks strange, as I approach it and inspect it closely.

"Oh my God! I think that's a tree against the window!"

The very strong hurricane glass is cracked from the impact of the tree. I step closer and the roar of a train gets louder. Anisa can't resist looking at it up close, it looks surreal. As we watch, the noise reaches a crescendo and the house vibrates in time with the noise. With a great scraping sound as it rubs against the house, the tree begins to lift.

I realize what's happening and I step back from the glass. I get to the doorway and brace myself in the frame. Even though she's a horrible monster, I can't let her die.

I yell at Anisa, "Get away from the window! It's a tornado!"

The tree smashes back against the windowpanes and they shatter before she can get out of the way. The tree slams downward and the wind and rain and thousands of leaves rush through the opening. Thankfully the glass is shatter resistant and it falls to the ground in a clump. I don't wait to see what happens next. I run. I grab her raincoat as I fling open the door and rush into the center of the mayhem of flying leaves still attached to their branches and rain. The water is lapping at the top step, the waves are crashing onto the porch. There's nowhere to go, no way to escape. I brace myself into the corner, where the wall juts out, and hunker down beneath the raincoat. I squeeze into a tight ball and protect my head.

The door crashes open and almost closes until Anisa runs through it and past me. She doesn't see me in the corner behind her, so I remain still. When I see her feet, I raise my head enough to watch her. Her hair is swirling in the air above her head. It's broken free of its bun and she looks like Medusa with her head of snakes. Her clothes are instantly soaked and cling to her skin.

She waves the gun in the air and screams, "Peyton!! You bitch!" She approaches the stairs and looks over the steps and into the water. Not finding me, she turns back towards the house and sees me. She aims her gun at me. It's a disturbing sight. Her hair waving in the wind, her face scrunched into an angry scowl, and the dark clouds rushing and circling above her. The gun in her hand isn't the most menacing thing in this image.

"Nice try, now get back inside! Move!" She has to scream to be heard. I try to think of some way to get out of this terrifying situation.

"Now!" She fires a shot into the air and I jump to my feet and brace against the wind. As I open my mouth to say something to her, a big sheet of wood barrels through the air and hits her in the forehead. It spins from the impact, and I see a flowery, smiling skull painted on the other side as it continues its flight, fluttering on the gusts.

Blood instantly gushes from her wound; the gun leaves her hand and disappears under the waves. She looks stunned for a moment as she falls backwards off of the porch and into the icy depths of Hurricane Isaac. She surfaces a moment later, her hair covering much of her face is mixed with blood as it continues to leak from the gash on her head. She looks like the star of a horror film, well, at least the villain. I rush to the top of the steps to help her as she's dragged back beneath the cresting waves.

A moment later she surfaces again, and I reach out for her while I hold onto the railing. She flails her arms as if she's fighting off a sea monster. She screams like she's being chomped on by the shark in Jaws.

"Take my hand! Here, Anisa!" I scream, desperately trying to reach her. She goes under again and I watch for her to come back up. I'm braced and ready to make a grab for her when she resurfaces. When she comes up again, her face is twisted in pain, she flings off something that's wrapped around her hand. At first, I think it's a vine, but as I witness her struggle, I see the telltale black and red, separated by yellow bands of a deadly poisonous coral snake. My own mouth falls open in shock as I watch it swim away. Anisa vanishes beneath a wave and does not resurface.

I fall to my knees and sob. It's part terror and part relief. I don't know how long I sit there. I'm numb to the cold and wetness. My tears are washed away by the harsh raindrops. At some point the rain slows, the wind eases to a breeze, and the sun begins to peek through the clouds.

An engine breaks my stupor. I lift my head and see three men in a boat. The boat is bright red and the men are dressed in black rain gear and helmets. One of them has a rifle in his hands and I vaguely acknowledge they have my three favorite letters across their chests, FBI. They come right to the porch and the one in front jumps off and runs to me. He removes his helmet and I see the love of my life. I jump into his open arms and comfort floods me as I breathe in his familiar scent.

"Thank God! Are you hurt?" he asks as he assesses me. I can tell when he sees my nose injury, "Dammit! Who did this to you?"

"It was Anisa. It was all Anisa." I see understanding dawn in his eyes and he kisses my head, he lifts me in his strong arms and carries me to the boat. I shut down, I'm safe and secure in his embrace, and that's all I need to know.

Micah

“I love you, Eagle.”

“I love you, Radiohead.”

I can’t believe she was here. Thank God she’s mostly okay. I can see her nose is injured, her ankle is swollen, and she’s favoring her ribs. I wrap her in safety blankets and hold her close to keep her safe until we arrive back at the Hummer. Ramirez was able to call for medical to meet us. It’s surreal the way the sky turns blue and the sun shines down. We don’t have much time; the eye of the storm is almost past. Rain is sprinkling down on us once again and the gusts are getting a little stronger each time they blow. In no time, we’ll be back in the eyewall, the worst part of the storm.

Medical can't get to the hospital because of the downed trees and high water so they took us to the warehouse containing our base. Everyone’s been alerted that she’s found and they’re arriving from every direction back at base. They’re able to raise the large overhead door so the medical guys pull their truck right into the warehouse. Peyton is strapped to the gurney inside.

I spy Rhett and brace for impact. He rushes inside and he wants to dive on her and hug her, I see it in his eyes. He restrains himself and settles for holding her hand and kissing her forehead. Turns out her temple is injured as well.

I ask the medic treating her to check her ribs and she freezes. I inspect her face and see the trepidation in her eyes. Rhett's absorbed in a conversation with Orlando, he doesn't notice. I check her over carefully and something is definitely wrong.

"What's up, babe?" Tears pool in her eyes and she won't meet my gaze. I gently place my hands on her cheeks and aim her face to mine.

"Baby, what is it?"

She starts crying, "I'm afraid you won't love me anymore," she blurts and looks away.

I chuckle, "There's nothing you could ever do to make me stop loving you. Whatever happened, it wasn't your fault. Those monsters took you against your will. You've done nothing wrong."

She cries harder, her face is pinched in an ugly crying mask. It must hurt her swollen nose. What the fuck? Oh no. Did those fuckers touch her? Was she assaulted? Should I call in a female to talk to her? No, I love her. I'm the best person to help her.

I clear my throat, "Hey, guys? Could you all clear out for a few minutes, give us some privacy? Please?" Rhett presses a kiss on her cheek and then ushers everyone out. I can tell by the concern engraved on his face he's worried about the same thing as me.

She won't lift her head; tears are dripping rapidly from her chin. I squat down so I can look up into her face. Her eyes are closed, and her face is twisted in pain. I gently place my hand on her knee, she jolts in response.

I carefully touch her chin as I whisper softly, "Baby, whatever it is, you can tell me. I love you more than anything on Earth. Nothing will change that, absolutely nothing. Please tell me."

I hold my breath waiting for her. I'll wait as long as it takes. She's my everything, I'll wait for her, kill for her, whatever she needs. She's trembling and I want to pull her into my arms but I'm afraid of hurting her. I'm even more afraid of her rejecting me.

She makes a sobbing sniffling sound that ends on a hiccup before she says, "He...he carved into my r-ribs, I'm going to be s-scarred f-forever. I'm ugly. Y-you're going t-to see his m-marks on me every t-time you see me."

New sobs wracked her whole body. I no longer fear her rejection. I climb onto the gurney and gently pull her into my lap. Her IV-line hits me in the face as she wraps her arms around my neck. I grab onto her lower back, as far as I know it's not injured and hold her close.

I speak in the softest, most soothing voice I can manage, "Eagle, you're my world, and you could never be ugly to me. I'm in love with you, and the person you are. Your beauty radiates from within. You're stunningly beautiful, but it's not all on the outside. Some scars would never even put a dent in how I feel about you. You know that right?"

She bobs her head in a shaky semblance of a nod. I rub her back as her sobs slowly calm. She leans her head under my chin and snuggles into me. I continue rubbing and mumbling how much she means to me until she finally speaks.

Her voice is rough, "He was a monster. I killed him." I freeze and my insides tighten, what the *fuck* happened to her?

"He kept cutting me and calling me *pet*. It hurt so much. I got the chance to hide a scalpel and when he leaned over me, I stabbed him." My breath leaves my body in a whoosh. I didn't imagine that she had to stab the fucker. I had an inkling she burned him up, but hands on stabbing, fuck. I place kisses on every part of her my lips can reach. She must've been so scared. My own eyes fill with tears for her suffering. Damn, who knew it would hurt this much to love someone.

"Baby, you did what you had to do to survive the worst possible circumstances. It's not your fault, they did this, not you. I'm actually so proud of you. You're a fucking badass. You're my beautiful badass."

We're both sniffling and she laughs through her tears. She moves back and looks into my watery eyes. I guess she's satisfied with what she sees there. I'm feeling nothing but love and awe.

"I love you, Radiohead. You could never do anything to change my mind either. I think you're stuck with me. Scars and all."

"No place I'd rather be, babe." We both chuckle, then she kisses me, and I return it with all the love I have for her. It seals our future, we're a team for life.

Peyton

I place the flowers in the vase on Nova's headstone. She's next to her beloved Henry in eternal rest. Knowing her she's causing all kinds of mischief while conducting her angel duties. I felt compelled to visit her as soon as I recovered enough. Micah wanted to come, but he understood my reasons for wanting to come alone. He's the best.

"Hey Nova, I've been feeling your presence lately and needed to come visit. I have so much to tell you, but I kinda feel like you might know some of it already." I fill her in on everything that's happened to me recently. I cry when I get to the part where I killed a guy and then Anisa died. Despite her trying to kill me, I still feel bad she didn't make it.

"So, Micah says it looks like Buzzard could get forty years to life for all of his crimes if he's convicted, including his involvement from what happened to Paige. He's in jail without bail for now. So is Diamond. She could get 20 years to life, and even if she's not convicted, she'll never work in the medical field again."

I dab at my eyes, it's hard to talk about the people who died regardless of if they were monsters. I've had too much death in my life.

"Rev could get thirty-five years, he and Tool had a drug lab in their workshop. No matter what he'll always suffer the loss of Tool, I feel bad for him losing his twin. He was caught in a canoe looking for Anisa. She wasn't found until the storm waters receded. Her heart and lungs stopped working from the venom of the snake bite, it caused her to drown. They found her in storm debris blocking a drain. They're still trying to figure out who Mr. Big is, if he's the guy who kept her trapped repaying her brother's debt, he probably runs a trafficking ring of his own. Micah's investigating it"

I sit on the grass. It's warm, the sky is blue with fluffy clouds, Isaac is long gone. We'll be cleaning up the mess he left behind for weeks.

"When they searched Anisa's place, they found tons of notes and journals about all of her plans. Apparently, she figured out my alarm code was Micah's birthday. It never occurred to me that someone close could easily figure it out and couldn't be trusted. She had more ketamine and pictures of me and everything. The worst part is how she casually documented Roger's murder, like it was just an errand. Denise Ramsay wasn't like the character Anisa she played at all. I miss Anisa. That's weird I guess, but she was fun when she wasn't trying to kill me."

Taking a sip of my drink, I decide to focus on some of the good things that have happened recently. Nova will be thrilled with my next bit of news.

"You'll be happy to know Rhett and Paige have decided to name the baby after my dad, Thadeus Warrior Baker and your Henry. They're going to name him Henry Warrior Baker and call him War. Your namesake is already calling Paige's belly, War. She can't wait to meet him. Also, they found some more of the money you hid in your property. They used it to open Nova's Savage Hope Foundation. The renovations for the shelters are almost finished. Paige hopes to get them opened before the baby comes."

I smile at a man and his dog. The dog is holding flowers in his mouth and must be visiting his owner's grave. Maybe the man's wife. I guess I'm not the only one who hangs out and chats with the dead. I watch the man sit and start speaking to the headstone on the grave he's visiting.

"Since they're getting the foundation running before I'm done with school, Dr. Bertman, my favorite professor, has agreed to oversee my work there until I'm licensed. Jake's decided to stay here too. He and Connor moved into Micah's old place and Micah's living with me now. Jake's going to work for the foundation too. He's going to help all of the trafficking victims from South, and Central America, and Mexico return home.

I'm glad, he and Connor are true friends and Micah, and I are really happy to have them around. Orlando and Ax are getting to be really close friends as well. It's nice to know I have real friends I can trust."

Even though it's almost Thanksgiving, it's very warm and sweat beads on my temple. I dab it with my tissue.

"Oh! I also got a tattoo. You'd be proud of me for living a little. Micah and I want to get matching tattoos once my wounds are totally healed. I want to cover it over with something I choose versus the scars someone else chose to make. We're getting hearts with infinity symbols that say: *Lucky in love with my best friend.* Since Micah already has a tattoo on the other side of his ribs, I got one on mine. It's an eagle and the logo for the band, Radiohead. It's my nickname for Micah. Not sure I ever told you about that. He was a little obsessed with the band when we first became friends. I teased that I was going to call him *Radiohead* and it just stuck. The logo is cool, sort of a big mouse head with big eyes and teeth. It looks better than it sounds. I put a few music notes and hearts around it. The eagle represents me, it's my nickname. It's short for *legal eagle.* I love it and I can't wait to cover my scars with our matching tattoo. You know, I saw your tattoo once. It was at the dress shop when we were looking for bridesmaid's dresses. I thought it was badass. I miss you, Nova."

My eyes water and I'm embarrassed to say the final thing on my mind. I look around and make sure nobody is close enough to hear me. When I'm satisfied the guy and his dog are busy, and the ladies at another grave are too far away to hear, I take a deep breath.

"So, there's one last thing. When I was struggling through all this stuff, there were a few times I heard your voice in my head. I mean as clear as if you were standing here. I don't believe in ghosts, or angels, but now I'm questioning my conviction. I know you believed in lots of supernatural stuff, especially that Henry was around. If it was really you, I just wanted to say thank you. I don't know if I would've survived without your help.

If it wasn't you, but just your memory, thank you anyway. You were an amazing lady and I think you saved my life. I love you, Nova Gestwicki!"

With that off my chest, I pat her headstone and head back to my car. Micah's waiting for me at Rhett's. I'm thankful for my life and all of the people in it. Especially Micah, he's my forever.

Afterword

Dear Enchanting Reader-

I hope you enjoyed Micah and Peyton's story. They'll be around in the next book, you haven't seen the last of them. The series will continue with more tales of the Savage crew and beyond.

Orlando and Ax have stories of their own to tell. Please subscribe to my newsletter so you won't miss updates about new releases for each new book and series. I also have a duet horror story coming soon! VioleNt and the Origin of Violet, will be out in October 2024!

Visit https://www.enchantingauthor.com to subscribe. You'll get all the updates on new releases and special events and discounts. Also, find me on Facebook, Instagram, Threads, TikTok, X, YouTube, and LinkedIn. Join my special group for readers on Facebook, Enchanting Reads.

As always, thank you for reading, please leave a review on Amazon, Goodreads, and your favorite social media!

Warmest regards,

E.N. Chanting

Also by E.N. Chanting

Forces of Nature Series- romantic suspense
Force of Corruption Book 1
Force Majeure Book 2
Force of Attraction Book 3 (coming soon)
Southern Suns MC Series- biker romance
Ax (coming soon)
Horror Duet plus
Origin of Violet: Book .5 (novella horror-coming 2024)
VioleNt: Book 1 (romantic horror- coming 2024)
Vile: Book 2 (romantic horror-coming 2025)
Short Stories
Haunted Hunting Camp (horror)
Deadly-Go-Round (horror- coming 2025)
The Devil's Affair (romantic suspense)

www.ingramcontent.com/pod-product-compliance
Lightning Source LLC
Chambersburg PA
CBHW032111310726
48972CB00001B/179